20x94
0x03

D0055545

The Harafish

*The following titles by Naguib Mahfouz
are also published by Doubleday
and Anchor Books:*

THE THIEF AND THE DOGS

THE BEGINNING AND THE END

WEDDING SONG

THE BEGGAR

RESPECTED SIR

AUTUMN QUAIL

THE TIME AND THE PLACE and Other Stories

THE SEARCH

MIDAQ ALLEY

THE JOURNEY OF IBN FATTOUMA

MIRAMAR

ADRIFT ON THE NILE

The Cairo Trilogy:

PALACE WALK

PALACE OF DESIRE

SUGAR STREET

NAGUIB MAHFOUZ

Translated by Catherine Cobham

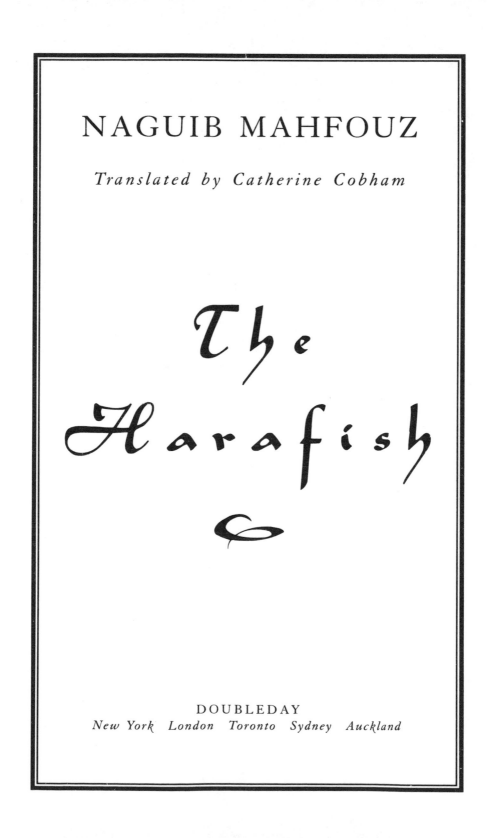

The Harafish

DOUBLEDAY
New York   London   Toronto   Sydney   Auckland

PUBLISHED BY DOUBLEDAY
a division of Bantam Doubleday Dell Publishing Group, Inc.
1540 Broadway, New York, New York 10036

DOUBLEDAY *and the portrayal of an anchor with*
a dolphin are trademarks of Doubleday,
a division of Bantam Doubleday Dell
Publishing Group, Inc.

The Harafish *was first published in Arabic in 1977,*
under the title Malhamat al-harafish.
Protected under the Berne Convention.

This translation is published by arrangement with
The American University in Cairo Press.

Library of Congress Cataloging-in-Publication Data

Mahfūz, Najīb, 1912–
    [Malḥamat al-harāfīsh. English]
    The harafish / Naguib Mahfouz; translated by Catherine Cobham. — 1st ed.
    p.   cm.
    I. Title.
    PJ7846 .A46M2813   1994
    892'.736—dc20   93-7782
                                                                CIP

ISBN 0-385-42324-1
Copyright © 1977 by Naguib Mahfouz
English translation copyright © 1993 by Catherine Cobham

Book Design by Gretchen Achilles

ALL RIGHTS RESERVED
PRINTED IN THE UNITED STATES OF AMERICA
APRIL 1994
FIRST EDITION
10   9   8   7   6   5   4   3   2   1

CONTENTS

TRANSLATOR'S NOTE

The historical meaning of *harafish* is the rabble or riffraff. In the novel it means the common people in a positive sense, those in menial jobs, casual workers, and the unemployed and homeless.

I am grateful to Sabry Hafez for help and encouragement, and to Mohamed Malek for the transliterations of the lines of Persian poetry.

CATHERINE COBHAM
St. Andrews
October 1992

Ashur al-Nagi

ↄ

The first tale in the epic

of the harafish

1.

*I*n the passionate dark of dawn, on the path between death and life, within view of the watchful stars and within earshot of the beautiful, obscure anthems, a voice told of the trials and joys promised to our alley.

2.

He felt his way along with his rough stick, his guide in his eternal darkness. He knew where he was by the smell, by the number of steps he had taken, by how well he could hear the chanting, and by his own inspired instincts. Between his house by the graveyard and the alley was the hardest but also the most delightful part of his route to the Husayn mosque. Unexpectedly there came to his sharp ears the cries of a newborn child. It could have been an echo, magnified in the silence of the dawn. It roused him unceremoniously from the intoxicated visions inspired in him by the sacred chanting. At this hour, mothers are supposed to be totally preoccupied with their children! The noise was growing louder and nearer and he would soon be level with it. He cleared his throat to fore-

stall a collision in the quiet landscape of dawn, wondering when
the child would stop crying so that he could revert to his state of
calm repose. Now the crying came insistently on his left-hand side.
He moved over to the right until his shoulder brushed the wall of
the dervish monastery. He stopped and called out, "Woman! Feed
the child!"

But nobody answered him. The crying continued. "Woman!
Hello! Is anybody there?" he shouted.

All he could hear was the sound of crying. He was filled with
misgivings. Gone was the innocence of the dawn. Very cautiously
he advanced in the direction of the sound, keeping his stick close in
to his side. He bent forward a little, extending his hand gently until
his forefinger touched a bundle of clothing. It was just what he'd
expected. He moved his fingers around in its folds until he felt a
soft moist face, convulsed with tears.

"The wickedness of human hearts!" he exclaimed under his
breath. Then he raised his voice in anger. "May they rot in hell!"

He thought a little but decided not to ignore the bundle even
if it meant missing the dawn prayer at the Husayn mosque. The
breeze was chilly at this time on a summer's morning, there were a
lot of lizards and suchlike about, and God tested his servants in
unforeseen ways. He picked the bundle up gently, then resolved to
return home to consult his wife. He heard the sound of voices. It
was probably worshipers on their way to the dawn prayer. He gave
another cough to warn of his presence.

"God's peace on the faithful," came a voice from the darkness.

"And on you," he answered quietly.

The speaker recognized his voice and said, "Sheikh Afra
Zaydan? What's holding you up?"

"I'm going back home. It's nothing serious."

"I hope not, Sheikh Afra!"

He hesitated, then said, "I found a newborn child at the foot
of the old wall."

There was the sound of muttering between the men.

"May they rot in hell, the criminals!"

"Take it to the police station!"

"What are you going to do with it?"

"God will guide me," said Afra with a calm inappropriate to the situation.

3.

Sakina held the lamp up in her left hand. She was alarmed when she saw it was her husband. "Why have you come back?" she demanded. "I hope nothing's wrong?" Then she saw the baby. "Whatever's that?"

"I found it on the path."

"Merciful God!"

She took the child gently and the sheikh sat on the sofa between the well and the oven, mumbling, "There is no God but God."

Sakina began rocking the child in her arms. "It's a boy, Sheikh Afra!" she said tenderly.

He nodded silently.

"He must need food," she went on anxiously.

"What do you know about it? You've never had children."

"I know some things, and I can always ask. What are you going to do with him?"

"They told me I should take him to the police station."

"Do you think they'll feed him there? Let's wait until someone comes looking for him."

"Nobody will."

A tense silence followed. "Isn't it wrong to keep him any longer than we have to?" muttered the sheikh at length.

"The wrong's already been done," said his wife with passionate energy.

Then inspiration came to her; she welcomed it delightedly. "I can't hope to have a child of my own now."

He pushed his turban back to reveal a protruding forehead like the handle of a washbowl. "What are you thinking, Sakina?" he demanded.

"How can I refuse what God has provided?" she said, intoxicated by her idea.

He wiped his closed eyes with his handkerchief and said nothing.

"It's what you want yourself!" she cried triumphantly.

"I've missed the dawn prayer in al-Husayn," he complained, ignoring her.

She smiled broadly and without taking her eyes off the swollen little face said, "Dawn's only just breaking, and God is forgiving and merciful."

The sheikh got up to pray as Darwish Zaydan came downstairs, his eyelids heavy with sleep, saying, "I'm hungry, sister-in-law."

He noticed the baby and looked astonished, as a boy of ten might. "What's that?" he asked.

"A gift from God," answered Sakina.

He stared hard at it. "What's its name?"

After a moment's hesitation, the woman said almost inaudibly, "Let him take my father's name, Ashur Abdullah, and may God bless him."

In the background Sheikh Afra recited the dawn prayer.

4.

The days went by to the sound of the beautiful, obscure anthems. One evening Sheikh Afra Zaydan said to his brother Darwish, "You're twenty years old. When are you going to get married?"

"All in good time," answered the youth nonchalantly.

"You're a fine strong porter. They make a good living!"

"All in good time."

"Aren't you frightened of being led astray?"

"God protects the faithful."

The blind Quran reciter shook his head. "You got nothing from Quran school," he said regretfully, "and you don't know a single chapter of God's book by heart."

"Work is what counts, and I earn my living by the sweat of my brow," said Darwish irritably.

The sheikh pondered for a few moments. Then he asked, "Those scars on your face, how did you get them?"

Darwish realized that his sister-in-law must have betrayed him and scowled at her. She was trying to light the oven, helped by Ashur.

"Darwish, do you really expect me to keep it a secret from your brother if you're being harmed?" she smiled.

"So you're modeling yourself on the men of evil and violence?" said the sheikh reprovingly.

"If they pick a fight I'm obviously going to defend myself."

"Darwish, you've been brought up in the house of a servant of the Quran. Why don't you behave more like your brother Ashur?"

"He's not my brother!" snapped Darwish fiercely.

The sheikh withdrew into angry silence.

Ashur had been following the conversation intently. He was shocked, although he had been expecting it. He did what he could to contribute to the household and was never asked to do more. He cleaned the house, shopped in the market, accompanied his benefactor to al-Husayn every morning for the dawn prayer, drew water, lit the oven, and in the late afternoon sat at the sheikh's feet while he instructed him in the Quran and taught him how to lead a decent life. The sheikh loved him and was pleased with how he was turning out. Sakina used to gaze fondly at him and remark, "He's going to be a good, strong lad."

"May he use his strength to serve his fellows, and not the devil," the sheikh would say.

5.

The heavens showered their blessings on Ashur and as the years went by the sheikh rejoiced in him as much as he despaired of Darwish, his own brother and foster child. Why, Lord, when they were reared under the same roof? But once he had set his heart against learning, Darwish moved out of reach of the sheikh's influence as he went in search of a living. He set off into the world a fresh-faced boy and was schooled by harshness and violence before he was fully grown, and before his spirit had acquired strength and purity. Right from the beginning, Ashur responded to the beauty and radiance in the world, to the harmonies of the sacred anthems. He grew huge like the monastery door, tall and broad, with arms as solid as the stones of the old city wall and legs like the trunks of mulberry trees. He had a large, noble head and strong well-proportioned features where the sap of life flowed abundantly. His strength showed in his zeal for work, his endurance, his cheerful persistence. The sheikh often said to him, "May your strength be used to serve your fellows, and not the devil."

One day the sheikh announced that he wanted to make him a reciter of the Quran like himself.

"Don't you think the sight of his huge frame would be enough to frighten off his audience?" laughed Darwish scathingly.

The sheikh ignored this remark but was forced to abandon his plan when it became clear that Ashur's voice was not up to it. It went out of tune easily, had no sweetness or flexibility, and lacked clarity, so that it sounded as if he were singing in a tunnel. Furthermore, he was incapable of learning a long chapter by heart.

Ashur was content with what he did, happy with his life, and imagined he would remain in this paradise till the end of time. He believed what he was told, that the sheikh had taken charge of him at the death of his parents, good people cut down in their prime, and thanked God that in His mercy and might He had provided him with a home whose kindness was unrivaled by any other in the alley. Then one day Sheikh Afra decided his upbringing and education were complete and it was time to send him to learn a trade. However, events overtook the sheikh, he fell ill with a fever which popular remedies failed to cure, and went to join his Maker. Sakina found herself with no income or means of supporting herself, and went back to her village in Qalyubiyya. She and Ashur parted tearfully. She kissed him, uttered a charm to protect him from evil, and left. All at once he felt alone in the world, at the mercy of his inflexible new master, Darwish Zaydan.

He closed his heavy eyelids, deep in thought, feeling that things were sliding into a gulf of emptiness, that he wanted to climb the sun's rays, melt away in a dewdrop, or ride the wind that

rumbled through the archway; but a voice in his heart told him
that the emptiness would be filled with the power of God's spirit
and the earth would live again.

6.

Darwish examined him as he squatted dejectedly by the oven.
What a giant! With the jaws of a beast of prey and mustaches like a
ram's horns. A redundant, shiftless power, doomed to lie fallow.
Lucky he had never learned a trade, but he should guard against
underestimating him. Why did he dislike him? As he sat hunched,
rooted to the floor, he reminded him of a sharp rock blocking the
way, a dust-laden blast of hot wind, an open tomb on a feast day,
disquieting and provocative. Damn him! He ought to use him
somehow! "How will you earn a living?" he asked, not looking at
him.

Ashur opened his large deepset eyes and said resignedly, "I'm
at your service, master Darwish."

"I don't need any help," said Darwish coldly.

"Then I'll have to go away."

He hesitated, then added hopefully, "Won't you let me go on
living here? It's the only home I've known."

"It's not a hotel."

The oven's mouth gaped, dark and lifeless, and from the shelf
above came the rustle of a mouse scampering over dry garlic stalks.

Darwish cleared his throat. "Where will you go?"

"The world's a big place."

"And harsher than you think. You don't know the first thing
about it," said Darwish scornfully.

"At least I'll find work and get a living."

"Your body's the biggest obstacle. You won't find lodgings
and no tradesman will take you on. And you're almost twenty. Too
old to learn a trade."

"I've never used my strength to harm anyone."

Darwish laughed loudly.

"No one will trust you all the same," he said. "The clan chiefs
will see you as a rival, and the merchants as a bandit and a thug."

Then he added evenly, "You'll starve to death if you don't make use of your strength to survive."

"As God's my witness," exclaimed Ashur with passion, "I'll gladly give it in the service of others."

"If you don't get rid of your stupid notions, it will do you no good at all."

Ashur gave him a bewildered look, then said, "Let me work as a porter with you."

"I've never been a porter in my life," Darwish replied derisively.

"But . . ."

"Forget it. What did you expect?"

"What is your job then?"

"If you're patient, I'll find you some work. Take it or leave it."

Sounds of a funeral ceremony could be heard from the graveyard. "Ashes to ashes, dust to dust," remarked Darwish.

"I'm famished!" said Ashur, losing patience.

Darwish handed him a small coin. "That's the last time I give you charity," he warned.

Ashur left the house as dusk settled over the graves and the open country. It was a summer's evening and a gentle breeze blew, smelling of damp earth and basil. He went along the path to the little square. He could make out the archway in the darkness and the dim shapes of the mulberry trees over the walls of the monastery gardens. The songs rose into the air, impenetrable as always, and he resolved to lay his cares aside.

"Don't be sad, Ashur," he told himself. "You have countless brothers in this world."

The singing echoed in his head:

Ay furughe mahe hosn az ruye rakhahane shoma
Abruye khubi az chahe zanakhdane shoma

7.

Ashur took deep breaths of the night air. The stars' bright gaze flowed into his heart. His soul soared up to the clear summer sky.

What better night could there be than this to fall to his knees in worship, give voice to hidden desires, call upon loved ones beyond the veil of the unknown?

A shadowy figure stood a few paces from him, clouding his serenity, dragging him back to the world of trouble.

"What are you doing here, master Darwish?" he inquired in his husky voice.

Darwish punched him in the chest.

"Lower your voice, you fool!" he said in an angry whisper.

The two men stood close up against a hedge bordering the graveyard, on the side that overlooked the desert. The hills were far to their right, the graves to their left. There was not a sound, nobody passing by. Even the souls of the dead seemed absent at this hour of the night. Vague notions took on substance in the darkness and became forebodings, and Ashur's heart beat anxiously.

"Tell me what you're up to, for the love of God," he whispered.

"Wait," scolded Darwish. "Can't you be patient?"

He leaned toward him and went on, "I'm not asking you to do anything. I'll do it all. Just cover my back if you need to."

"But I don't know what you're going to do."

"Shut up. Nobody's forcing you to stay."

A sound floated up from the desert. The scent of a living creature was carried on the breeze and an old man's voice apparently encouraging an animal.

Soon they could make him out, sitting astride a donkey. As he drew level with them Darwish jumped on him. Ashur was astonished. His worst fears were realized. He could see nothing clearly, but he heard Darwish's voice threatening, "Hand over your money."

"Have mercy. You're hurting me," said a voice trembling with old age and terror.

Ashur rushed forward without stopping to think. "Let him go!" he shouted.

"Shut your mouth!" screamed Darwish.

"I said let him go."

He wrapped his arms around Darwish's waist and hoisted

him off his feet. Darwish elbowed him frantically in the chest and cursed loudly. Ashur immobilized him so that only his tongue still moved, then turned to the old man. "Go in peace," he said.

Only when he was sure the man had escaped did he release Darwish. "I'm sorry if I was rough," he said apologetically.

"Ungrateful bastard!"

"But I saved you from doing something you'd regret."

"You miserable idiot! Begging's all you're fit for!"

"God forgive you."

"Dirty bastard!"

Saddened, Ashur fell silent.

"You're a bastard. Don't you understand? It's the truth."

"Don't let your anger get the better of you. The sheikh told me where I came from."

"I'm telling you the truth. He found you on the path where your whore mother left you," said Darwish venomously.

"God rest them all."

"On my honor and my brother's soul, you're just a bastard. Why else would they have got rid of a newborn baby in the middle of the night?"

Offended, Ashur said nothing.

"You've wasted my good work. Thrown away an opportunity to make some money. You might be strong, but you're a coward. You've just proved it."

He landed a punch full in Ashur's face. Ashur, stunned by his first direct experience of physical violence, did nothing.

"Coward! Weakling!" shouted Darwish in a fury.

A wave of anger swept over Ashur, its violence shattering the sanctuary of night. With the flat of his great hand he struck his master on the head. Darwish sank to the floor, unconscious. Ashur struggled with his anger, forcing himself to calm down, and realized the gravity of what he had done.

"Forgive me, Sheikh Afra," he muttered.

He lifted Darwish in his arms and made his way among the graves to the house, where he laid him down on the sofa, lit the lamp, and stood watching him, full of anxiety and remorse. The minutes dragged by. At last Darwish opened his eyes and moved his head feebly.

Rage flickered in his eyes, showing that he remembered. The two men looked at one another in silence. Ashur felt as if Afra and Sakina were there, watching them sorrowfully.

He left the house. "God knows what's going to happen to me now," he murmured.

8.

Ashur wandered here and there. He slept on the ground, which is father and mother to the homeless, getting food where he could. On warm nights he slept below the wall of the monastery and on cold nights under the archway. He finally believed what Darwish had told him about his origins. The bitter truth hounded him and closed around him. A few nights in Darwish's company had taught him more about the realities of the world than twenty years spent under the wing of the good sheikh Afra. The wicked are harsh but honest teachers. He was a child of sin. The sinners had vanished, leaving him to face the world alone. Maybe he lived on as a painful memory in some restless heart.

His grief made him listen to the songs from the monastery more eagerly than ever. The meanings of their sweetly intoned cadences were hidden from him behind a veil of Persian, just as he imagined his mother and father were hidden behind the faces of strangers. One day he might find his mother, or his father, or discover the meanings of the words. Perhaps some of the riddles would be solved, he would cry tears of happiness, find cherished desires realized in the person of someone he loved. He spent hours gazing at the monastery garden, with its graceful, arching trees, grassy lawns, and trilling birds, and at the dervishes moving nimbly in their flowing robes and tall felt hats.

"Why do they do menial tasks like the poor?" he mused one day. "They sweep, lay the dust, water the plants. Perhaps they need a reliable servant."

The great door was calling him, whispering to him to knock

and enter. The joy and serenity of the place scared him. He was in the garden, a fruit swollen with sweet juices, leaves yielding silk. A pure hand will come to pluck you in ecstasy.

The soft whisper won him over. He approached the door and called out modestly, politely to the men of God.

He called again and again, to no avail. They were hiding. No one answered. Even the birds regarded him suspiciously. The men of God didn't know his language, nor he theirs. The stream stopped flowing; the grass and flowers stopped dancing. Nothing needed him.

His enthusiasm waned. His inspiration was stifled. He was covered in confusion. He reproached himself for the strength of his feelings and struggled to control his will.

"Don't let yourself become the talk of the neighborhood," he told himself, tugging on his splendid mustache. "Forget about people who refuse your help and look for someone who needs you."

After this he earned his living any way he could, helping at weddings and funerals, acting as a porter or an errand boy, grateful for the odd coin or loaf of bread, or even a kind word.

One day an ugly man with a rat face accosted him: "Hey, boy!"

Ashur went up to him politely, ready to help.

"Don't you know me?" asked the man.

"Forgive me. I'm a stranger," answered Ashur, embarrassed.

"But you come from this alley?"

"I've only lived in it a short time."

"Kulayb al-Samani. I'm one of the clan chief's men."

"Pleased to meet you, master."

The man stared hard at him, then asked, "Will you join us?"

"I haven't the stomach for it," replied Ashur, without hesitation.

Kulayb laughed scornfully. "The body of an ox and the heart of a bird," he said, turning to go.

Ashur used to see Zayn al-Naturi's donkey tied up in the stable after a hard day's work. He took to brushing her, feeding her, sweeping the yard and sprinkling it with fresh water, never asking anything in return.

One day Zayn called him over. "You're Sheikh Afra's boy, aren't you?" he inquired.

"Yes. God rest his soul," answered Ashur humbly.

"I heard you refused to join Qanswa's clan?"

"There's nothing in it for me."

Zayn smiled and offered him a job as a donkey boy. Ashur accepted on the spot, his heart dancing for joy.

He led the donkey to work with energy and enthusiasm. As each day passed Zayn grew more sure of his good conduct and his piety, while Ashur for his part was glad to prove that he was trustworthy.

While he was working in the courtyard of Zayn's house, he carefully avoided looking anywhere he might catch a glimpse of his master's wife. But he saw his daughter Zaynab going out one day. He glanced for a few brief moments, and regretted it immediately. His remorse grew as a hot flame burned through his chest and innards and settled in his groin, blazing with unbridled desire.

"God save me," he murmured, intoxicated by a rich, wild craving.

For the first time he had mentioned God's name while his thoughts were somewhere quite different. This sexual experience, limited and basic as it was, sent through him a shudder of embarrassment, anxiety, and strangeness.

Zayn al-Naturi decided he would make a dependable watchman. "Where do you live, Ashur?" he asked.

"By the monastery wall or under the archway."

"Wouldn't you like to sleep in the stable here?"

"Thank you, master," answered Ashur happily.

9.

He used to wake at dawn. He liked the darkness streaked with smiling light, the hum of activity from the pious and the dissolute, the pure breathing of existence still wrapped in dreams. He would push aside Zaynab's provocative image, say his prayers, swallow a flat loaf with pickled olives and onions, pat the donkey affectionately, then drive it ahead of him to the main square, looking forward to earning his daily bread. He was overflowing with vitality and full of boundless confidence in his ability, his powers of endurance, his control over the unknown. At the same time he was caught up in a vortex of feelings which threatened to uproot him: Zaynab was always ahead of him, triumphantly drawing him with her secret call. She had a pale face with a prominent nose and thick lips, and a small, solid body, but she had a bewitching effect on him. A fire burned constantly in his entrails. Sometimes he was oblivious to the donkey and its rider.

When he broke for a rest he would stand in front of the house, watching the stream of passersby: market traders, barrow boys, hawkers and peddlers, vagrants and tradesmen in search of work. Were his father and mother there somewhere? Were they still alive? Did they know him? Who had bequeathed him the giant frame, filled out by the benevolence of Sheikh Afra Zaydan? He chased away these futile thoughts and was immediately accosted by Zaynab al-Naturi's secret call.

"Nothing stays the same," he said to himself. "Something must happen. Let God be on my side as a reward for my pure intentions."

The furious voice of Zayn al-Naturi broke in on his thoughts. He saw him in the yard, locked in a verbal confrontation with a customer.

"You're nothing but a thief," he shouted.

"Watch your tongue!"

Zayn slapped him around the face and grabbed his collar. Ashur rushed up to them, shouting at them to stop, and threw himself between them. Swearing viciously, the customer kicked out. Ashur held him pinned until he screamed in pain. Relaxing his grip, he said, "On your way, or you'll regret it."

He took to his heels as the women crowded to the window and Zaynab's mother shouted, "Next we'll be raped in our beds!"

Zayn al-Naturi fixed grateful eyes on Ashur. "God bless you, son," he murmured, doing his best to hide his embarrassment.

He went indoors. Only Zaynab was left at the window. Ashur returned to his place by the door, thinking that it was only a matter of time before their eyes met.

He leaned back against the wall and noticed a cat preparing to terrorize a black dog. The dog turned aside to avoid a fight.

"Take care, Ashur," he said to himself. "This is a warning from your parents!"

Then he abandoned himself to the caresses of pleasant dreams until the sun's rays burned him.

10.

"Are you sure he can be trusted?" said Adlat to her husband, Zayn al-Naturi.

"Of course. He's become like a son to me."

"Fine. Marry him to Zaynab," she said impatiently.

Zayn al-Naturi frowned thoughtfully. "I'd hoped for someone better."

"We've waited too long. Every time someone comes asking to marry one of her half sisters, you refuse because Zaynab's the oldest."

"If she was your own flesh and blood you wouldn't say that."

"She's spoiling my daughters' prospects. She's twenty-five years old, she's ugly, and she's getting more ill-natured from day to day."

"If she was your own flesh and blood you wouldn't say that," he repeated morosely.

"Isn't it enough that you trust him? You need someone you can trust in your old age."

"What about Zaynab?"

"She'll be delighted. Save her from her desperation!"

11.

Ashur heard Zayn calling him from his sitting room. He made room for him on a wooden sofa covered with a sheepskin rug. After a moment's hesitation Ashur sat down.

"Isn't it time you thought of getting married, Ashur?" his master asked him gently.

Light and joy: when the dream becomes a blessing, a song in the ear and the heart, and the faces of men shine with tolerance, and even insects no longer sting.

Ashur went to the Sultan baths and shaved and washed away the sweat, combed his hair, trimmed his mustache, sprinkled himself with rose water, and cleaned his teeth with a polished walnut twig. Then he strolled out in a flowing white robe and red leather slippers made especially for his huge feet.

The wedding was celebrated in the normal way in the al-Naturi house, and afterward the bride and groom set up home in a basement flat across the alley, composed of one room and an entrance hall. Ashur was overflowing with love, and some degenerate citizens, leaving the smoking dens well after midnight, would crouch in the darkness close to the basement window, listening and dreaming.

As time passed Hasballah, Rizqallah, and Hibatallah were born, Zayn and his wife died, and their daughters married.

Ashur was happy in his married life. He continued to work as a donkey boy with the animal al-Naturi had given him as a wedding present. Zaynab learned how to raise chickens and sold the eggs in the market. Life became easier and the hallway smelled of garlic, coriander, and cooking butter.

As the boys grew up they all learned different trades: Hasballah was apprenticed to a joiner, Rizqallah to a tinsmith, and Hibatallah to a laundryman. None of them was endowed with the giant stature of his father, but they were strong enough to win respect in the neighborhood. Ashur himself was known to be slow to anger and gentle, but none of Qanswa's men dared pick a quarrel with him. Zaynab did not share his pleasant nature: she was tense, suspicious, and sharp-tongued, but always hardworking and faithful.

She was five years older than he and while he preserved his youth and vitality she changed rapidly and faded before her time. But he only had eyes for her and never stopped loving her.

The years went by. With the money they had both earned Ashur bought a cart and progressed from donkey boy to driver. Zaynab remarked wryly, "Your customers were always men. From now on they'll all be women!"

"I hope they won't all be visiting the cemetery," he laughed.

"I'll know if you're up to anything," she warned.

It saddened him that he had begun to forget the Quran and remembered only the little bits he recited in his prayers. But his love of what was good had never wavered. He knew that Darwish Zaydan was not the only evil person in the world; that life was full of deceit and violence and villains like him. In spite of this, he persisted in trying to lead a decent life and judged himself harshly whenever he was involved in any wrongdoing. He never forgot that he had appropriated all Zaynab's savings and some of his sons' wages to buy the cart, and had made life hard for them sometimes and flown into violent rages.

He noticed some of his neighbors were having trouble from the clan chief and his men. He suppressed his anger, consoling the victims with futile words and calling for restraint. At last someone said to him, "It's true you're strong, Ashur, but what good is it to us?"

What were they blaming him for? What did they want him to do? He'd refused to join the oppressors. He'd only used his strength to help people. Wasn't that enough for them?

But his conscience troubled him like flies on a hot summer's day. People didn't understand him, he thought, and asked himself sadly how he would ever be at peace.

13.

He squatted in the little square in front of the monastery, watching the last of the daylight disappear, greeting the evening and waiting for the anthems to fill the air. A chill autumn breeze, smelling of sorrow, slipped over the ancient wall, dragging the phantoms of night in its wake. Ashur appeared completely calm. There was not a single white hair on his head. He bore the burden of forty years of existence but these years seemed to have given him the grace of the immortals.

A vague premonition made him look toward the graveyard path and he saw a man turning out of it with an indolent gait. He stared harder and in the fading light recognized who it was. His heart thumped and his pleasure ebbed away. The man came toward him and stopped in front of him, blocking out the monastery, smiling.

"Darwish Zaydan!" mumbled Ashur.

"Aren't you going to say hello? Good evening, Ashur!" said Darwish reprovingly.

Ashur stood up, extending his hand. "Hello, Darwish," he said in an expressionless voice.

"I don't think I've changed that much."

The resemblance to Afra was painful, but his features had grown coarser and harder.

"No."

Darwish stared at him meaningfully and said, "Although everything else is changing."

Ashur ignored this remark. "Where have you been all this time?" he asked.

"In prison," he said casually.

"In prison!" exclaimed Ashur, although he was not surprised.

"I was just unlucky."

"God is forgiving."

"I hear things are going well for you?"

"I get by."

"I need cash," Darwish said laconically.

Ashur felt annoyed. He stuck a hand in his breast pocket and brought out a coin. "It's not much, but it's all I can afford."

Darwish took it with a sullen expression, then said seriously, "Let's say a prayer for my brother's soul."

They recited the prayer.

"I visit his grave regularly," murmured Ashur.

"Can I stay with you until I get back on my feet?" asked Darwish boldly.

"I don't have room for a stranger," Ashur snapped back.

"A stranger!"

"I only shook hands with you for Sheikh Afra's sake," Ashur said stubbornly.

"Lend me a bit more," persisted Darwish, "and I'll pay it back when things are easier."

Ashur gave him as much as he wanted, even though he was extremely hard-up. Darwish went off toward the archway without a word while a sweet voice sounded from the monastery, singing:

Ze geryeh mardome chesh nesheste dar khunast.

14.

As Ashur drove along in his cart one day he noticed a group of men on some waste ground near the top of the alley. When he drew closer he saw they were building workers congregating around piles of sheet metal, wood planks, and palm branches. Among them was Darwish Zaydan. His heart sank: the man must be building himself a house there. As he passed, Darwish shouted to him, "I'm doing what I can to help the neighborhood."

"A man needs a roof over his head," Ashur responded dryly.

Darwish laughed loudly. "This is going to be a shelter for the homeless!"

15.

"The story's out. The man's building a booze joint," said Hasballah to his father.

"A bar?" demanded Ashur in shocked tones.

"That's what everyone says," agreed Rizqallah.

"Lord!" exclaimed Ashur. "My cash helped build it!"

"Deeds are judged by the intentions behind them," quoted Hibatallah.

"What do the authorities have to say?"

"He must have got a license, I suppose."

Ashur remarked sadly, "We haven't managed to build a drinking fountain or a mosque for the alley yet. So how can they put up a bar?"

But the bar was well and truly built, and baptized by Qanswa and his men.

"He's got protection too," observed Ashur dejectedly.

16.

There was an uproar in the street outside the basement window. Why were they always fighting round here? Ashur sipped his coffee on the only sofa in the room. The lamp was not lit. A wintry blast rattled the window. Zaynab looked up from her ironing and said anxiously, "That's Rizqallah's voice!"

"Do you think it's the boys fighting?"

Zaynab rushed outside.

"You're crazy! Aren't you ashamed of yourselves?" he heard her shouting.

Ashur jumped to his feet. In a moment he was standing between his sons. They were quiet but the anger remained in their faces.

"Are you pleased with yourselves?" he demanded.

Glancing down, he saw a draught board and draughts scattered on the ground.

"Were you playing for money?" he inquired sharply.

No one answered. "When will you grow up?" he roared, ablaze with anger.

He drew Hasballah roughly to him. "You're the oldest, aren't you?"

From Hasballah's mouth came an alien smell, filling his nostrils, troubling him. He pulled the others to him, smelling their breaths. Ah! He wished the earth would perish with all its creatures.

"You're drunk! Bastards!"

He took hold of them by the ears, squeezing hard, his face

twitching with rage. A group of lads formed, watching with interest.

"Let's go indoors," implored Hasballah.

"You're embarrassed before these people and not before God?" roared his father in his hoarse voice.

Zaynab tugged at his arms.

"Don't make a spectacle of us in front of this rabble."

He let himself be led inside, muttering, "My sons are the rabble."

"They're not children," she whispered fiercely.

"They're no good. Just like their mother."

"The bar's not short of customers!"

He sank down on the sofa. "It's no use expecting any help from you."

She lit the lamp and put it in the window.

"I work harder than you," she said mildly. "If it wasn't for me you wouldn't have the cart, and there'd be no one to light the stove for you."

"All you've got is a tongue like a lash," he said irritably.

"The boys have worn themselves out for you," she shouted back angrily.

"They've got to be taught a lesson."

"They're not children. They'll leave."

She knew the quarrel would soon die down; hurtful words and loving whispers were two sides of the same coin.

Ashur wondered anxiously what could be done about his children. None of them had done well at Quran school. He and Zaynab had been too taken up with work to give them the attention they needed. Unlike him, they had had no Sheikh Afra to watch over them. They had absorbed the violence and superstitions of life in the alley and its virtues had passed them by. They hadn't even inherited his physical strength. They were not close to him or Zaynab. Whatever affection they felt was superficial and capricious. In their hearts they had turned against them long ago, although they had said nothing. They possessed no special talents and would remain apprentices all their lives. And here they were rushing to

drink in a bar at the first opportunity and not knowing when to
stop.

Sadly he said, "They'll only bring us trouble and grief."

"They're men," she replied resignedly.

17.

One day as he drove by the bar he heard Darwish's voice calling
out a greeting. This time he did not ignore him, despite the loathing he felt for him. He brought the donkey to a halt and jumped
down and stood in front of Darwish.

"This work is not fitting to your brother's memory," he said
sternly.

Darwish smiled sarcastically. "Isn't it better than mugging
people?" he said.

"Just as bad."

"Sorry, but I like risky ventures."

"There's more than enough evil in this alley."

"Drink makes bad men worse but it makes good men better.
Come in and see for yourself."

"It's a curse!"

He noticed a female figure moving swiftly around in the bar.
"Are there women in there too?" he asked in surprise.

"It could have been Fulla."

He had not seen the woman clearly enough to identify her.
He asked again, "Do you have women customers as well?"

"Of course not. She's an orphan I've adopted. You can't imagine I'm capable of doing good, can you? But isn't adopting an
abandoned child better than building a mosque?" he added significantly.

He accepted the taunt without protest. "Why bring her to the
bar?"

"So that she can earn her keep by doing a bit of hard work!"

"What's the use?" murmured Ashur dispiritedly.

He jumped up into the driver's seat with a shout to the donkey, and the animal was off with a musical clip-clopping of its
shoes on the cobbles.

18.

Now Ashur could not see beyond the dust of daytime and the dark of night. Every time he came to a bend in the road, he expected a hitch. His eyes would flicker. He would mumble under his breath, "God, let it be good."

Was the structure of life irreparably damaged?

He was about to get into bed just after midnight when he heard a cry outside the window. "Ashur! Ashur!"

He rushed to open it, muttering, "The children!"

A shadowy figure peered through the window bars.

"What's going on?" he asked.

"Come and get your sons. They're in the bar fighting over the girl Fulla!"

Zaynab blocked his path. "Let me go. You stay here," she begged.

He pushed her out of his way, stuck his feet into his slippers, and was off like a tornado.

19.

His frame filled the doorway. The eyes of drunken men reclining around the walls turned to focus on him. Darwish bounded toward him. "Your sons are going to wreck the place," he shouted.

He saw Hibatallah sprawled helplessly on the floor. Hasballah and Rizqallah were locked in a vicious struggle, while the other customers looked on indifferently.

"Stop!" he roared in a dreadful voice.

The two youths separated, looking toward the source of the voice in terror. With the flat of his hand he struck one, then the other, and they crashed down onto the bare earth floor. He stood looking defiantly around at his audience. Nobody said a word. He threw a withering glance at Darwish. "To hell with you and this foul hole of yours!" he shouted.

Fulla suddenly materialized from nowhere. "I'm innocent," she muttered.

"She was just doing her job. But your sons were after her," said Darwish.

"Shut up, you pimp!" shouted Ashur.

"God forgive you," said Darwish, backing away.

"I could bring this place down around your ears."

Fulla took a step forward and stood directly in front of him. "I'm innocent," she persisted.

"Get out of my way!" he said roughly, hardly able to keep his eyes off her.

He sent his sons staggering through the door one after the other.

"Don't you believe I'm innocent?" Fulla asked again.

Again he had to tear his eyes away from her. "You're small fry." Then he turned on his heel to go, without looking at her again.

In the darkness outside he breathed deeply. He felt that he'd escaped the clutches of evil. The darkness was thick and unseeing. He squinted, trying to make out his sons' shapes but they had vanished.

"Hasballah!" he shouted.

Nothing but silence and darkness. A glimmer of light from the café as he passed, and then nothing. In his heart he knew they would not be back. They would flee their birthplace and his authority. In future they would seem like strangers. Only the sons of eminent families stayed close to their roots in this alley.

As he made his way in the darkness, he felt that he was bidding farewell to security and peace of mind. He was caught up in a whirlpool of troubled emotions, and fear overcame him, as hard to resist as deep sleep. He told himself the girl must have overwhelmed them with her beauty. He himself had been struck by it. Why hadn't the idiots married? Wasn't marriage a religious act, a safety device?

20.

Zaynab was waiting for him at the door. Her lamp on the step guided him home.

"Where are the children?" she asked anxiously.

"Aren't they back?"

She sighed audibly.

"Let's hope it's for the best," he muttered.

As he sank down on the sofa, she said angrily, "You should have let me go."

"To a bar awash with drunks!"

"You hit them. They're not children. They'll never come home."

"They'll wander around for a day or two, then they'll be back."

"I know them better than you do."

He subsided into silence and she started off on another tack.

"Who's this Fulla Darwish keeps going on about?"

He avoided her eyes and said carelessly, "What's it to you? She's a barmaid!"

"Is she pretty?"

"She's a whore."

"Is she pretty?"

He hesitated. "I didn't look at her."

She let out a despairing breath. "They'll never come back, Ashur," she said.

"Perhaps it's for the best."

"Don't you know how young men behave?"

He said nothing.

"We have to be tolerant of their mistakes."

"Really!" he returned incredulously.

Suddenly she looked withered, faded, old like the wall by the path, and he mumbled in embarrassment, "I'm sorry for you, Zaynab."

"No doubt we'll feel sorry for each other a lot in the years to come," she said irritably.

"In any case, they don't really need us anymore."

"There's no life in the house without them."

"Poor Zaynab."

She rested her head in the palm of her hand and said miserably, "I've got to work early in the morning."

"Try to sleep."

"On a night like this!"

"Whenever you want then!" he said in exasperation.

"What about you?"

"What I need is a breath of fresh air."

21.

The darkness again. Haunting the archway. Hiding beggars and tramps. Humming with silence. Embracing angels and demons. Night where the troubled man goes to escape his obsessions, only to become submerged in them. If fear can seep through the pores of these walls, then deliverance is a joke.

22.

He emerged from the archway into the little square. He found himself alone with the chanting from the monastery, the ancient wall, and the star-studded sky. He squatted with his head between his knees. More than forty years ago someone had crept along and hidden him in the darkness here. How and where had the sin been committed? What were the circumstances? Was he the only victim? Try to imagine your mother's dreamy face and your father's, inflamed with passion. Imagine the honeyed phrases of seduction, and the moment when your fate was decided. There's an angel and a devil standing beside them but desire is defeating the angel. What does your mother look like? Perhaps like . . . To arouse such a conflict she must have had clear skin, dark eyes outlined with kohl, delicate features like flowers opening, a slender, magical body, and a gentle voice. And underlying all that there must have been this hidden, blind-rushing, treacherous, rapacious energy, without scruples, admirably suited to its purpose.

An enticing bait lying in wait while fate looked on expectantly.

Fifteen years of a man's life put paid to in an instant.

He knocked at the monastery door, but it remained closed. He could have forced it easily enough, but he had no desire to. A man wedded to life may as well embrace its children, perfumed with lust. But he was forced to admit that what was happening was hard to believe, and suffer the feelings of a runaway who had finally been trapped. Laughter and tears are equally the stuff of fate. He was a new creature now, plagued by blind desires, madness, and remorse. He begged help from the Almighty, and the wine of temptation flowed through his veins.

His head grew heavy and he drifted into unconsciousness.

He saw Sheikh Afra Zaydan standing before his grave. He took Ashur in his arms.

"Are you taking me into the grave, my lord?" asked Ashur uneasily.

But he carried him along the path, across the square, and under the archway.

Something woke Ashur. He opened his eyes and heard Zaynab saying, "Just as I thought. Are you going to sleep here till morning?"

He jumped up in fright, gave her his hand, and the two of them went off in silence.

23.

Suddenly his huge frame filled the doorway. The drinkers' heavy eyelids flickered and behind their clouded eyes silent questions were exchanged:

"What's he come back for?"

"Is he chasing his sons?"

"Don't expect any good to come out of it!"

He swept his eyes around the place and found a space on the left-hand side of the bar. He crossed over and dropped onto his haunches, acting casually to cover his embarrassment.

Darwish hurried up to him. "Nice to see you." He smiled. "Who would have thought it!"

Ashur ignored him entirely. Fulla came over with a calabash and a paper cone of spiced lupin seeds. He lowered his eyelids and remembered the story of the flood. Then he pushed the calabash aside and paid for the drink without a word.

Darwish began to look at him strangely. "We're here to get you whatever it is you want," he whispered and left him on his own.

The other customers quickly disregarded him. Fulla wondered what made him keep off drink. She went up to him again and gestured toward the untouched calabash. "It's really good," she said encouragingly.

He inclined his head as if to thank her.

"I'd keep out of his way," called a drunk.

"Don't you think he's like a lion?" she answered, laughing, loud enough for Ashur to hear.

A childish joy descended on him, but he kept his features immobilized. His clothes no longer shielded his nakedness from prying eyes. The whole course of his life, between the day he was found tucked away at the side of the path and this moment as he sat at the bar, shrank to nothing. Its twists and turns were all swallowed up in the surging waves of a new song. In no time he gave in to defeat, exhilarated at the sense of victory it brought him.

Fulla was standing among the earthenware containers looking at him with interest when Hasballah, Rizqallah, and Hibatallah burst through the door.

Little trickles of expectation spread through the lazy air and the customers craned their necks to have a better view. Hasballah shouted a greeting. Then he noticed his father. He swallowed and froze. Rizqallah and Hibatallah looked as if the air had been let out of them. All three stood there for a moment in shock, then turned on their heels and vanished. A sarcastic laugh broke the silence. Fulla looked in Darwish's direction. He said nothing, but annoyance was written all over his face.

24.

"Is this going on forever?" asked Zaynab, her face registering protest.

"What do you suggest?" replied Ashur dully.

"It's all very well to ban them from the bar, but is it worth the price you have to pay?"

He moved his big head in an indecisive gesture and said nothing.

"It means that you've begun to prop up the bar at Darwish's all day long," she cried angrily.

25.

He was driving along when Fulla came out of the bar and stood in his path. He pulled on the reins, muttering a little prayer for divine mercy. Without a word she leapt gracefully aboard the cart and sat next to him, winding her black wrap around her. Her face was unveiled. He looked at her questioningly.

"Take me to Margoush," she said sweetly.

Darwish appeared in the doorway with a smile on his face and said, "Look after her. I'll pay her fare."

Ashur saw the web closing around him and he didn't care. He was so happy he felt drunk. All he had learned from Sheikh Afra was crushed under the donkey's hooves as he drove along, his back molten in the heat.

"You could easily be chief of the clan, if you wanted," she said suddenly.

His face lit up. "Do you think I'm that bad?"

She laughed softly. "What's the point of being good when you're dealing with people who don't know the meaning of the word?"

"You're still young."

"No one's ever treated me like a child," she replied caustically.

He frowned. The attentive stares directed at his precious cargo had not escaped him. "Why are you going to Margoush?" he asked her abruptly.

When she did not answer, he regretted his slip of the tongue. She asked him to stop at the entrance to Margoush alley. "I wish the ride had been longer," she said. Then as she started to walk away, she looked back and added, "But it will soon be nighttime!"

Ashur patted his donkey on the neck and whispered in its ear, "Your master's finished."

26.

At first light he stormed into the bar. Darwish woke up, protesting loudly. He was taken aback when he saw who his visitor was.

"What brings you here?" he asked.

Ashur pulled him to his feet and stared wildly at him. "There's no way out," he muttered.

"Why have you come, Ashur?"

"You're malicious and evil. You know very well why I've come," said Ashur roughly.

Darwish rubbed the back of his neck, squinting at him through reddened eyes.

"I should be starting work," he mumbled.

"I've decided to take her," said Ashur, jumping in with both feet.

"There's a time for everything," smiled Darwish.

"But as my lawful wedded wife . . ."

Darwish's eyes widened in surprise and the two men glared at each other silently. "What's this all about?" murmured Darwish.

"It's not what you think."

"Have you gone mad, Ashur?"

"Maybe."

"I can't manage without her," said Darwish, tiring of the conversation.

"You'll have to!"

"Have you thought of the consequences?"

"It makes no difference."

"Don't you know that all the men in the neighborhood . . ." began Darwish with a vicious air.

Fulla interrupted him from her couch, making it clear that she had heard the whole conversation. "What are you trying to tell him? If he'd wanted you to give evidence, he'd have asked you!"

"You'll be the laughingstock of the whole place," shouted Darwish, erupting into anger.

"He can look after himself," Fulla shouted back.

Darwish fell on her, striking her so hard that she cried out in pain. Ashur sprang toward him, locked him in his arms, and squeezed him until he begged for mercy. Then he let go of him, growling with rage, and Darwish sank to the floor, doubled up. "To hell with you!" he shouted.

27.

Ashur put his plan into action with blind resolve. Even the sadness he felt on Zaynab's behalf, and his memories of his life with her did nothing to stop him.

"I can't help it," he said, head bowed.

She looked at him with innocent curiosity.

"I'm going to marry another woman, Zaynab."

Zaynab was dumbstruck. She felt as if she was losing her mind and flocks of twittering birds were pouring out of her head. "You! The paragon of virtue!" she shouted.

"It's God's will," he said contritely.

"Why do you make a mockery of God's name?" she demanded. "Why don't you admit it's the devil? Do you think you can palm me off with that?"

"You won't lose any of your rights," he said confidently.

"You're leaving me all alone," she said, choking on her tears. "You traitor! How can you turn your back on everything we've been through together?"

28.

Fulla and Ashur had a quiet wedding. He rented her a basement at the end of the alley near the main square. He was so happy in his marriage that he looked like a young man again.

29.

News of the marriage swept through the quarter like wildfire.

"Couldn't he have done the same as everybody else does?" people asked.

Hasballah said sourly, "So he was banning us because he wanted her for himself!"

Ashur's reputation as a good and upright man was diminished when people heard the news. Is this how the good fall? Where was his gratitude to Zayn al-Naturi? Who made him a donkey boy, then gave him a cart to drive? Who took him in off the streets in the first place?

"If I wasn't who I am, I wouldn't have bothered to marry her at all," said Ashur defensively.

As the days passed, his happiness grew, and he learned to ignore the gossip. Fulla was fonder of him than he had dreamed possible and determined to prove to him that she was a good house-wife, docile and anxious not to arouse his jealousy. One of the things that made her more exquisite in his eyes was his discovery that she, like him, had never known her mother or father. Because he loved her so much he excused her for her ignorance of many useful things and tolerated her bad habits. From the beginning he realized that she only paid lip service to religion, had no conscious moral values, and simply followed her instincts and copied those around her. He wondered when there would be time to correct the serious omissions in her life. Love protected her now, but would it always be enough?

He preserved relations with Zaynab and respected all her rights. She began to grow accustomed to her new life, resigned herself to her pain, and tried not to spoil his visits to her.

Darwish watched events unfolding and said spitefully to him-self, "The scorpion adores him so far, but when will she turn around and sting him?"

After some time had passed Fulla gave birth to a son named Shams al-Din. Ashur rejoiced as if it had been his firstborn.

The days passed in happiness and serenity, the like of which Ashur had never known in his life before.

30.

What's happening to our alley?

Today is not like yesterday, nor yesterday like the day before.

Grave events are taking place. Did they descend from heaven or explode out of the depths of hell? Or are they the product of mere chance? However, the sun still rises each morning and makes its daily journey through the sky. Night follows day. People go about their business. The mysterious anthems rise into the air.

What's happening to our alley?

He watched Shams al-Din, ecstatically suckling from his mother's breast and smiling, oblivious to events around him.

"Another death. Can't you hear the wailing?" he said.

"I wonder who it is," said Fulla.

He peered out between the window bars, trying to hear where the sound was coming from.

"It might be from Zaydan al-Dakhakhani's house," he muttered.

"There've been so many deaths this week," said Fulla anxiously.

"More than there usually are in a year."

"Sometimes a year goes by without a single person dying."

The crisis showed no sign of abating.

One morning Ashur was driving along when Darwish accosted him. "Have you heard what they're saying, Ashur?"

"What?"

"That people vomit, have uncontrollable diarrhea, collapse and die like flies."

"People say anything around here," muttered Ashur irritably.

"Yesterday it happened to one of my customers. He made the place filthy."

Ashur regarded him scornfully and Darwish went on, "Even the rich aren't safe. Bannan's wife died this morning."

"Then it must be the wrath of God!" said Ashur as he drove away.

31.

The emergency reached gigantic proportions. The path leading to the graveyard hummed with new life. Mourners thronged down it as one coffin followed another and queues of bodies waited to be buried. Every house was in mourning. Not an hour went by without a death being announced. Death swept through the alley, attacking rich and poor, weak and strong, men and women, old people and children indiscriminately, pursuing all alike with the sword of destruction. Other alleys nearby were similarly affected and the whole area was cordoned off to contain the epidemic. Night and day, fractured voices rose in prayer, imploring saints and angels to stop the disaster.

Amm Hamidu, the sheikh of the alley, stood before his shop beating a drum to summon his flock. Dropping whatever they were doing, they rushed to hear his announcement. "It's the plague," he said gravely. "It strikes without warning and no one is spared, unless God has decreed it."

A fearful silence settled over the audience and he hesitated a little before continuing, "This is what the authorities advise."

They listened intently. Could the government save them from this catastrophe?

"Avoid all public gatherings and crowded places."

They looked at one another in astonishment. They lived their lives in the street. At nights the harafish congregated under the archway and in derelict buildings. How could they avoid crowds?

The sheikh elucidated: "Avoid the cafés, the bars, the hashish dens!"

Escape death by dying! How cruel life is!

"And hygiene! Always remember to take precautions!"

The mocking eyes of the harafish looked at him from behind masks of caked dirt.

"Boil the water from wells and water skins before using it. Drink lemon and onion juice."

The silence returned. The shadow of death hovered above their heads.

"Is that all?" someone asked eventually.

Amm Hamidu replied in a tone which invited no further discussion, "Say your prayers and accept the Lord's judgment."

The crowd broke up despondently. The harafish went off to

their slums exchanging sarcastic jokes. The funeral processions went on without a break.

32.

Anxiety drove him to the monastery square in the middle of the night. Winter was coming to an end. A gentle, invigorating breeze blew and the clouds hid the stars. In the darkness the anthems floated from the monastery as clearly as ever, their serenity undisturbed by a single elegiac note. Don't you know what's happened to us, gentlemen? Have you no cure? Haven't you heard the wailing of the bereaved? Seen the funeral processions going by your walls?

Ashur stared hard at the outline of the great arched door until his head spun. It grew until its top disappeared in the clouds. What's going on, Lord? The door undulated slowly in its place and seemed ready to fall. A strange smell reached his nostrils; it was earthy, but governed inexorably by the stars. For the first time in his life Ashur was afraid. He rose to his feet trembling and made for the archway, conscious that he had encountered death. As he went home he wondered sadly why he should be so terrified of death.

33.

He lit the lamp and saw Fulla asleep. Only Shams al-Din's hair showed above the bedcovers. Fulla had abandoned her beauty to sleep: her mouth was half-open, without the trace of a smile, and her scarf had slipped back, allowing strands of hair to escape. Fear aroused his slumbering desire. A silent call licked around him like a tongue of flame.

Frantic with lust, he went forward impetuously whispering her name until she opened her eyes. When she realized who it was, and understood from the look in his eyes and the way he was standing, she stretched voluptuously beneath the covers, smiled, and asked, "What were you doing out at this hour of the night?"

But he was too agitated to answer her: a sensation of violent grief swelled in his huge chest.

34.

He fell asleep for a couple of hours.

He saw Sheikh Afra Zaydan in the middle of the alley and rushed toward him, wild with hope. The sheikh turned and began to walk away, taking two steps for every one of his, and so they progressed along the path and through the graveyard out into the hills and the open country. He tried to call out to the sheikh but his voice stuck in his throat and he woke up in the depths of depression.

He told himself that there must be a reason for this dream and thought about it at length. By the time the dawn light came flooding through the window he had reached a decision. Cheerfully he rose and woke Fulla. Shams al-Din began to cry. She changed him and thrust her full breast gently into his open mouth, then turned reprovingly to her husband.

He stroked her hair tenderly. "I had a strange dream."

"I want to go back to sleep," she protested.

"We have to leave the alley without delay," he said with a severity which surprised her.

She stared at him in disbelief.

"Without delay," he repeated.

Frowning, she asked, "What on earth did you dream about?"

"My father Afra showed me the way."

"Where to?"

"The hills and the desert!"

"You're off your head."

"No. Yesterday I saw death. I smelled its smell."

"It's not for us to resist death, Ashur."

He looked down in embarrassment and said, "We have a right to resist death as well as to die at the appointed time."

"But you're running away from it!"

"Flight can be a form of resistance."

"How will we survive in the open country?" she asked anxiously.

"Survival depends on how hard you work, not where you live."

"People will laugh at our stupidity," she sighed.

"The sources of laughter have run dry," he remarked sorrowfully.

She burst into tears.

"Are you abandoning me, Fulla?" he asked anxiously.

"I've got no one but you," she answered tearfully. "I'll go where you go."

35.

Ashur went to see his first wife Zaynab and his sons Hasballah, Rizqallah, and Hibatallah. He told them of his dream and his decision to flee the area. "You must come too. There's no time to lose," he urged.

They looked at him in amazement, refusal etched on their faces.

"Is this a new way of avoiding death?" asked Zaynab sarcastically.

"We earn a living here. We can't just drop it all," said Hasballah.

"We've got the strength of our arms, and the donkey and cart," said Ashur angrily.

"Doesn't death exist out there, father?" asked Hibatallah.

"We have to do all we can to prove to my lord Afra that we're grateful for his blessing," said Ashur, his anger mounting.

"The girl's turned your head," exclaimed Zaynab.

He looked at each of them in turn and asked them finally, "What are you going to do?"

"Sorry, father," replied Hasballah. "We're staying. Let's hope it turns out for the best!"

Overcome with grief, Ashur left them.

36.

Hamidu, the local sheikh, looked up from his desk to see Ashur towering over him like a mountain. "What do you want, Ashur?" he inquired sharply. Before Ashur could reply he went on, "Hasballah told me what you intend to do. I've heard some funny things in my time . . ."

Strangely calm, Ashur continued, "I came to ask you to try and persuade the people yourself. They're more likely to listen to you."

"Have you gone mad, Ashur?" shouted the sheikh. "Perhaps you imagine you know more than the authorities?"

"But . . ."

"Take care you don't put people's livelihoods at risk preaching anarchy."

"But I saw death and had a dream of salvation."

"This is madness incarnate! Death is invisible and most dreams come from the devil."

"I'm a good man, Master Hamidu . . ."

"Didn't you go to the bar one day to save your sons from a woman, then fall in love with her and keep her for yourself?"

"I saved her from evil," returned Ashur angrily, "and anyway I'm not saying I've never committed any sins."

"Do what you want," cried the sheikh in exasperation, "but try to influence anyone else and I'll report you to the police."

37.

Ashur fled at dawn. He drove out through the archway toward the cemetery as if it was a feast day. Behind him on the swaying cart sat Fulla with Shams al-Din in her arms, hemmed in by bundles and packages, bags of peanuts, jars of pickled lemons and olives, and sacks of crusty bread. As they drove out into the monastery square, they were greeted by the last strains of the night's chanting:

Joz astane tovam dar jahan panahi nist.
Sare mara bejoz in dar havale gahi nist.

Ashur listened to it sadly, then prayed for the alley with all his heart.

He drove down the long track, then made his way between the tombs, seldom closed for long these days, and out into the open country. A cool breeze enveloped him, kindly and refreshing. "Make sure you and the child are well wrapped up," he said to Fulla.

"There's not a living creature in sight," she complained.

"God is everywhere."

"Where are we going to stop?"

"In the foothills."

"D'you think we'll be able to stand the climate?"

"We'll be fine. And there are plenty of caves."

"What about bandits?"

"Just let them try!" he joked.

As the cart drew nearer to its destination the darkness began to lift. The shadows dissolved in the rosy, translucent, liquid air and new worlds were revealed between heaven and earth. Strange colors streamed from them, blending together and staining the horizon a pure brilliant red, which merged into the clear blue of the sky's arch. The first rays of sun broke through, bathed in dew, and the mountain appeared, lofty, calm, enduring, indifferent.

"God is great!" exclaimed Ashur.

He looked at Fulla and said encouragingly, "The journey's over." Then with a laugh he added, "The journey's just begun."

38.

They spent about six months in the open. Ashur only left the cave where they had settled and its immediate area to take water from the public drinking fountain in Darasa, or buy fodder for the donkey and such basic necessities as their slender means allowed. Fulla suggested they should sell her gold earrings but he refused, without telling her why: she had worn them before he married her, so they had been bought with tainted money.

The early days in the cave seemed like a picnic, an adventure, an excursion. In the shadow of her giant of a husband she felt no fear. But very soon life appeared empty, monotonous, unbearable. Have we come here to count the seconds as they crawl steadily over our skins, the grains of sand in the day, the stars at night?

She said to Ashur, "Even heaven would be unthinkable without people or work to do."

He did not contradict her. "We have to be patient," was all he said.

He spent much of his time in prayer and meditation, and in thinking about the family he had left behind and the people of his alley. "I've never loved other people as much as I do now," he confessed to his wife.

He slept part of the day and stayed up all night. He thought so long and deeply that he had a strange presentiment he would soon hear voices and see figures from the spirit world. He became the companion of the stars and the dawn. Nothing separated him from God. Why did the alley's inhabitants give in to death and believe that human beings were powerless? Wasn't this a kind of blasphemy? He was involved in endless silent conversations with figures from his past: Sheikh Afra, Sakina, Naturi, Zaynab; and in sad confidences with his three sons. Hasballah was the one he would have chosen as his friend every time; it was a pity he had missed so many chances with him. Rizqallah was a lost cause, but he was smart, while Hibatallah was so attached to his mother that it was almost unhealthy. All the same, he decided that they were better than many of their peers and prayed long and earnestly for them and their mother. His alley seemed like a jewel stuck in the mud. He loved it now with all its faults. However, it was borne in on him in the course of his devotions that people bring their sufferings upon themselves. The notables, the harafish, Darwish, all revolve around a twisted axis, bent on mastering its awkward secret. And now God is punishing them, as if he has lost patience with them. Yet the dawn still reels in rosy bliss, the rays of light dance in everlasting joy.

Soon he would hear voices, see spirits; he was about to be reborn.

39.

The occasion arose at last to make Fulla a believer. She was a young and beautiful woman without religion. She knew nothing of God or the prophets, of virtue rewarded or sin punished. All that protected her in this terrifying world were her love and her maternal instincts. Fine, he would bend all his efforts to educating her. If she hadn't had such confidence in him she wouldn't have believed a word he was saying. With great trouble she learned some chapters of the Quran so that she could say her prayers. She would burst out laughing in the middle and interrupt herself, but she prayed obediently, trying not to provoke her husband's anger and anxious to please him.

"Why does God let death destroy people?" she asked him innocently.

"Who knows?" he answered fiercely. "Perhaps they need to be taught a lesson."

"Don't get angry, like God!" she teased.

"When will you learn to keep a decent tongue in your head?"

"All right, so why did He create us with so much evil in us?"

He struck the sand with his palm. "Who am I to answer for the Almighty?" he demanded. Then, imploringly, "We just have to believe in Him and serve Him with all our strength."

She abandoned the discussion. "Time's passing and this loneliness is more terrible than death," she complained.

Silently he looked away from her. She was threatening to rebel. Would she run away, taking Shams al-Din with her? There would be nothing left in his life.

Shams al-Din at least was content. He crawled around on the sand, sat and played with pebbles, slept well, was never bored, and grew in the wind and sun, feeding abundantly on his mother's milk. The donkey too was happy, eating well, working little, swishing its tail at the flies, and roaming its kingdom with infinite patience. Ashur watched it with tenderness and respect: it was his friend and companion and his source of income; a firm bond of affection united them.

40.

The days went by. They came close to the edge of collapse in their relationship.

Then one day on his return from Darasa, he announced, "They say the disaster is under control."

Fulla clapped her hands and cried, "Let's go back at once!"

"Let's wait till I make sure it's true," he said firmly.

41.

The cart crossed the cemetery as dawn approached. Under the pale stars its passengers' hearts overflowed with joy and trembled in gratitude for their escape. When they turned onto the path and were met by the sound of the chanting, tears sprang into their eyes; the songs said that everything would be as it always had been.

Here was their alley immersed in sleep: people, animals, and things. As strange in its lethargy as in its wakefulness, it would always tantalize Ashur. As they passed Zaynab's his heart stopped, but he didn't want to disturb them and postponed the embarrassment of seeing them again till later. In their hearts he and Fulla blew dancing, joyous kisses to the walls, the earth, the cheeks of loved ones. Death had not conquered life, or he himself would be dead, but still he felt some regret and shame.

At last they were in their own room, inhaling the odors of dust and decay. Fulla rushed to open the window. "What sort of welcome do you think you'll get, Ashur?" she asked apprehensively.

"Let them do as they think right," answered Ashur with a defiance he did not feel.

42.

He squatted down behind the window bars patiently waiting for the last of the darkness to disappear. Light began to settle on the buildings so that their features emerged, familiar as the faces of old friends. He wondered who would be the first to come by. The milkman perhaps, or a servant at one of the big houses. He would greet him resoundingly and take whatever sarcasm came his way. Daylight was streaming into the alley by now and the bean seller was not even open for the breakfast trade yet. He moved away from the window uncertainly.

"Government regulations seem to have changed the habits of the alley," he said.

He pushed his feet into his leather slippers and added, "I'm off to visit the children."

43.

He walked along the deserted alley between locked doors and windows, stopped in front of Zaynab's, pushed the door, and went in. The room was empty and gave off an odor of melancholy. The bed was made in the normal way, but covered with a layer of dust. The single sofa was strewn with worn clothes, the wooden bench overturned; under the bed were pots and pans, crockery, the cooking stove, and half a basket of coal; in the chest a black wrap, a dress, a comb, a mirror, a towel.

They must have fled. But why had they left their clothes behind?

In vain he tried to fight off the sense of impending disaster. He struck his forehead with the palm of his hand, sighed, and began to weep silently. Then he told himself that he would hear what had happened from other people, that it was too early to lose hope, and walked unsteadily outside.

44.

He followed the alley to the main square. How silent it was, how empty! Not a door or window open. He went forward slowly, stupefied. The bar, the caravanserai, the café, the houses, all were closed and shuttered. Nothing stirred. No sign of a cat or a dog, not a breath of life anywhere, and the dusty buildings all sunk in the same desolation.

The sun shone for nothing, the autumn wind blew aimlessly. In his hoarse voice he shouted tearfully, "Is anyone there?"

Nobody answered. No windows opened. No heads looked out. There was only the stubborn silence of despair, defiant fear, and leaden misery.

He went through the archway to the little square and the monastery rose before him, unchanged. The mulberry leaves gazed at him and he saw their nectar running like blood. The anthems were silent, cloaked in indifference. He stared for a long time, sorrow tearing his heart from its moorings, tears flowing down his cheeks.

In a voice like a roar of thunder he shouted to the dervishes in the monastery.

It seemed to him that the branches bent and swayed to his voice, but no one answered. He began to shout unrestrainedly, to no effect. He cackled like an idiot.

"Who listens to your songs every day?" he called. "Don't you know who I am?"

45.

"There's not a soul about," he said to Fulla, drying his tears.

From her own reddened eyes he saw that she too suspected a disaster.

"From one wasteland to another, Ashur," she remarked with a catch in her throat.

He sighed helplessly.

"Let's go somewhere else," she suggested.

He looked at her in silent amazement.

"Do you want us to stay in this graveyard?" she asked sharply.

"We'll move around in the cart. We won't stay here all day. But this is the only home we have."

"An abandoned alley!" she exclaimed.

"It won't always be like this," he cried angrily.

46.

Neither sorrow nor joy lasts for ever.

Ashur returned to his trade as a driver. Fulla and Shams al-Din rode with him all day and part of the night, protected by this giant of a man.

He realized that the alley must have been forgotten in the tide of weightier responsibilities inundating the authorities as the plague spread far and wide. No one would suspect his presence in this desolate corner. But they would come. One day they would come. People from here and there breathing new life into the alley, dispelling its blank chill.

Whenever he went out in the early morning to fetch the cart, his eyes were drawn to the Bannan's house. Its purple dome, its awesome bulk, its air of mystery fascinated him. What treasures were left inside? Would a member of the Bannan family bother to come and retrieve them?

Temptation took root in his heart and gave rise to entrancing dreams. He was as curious as he had once been to see the secrets of the monastery. The difference was that the Bannan house was accessible and there was no one else around. A single action, entirely without danger, was all that stood between him and the fulfillment of his dream.

47.

He shrugged his broad shoulders disdainfully, and pushed open the door. Dust covered the mosaic of the wall tiles and the marble floor. Dust was the dominant presence everywhere. He stood dumbstruck on the threshold of the reception hall. It's like a city square, Ashur! The ceiling was higher than a jinn's head with a chandelier like the huge dome of Sultan Ghury's palace in the middle and lamps hanging from each corner. Ornately patterned rugs covered wooden couches ranged around the sides of the room. Sumptuous hangings and framed verses of the Quran illuminated in gold lined the walls.

He heard Fulla's voice calling him and ran out to her. She looked at him in astonishment. "Whatever are you doing?" she asked.

"Satisfying a whim," he answered, shamefaced.

"Aren't you scared the owners will find out?"

"There aren't any."

She hesitated, torn by conflicting desires, then indicated the cart and said, "We're late."

"Come and have a look around, Fulla," he begged shyly.

They spent the day going from room to room, exploring the bathroom and kitchen, trying out the divans and chairs and couches. A mad light sprang into Fulla's beautiful eyes. "Let's spend the night here," she said.

Ashur said nothing. He felt weaker than ever.

"We could wash in that amazing bath, wear new clothes, sleep in this bed. Just for one night, then go back to our normal life."

48.

But it wasn't just for a night.

They would leave the house at dawn and slip back in as night fell. During the day they drove the cart from one district to another and ate lentils, beans, and ta'miya; at night they floated about in cotton and silk, lounged on divans on the ground floor, and slept in a luxurious bed reached by a short flight of ebony stairs. Fulla stroked curtains, cushions, carpets, and exclaimed, "Our life was just a nightmare!"

At night through the carved lattices the alley looked a gloomy place, haunted by wretched phantoms. "Divine wisdom is hard to comprehend," muttered Ashur sadly.

"But God is generous to those he chooses," Fulla answered defiantly.

Ashur smiled, wondering how long the dream would last, but she was thinking of other things.

"Look at all these precious objects around us," she said. "They must be worth a lot. Why don't we sell some of them so that we can eat food more in keeping with our surroundings!"

"But it's other people's money," he said gently.

"Nobody owns it. You can see that. It's God's gift to us."

Ashur pondered for some time. Temptation stole over him like sleep over a weary man. He resolved to find a way out of the crisis and arrived at a new formulation. "Money is forbidden when it is spent on forbidden things," he announced.

Eager to advance the debate, she said, "It's a gift, Ashur. We only want to eat."

He began pacing the floor uncertainly. Finally he murmured, "It's all right as long as we spend it honestly."

49.

With the passing of time their scruples eased and Ashur and his family took up permanent residence in the Bannan house. The donkey grazed in the courtyard at the rear and the cart was stowed away in the basement. Ashur swaggered about the house like a rich man, with an elegantly rolled turban, a flowing robe, and a gold-handled cane. Fulla blossomed in her new life of ease, the most beautiful notable's wife the alley had seen. Shams al-Din peed on the costly Shiraz carpets. From the gentle warmth of the kitchen floated the scents of grilled and roasted meats and spicy stews.

The days went by and life began to steal back into the alley. The harafish came to squat in the derelict buildings. Every day a new family moved in to an empty house. Shops began to open their doors. Life breathed again, the chill vanished, voices called to one another, dogs and cats appeared, the cock began to crow at dawn, and only the houses of the rich remained empty.

Ashur was known as the only notable in the neighborhood.

People greeted him respectfully, addressing him without irony as "Lord of the Alley."

He was widely rumored to be the sole survivor of the plague and given the name Ashur al-Nagi, Ashur the Survivor. People were eager to sing his praises, seeing him as a good, kindly, and charitable man. He was the protector of the poor: not content with heaping alms on them, he bought donkeys, baskets, and handcarts and distributed them to the unemployed until only the old and the insane were without work.

They had never known a rich man like this before and they raised him to the ranks of the saints, saying God had singled him out and spared him for this purpose.

Ashur grew calm and his conscience eased. He began to fulfill dreams which had beguiled him in the past: he hired workers to clean the little square and the pathway and rid them of piles of dirt and rubbish. He built a trough for the animals, a drinking fountain, a small mosque, features which became as deeply embedded in the consciousness of our alley as the monastery, the archway, the graveyard, and the old city wall, and made it the jewel of the whole neighborhood.

50.

The sound of unfamiliar activity from the direction of the bar caught his ear one day. He was on his way to the Husayn mosque and stopped dead in surprise. Builders were reconstructing the place, restoring it to life. He leaned through the doorway and called, "Who are you working for?"

"For me, sir," came a voice from a dark corner to the right of the entrance and Darwish materialized before him from out of the gloom.

He was gripped by a violent shudder of shock and distaste, closely followed by a surge of anger. "So you're alive, Darwish," he exclaimed.

Inclining his head gratefully, he said, "Thanks to you, Lord of the Alley." Seeing that Ashur was in need of enlightenment, he went on sarcastically, "I followed your advice and fled into the desert. I was quite close to you all the time."

Ashur decided to take the bull by the horns. "I forbid you to reopen the bar," he said.

"You might be lord of the alley and the only notable around, but you're not the law or the clan chief!"

"Why don't you go somewhere else? Anywhere but here?" demanded Ashur angrily.

"My home is here, Mr. Notable."

They looked at each other in silence until Darwish said, "What's more, I expect to profit from your general munificence!"

Was he planning to fleece him? Trembling with anger, Ashur drew him outside and said, "Perhaps I can't close you down, but I warn you, I won't give in to threats."

"I thought you helped anyone in need?"

"To do good, never harm."

"You're free to spend your money as you want, of course," said Darwish, emphasizing the "your" suggestively.

Ashur shrugged his shoulders. "Maybe you'll get the urge to expose me," he said. "Maybe. But do you know what will happen to you if you do?"

"Threats, Ashur?"

"I'll batter you to a pulp, I swear by the head of Husayn. When they come to scrape you up, they won't know your head from your feet."

"Are you threatening to kill me?"

"You know I'm quite capable of it!"

"Just to keep your hands on money that's not yours in the first place?"

"It's mine as long as I spend it on things that benefit people."

Again they stared silently at each other. Weakness flickered in Darwish's eyes. "All I want is for you to give me handouts like you give the others," he said pleasantly.

"Not a penny to people like you."

A heavy silence descended.

"Well?" demanded Ashur impatiently.

"So be it," murmured Darwish with regret. "Although we're brothers, we'll live side by side like strangers."

51.

Fulla received the news agitatedly, her sweet face sullen with misery.

"Use different tactics with him," she pleaded. "Give him what he wants so we're not haunted by the specter of betrayal."

"Didn't the desert air purge you of such weakness?" frowned Ashur.

She brandished her Damascus silk shawl at him. "This is what I'm afraid for."

He shook his head crossly.

"We're not safe anymore, Ashur."

"He's evil, but he's a coward," replied Ashur with scorn.

52.

The sun shone again after a cold, stormy night. The shop belonging to the sheikh of the alley opened its doors. The new sheikh was called Mahmoud Qatayif. The people sensed that the government was beginning to recover from the onslaught of death and destruction and replace those of its officers who had perished in the plague.

Many saw this as a good sign but the reaction was different in Ashur's household. Ashur was full of misgivings and Fulla, horrified, held Shams al-Din close to her and murmured, "Things look bad."

"Surely what's past is past," Ashur said worriedly.

"You're as frightened as I am, Ashur."

"What have we done wrong? We found some money that didn't belong to anybody and spent it in a way which benefited the community."

"But isn't that man threatening to harm us?"

Ashur's anger flared. "Let's trust in God," he shouted. "He's the true owner of the money."

Fulla cradled Shams al-Din in her arms. "All I want is for the river of bounty to flow on until this child can swim in it."

53.

Ashur decided to confront the threat without further delay. He went to introduce himself to the new sheikh, who received him warmly: "Welcome to our lord and protector."

Joy filled Ashur's heart as he returned the greeting.

"Do you know, master," went on the sheikh, "I was about to come and see you."

Ashur's heart jumped but he said evenly, "You're welcome at any time."

"I need to hear al-Nagi's version of events—the man best placed to tell me how the alley was wiped out."

54

Thus Mahmoud Qatayif entered Ashur's house. The two men sat side by side on the divan in the reception hall, while Fulla hovered behind the half-open door. They sipped coffee and exchanged pleasantries, then the sheikh came to the point: "I need the opinion of the man the community regards as its benefactor."

"I'm at your disposal," replied Ashur unenthusiastically.

"A commission has been set up recently to make inventories of the houses of the rich . . . yours among them."

"God have mercy on the souls of the dead."

"We've discovered that a number of these houses have been looted."

"But there wasn't a soul about!"

"The inventories show that looting has taken place."

"How strange! I pray God the money went to those who deserved it."

"Deserved it?"

"The poor, I mean."

Mahmoud Qatayif smiled. "That's a theory, I suppose, but not one the government subscribes to."

"What's their theory?"

"These houses are to be considered Treasury property and put up for auction."

Ashur looked sharply at him. "What about the looting?"

Qatayif shrugged his shoulders. "The commission's decided to overlook it, to avoid accusing innocent people."

Ashur realized that the looters were none other than the members of the government commission. Although he was disgusted, much of his confidence returned. He said jokingly, "Perhaps the commission is applying my theory, sheikh!"

"One problem remains," said the sheikh regretfully.

Ashur looked inquiringly at him, still sure of his own position.

"The commission wants to examine the documents relating to your ownership of this house. Then it will have done its job."

With one treacherous blow his sense of security was destroyed. For an instant his eyes met Fulla's behind the door.

"Do you have any doubts that I'm the legal owner?"

"God forbid! But orders are orders."

"I want to know what's behind these orders," he said in his hoarse voice.

"In neighboring areas there have been cases of people taking over houses that don't belong to them," murmured the sheikh.

A silence, fraught with apprehension and doubt, enveloped the two men. Then Ashur suddenly spoke: "Supposing I'd lost them in the chaos of death and exile?"

"That would be extremely awkward," muttered the sheikh uneasily.

"Awkward!" roared Ashur in anger. "Aren't they satisfied with what they've taken already?"

The sheikh trembled at the force of Ashur's voice. "I'm only carrying out orders," he said apologetically.

"You must have more information. Tell me what you know."

"The problem is that one of the members of the commission has some reservations."

"To hell with him!"

"The documents would resolve all doubt."

"They're lost."

In a soft, fearful voice the sheikh said, "This will cause problems, Master Ashur."

At this point Fulla burst furiously into the room. "That's enough beating about the bush," she stormed at the sheikh.

The man rose to his feet in embarrassment. "You've got nothing to lose. Let's settle this between ourselves," she said, her words as plain as a blow from a club.

"If it was only up to me, it would be easy," said the sheikh sadly.

Ashur jumped up in annoyance. "Let's get it over with," he said.

55.

Things were going on both openly and behind the scenes which the alley, absorbed in its daily activities, never suspected. Few of its inhabitants could notice something without drawing conclusions. But their hearts, drunk with hope, trusted in the light which surrounded them.

One morning the giant figure of Ashur al-Nagi appeared in their midst in handcuffs, his head bowed. It was him; it couldn't be anyone else. Surrounded by soldiers with an officer at their head and Mahmoud Qatayif bringing up the rear.

Angry astonishment spread like sparks from a fire, drawing people from their shops and houses and bringing curious faces to fill the windows.

"What's going on?"

"What's happening to the world?"

"A saintly man like that in handcuffs!"

"Clear the way!" roared the officer.

But they flocked together at the rear of the procession, sticking to it like a shadow, until the officer shouted, "Anyone who comes near the police station will be in trouble."

Darwish could not believe what he was seeing and in a loud voice, clearly intended for Ashur to hear, he said, "By my brother's life, I never said a thing!"

Fulla was a model of grieving beauty, with Shams al-Din on her hip and a bundle over her shoulder, her eyes red from weeping.

56.

Ashur's trial was one of those events which sticks in the mind for years afterward. A huge crowd from the alley attended, following each twist and turn with beating hearts. For the first time they were united in their love and affection. Ashur stood in the dock, glowing with pride at the warmth round about him. Perhaps the judges admired his giant's body or leonine features; in any case the people would never forget the sound of his hoarse voice as he spoke in his own defense: "I am not a thief. I have never robbed anyone, believe me. Death had ravaged our alley. I returned from the desert to find it empty and abandoned. The house no longer had an owner. Isn't it fitting that it should be given to the sole survivor? And I didn't keep the money for myself. I thought of it as God's, and of myself as His servant entrusted with spending it to His greater glory. There are no starving or unemployed left in our alley and we want for nothing. We have a drinking fountain, a trough for the animals, a small mosque. So why have you arrested me like a common thief? Why do you want to punish me?"

The public chorused their agreement. Even the judges smiled inside themselves all the time he was speaking. They sentenced him to one year in prison.

57.

Fulla returned to the basement room without a penny. She found people genuinely ready to care for her. They brought her food, water, firewood. The air was fragrant with kind words.

The disclosure of Ashur's secret did nothing to detract from the love and respect people felt for him. On the contrary, it may have helped to create a legendary figure of him, braver and more heroic than before.

All the same, Fulla decided not to live off charity, and went to work in the Darasa market, far from prying eyes.

One day Darwish stood blocking her path. "You have my sympathy, Mother of Shams al-Din," he said in a gruff voice.

"You must be enjoying this, Darwish!" she retorted sharply.

"I had nothing to do with it," he said vehemently, "Mahmoud Qatayif will testify to that."

"It must be convenient for you, though."

"God forgive you! What do I gain from him being in prison?"

"Don't pretend you're not pleased, Darwish."

"God forgive you . . . But let's stop quarreling," he said, suddenly ingratiating, "and let me give you some advice."

"Advice?"

"It's not right for you to work alone in the Darasa market."

"Do you have a better idea?" she scoffed.

"You could work where I could keep an eye on you."

"In the bar!"

"At least you'd be quite safe there."

"To hell with you!" And she walked off without saying good-bye.

The same evening she heard that he had formed a gang to get himself appointed chief of the local clan.

58.

When she visited Ashur and saw him in prison clothes her eyes filled with tears. Shams al-Din bounded happily forward so that his father could kiss him through the bars. Ashur asked how she was. "Everything's fine. I'm working in the Darasa market," she assured him.

He seemed angry and resentful. "The injustice is harder to take than prison," he said. "I've done nothing to deserve this."

He repeated this last sentence several times over, then, the note of protest rising in his voice, he added, "Not one of the men in here is as evil as Darwish."

"And do you know what?" she broke in scornfully. "He asked me to come back and work for him!"

"Bastard! What about the sheikh?"

"He treats me with respect."

"He's a bastard too. And he really *is* a thief."

"You can't imagine how many people send their greetings."

"Bless them! How I miss hearing the anthems!"

"You'll soon be back listening to them. The animal trough and the fountain and the mosque have become reminders of you. Linked with your name forever."

"They should remind people of God."

Fulla smiled wanly. Then she said, "The bad news is that Darwish has become our new chief."

Ashur frowned. "That won't do him any good."

Fulla was amazed at how healthy and rejuvenated he appeared, against all the odds.

59.

Ashur al-Nagi was never far from people's thoughts throughout his stay in prison. The harafish waited impatiently for the day he would return. Others took elaborate precautions. Darwish surrounded himself with hangers-on, keeping them loyal with cash from the protection rackets he ran. Mahmoud Qatayif encouraged him. "It's numbers that count, no matter how strong the individual."

The rich supported him, alarmed at the affection shown for the absent Ashur. The general consensus was that he should be restrained or done away with.

Season followed season. The dervishes in the monastery continued to chant their mysterious anthems. At last the appointed day arrived.

Sheikh Mahmoud looked about him. "God Almighty!" he breathed angrily.

Flags fluttered on the rooftops and over shop doorways. Lamps were strung across the alley, bright sand strewn on the ground, and congratulations rippled through the air.

"All this because a thief is coming out of prison," he grumbled.

He saw Darwish approaching. "Everything ready to welcome the king?" he hailed him.

"Haven't you heard the news?" said Darwish in a low, troubled voice. He proceeded to tell him how his gang had abandoned him and gone off to the main square to welcome Ashur. Not one of them had stood by him.

The sheikh blanched. "Bastards!" he muttered. Then he whispered in Darwish's ear. "We'll have to think again."

As he moved away, Darwish was saying, "He's the new chief. He didn't even have to fight for it."

From the main square came the sounds of drumming and piping. At once men, women, and children surged out into the alley. A procession came into view, leading a swaying carriage where Ashur sat enthroned, surrounded by the erstwhile members of Darwish's gang.

The onlookers cheered, applauded, and danced for joy. So great was the crush that the cart took about an hour to cover the distance between the entrance to the alley and the little mosque.

The drumming and dancing went on until dawn the next day.

Epilogue

Ashur al-Nagi became clan chief without a fight. As the harafish expected, he set about his duties in an entirely different manner from his predecessors. He returned to his trade as a carter and lived in the basement room of his earlier days. He obliged all his followers to work for a living, thus eliminating the thugs and bullies. Only the rich had to pay protection money, which was used to benefit the poor and disabled. He subdued the chiefs of neighboring alleys and gave our alley a new dignity. As well as the respect of the outside world, it enjoyed justice, honor, and security at home.

Ashur would sit in the monastery square late into the night, transported by the sacred melodies. Spreading his hands before him he would pray, "O God, preserve and increase my strength so that I can use it to protect your faithful servants."

Shams al-Din

*The second tale in the epic
of the harafish*

1.

Under the merciful shadow of justice pain is lost in the recesses of oblivion. Hearts bloom with confidence, drinking in the nectar of the mulberry trees, delighting in the sound of the anthems, without understanding their meaning. But will the brightness and the clear skies last forever?

2.

For the first time Fulla awoke and did not find Ashur asleep at her side. Her eyelids, heavy with sleep, flickered uneasily and her chest contracted with fear. She prayed God to protect her from a lover's forebodings. The sweet, safe world around her gave way to bleak emptiness. Where was the prodigious young man of sixty, still strong, energetic, black-haired? Had he fallen asleep during his nightly vigil in front of the monastery?

She called Shams al-Din. He woke up, grumbling. His handsome face looked inquiringly at her.

"Your father's not back yet," she said.

He took time to absorb her words, then pushed the cover back and stood up, slender, tallish. "What's happened to him?" he muttered anxiously.

"Perhaps he fell asleep," she answered, fighting her apprehensions.

As he dressed, his grace and beauty became more apparent, crowned with the innocence of early youth.

"How can anyone want to stay up till daybreak in autumn?" he said as he went out of the door.

3.

Outside a damp breeze blew. The last strands of mist were vanishing and life began to stir. Before long he would find his father asleep with nothing over him. He would scold him gently, which the intimacy between them allowed him to do.

He went through the archway to the monastery square, peering in front of him as he prepared himself for the saga of their meeting. However, he found the place deserted. He looked about him in troubled silence: the square, the monastery, the ancient wall, but no trace of a human being. This was the spot where his giant of a father usually sat. Where had he gone?

He threw a furious glance at the monastery; as usual it gave nothing away. Where had he gone?

4.

Perhaps he would find out the answer from Ghassan or Dahshan, Ashur's right-hand men. But they were surprised to see him and said Ashur had gone to the square a little before midnight and stayed an hour or two, no more.

"Could he have arranged to meet somebody?" ventured Shams al-Din, but they claimed to know nothing more of his movements.

After some hesitation he went to see Sheikh Mahmoud, who received the news with surprise and became lost in thought.

"So the lion's vanished," he said finally. "Don't worry. He knows what he's doing. He'll be back before morning."

5.

Fulla's strength of will abandoned her. She cried out, "Receive me in your arms, Lord! Spare me from my fears!"

Shams al-Din sat with his father's men in the café, talking and waiting. From time to time they glanced toward the archway or the corner of the alley, where it joined the main square. Autumn clouds filled the sky, silvery from the light behind them. Midday came and there was still no sign of Ashur. The men split up and went off in different directions in search of clues. By now the whole alley had heard the news and was consumed by it; nobody bothered to work.

6.

The well-off and the merchants were astounded by the news. Magic filled the air they breathed like a miracle. For when people are caught in the grip of an unyielding force and see no chance of escape, they are desperate to believe in miracles. Had they not feared their hopes would soon be dashed, they would have dropped their guard and gloated openly. Only a miracle could deliver them from the tyrant's authority, from his eternal youth, his iron will! So they prayed for his absence to last, the legend to be buried, the present order reversed once and for all.

"Where's he gone?" Darwish inquired of Sheikh Mahmoud.

"Do you think I've got second sight?" said the sheikh scathingly.

Darwish shook his white head. "There's one possibility we shouldn't overlook," he murmured, "and that's his weakness for women."

The sheikh smiled in a superior way but made no comment and Darwish went on, "I thought he'd be around for a hundred years!"

"He creates that which ye do not know," intoned the sheikh under his breath.

7.

Evening fell. The night drifted in, unexpectedly cold, and there was no sign of Ashur. The café, the bar, the hashish dens, were cloaked in gloom. His family and his followers watched and waited, unable to sleep.

"There are so many of them and yet they're helpless," sighed Fulla.

"Have we forgotten something? Is there anything else we can try?" asked Shams al-Din dejectedly.

She let her tears flow unhindered. "Right from the start I knew it was wrong to have false hopes!"

"I don't like people who fear the worst always," he shouted angrily. "Nobody's made off with him. He's not some toy. And he's too shrewd to fall into a trap. I'm only worried because the trails have all gone cold."

8.

The following morning Ashur's men gathered in the café together with Shams al-Din and Fulla; they were joined by Sheikh Mahmoud and Husayn Quffa, imam of the little mosque. All were perplexed and full of foreboding, but none dared to express his fears.

"In twenty years the chief's never altered his routine," said Dahshan.

"He must have a secret!" said Husayn Quffa.

"He doesn't have secrets from us," said Ghassan.

"And certainly not from me!" declared Fulla.

"Could he have joined the dervishes?" suggested Husayn Quffa.

"Impossible!" objected several voices.

"Something tells me he'll reappear as suddenly as he vanished," soothed Sheikh Mahmoud.

"It's hopeless," wailed Fulla.

At this Dahshan pronounced dramatically, "Perhaps he's been betrayed."

Hearts raced and eyes flashed angrily. "Even lions are sometimes betrayed," persisted Dahshan.

"Calm down," cried Mahmoud Qatayif. "Nobody bears a grudge against the finest man in the alley."

"There are always people with grudges."

"Guard against temptation and be patient. God is our witness."

9.

Darwish was handing a calabash to a drunken customer. The man suddenly gripped his arm and whispered in his ear, "I heard Ashur's men talking. They were saying that you're the only person who could have betrayed him."

Darwish hurried in alarm to Mahmoud Qatayif's shop and told him what he had heard. He was shaking with terror. Qatayif lost patience with him. "Stop acting like a woman!" he snapped.

"How can they suspect me when I'm in the bar night and day?"

The sheikh thought hard. "Run away," he said eventually. "You've got no choice."

Darwish suddenly vanished. Nobody knew if he had fled, or if someone had killed him. Nobody asked about him, and Sheikh Mahmoud appeared not to notice he had gone. Soon the bar was taken over by a local drug trafficker, Ilaywa Abu Rasain, and it was as if Darwish had never existed.

10.

The days passed without a glimmer of hope, slowly, heavily, shrouded in melancholy. They all despaired of seeing Ashur al-Nagi again, sadly remembering the giant figure going about the neighborhood, restraining the powerful, protecting the rights of the humble breadwinners, and creating an atmosphere of faith and piety.

Fulla wore mourning; Shams al-Din wept uncontrollably, and Ashur's men were sunk in sorrow and reflection. Some people thought that Darwish had betrayed Ashur, then killed him near the monastery, dragged his body to the cemetery, and buried him in an unmarked grave. There were those who insisted that Ashur would return one day and laugh at all their desperate notions; others imagined that because his disappearance aroused such strong feelings it was a miraculous event, and proved that he was a saint.

The harsh magic of custom began to have its effect on the sad episode, making it acceptable, ordinary, reducing its significance, thrusting it into the eternal stream of events where it vanished from sight.

Ashur al-Nagi had disappeared.

But time and fate will never stand still.

II.

A new chief had to be chosen before the regime crumbled completely or ambitious gangs from other alleys moved in. The choice was narrowed down to Ghassan and Dahshan as the strongest candidates and the closest to al-Nagi. Shams al-Din was not even considered: he was too young and delicate-looking. Each man backed his favorite, and they decided to follow the procedure normally adopted in such cases: the rival candidates were to fight it out in the Mameluke Desert and the winner would be made chief.

News of these developments reached Fulla and when she saw Shams al-Din dressing to go and watch the fight with the other gang members tears of self-pity sprang to her eyes. Irritated by his mother's reaction, he said, "The alley can't survive without a chief."

"Who can follow him?" she asked fiercely.

"There's nothing we can do."

"The place'll be run by thugs and tyrants like it was before."

"It won't be that easy for them to turn their backs on al-Nagi's legacy," said the boy with passion.

She sighed and seemed to be addressing herself: "Before, even though I was poor, I was a lady. Now I'm going to be just a sad

widow, abandoned by everybody, praying without hope, dreaming
of my lost paradise, hiding away at weddings, afraid of the dark,
wary of men, avoiding other women, bored and forgotten."

"I'm not dead yet!" he said reproachfully.

"God give you a long life. But your father's left you while
you're still a boy. A carter without money or status, or his giant size
which would have guaranteed you the leadership . . ."

"I have to go now," he muttered dispiritedly. He said goodbye, tucked his father's rough stick under his arm, and left.

12.

Shams al-Din had grown up in a Spartan household and knew only
hard work and a simple way of life. He remembered nothing of the
opulence of the Bannan house. His father used to take delight in
his handsome face, almost a copy of his mother's, and say, smiling,
"This boy's not cut out to be a chief."

He sent him to Quran school, poured life's sweetest melodies
into his heart, and did not neglect the physical side of his education:
he taught him horse riding, single-stick fencing, boxing, and wrestling, although he had no thoughts of preparing him to be chief. As
Shams al-Din became more aware of his surroundings, he realized
the extent of his father's power and influence and was brought
abruptly face-to-face with the sharp contrast between his greatness
and the miserable life he led. One year as a feast day approached he
declared boldly, "Father, I want to wear a cloak and headcloth in
the parade."

"Have you ever seen me in anything but a plain gallabiyya?"
asked his father sternly.

Like her son, Fulla was annoyed with the way they lived and
said to Ashur in his hearing, "Nobody would blame you if you took
enough from the taxes to ensure yourself a decent living."

"No," replied Ashur. "You should raise chickens if you want
to make us a bit more comfortable." Then, turning to Shams al-
Din, he added, "Surface gloss has no value in this life compared to
a clear conscience, the love of your fellow man, and the pleasure of
listening to the anthems!"

He trained him to be a carter and they shared the work until Ashur was approaching his sixties, when he handed most of it over to Shams al-Din. Shams al-Din admired and respected his father but at the same time longed for a life of ease; sometimes he supported his beautiful mother in her aspirations. Spurred on by these suppressed desires, he innocently accepted a feast-day bonus offered to him by the owner of the caravanserai and rushed out to buy a cloak, headcloth, and leather shoes with turned-up toes. On the morning of the feast he sauntered proudly through the alley in his new attire. When Ashur saw him, he grabbed him by his collar and marched him into the basement, then struck him so hard that his head spun.

"They'll use your weakness to get at me, now they've failed to make me back down," he shouted.

He made him take the clothes back to the shop and return the bonus. Shams al-Din realized that he was powerless in the face of his father's anger. He felt ashamed of himself and disillusioned with his mother who dared not defend him or take his side.

But it was love, not force, which bound Shams al-Din to his father as his pupil, confidant, and friend; he was saturated with his words, inspired by his piety, and shared his passion for the sacred songs and the stars. He drove his cart proudly, quelling the flashes of weakness which stirred in his depths every now and then.

In spite of their poverty they had been received with affection and esteem wherever they went. Would things change now? For here was his mother looking at the future with eyes full of apprehension!

13.

In the vast wildness of the Mameluke Desert the men looked like a few scattered grains of sand. This was the territory of robbers and fugitives, home to jinns and reptiles, graveyard of countless anonymous bones. Ghassan approached, surrounded by his men, and stood face-to-face with Dahshan and his supporters. Eyes met under the burning sun, tortured by the fierce blaze of heat rising from the sand. The surrounding emptiness looked on coldly, mockingly, without pity, promising the loser eternal ruin.

Shams al-Din came up quietly and chose a position equidistant between the two groups, thereby proclaiming his neutrality and, at the same time, his readiness to rally to the winner's flag. He raised his hand in greeting and cried in his loud, hoarse voice—the only trait he had inherited from Ashur—"The peace of God on the people of our alley."

Lips dry with dogged anticipation muttered back, "The peace of God on the great man's son."

It occurred to Shams al-Din that neither side had asked him to join them or sought his mother's blessing. On the cruel field of battle women and inexperienced youths were irrelevant.

Shaalan the One-Eyed came and stood beside him. Once a clan chief himself, in his old age he acted as arbitrator, impartial and reliable. He announced, "The contest between Ghassan and Dahshan will begin. Let every man present remember his duty."

He gestured warningly and carried on, "Keep in your places, abide by the result. Going against it means disaster for all."

Nobody spoke. The desert watched with its cold, hard, mocking stare. A raven croaked in the clear blue dome of the sky. Shaalan the One-Eyed said, "May the best man win. Everyone will owe him allegiance, including the loser."

The sweat-stained faces acquiesced without protest and Shaalan turned to Ghassan: "Do you swear to submit if you are defeated?"

"I swear, as God is my witness," said Ghassan.

"And you, Dahshan?"

"I swear, as God's my witness."

"A touch is enough to decide the winner. Avoid violence at all costs. It only causes ill feeling."

The circle opened out, leaving Ghassan and Dahshan alone in the ring: two sturdy bodies tensed and ready to spring, they brandished their sticks like magicians. Ghassan jumped forward and Dahshan attacked. Their sticks clashed, turning around each other, whirling with cunning grace. Each player struggled for a touch, blocked, parried, and ducked, their tension and determination

mounting as the fight reached its climax. The infernal heat of the
sun fell on their heads in benediction.

With a sudden swift lunge, Ghassan caught Dahshan off his
guard, struck home, and touched his collarbone. Wild with enthusiasm, his supporters cried, "Ghassan! Ghassan! God bless Ghassan!"

Dahshan slumped, panting, swallowing his disappointment.
Ghassan held out his hand and said, "My brother!"

Dahshan shook it, muttering, "My chief!"

"God bless Ghassan! God bless Ghassan!" chanted the crowd.

Ghassan turned in a circle, elegantly, exultantly, as he addressed them. "Does anyone wish to object?" he demanded.

The crowd roared their allegiance. As the storm of support
died down, a voice spoke: "I object, Ghassan."

14.

All eyes turned in amazement to Shams al-Din. He stood apart a
little, tallish and slender, his handsome face raised in pride, his skin
suffused with the sun's burning rays.

"You, Shams al-Din?" gasped Ghassan.

"Yes, me, Ghassan," he answered firmly.

"Do you really want to be clan chief?"

"It's my duty and my fate."

One-Eyed Shaalan said kindly, "Your father himself didn't
prepare you for it."

"I've learned a lot, and I know things other chiefs don't."

"Goodness isn't enough by itself!"

Shams al-Din attempted a few moves with his father's club,
every gesture full of elegance and charm.

"I can't harm you!" Ghassan shouted.

"Let the weapons do the talking!"

"You're just a lad, Shams al-Din!"

"I'm a man like my father."

Ghassan raised his face to the burning sky and cried, "Forgive
me, Ashur!"

Nobody felt happy at this turn of events. Lips curled in displeasure. The desert appeared colder, harsher, more disparaging than ever.

Shams al-Din made the first move and the battle started. In its opening explosive moments a miracle occurred: Shams al-Din's weapon found its way to Ghassan's leg and scored a hit. Ghassan stopped fighting in disbelief. Apparently he had underestimated his opponent and was paying the price, or so thought many of the spectators. But the battle had scarcely begun. How could it end just like that? Ghassan, still incredulous, prepared to go on fighting. The crowd was silent. Shams al-Din held out his hand. "My brother," he said.

Ghassan ignored him, anger leaping into his eyes.

"Your hand, Ghassan," cautioned One-Eyed Shaalan sympathetically.

"He was just lucky," shouted Ghassan.

"God wanted him to win."

"The contest is decisive only when the contestants are equally matched," persisted Ghassan, "but Shams al-Din is still a sapling, ready to crack. Or do you want to be easy meat, a toy in the hands of any powerful chief around?"

At this Shams al-Din threw down his club, stripped to his loincloth, and stood waiting, his slender body glistening in the shimmering air.

Ghassan smiled confidently and did the same. "I'll protect you from your evil urges," he said.

Cautiously they approached one another until their bodies touched, then they clinched and grappled, each one using all his strength and will, until their muscles bulged and their veins stood out. Their feet sank into the sand. Each one was possessed by a huge, inflexible desire to crush the other until the last breath of life left his body. The crowd watched in stunned silence, waiting for the blood to flow. The seconds passed, molten in the furnace of the sands. The crowd held its breath and not a sound was heard. Ghassan's brows met in a furious scowl. He appeared to be challenging the impossible, resisting fate. Struggling like a drowning man. Fighting the unknown like a madman. Unleashing blind fury against creeping despair. And yet he weakened, despite his persistence and pride and anger. He lost his footing, staggered, and, with a rasping intake of breath, began to sink. Shams al-Din showed him no mercy until his arms sagged, his legs buckled, and he collapsed on the ground.

Shams al-Din stood panting, bathed in sweat. The shocked silence prevailed, broken only when One-Eyed Shaalan handed him his clothes and cried, "Long live our young chief!"

Then the crowd roared out, "God bless him! God bless him!"

"Ashur al-Nagi has risen from the dead!" exclaimed Dahshan.

"His new name shall be Shams al-Din al-Nagi," pronounced One-Eyed Shaalan.

The vast unchanging desert bore unimpassioned witness to his glory and might.

15.

The alley was waiting for the victory parade. Many people had put their money on Ghassan and almost as many on Dahshan, but no one had thought of the nice young Shams al-Din. The initial feeling of shock which the news provoked quickly turned to absolute joy. The harafish danced in the street and said it meant that Ashur lived on.

"Has the age of miracles returned?" asked Mahmoud Qatayif with angry sarcasm.

Shams al-Din received a splendid welcome. Even Fulla trilled for joy although she was in mourning.

Sheikh Mahmoud heard the story of the contest from One-Eyed Shaalan and was secretly filled with gloom. "Does this mean the age of poverty and depression will continue?" he said to himself.

16.

"I prepared myself for this," confided Shams al-Din proudly to his mother.

"Even your father didn't believe it possible," said Fulla wonderingly.

"It'll be hard for someone like me to succeed him."

"Watch out for Ghassan. He's your enemy now. But you can win your men's hearts if you play your cards right!"

"I'm the people's only hope now. I can't disappoint them."

"Moderation is chief of virtues," she said provocatively.

"I can't disappoint them," he repeated doggedly.

17.

The days passed, pulsating with happiness. The people truly believed that Ashur al-Nagi lived on. Ghassan spent his evenings in the bar and when he was drunk he would sing:

> *If your luck turns*
> *It's not enough to be smart.*

One night Shaalan rounded on him. "Haven't you had enough of that stupid song? You ought to get rid of the bitterness in your soul."

"He's sold it to the devil," teased Dahshan.

"You can't forgive me for beating you, Dahshan," said Ghassan roughly.

"Go to hell! At least I stuck to the rules."

"If you hadn't had it in for me, you'd never have accepted a boy as chief."

"He was a worthy winner, wasn't he?" said Dahshan resentfully.

"Something tells me our new chief will be a good customer of mine," interjected Abu Rasain.

Ghassan guffawed. "I'll shave my mustache off if that ever happens," he said. "All we'll get from him is poverty."

"This evening's going to turn out badly," moaned One-Eyed Shaalan.

"You've had too much to drink, Shaalan," said Ghassan scathingly. "It'll be just like any other evening. Like all those happy evenings in the good old days when the best whore of the lot paraded around in front of the drunks in all her glory!"

Dahshan flung his calabash at him, hitting him full in the chest. "Bastard!" he roared in his face.

Ghassan stood up menacingly but Shaalan bounded toward him and said in a stern voice, "You're not wanted here anymore, Ghassan."

Although he was drunk, Ghassan realized he had gone too far, and staggered out of the bar.

18.

Nobody thought it necessary to tell Shams al-Din that his mother had been insulted.

"It's ancient history. The boy never knew about it," said Shaalan to Dahshan.

"But we should tell him Ghassan's opposing him," said Dahshan.

Shams al-Din decided to resolve the matter straightaway and confronted Ghassan as he sat in the café. With anger in his eyes he demanded, "Ghassan, do you think you can be faithful to me like you were to my father?"

"I've already given you my word," said Ghassan flatly.

"But you're a liar. I can't trust you."

"Don't believe those traitors."

"I believe people I know are loyal." He leaned toward him. "From today you're out of the clan."

And Ghassan was never seen in the alley again.

19.

Nothing was changed from Ashur al-Nagi's time. Like him, Shams al-Din protected the rights of the harafish and muzzled the rich and powerful, kept up his trade in spite of being chief and expected his men to do the same. He continued to live in the cramped basement flat, turning a deaf ear to his mother's whispered entreaties. He was suffused with true greatness and he quenched the thirst in his heart with the people's love and admiration. He began frequenting the little neighborhood mosque and made friends with the sheikh, Husayn Quffa. From the protection money paid by the rich he renewed the mosque furnishings, and at the sheikh's suggestion founded a new Quran school beyond the fountain.

He never forgot his responsibility to the alley and its people, sharing the weighty burden of the trust placed in him with his most dependable followers. With the disappearance of Ashur, the venerable giant, neighboring chiefs had caught their breath and began to pick quarrels with street vendors from the alley. To establish his power and banish any lingering doubts, and to prove that his gentleness and delicate physique in no way detracted from his qualities as a chief, he decided to challenge the strongest of his rivals, the chief of the Atuf clan. An opportunity arose when an Atuf wedding procession passed through Citadel Square. Shams al-Din and his men held it up and a fierce battle followed, from which they emerged the undisputed victors. The news swept through the surrounding area and all who had toyed with the idea of challenging Shams al-Din were convinced that he was no less brave and strong than his father had been.

So the alley continued to live under its exemplary regime and preserved its reputation in the world beyond the square.

20.

Nevertheless, Shams al-Din returned from fighting the Atuf with an anxious heart. There was dust and dirt in the hurricane which had swept him drunkenly to power. As the Atuf chief squared up to him, he had shouted, "Come on, son of a whore! Your mother was a slut in Darwish's bar! Who do you think you are?"

Everyone had heard these insults; the Atuf men cheered while the others roared with anger. Was he just working himself up for the fight, or talking about things that had really happened, things he was too young to know about? He went privately to see One-Eyed Shaalan to ask him what the man had meant.

"Just the yelping of a wounded dog," said Shaalan firmly. "A woman chosen by Ashur al-Nagi to be his wife and produce his offspring is above all suspicion."

He felt reassured, but not for long; he still hadn't regained his peace of mind. Misgivings piled up in his heart like clouds on a rainy day. In his free time he watched Fulla surreptitiously. She was about forty, perhaps slightly less, very beautiful, small, slim, seductive, with eyes radiating sheer fascination. She was also pious and respectable with an impressively strong personality. He couldn't imagine she was impure and cursed the man who had made him doubt her. He had been almost infatuated with her: Ashur had actually said to him one day, "A real man is not so attached to his mother." And when he was still a little boy his father had taken him with him to work; Shamṣ al-Din had eaten and slept in the cart, his life revolving around his father's life, well out of reach of his mother's warm embrace.

Still, he wondered what had gone on in Darwish's bar. Were there men who knew things they shouldn't about his mother's past? He mumbled angry curses under his breath at those who dared profane her.

21.

One day he saw a face which transported him back into his childhood. He was driving his cart toward the main square when an unusual fight between a boy and girl blocked his way: the girl sprang at the boy like a tigress, striking him, spitting in his face, hurling a stream of abuse at him while he dodged out of her way, swearing back in even fouler language, and a group of curious onlookers stood laughing at them.

Seeing Shams al-Din, they greeted him, the fight stopped abruptly, and the boy ran off. The girl bent to pick up her black wrap from the ground and wound it tightly around herself, raising her eyes timidly to look at him. Shams al-Din liked her energy, her glowing face, her supple body. She noticed him staring at her and said apologetically, "He behaved badly, master. I was teaching him a lesson."

"You did the right thing," murmured Shams al-Din, smiling. "What's your name?"

"Agamiyya." Then, looking even more embarrassed, "Don't you remember me?"

All at once he did, and said with surprise, "Of course I do. We used to play together."

"But you didn't recognize me!"

"You've changed a lot. Aren't you Dahshan's daughter?"

She inclined her head and walked off.

Dahshan's daughter! What a change!

She had set his senses alight and his young blood pumped through his veins, burning like the midday sun.

22.

On the outskirts of the quarter of al-Ghuriyya, he saw Ayyusha, the door-to-door saleswoman, signaling to him. He stopped and noticed another woman with her, a splendid creature who was attracting the attention of the passersby: she wore a wrap of fine crepe material and a face veil with a gold nosepiece; her beautiful eyes were outlined with kohl and her body was firm and succulent. The two women took their seats in the cart and Ayyusha said in her old woman's voice, "Darb al-Ahmar, master!"

He sprang to the driver's seat, hoping to catch another glimpse of his mysterious passenger, while Ayyusha remarked, "How nice to see our chief driving a cart! And to think, if you wanted, there's nothing to stop you living in the lap of luxury!"

He felt happy at her words but said nothing. He was enjoying the warmth of being in love and was suffused with the fragrance of true greatness, so he chased all notions of weakness and temptation from his head. He waited for the beauty to say something but she was silent the whole journey. When she descended in Darb al-Ahmar he was able to have a good look at her, keeping her in sight until she went off in the direction of Sheikhs' Cloister.

As Ayyusha stayed where she was he turned toward her inquiringly. "To the citadel," she muttered.

The cart went on its way. He remained silent even though he longed to speak. Suddenly the old woman asked him, "Is that the first time you've seen Qamr?"

"The very first," he answered, grateful to her for initiating the conversation.

"That's the way it is with virtuous women!"

"Is she from our alley?"

"Yes. A widow. Extremely beautiful and extremely rich!"

"Why doesn't she hire a carriage?"

"She had a craving for our chief's donkey cart!"

He turned to look at her and caught the hint of a sly smile in her dull eyes. His senses caught fire for the second time that day. He summoned Agamiyya's image and the two women danced together in his mind until he felt drunk.

"You liked her then?" asked Ayyusha.

"What are you talking about, woman?" he said, pretending to be harsh.

Laughing, she said, "My trade is selling clothes and happiness."

He decided not to pursue the conversation, for fear of where it might lead.

As she got down at Citadel Square she said, "We've still got things to discuss. Remember Ayyusha's there if you need her!"

23.

She rode on his cart again often, Ayyusha the saleswoman. The desire for conquest tempted him strongly, but his true weakness lay in his adolescent heart and his fiery youthfulness. Qamr disturbed him with her dazzling beauty, but so did Agamiyya with her youth. Perhaps he was going to spend his adolescent years trying to work out what it would mean to marry on the one hand a woman of Qamr's standing, and on the other a young girl like Agamiyya. A storm was gathering on the horizon. Better to let it break and expose himself to its fury if this was the only way to have peace in the end.

One evening after dinner he saw that his mother was not her usual self. Her beautiful eyes glittered craftily, penetrating the whirlpool of his thoughts.

"What's going on behind my back?" she asked sharply.

Fine. He was glad to be found out, longing to divulge the secrets of his rebellious heart. "What do you mean?"

She tilted her chin proudly, scorning the deception, and asked, "What's Ayyusha up to?"

No secret was safe in Ayyusha's toothless mouth, he thought, and smiled resignedly, murmuring, "She was just doing her job."

"Qamr's old enough to be your mother and she's infertile," retorted Fulla.

"But she's rich and beautiful," he replied, with the sole aim of provoking her.

"Her beauty won't last much longer, and if you really want to be rich there's nothing to stop you."

"Do you want me to betray Ashur's memory?" he asked reprovingly.

"Getting rich through a woman is no less shameful."

"I don't agree," he lied, to enrage her further.

"Really! Then let me find you a rich man's daughter to marry."

"That would still be getting rich through a woman!"

"But in a normal way. There wouldn't be anything perverted about it. To tell you the truth, it's what I've dreamed of!"

He studied her anxiously. "I know you only accept our way of life because you have to. Do you really think I could take the people's love lightly and turn my back on true greatness?"

"Then you were playing tricks on me?"

"Just teasing you!"

"I'm not as selfish as you think," she said crossly. "Only yesterday I refused a rich man's offer of marriage!"

He frowned uneasily, the blood rushing into his face.

"Ayyusha was the go-between there as well," she added.

"Damn her!"

"I told her Ashur's widow can't accept another man in his place."

"That's the least you could have said," he grunted, distaste written all over his face.

"I said it out of respect for your father, not because I was scared of you."

"Who was this scoundrel?"

"He's not a scoundrel, and he's got every right to ask."

"Who was he?"

"The wood merchant, Antar al-Khashshab."

"He's married already, and he's not much older than me."

She shrugged her shoulders carelessly. "That's who it was. The trouble is, while we're trying to ensure justice for others, we forget to look after ourselves."

"I have to carry on my father's work," he said firmly.

She was ambitious and rebellious, he realized that. Again he wondered about the past of this woman he loved more than anyone else in the world.

24.

Shams al-Din acknowledged that his mother was strong and stubborn, and also that he loved and respected her not only as his mother but as the widow of Ashur, who was much more than just his father. He loved this reality embodied in Ashur more even than he loved him as a father: it was the focus of his life, the object on which he pinned his hopes, the secret of his fascination with the concept of true greatness.

This was why he had decided to make directly for his goal, avoiding fruitless detours.

That evening he went to the monastery square with his friend Dahshan. It was a clear summer's night; the sound of chanting rose sweetly in the air and the stars above shone peacefully.

"This was where Ashur used to come to be alone and think his most sublime thoughts," said Shams al-Din to Dahshan.

Dahshan muttered a prayer for his old master's soul. Shams

al-Din continued, "I've chosen it so that he'll bless what I'm about
to ask you."

"I'm at your service. He'll bless it," muttered Dahshan, embarrassed.

Calmly Shams al-Din announced, "I want to marry your
daughter, Agamiyya."

Dahshan was taken completely by surprise and was unable to
speak.

Gently Shams al-Din prompted him, "What do you say, Dahshan?"

"I'd never have dreamed of such an honor, master."

Shams al-Din held out his hand. "Then let's recite the prayer
to clinch the deal."

25.

On his way home Shams al-Din experienced some sharp pangs of
regret at having defied his mother's authority, so gentle and so
powerful. Later, as he sat with her in the peaceful gloom, he said,
"Mother, Dahshan has agreed to let me marry his daughter."

For a moment Fulla seemed not to understand, then she
glared at him, astonished. "What did you say?"

Hiding a sudden feeling of dislike for her, he repeated what
he had said.

"I suppose this is another of your jokes?"

"No. It's true."

"Don't you think you should have consulted me first?" she
protested.

"She's a suitable girl and her father's an honest man."

"I agree, but you should have spoken to me first."

"I knew in advance what you thought and it's out of the
question."

"What a waste!" she murmured sadly.

"Aren't you going to congratulate me?" he smiled.

She hesitated, then went up and placed a kiss on his forehead.
"The Lord bless you in all you decide to do," she muttered.

26.

Sheikh Mahmoud Qatayif asked to see Shams al-Din. Remembering just such a meeting in the past, Fulla cursed to herself, but her
son welcomed him and sat him at his side on the only couch in the
room. Although he was over sixty he seemed healthy and full of
energy, his body so slender and sprightly that he looked as if he
could live forever. Fulla served coffee, her head draped in a black
veil, and inquired politely, "How are you, Master Mahmoud?"

The man returned her greeting and went on, "If only you
would honor us with your presence, we could benefit from hearing
your point of view!"

Fulla exchanged glances with her son, then perched on the
edge of the bed. Shams al-Din prepared himself to listen, fearing
the worst. He counted Mahmoud Qatayif among his secret detractors, like the notables and all those who had lost power and status
under his regime.

"Tolerance is the chief of virtues and integrity the privilege of
the powerful," began Mahmoud.

Shams al-Din nodded his head without speaking and the
sheikh went on, "To tell you the truth, I've been sent by the notables."

"What do they want?" demanded Shams al-Din.

"They have an honorable and sincere desire to hold a wedding
celebration for you."

"I'll celebrate my wedding according to my means as a
carter," stated Shams al-Din simply.

"But you're also our chief, aren't you?"

"That will never make me change my view, as you know."

"You're everybody's chief. You're answerable to the rich as
well as the little people. Each group has the right to honor you in
its own way." Then, turning to Fulla, he added gallantly, "What
do you think, madame?"

"It's an honor he deserves, but it's up to him," replied Fulla
shrewdly.

"Well said, as usual," breathed Mahmoud Qatayif with relief.

Shams al-Din looked grim. "How can I accept an honor from people I know hate me?" he said.

"Not at all. No one hates justice. They just want to clear the air."

"Such frivolities won't help. I suppose there's a lot more to it. Tell me what you know!"

Mahmoud looked disconcerted for a moment, then declared, "They say that everyone enjoys justice and fair treatment except the rich and those who really work hard for a living. Is that justice?"

So the shadowy armies were on the move, determined to snuff out the torches lighting up the little lanes and dark corners of the alley. They imagined him to be a raw youth, attracted by fine trappings just like his pretty mother. Raise high Ashur's knotted club and strike at the specters of illusion and sedition!

Roughly he asked, "Don't they enjoy security and peace of mind?"

"Tolerance, master! Why do you only take protection money from them?"

"They're the only ones who can afford it."

"But people interpret it as it suits them and despise them!"

"They're only interested in promoting themselves, and to hell with other people!" cried Shams al-Din angrily.

Mahmoud Qatayif lapsed into silence for a while, then said, "It's their right to demand respect commensurate with their achievements."

"What do you mean?"

"Where would we be without them? Their houses adorn the alley, their names shine like stars in the neighborhood, their shops keep us abundantly supplied with food and clothes, and the mosque, the fountain, the trough, and the new Quran school have all been built with their money. Isn't that enough?"

Furiously Shams al-Din burst out, "If it hadn't been for my

father, no one would have seen a penny of their money. Take a look at what happens in other alleys!"

Again the sheikh fell silent. He seemed uncertain what to say next. "Speak," urged Fulla. "The messenger only has to deliver the message."

Taking heart from her words, he went on, "They think they're unfairly treated, and they think you and your men are too. They say power should be in the hands of the rich and influential whom God has favored, without denying for a moment that the poor have a right to justice."

"Everything's clear now," exclaimed Shams al-Din. "They're trying to make me go back on my word and throw in my lot with thugs and criminals."

"God forbid!"

"It's the truth and you know it."

"God forbid, master," pleaded the sheikh.

"This is my last word . . ."

The sheikh interrupted him, getting to his feet as he spoke: "Give it a little thought," he begged. "All I'm asking is that you postpone your decision until you've thought a bit more about it."

And he rushed out of the door, as if he was glad to escape.

27.

Mahmoud Qatayif left behind him an odor of tobacco and sweat. In the silence that followed his departure their eyes met and parted. There was conflict between mother and son, between the youth and his instincts. The world's dazzling sweetness lured him with its pungent aroma of forbidden passions. In this mean room flamboyant dreams of comfort and voluptuous intimacy blazed fiercely. The promptings of his spirit made him blush for shame at the thought of his beautiful rebellious mother with her bewitching sidelong glance. Her beauty, of unknown origins, was the embodiment of his odious hidden weakness.

Aggressively he said to her, "As you know, the clan chief is the guardian and protector of the alley, the man responsible for restraining the forces of evil in it."

"And yet you can't tell him apart from any old beggar," she sneered.

"Mother! Be on my side, not against me," he said passionately.

"I am, as God's my witness."

"I want to be worthy of al-Nagi's name," he exclaimed, vexed with himself and his mother at the same time.

"Ashur didn't hesitate to take over the Bannan's empty house," she returned triumphantly.

"And look how that turned out," he said angrily.

"He set a precedent for us, in any case."

"The time will come," he said disparagingly, "when we attribute all our weak impulses to the great Ashur."

28.

Shams al-Din walked along beside his donkey, calm and spent by the struggle. He always noticed how the sun shone cheerfully after clouds and rain. There was no shame in weakness if you overcame it. What was the point of strength if not to subdue these impulses of frailty? He felt the sublime nectar of life coursing through his veins once more.

In front of Mahmoud's shop he pulled on the reins and brought the cart to a halt.

The man rushed out to him eagerly. Shams al-Din gave him a cold look, then said firmly, "Ashur al-Nagi is not dead!"

29.

Shams al-Din was going home one evening when the figure of a woman loomed up in his path.

"Good evening," she murmured.

"Ayyusha? What brings you here?"

"Won't you come back with me?"

His heart beat faster. The invitation frightened him, aroused his curiosity, set his young blood on fire. Meekly he followed her.

30.

As she led the way into the entry she whispered, "I don't understand you."

"What?"

"Aren't we entitled to ask why the moon in all its glory is refused?"

She opened the door into the room and lamplight fell on the ground. She stood aside for him, pushing him forward. He saw Qamr sitting on the edge of the bed, the only place there was to sit, veiled, her black wrap drawn tightly around her, her eyes downcast in embarrassment.

He stood staring at her, overcome with emotion.

From her place in the doorway, Ayyusha asked, "Have you heard bad reports of us?"

"Not at all," he answered in confusion.

"Is there some flaw in our beauty?"

Warning lights flashed in his head as he said, "God forbid."

"Has exposing our secret lowered us in your eyes?"

He mumbled deprecatory noises, his mouth dry.

The old woman went out, closing the door behind her, leaving him on the edge of the abyss.

"I'm ashamed," whispered Qamr in a voice that was barely audible. "I don't know what I've brought upon myself."

"Nothing to be ashamed of," he said stupidly.

"Don't think badly of me."

He collapsed under the deluge and his desire engulfed the universe. Rashly, proudly, blindly he succumbed to its imperious, arrogant power.

Qamr barely resisted. "Don't think badly of me," she whispered.

31.

Shams al-Din found himself in the hall once more with the door shut firmly behind him. The place was bathed in darkness and it crept into the recesses of his soul. The fire had burned out, leaving the acrid fumes of cold ashes, and the world sighed in weary sorrow.

At the end of the passage he saw Ayyusha's form against the pale light of the stars. As he passed her on his way out, she said softly to him, "You can't disappoint a lady."

He glowered at her and went off with a heavy heart.

32.

He had sinned, but others had sinned more gravely. His mind was confused; she was a cunning woman. But he wasn't going to fall into the trap like an idiot or risk the precious gifts nature had given him, however much trouble and pain he had to bear. The forces of darkness were conspiring against him—like his mother and his moments of weakness—but he was ready to fight.

33.

Agamiyya Dahshan married Shams al-Din al-Nagi.

"Tonight, everything's allowed," announced One-Eyed Shaalan, and carried the message from Khalil Sukkar's hashish den to Ilaywa Abu Rasain's bar.

The traditional procession went all around the neighborhood, led by flutes and drums and escorted by a guard of honor with clubs raised high in salute. No other clan tried to stop it, and it reinforced the great chief's dignity.

Shams al-Din felt as if he was flying. Every time the procession came to a halt he was gripped by a feeling of rapture and inspiration: Ashur al-Nagi descended to bless him astride a green mare; angels sang to him from above the wisps of cloud, the

monastery door opened and heavenly melodies laden with the nectar of ripe mulberries came pouring out.

Agamiyya was borne along on a camel litter behind brocade
curtains. Fulla received her with a radiant expression and a dismal
heart.

34.

In the morning he sat on his favorite sofa in the café doorway.

Ayyusha slipped up to him and squatted down at his right-
hand side. A cloud blotted out the sun. "Congratulations," she
lisped.

He thanked her and she continued, "Even though I didn't go
to the wedding."

"You've got an open invitation to all weddings," he replied
indifferently.

"In any case, we're expecting justice from our chief, just like
everyone else."

"What's your complaint?"

"I'm defending the weakness of an honorable woman."

"You led me astray," he grumbled.

"Is a strong and trusted leader open to temptation?"

"Go to hell," he muttered angrily.

She clambered to her feet. "We'll wait patiently till justice is
done."

35.

The days passed. The storms at the end of winter were followed by
the hot dusty winds of early spring. Banks of cloud gave way to
clear blue skies.

From the first month of the marriage, a fierce conflict had
blazed between Fulla and Agamiyya. It grew worse, with no hope
of a truce in sight, while the young bride gave birth to one child
after another. Shams al-Din pretended to ignore it, as wary of
supporting the oppressed as he was of chastising the oppressor. He
was convinced that gang warfare was safer than interfering be-

tween two hostile women. Fulla was stubborn, spiteful, merciless, while Agamiyya, despite being hardworking and devoted to her husband and children, showed herself quite strong enough to stand up to Fulla and had a vicious tongue when roused.

One day he heard Fulla insulting his wife, calling her grandfather a thief. "You can't talk," shouted back Agamiyya at once. "You were brought up in a bar!"

At this he lost his head and struck his wife so hard he nearly killed her.

He took himself off to the monastery square to be alone in the dark. He was deaf to the sacred melodies, blind to the stars, consumed by the fire raging inside him. So it was true. Friends and enemies alike knew all about it. Were it not for the strength of his authority, his detractors would shout it from the rooftops. It was sure to be their favorite topic of conversation behind closed doors. He was on the brink of madness, but refused to despise his mother. Ashur al-Nagi would not have married her unless she was innocent and virtuous. Her union with Ashur was a permanent testimony to her virtue and had made a new creature of her. He cursed those who had dared touch her. But the reality remained, an open bloody sore. The plague had wiped out all the men who had fooled around with her. But the reality was unchanged. Life, even at its happiest moments, was tainted with poison. He cursed the troubled waters of sorrow. His sadness weighed so heavily on him that he felt as if the ancient wall had collapsed on his shoulders.

36.

In spite of everything, his mother considered that he had disregarded her rights. Giving way to her anger, she delivered an unexpected blow. She took advantage of Agamiyya's absence from the house one day to declare boldly, "I've decided to marry again."

Amazed, he stared furiously at her. "What?" he demanded.

"I've decided to get married."

"You're joking."

"I'm quite serious."

"It's madness!"

"It can't be mad if God allows it."

"It will never happen while I'm alive," he shouted.

From then on he considered Antar al-Khashshab his rival, and humiliated him and threatened him until he was forced to stay indoors. "Look how our just chief behaves," Antar was heard to say to his friends. "He even defies the law of the Almighty."

Shams al-Din grew angrier and sadder. He felt the earth was moving violently under his feet, and he was straying off the road.

Fulla caught a fever and went into a decline. The herb doctors could do nothing for her. She gazed at him in silence, unable even to cry, and gave up the ghost in the dead of night.

37.

He felt as if he had been torn up by the roots. The sun was no longer shining. Rumors flew around the alleys of hostile clans that Shams al-Din had poisoned his mother to prevent her remarriage or had discovered an illicit relationship between her and Antar. He went about in a fury, initiated bloody battles, and was viewed in the area as a ruthless tyrant.

Melancholy attacked him constantly like a chronic illness. Inwardly his uncharacteristic behavior terrified him: he mulled incessantly over regrettable episodes with Qamr, Fulla, and Antar, and wondered about the demonic violence unleashed in him when he was fighting. He began to say sadly of himself that he had al-Nagi's name but none of his attributes.

One night he was so agitated by all that had happened that he found himself going like a sleepwalker to Ayyusha's flat. He sat down on the edge of the bed without looking at her while she stared at him in surprise. Without any emotion in his voice, he said, "Go and fetch Qamr."

38.

The days went by.

The children grew up and were apprenticed in various trades. Mahmoud Qatayif died and was replaced by Said al-Faqi.

One-Eyed Shaalan died and Dahshan retired from active life. Husayn al-Quffa, the imam of the local mosque, died and was replaced by Sheikh Tulba al-Qadi. Ilaywa Abu Rasain died and Uthman al-Darzi bought the bar.

Agamiyya gave birth to the last of the bunch, Sulayman. He grew at an extraordinary rate and reminded his father of Ashur. He decided to educate him to be chief of the clan and a worthy successor to al-Nagi.

Despite his lapses Shams al-Din retained unchallenged his hold on the alley. His prestige and his advanced years did not deter him from working as a carter and protecting the interests of the harafish with compassion, justice, and love. He was known for his piety and devotion and the sincerity of his faith. The people forgot his past errors and extolled his merits and the name of al-Nagi became synonymous with goodness, happiness, and firm rule.

39.

The cart glides along discreetly, garlanded with flowers. No one notices the creaking of its wheels. People only hear what they want to hear. The powerful believe they are joined in eternal union with the world. But the cart never stops and the world is an unfaithful spouse.

40.

Agamiyya went on putting henna on her hair. She had started to go gray when she was fifty and by the time she reached her sixties there was not a single black hair left on her head. The henna gave her hair moisture, like dew at twilight, and added a fine proud warmth to it. She was still strong, brimming with vitality, never slacking, working all the hours of daylight and sometimes by moonlight too. Her fresh bloom had not left her and with the passing of time she had grown superbly plump. There was nothing about her strong frame to give rise to alarm.

Noticing the henna powder one day Shams al-Din said teasingly to her, "What's the point of trying to hide it, my lady?"

"If gray hair's really a sign of old age," she retorted, "why's your hair still black?"

Coal-black hair and a physique composed of beauty, strength, and grace—she felt boundless love and admiration for him, tinged with fear and jealousy. He had never taken a second wife and had only been unfaithful once or twice with a woman the age of his mother. But who knew what the future had in store?

41.

One morning as he was combing his hair Agamiyya suddenly stared hard at his head and with ill-concealed joy exclaimed, "A white hair!"

He turned toward her, suddenly alert, as he would turn when the signal for battle was given. He shot her an irritated look, and she said, "I swear it was a white hair."

He squinted into the little mirror he held in his hand. "Liar," he muttered uncertainly.

She approached him, eyes fixed on her goal like a cat stalking a mouse, detached a single hair from his abundant crop, and pronounced triumphantly, "There it is."

He examined his hair in the mirror again. There was nothing he could do, no point resisting. It was as if he had been caught doing something wrong. Like years and years ago when he was sneaking into Ayyusha's basement. His heart filled with anger, resentment, and shame. He avoided meeting her eyes. "So what?" he said scornfully. "You're just jealous!"

42.

This episode did not simply pass harmlessly into oblivion, as Agamiyya had expected. He made a thorough examination of his head every morning after that and she regretted opening her mouth.

"Having gray hair doesn't mean you're not strong and healthy," she said soothingly.

But he began to wonder about his age. How had he got so

old? Where had all the time gone? Wasn't it only yesterday he had defeated Ghassan? How was it Dahshan had already gone senile and started to walk like a small child? What good was a chief who had lost his strength?

"All we can do is pray God we keep healthy," went on Agamiyya.

"Why do you keep repeating these meaningless clichés?" he asked in exasperation.

She laughed, trying to soften the effect of his anger, and said, "There's nothing wrong with men dyeing their hair."

"I'm not completely stupid!" he exclaimed.

For the first time he began to brood on what was past and what was to come. He thought about people who had died, about saints who had lived for a thousand years. About the processes of decay which turn strong men into objects of ridicule. Betrayal was not only caused by spiritual weakness or the acts of men. It was easier by far to wreck an armed parade than to unsay things that should never have been said. You could rebuild a ruined house, but not a human being. The pleasure of the music is only a short-lived veneer on the song of parting.

He wrapped his headcloth around his head and asked her, "Do you know what I'd pray for?"

When she was silent he said, "People to die before they get old."

43.

After he had gone out Agamiyya said to herself that all people could do was have faith.

When she was told that her father had died she shrieked so loudly that the window bars shook.

44.

She wept bitterly for her father. She used to say that a person who has lived for a long time becomes a precious habit, without which life is hard to imagine. Shams al-Din grieved for the loss of a friend

who had been his father's friend before him, but it was the death of
the wood merchant, Antar, which upset him most. Antar was
roughly his own age, his generation, and his health had deteriorated rapidly after a sudden stroke. However, death did not concern him as much as old age and frailty. He hated the idea of
beating all the other clan chiefs only to succumb helplessly to the
mysterious sorrow of age.

"Wasn't Ashur al-Nagi lucky simply to vanish at the height of
his powers?" he marveled.

45.

As he sat in the café a friendly struggle took place under his nose
between his son, Sulayman, and another youth in the clan called
Atris. For the first few minutes their strength and skill were perfectly matched, but eventually Sulayman came through and beat his
friend.

Shams al-Din seethed with anger. He found it intolerable that
Atris had held out against Sulayman for more than a few seconds
and took no pleasure in his victory. Sulayman was strong enough,
being the same build as Ashur, but had none of his agility and skill.

46.

Shams al-Din took Sulayman up onto the roof of their building
and stripped down to his loincloth. He stood bathed in the golden
rays of the setting sun. "Now you do the same," he said.

"Why, father?" asked the boy hesitantly.

"Because I say so."

They stood face-to-face, Shams al-Din strong and graceful,
Sulayman built like a giant, the living image of Ashur.

"Now fight me with all the strength you've got," ordered
Shams al-Din.

"Spare me the shame."

"Come on! You'll find out strength isn't everything."

He grabbed hold of him with force and persistence. They
grappled, their muscles bulging.

"Don't hold back!"

"I spun it out with Atris to be friendly. I could have beaten him right at the start."

"Don't hold back, Sulayman," roared Shams al-Din.

Shams al-Din felt as if he were wrestling with the ancient city wall and as if its stones, sated with the nectar of history, were pounding him like the assaults of time. The struggle grew fiercer; he seemed to be resisting a mountain. It was ages since he had been in a fight. His strength lay dormant in the shadow of his glorious reputation. He tried to forget he was meant to be coaching his own son. Better to die than retreat now. Suddenly he felt determined, single-minded; he flexed his muscles arrogantly and lifted his son's huge frame clean off the ground and threw him flat on his back at his feet. Then he stood looking down at him, panting, smiling, sore in every part of his body.

Sulayman got to his feet, laughing. "You're a genuine Nagi, powerful and unbeatable," he said.

Shams al-Din put his clothes on, full of conflicting emotions. He was neither happy nor sad. The sun went down and perfect calm descended with the dusk.

47.

Shams al-Din settled on the couch. Sulayman did not leave his side. Why was he staying? Did his face show his anguish?

"Why don't you go now?"

"I'm ashamed of what happened," mumbled Sulayman.

"Go. Don't worry."

He wanted to repeat the order but his tongue refused to obey him. Night fell earlier than usual.

48.

Shams al-Din al-Nagi lost consciousness.

When he opened his eyes he saw red hills under a dust-laden sky. A memory caressed him and vanished. He was breathing in a cave haunted by indifference. The fog rolled away to reveal the faces of Agamiyya and Sulayman. Consciousness assaulted him rudely with a jaundiced laugh. He smelled rose water from his head and neck.

"We were frightened out of our wits," whispered Agamiyya, white-faced.

"Are you all right, father?" Sulayman asked in a trembling voice.

"Thanks be to God," he murmured, then added apologetically, "Even Shams al-Din can't escape illness."

"But you never complained," said Agamiyya, bewildered.

"I hate to complain." Then anxiously he asked, "Has the news got out?"

"Of course not. You were only unconscious for a couple of minutes."

"Very good. No one must know, not even my men." He looked at Sulayman and said, "Forget all that's happened the moment you go out of the door."

He nodded his head obediently.

"Are you sure you're all right?" asked Agamiyya.

"Fine."

"The herb doctor will have something to put you back on form."

"He's one of our enemies," he said crossly.

"What about the barber surgeon? He's a friend."

"I said there's no need for anyone to know. And I'm fine now."

"But why did it happen at all?" asked Sulayman uneasily.

"Strenuous activity after too much to eat," said Shams al-Din with a bravado he did not feel.

As he recovered, his confidence returned. He got up and took a few paces around the cramped room. It would be good for him to sit up part of the night in the monastery square as Ashur used to do. But he was overcome by an irresistible desire to sleep.

49.

He made for the square in the late afternoon. The sun's last rays
lingered on the rooftops and the minaret. He passed Atris leading
his donkey to drink at the trough. The young man greeted him, the
apprentice addressing his revered master. In the alcove housing the
fountain he came upon Sheikh Said and stopped to exchange a few
words with him. As he stood hidden from view he heard Atris'
voice saying, "Our master Shams al-Din isn't himself."

"Perhaps he's ill," said another voice sadly.

"Or perhaps it's old age," said Atris in the same regretful tone.

A hot blast of anger swept over Shams al-Din. He retraced his
steps shouting, "Imbecile!" He took hold of Atris, lifted him high
in the air, and threw him into the trough. The crowd dispersed,
abandoning their donkeys who had started away in fright at the
commotion as the body hit the water.

It was pointless to go to the square now. He rushed blindly to
the bar, hurtling through the doorway like a tornado. The drink-
blurred voices fell silent; the eyes looked at him in astonished expectation. He looked back defiantly; mystified, they rose to their
feet, unsteady but deferential.

Diabolical thoughts whirled around in his head. Uthman al-
Darzi hurried up to him. He came to his senses and his wild
schemes evaporated. He realized he was being foolish. He had no
intention of tilting at windmills, or committing further stupid excesses. A better chance would come and he'd take it. It needed the
right moment.

He went out again without having uttered a single word,
leaving the bar's clientele in complete bewilderment.

50.

One day followed another. Destiny appeared on the horizon, moving steadily closer all the time. Nothing delayed its progress. He
flexed his muscles, honed his will, and waited. But why persist in
using force, when you never really believed in it? The white hair

was spreading and there were wrinkles around the mouth and under the eyes. The sight was dimmer, the memory less clear.

The changes in Agamiyya happened faster, more abruptly. Her appetite diminished, her digestion was poor. She had mysterious pains in her back and legs. She grew thinner, shrunken, and took to her bed. What had happened to this powerful woman? She tried one cure after another, but some essential ingredient was missing.

He sat in the café more and more frequently, and left the cart to Sulayman. He met with his men, heard the latest news, evaluating his power daily, testing his authority and influence.

"There's a new chief in Atuf," announced one of his followers one morning.

"Perhaps fate has blinded him to his true worth. Let's teach him a lesson," he said disdainfully.

In the evenings he sat alone in the square for an hour or two listening to the anthems, then hurried home to sit with Agamiyya. It was clear she was going from bad to worse. Was he destined to spend his last years alone? She had tried every remedy and continued to deteriorate.

51.

He was going home one noontime when he accidentally kicked a child's spinning top.

"You stupid old man! Are you blind?" shouted the child in a fury.

He whipped around and saw the boy, as straight as a lance, staring at him defiantly. He wanted to squash him underfoot but swallowed his anger and walked away. This generation knew nothing about him. They were alive thanks to him, and yet they were unaware of his existence. Without thinking they expressed what the adults kept to themselves. Wouldn't it be better to be dead?

52.

At dawn the next day he was woken by a sudden movement from
Agamiyya. He lit the lamp and found her sitting up in bed, glow-
ing with unexpected vitality. He felt renewed hope. "You're better,
Agamiyya," he said to her.

But she didn't answer. She stared unseeing at the wall and
whispered, "Father."

He was filled with dejection. "Agamiyya," he called in low,
pleading tones.

He saw her drifting off into the unknown and shouted desperately, "Don't leave me alone."

He held her to his chest. His lifelong companion was dying.
His whole body was racked by a fit of weeping but not a single tear
fell.

53.

His sons' wives took it in turn to look after him. The house was
never empty but he would whisper to himself, "How terrible this
loneliness is."

Agamiyya's death did not cause him as much distress as he
had expected. He felt she was just a few steps away from him. At
his age there was no point in being sad. He feared not death, but
weakness. He was old; the day would come when all that was left
of his reign as chief was the name and the memory of what once
had been.

Bakri Samaha, who was over fifty, said to him one day,
"You've earned a rest."

"We're all ready to help," added others.

"What are you getting at?" he demanded angrily.

No one spoke, and he went on, "If I wasn't sure of my
strength, I would have retired already."

"Let Sulayman take over," began Samaha.

But Sulayman interrupted: "My father's still the stronger."

He glanced gratefully at his son, then turned back to the others. "What do you know of the curse of old age?" he demanded.

"It can turn into a boon if you take it easy," said Samaha.

"With others coveting your position. It's horrible, the slide downhill."

Again nobody spoke until at last he said irritably, "Thank you. You can go now."

54.

Salahe kar koja va mane kharab koja
Bebin tatavote rah az kujast ta bekuja.

He sat immersed in the chanting under the light of the full moon, by whose alchemy the paving stones in the square were changed to silver.

Shortly before midnight he started for home; as he passed Sheikh Said's shop the sheikh came out to speak to him: "Have you heard the news, master?"

He looked blank and the sheikh said, "Your men have ambushed the Atuf clan. Their new chief's victory parade!"

He started angrily. "Impossible!" he shouted.

"It's true. And they'll beat them, God willing."

"Where?"

"At Mitwalli Gate. To put the new chief in his place."

"Behind my back?" he fumed.

He struck the ground with his knotted stick and strode off into the darkness. Said al-Faqi watched him until he had disappeared from view. "Incontinent old fool," he muttered scornfully as he turned to go back into his shop.

55.

The battle had begun a few minutes before he arrived. Some of his men saw him and cried, "Shams al-Din al-Nagi!"

The procession had erupted into a series of running fights and the clash of sticks filled the air. Sulayman was working wonders.

The Atuf chief attacked with accuracy, striking confusion into Shams al-Din's men.

Shams al-Din hurled himself into the thick of the battle. He leapt nimbly in front of his son and came face-to-face with the Atuf chief. Dodging a heavy blow, he began to wield his stout stick with speed and dexterity. A strange power possessed him and he fought better than ever. He appeared exuberant, inspired, fearless. His men's enthusiasm increased in leaps and bounds and the clatter of weapons rose to a frenzy. Drunk on the heady wine of battle he performed miracles. Blows rained down on him but he was immune, unstoppable. His rival was put out of action and from then on the Atuf men lost their spirit and fell back defeated.

In less than an hour the victory parade had turned into a funeral. The colored lights were broken, flutes and tambourines lay smashed on the ground, flowers were trampled underfoot, and the men had all fled.

Shams al-Din stood panting, his forehead covered in blood. His men encircled him; Sulayman came forward and kissed his hand, but he motioned him away. "You owe me an explanation," he said.

"It was loyalty, not treason," said Sulayman apologetically.

The men cheered and shouted, "God bless Shams al-Din."

56.

They went home with Shams al-Din at their head, braving the darkness with flickering candles, and chanting in voices to waken the dead, "God bless him! God bless him!"

Then someone sang in a tuneful voice:

O sweet carnation in a garden full of mint.

But Shams al-Din did not enjoy his resounding victory for long. He soon became detached from the group and found himself in exalted, dreary isolation. He had heard it said that everything was worthless, even victory. And that if there were a lot of people cheering you, there were always many more listening to them cheering. Ashur al-Nagi came toward him, carrying his beautiful mother in her cumin-colored shroud. He was overjoyed to see Ashur after his long absence and told him he'd been certain he would come back someday; but hadn't his mother been buried already?

In happy moments a cloud would descend and bear him up into the vault of heaven. Then he would take no notice of the waves of depression which tried to drag him toward the unknown. It mattered little whether his legs carried him along or failed him. But he was alone. Alone, and suffering. What was the weakness slowly stealing over him? The lights were fading. The closer he got to the alley, the farther away it went. He was going toward infinity. His greatest ambition now was to reach his bed. The cries rang out: "God bless him! God bless him!"

Alone, Shams al-Din wrestled with the unknown. It blocked his path, made the ground rise up in front of him, snatched away his great victory with a mocking grin; it clenched its fist and struck him in the chest with a force he'd never experienced before.

Shams al-Din moaned and fell and his men caught him.

Love and Iron Bars

C

The third tale in the epic

of the harafish

1.

$\mathcal{T}$he whole neighborhood was upset by Shams al-Din's death and everybody contributed to building a tomb which would be a worthy resting place for him. Not a soul was absent from his funeral cortege. His heroic fortitude became the stuff of legend, ranking with the miracles of the saints, and he was given the title of "Vanquisher of Old Age and Illness." His just reign, free from corruption, was remembered forever alongside that of his father, the great Ashur. He was forgiven for his romantic escapades but no one forgot that he had always worked hard for a living and died in poverty.

Thanks to him and his father the alley existed as an ideal in people's minds for years to come.

2.

Sulayman Shams al-Din al-Nagi succeeded his father as clan chief. He was a giant like his grandfather, without the grace and beauty of his father, but he had all the charms of a typical man of his people. No one came forward to contest his election and Atris

joined his clan with enthusiasm and devotion. The nature and
quality of life was unchanged. For a few days hope flickered in the
hearts of the notables, then died away. Sulayman was no more than
twenty but he followed in his father's footsteps without hesitation.
Protector of the harafish, he muzzled the rich, fought criminals and
thugs, and was content to carry on his father's trade.

As was to be expected the chiefs of the neighboring clans
challenged him and he fought battle after battle against them, always winning; true, his victories did not have the same aura as
those of his father and grandfather, but they were sufficient to
secure peace and enhance the alley's prestige. The fighting left him
with permanent scars on his forehead and neck, but they were fine
evidence of his courage.

It would be fair to say that he was sometimes tempted to a life
of ease and opulence and that he read similar desires in the eyes of
his brothers and helpers, but he frowned on such weakness, discouraged it, and made his tender heart receptive to the fascination
of true greatness.

3.

Fathiyya—his friend Atris' sister—had been at Quran school with
him. His father's funeral was the first time he had seen her for
years. Despite his grief he took a fancy to her. She was about his
age and full of life, with a flat nose, dark brown skin, and beautiful
eyes. He felt marriage would protect him from behaviors unworthy
of a chief. So he asked Atris for her hand and they were married at
once. The people of the alley rejoiced at the news: they counted it a
victory for the harafish and a triumph of virtue.

4.

Ten peaceful years went by. Sulayman did his duty with the feeling
that being chief was a heavy burden and only on rare occasions was
there any joy in it. Fathiyya bore one daughter after another.

In the last of his peaceful years Sulayman saw Saniyya al-
Samari.

As he sat in the café resting after work she would pass in the carriage belonging to her father, a rich flour merchant. She looked radiant in her fine dress, her white veil emphasizing the calm, dark magic of her eyes, and her fleeting presence filled the air with warmth and inspiration.

He looked at the carriage, then at the Samaris' tall house. The bells on the horse's harness made him think of chiefs dancing after winning battles. Suddenly his cart seemed poor and mean for a man in his position. Few rose to their feet out of deference to him. The monastery door was not the only one to shut in his face. Weakness was repugnant, but hadn't Ashur been madly in love with Fulla? Wasn't the Samari house more salubrious than Darwish's bar? Would Ashur have held back if Fulla had been the Bannan's daughter? Did the fact that he took over the Bannan's house compromise his goodness and honesty? He could destroy his enemies, resist temptation, but love was destiny. Even Shams al-Din had fallen in love with Qamr. The harafish would be alarmed, the rich would rejoice, but Sulayman would never change. In any case, since he was fated to love Saniyya, he could do nothing about it. Of course, Fathiyya was still his faithful wife and mother of his children. She was also the sister of his loyal friend Atris. His new love swamped her like crashing waves but she was firmly rooted in her place. How sweet were the trials of a fierce and irresistible passion!

5.

After the Friday prayer Sheikh Said appeared at his side. They walked along together and as they reached the café the sheikh said, "I had a strange dream, master."

Sulayman looked at him inquiringly and he said, "I dreamed some good people wished to come and see you."

Sulayman's heart jumped nervously and he felt as if he had suddenly been stripped naked. To hide his confusion he murmured sarcastically, "What a diabolical dream!"

Earnestly the sheikh continued, "But they thought the first move should come from you."

"What did they want from a humble carter?" Sulayman asked craftily.

"They wanted him to lead them to the undisputed lord of the alley!" answered the sheikh.

6.

Temptation rose like a mountain in his path. He summoned Atris to the café. "I have a secret to tell you," he said.

Atris waited attentively and Sulayman said, "You're my friend. What would you think if I married again?"

"You want to get rid of Fathiyya?" asked Atris simply.

"Not at all. She'll still have pride of place."

Atris burst out laughing. "You know very well I've just got married for the third time!"

"We're not going to argue about one woman more or less, but there's a bit of a problem with this one . . ."

Smiling, Atris broke in: "You mean she's upper class?"

"Does everyone know, then?" exclaimed Sulayman in alarm.

"Love has a powerful scent!"

"What do people say?"

"Who cares what they say?"

"What do the harafish say?"

"To hell with the harafish," said Atris exuberantly. "Your faithful followers will dance with joy."

Sulayman interrupted him sternly. "You've got the wrong end of the stick, Atris," he said, "Sulayman al-Nagi will never change."

The glow of enthusiasm faded from Atris' face. "The lady's going to share Fathiyya's basement, is she?"

"Whatever happens, Sulayman won't change. The truth of the matter is," he went on after a pause, "that you're all as dissatisfied with justice and equality as the notables are!"

"What other clans put up with having as little as we do?"

"Sulayman will never change, Atris," he persisted.

7.

Said al-Faqi conveyed Sulayman's request to al-Samari who granted it with alacrity. In his heart al-Samari despised the carter and his humble origins but was eager for this alliance with the great chief, lord of the alley and oppressor of the rich. His only condition was that his daughter and her new husband should occupy a wing of his house until he could build her a suitable house of her own. Sulayman had no objection. Fathiyya was dumbfounded and wept bitterly but submitted to her fate. The rich were overjoyed, the harafish apprehensive, but Sulayman announced that he would not change.

The wedding was celebrated with a feast the like of which the alley had not witnessed before.

8.

Thus an alliance was formed between the clan chief Sulayman and the notable al-Samari.

"A holy alliance of power and prestige," commented Sheikh Said.

He had been well rewarded for his efforts, despite Sulayman's repeated declarations that he would never change. But life had taken on a new taste, and the clouds swelled with the waters of Paradise. Some women, Sulayman told himself, were like salty white cheese, others like butter and cream. The fragrant odor made him drunk; the smooth skin caressed and soothed him; the sweet voice sent him into ecstasies. Lighthearted elegance filled his life. Spending several days each week in the Samari house, he discovered the pleasure of family gatherings, the warmth of a soft bed, the smoothness of fine cloth, the splendid luxury of hot water in a comfortable bathroom, curtains, cushions, quilts, ornaments and objets d'art, carpets and rugs, jewelry and precious stones, and, above all, sumptuous meals, varied meats, magical sweets. The chief of the clan marveled at how this enchanting paradise could exist in a tumbledown corner of the alley. Outside he preserved his

normal appearance and insisted on continuing to work for a living
as usual. To the people of the alley he acted with the humility he
still associated with true greatness. But he noticed a new wind
beginning to blow in the calm air, stirring up sparks which threatened to start fires all over the place. Sharp eyes could see his gut
swelling with good food and drink. Around his secret paradise
people began to talk, especially his followers. For the first time he
felt obliged to distribute a share of the protection money to them on
feast days, in the greatest secrecy, and without doing noticeable
damage to the poor. He felt he was taking the first step down a
hateful, slippery road and beginning to stray from al-Nagi's way. It
appalled him as well that he was living in such luxury at the
Samaris' while Fathiyya and her daughters continued to eke out a
drab, bleak existence in the basement room. So once again he put
his hand in the public funds and showered them with presents,
descending a step farther down the slippery slope.

"I'm not really doing anything to harm the poor," he would
say to console himself.

But his conscience would not leave him in peace and his life
was clouded with nagging worries. Saniyya began to insist that he
give up his trade and hire someone else to drive the cart. He
proudly refused, trying to exert his authority like the strong man
he was. She pretended to give in, leaving the insidious, destructive
power of her love to do its work.

Whenever Sulayman felt he might be changing, he said resolutely to himself, "I haven't changed and I never will."

9.

At the Samaris' dinner table he came face-to-face with the men of
rank and prestige in the neighborhood. Previously they had
avoided him because they were afraid, or preferred a quiet life.
Now they looked at him trustingly, like people watching a lion at
the zoo.

They drank toasts and the blood coursed boldly through their
veins; the first glimmers of hope appeared.

"Perhaps you thought we could only submit to you if you used force," said the owner of the caravanserai. "Don't you know, master, that in the long run justice is valued by those who lose by it as well as by those who gain from it?"

"Who loses?" Sulayman asked hesitantly.

"You'll be glad to know you've saved us from hatred, envy, and from being robbed!"

"But," the coffee merchant picked up the thread, "we find in your perfect justice a hint of oppression."

"Oppression?" asked Sulayman, frowning.

"You oppress yourself and your followers."

"What's wrong in you having your fair share?" asked the herbalist.

"You shed your blood to defend our honor, after all," remarked his father-in-law.

"The chief and his men are notables, or that's how it ought to be," said the grain merchant.

"No!" objected Sulayman. "That's not how it was in my father's or grandfather's time."

"If your grandfather hadn't gone to live in the Bannan house the alley would never have known what it meant to be wealthy and successful."

"He was a greater clan chief than he was a notable," persisted Sulayman.

"The clan chief was made to be a notable. Strike me dead if I'm wrong!"

He laughed derisively, overcome by the wine's heat.

10.

Saniyya gave birth to two sons, Bikr and Khidr, and Sulayman enjoyed what he considered true fatherhood at last. The construction of Saniyya's new house was completed and he spent happy times there, marred only by his obligatory visits to Fathiyya's basement. Saniyya ruled his heart completely, just as she dominated the household. As time passed she worked on his emotions like a powerful drug. He stopped working and let one of his men take his place. He increased the handouts to himself and his followers, who little by little set up house closer to the notables and abandoned or neglected their simple occupations. The poor were not forgotten altogether but their share in the wealth diminished. The alley's glowing image changed; people began to ask what had happened to Ashur's legacy, to Shams al-Din's honesty. The clan was on its guard and threatened those who expressed their discontent. Saniyya raised Bikr and Khidr in luxury and comfort, then sent them to the Quran school and prepared them to go into business; neither of them showed any signs of wanting to succeed his father. When they were in their late teens she bought them a grain business and set them on the path to becoming respected and influential merchants.

Sulayman avoided fights whenever he could and eventually chose to make an alliance with the chief of the al-Husayn neighborhood to save himself the trouble of facing hostile attacks alone; the alley rapidly lost the dominant position it had enjoyed since the time of Ashur.

The giant's appearance changed completely: he wore a cloak and turban and used a light carriage for his outings, forgot his principles and drank to the point of depravity, and put on so much weight that his face swelled like the dome of a mosque and his jowl hung down like a snake-charmer's pouch.

Every feast day, when Sheikh Said came to wish him well he used to say, "May all your days be blessed, Master Sulayman . . ."

11.

The two brothers, Bikr and Khidr, were not much alike. Bikr had the beauty and grace of his mother and always appeared cheerful and arrogant. Khidr had inherited his father's prominent cheekbones and his height, but seemed more sensitive. He may have been less arrogant than his brother but nobody would have called him modest. From growing up in the Samari house the two of them had learned good manners and elegant, refined ways; their knowledge of the alley where they lived was confined to the view from the high balconies of their home, and they had never set foot on its uneven paving stones. They ran their business from a luxurious room in the house, only meeting the most important clients and leaving the daily transactions with the public to their subordinates. They didn't understand their father. Although they only saw him at his most imposing, they were not convinced of the worth of his position and did not entirely respect it. They had no idea that, without his influence, their business would have failed, and their employees and the merchants they dealt with would have made fun of their naiveté: they gained experience and skill in the most agreeable conditions, unaware of their good fortune.

12.

One evening the family sat around the silver-plated stove in the drawing room. January sat on its icy throne and a chill drizzle had been falling since early morning. Sulayman looked at his elegant, slender sons wrapped in velvet house robes, then, smiling faintly, said, "If Ashur al-Nagi could see you now, he'd disown you."

"Even a king would envy them," retorted Saniyya, gazing at them with love and admiration.

Sulayman said gloomily, "They're your sons. Neither of them will want to take my place."

"What makes you think I'd like them to?"

"Don't you have any respect for my position?" he asked dully.

"I respect it as I respect you," she said, changing tack deftly, "but I don't want to expose my sons to such dangers."

What was the point of quarreling? What was left of the covenant of the Nagis? His older daughters had married harafish; his youngest, brought up with the advantages of his elevated status, had married a so-called respectable man and her children would be as alien as her father had become to his origins. His conscience had relaxed, his greedy body had abandoned itself to temptation and abuses of the flesh. To object in these circumstances would be farcical.

His son Bikr said, "Anyhow, our ancestor Ashur liked the good life!"

"Who are you to think you understand Ashur?" asked Sulayman angrily.

"That's what they say, father."

"Only those whose hearts have been touched by the divine spark can understand Ashur."

"Didn't he take over the Bannan house?"

"It was the dream he had and the covenant that were miraculous," said Sulayman furiously.

"He didn't need a dream to tell him to run away from the plague," said Bikr rashly.

The blood rushed into Sulayman's face and he shouted, "Is that any way to talk about al-Nagi?"

The newly refined Sulayman turned abruptly into a wildcat and it was as if Ashur had been resurrected.

Saniyya started in fright and said sharply to her son, "Your great-grandfather was a holy man, Bikr."

"You'll never do anything worthwhile," his father raged at him.

He left them to retire to his room and Saniyya said to Bikr, "Never forget that you are Bikr Sulayman Shams al-Din Ashur al-Nagi!"

"That's right," murmured Khidr.

Still smarting from his father's rage, Bikr said, "But I'm also a merchant, and a Samari."

13.

Saniyya decided to marry off her firstborn. She liked the look of Radwana, daughter of Hajj Radwan al-Shubakshi, the herbalist, and proceeded to arrange the engagement. Bikr had never seen his fiancée but trusted his mother's judgment.

Radwan al-Shubakshi was very wealthy, had fathered many children, and loved music and entertainment.

The marriage was celebrated and the young couple settled in a wing of the Samari house.

14.

With Bikr's marriage a new beauty entered the house. Bikr loved her passionately from the first night. She was tall and slender with blue eyes and golden hair; the one thing that vexed Bikr—in a superficial way—was that she was the same height as him, and appeared taller when she wore high heels.

"You'll find she'll tend to fill out," his mother reassured him, "and with time she'll be as plump as her mother."

The young bride was embarrassingly shy and hardly looked anyone in the eye. But as time passed she began to take in her surroundings and fix her giant of a father-in-law and her brother-in-law Khidr with disconcerting stares.

"The bride's not settling in," said Khidr to his mother one day.

"She'll settle when she starts having children. I know these rich girls," she said, smiling. "Wouldn't you like me to find you a nice girl like her?"

"Not before I'm twenty," said Khidr. Then, noticing the dark Persian eyes gazing at him from a hanging rug, he hesitated, and added, "And I prefer golden hair and blue eyes."

Saniyya held out her coal-black plait of hair and asked him with a smile, "Is black hair no longer acceptable?"

15.

Radwana and Khidr struck up a brother-sister relationship and he helped her gladly whenever Bikr was away on a business trip. In this way he made the acquaintance of her youngest sister, Wafa. She was small and dainty and very beautiful, but she had chestnut hair and hazel eyes. It occurred to him that Radwana may have been suggesting indirectly that he marry her and he was afraid of annoying her if he refused.

One day his mother asked, "Do you like Wafa?"

"She's a nice girl, but she's not for me," he said firmly.

"I thought she'd be just right," murmured his mother regretfully.

"I'm afraid Radwana will be angry if she finds out," he told
her.

"Radwana has some pride. She wouldn't put her sister up for
sale," answered Saniyya, "and marriage is all a matter of luck
anyway."

16.

Bikr went away on a business trip which was to last several days.
When Khidr returned from the shop in the evening he found
Radwana standing at the door leading to her apartments. They
greeted one another and as he turned to go she said, "I want to ask
your advice."

He followed her into the sitting room and sat down on a
divan. She sat facing him and looked at him in silence as if not
knowing how to begin. The drowsy perfume of incense hung in
the air. He began listening to the rustle of the silence.

"I'm here to help," he prompted.

Still she said nothing. Then noticing his impatience, she began, "I don't know how to put it. Are you fed up with being with
me already?"

"Not at all. It's just that I'd like to help."

"I don't want anything more than that," she said mysteriously.

He waited, uneasy beneath the glow of the bright eyes. Con-
jectures jostled around in his head. Had he missed something? Was
she going to make an embarrassing suggestion?

"I'm at your service."

In a strange voice she said, "You don't know the situation I'm
in so I forgive you for trying to hurry me."

"Let me put your mind at rest."

"Do you think that's possible?"

"I don't see why not."

Avoiding his eyes, she asked, "Have you ever been defeated?"

"I don't think so. But what do you mean? Who's your enemy?"

"I have no enemy. It's a defeat from within."

He nodded his head, still confused.

"When you confront yourself and fail," she went on, more boldly. "When you accept that you're destroyed, I suppose you could say."

"God forbid!" he said, frowning. "Be honest with me, think of me as your brother."

"No," she said emphatically. "My brothers are somewhere different."

"But I'm your brother too."

"No, you're not. You should hear the whole story."

"I'm all ears," he said eagerly.

Clearly tense, she began, "When I was a girl in my father's house I used to see you from time to time and I heard someone saying you were one of the clan chief's sons."

He nodded without speaking, feeling strangely disturbed. Radwana continued, "I never saw Bikr at all. That's just the way it was. I didn't even know you had a brother. It's nobody's fault."

The strange presentiment grew stronger. Fears spilled into the incense-laden air and he summoned up images of Bikr, and his mother and father; the whole family came to hear the strange tale.

"Why don't you say something?"

"I'm listening to you."

She laughed with embarrassment and said, "But that's the end of the story."

"Then I didn't understand it."

"You mean you don't want to."

"I do," he protested, secretly despairing.

"Then I'll tell you in words of one syllable," she said with a bold, calculating glance at him. "One day my mother told me that Saniyya al-Samari had asked for my hand for her son."

She raised her eyes to the ceiling; her long white neck was like the silver candelabra. Something screamed at him that such beauty was created to destroy him. That sorrow was heavier than the earth, more pervasive than the wind. And that a man could only breathe freely in exile.

Gently, sweetly, submissively she confessed, "It was very hard for me to hide my joy." Then, almost as if she were singing a song, "I never doubted it was you."

He flinched and remained mute.

"That's the story. Now do you understand?" she demanded.

"You were lucky you got the better brother," he said in an unsteady voice.

"Are you talking like that because you're afraid?" she asked, gently reproving.

"No. Because it's safer."

"You've always been affectionate toward me."

"Of course. You're my brother's wife and he's very dear to me."

She came toward him in a graceful movement. Leaning closer to him so that her fragrant smell washed over him she said, "Tell me what you really feel."

He rose to his feet in alarm, saying, "I've been completely open with you."

"You're scared."

"I'm not."

"You're afraid of your brother, your father, yourself."

"Stop torturing me."

"Walls don't have ears or eyes."

"Goodbye," he muttered, making for the door. He walked blindly from the room, his mind and heart numb.

17.

Khidr avoided her. He had lunch in the shop and invented supper invitations. Saniyya noticed nothing out of the ordinary and the hours passed peacefully in the Samari household.

He was plagued with sorrow and anxiety. What should he do? He was alone with his problem, unable to ask anyone for advice. He felt tempted to flee the alley altogether. But where would he go and on what pretext? He had principles; Sulayman always said that he took after his great-grandfather—although he lacked his strength and authority—unlike his brother Bikr who loved business with all its risks and opportunities.

He suffered and did nothing, yielding bleakly to his fate.

18.

Bikr returned from his trip and stopped off at the shop before going home. Khidr welcomed him warmly. He came in beaming with pleasure at his success.

"Thank God, it was a profitable deal," he said.

Khidr smiled, welcoming the news, and Bikr asked, "How's business?"

"Great."

"You're not yourself. What's wrong?"

He shuddered inwardly, but mentioned some minor ailment by way of explanation. How could they have a good relationship again after what had happened? He entered the details of Bikr's transaction in the records, his head in a turmoil. Whether he told him his secret or kept it to himself it would be wrong. How could he get away?

Bikr stood up, saying, "I'm exhausted. I'd better go home."

19.

At this moment Bikr would be seeing Radwana again. Suddenly Khidr realized how wrong he had been to stay in the alley. He thought of her, bold and beautiful, receiving her husband. Would she be able to act the part of the longing, expectant wife? Would she go toward Bikr with the same graceful movement, passionately, eyes on fire? Would the curtain drop on her brief fancy and life return to its normal course?

Or would she succumb to hidden emotions and pretend to be ill? Would the rot spread in the new marriage, making life complicated and miserable?

He shuddered. "She could easily decide to have her revenge," he murmured to himself.

Bikr would ask her what was wrong and she would say, tearfully, "Your brother's a traitor!"

Such a lie would do incalculable harm!

Wait a minute. Why hadn't she told her father-in-law or her mother-in-law at least? She'd find someone to believe her and he'd never find anyone.

She was cunning and shameless: she would act sad and say cryptically, "I'd like to move away from here."

Bikr would ask her what was troubling her and she would screw up her face and say nothing. Did you have a fight with my mother, or my father? No, she'd say, no. Then that only leaves Khidr. Didn't he look after you nicely? She couldn't bear the sound of his name. What did he do wrong? And the false truth would emerge like the black night from under an overcast sky. She would resort to insinuations which Bikr might or might not believe but they would leave their mark. All she'd actually say was that she didn't like the way her brother-in-law looked at her; it made her uncomfortable, and that was why she wanted to move away.

How could he defend himself? Was he prepared to destroy his brother's happiness and his family's good name, or should he take the blame and run away?

But surely it was likely that his fantasies were the product of groundless apprehensions, and at this very moment the couple were enjoying the pleasures of love after a separation.

He heard the sound of hurried, angry footsteps. Then Bikr came in, slammed the door behind him, and stood there, quivering with rage.

20.

"You dirty bastard," shouted Bikr.

He fell on him like a wild bear and began to hammer him. Khidr stood there without reacting. Blood poured from his mouth and nose but still he made no response.

"Are you paralyzed with shame?" roared Bikr.

Khidr stepped back. "What's come over you?" he asked.

"You don't know? Really?"

"I've no idea."

"You want your brother's wife, and you've no idea!"

"You're crazy!" yelled Khidr.

At this Bikr fell on his brother again, pounding him savagely until some of their employees, alarmed by the cries, gathered in the doorway and people began to congregate in the alley outside the shop. In the distance Sulayman's voice could be heard scolding furiously.

21.

The crowd dispersed and the employees went back to work.

"If either of you raises a hand, I'll cut it off," shouted Sulayman.

Bikr stepped back and Khidr began to wipe the blood off his face with his handkerchief.

"He's a traitor. He needs to be taught a lesson," growled Bikr.

"I don't want to hear another word while we're in the shop."

He looked angrily from one to the other. "Follow me!" he ordered, and set off for the house like a wounded lion.

22.

They all stood before him: Bikr, Khidr, Radwana, and Saniyya.

"The truth!" he roared savagely.

Nobody said a word. "If you're hiding anything, you'll suffer for it," he threatened. He gave Radwana a sharp, commanding stare: "Talk, Radwana!"

She burst into tears.

"I don't like people crying," he said with irritation.

"All I said was that I wanted to move away," she sobbed.

"On its own that doesn't mean anything much!"

"From how she spoke I gathered she didn't want to live under the same roof as Khidr," said Bikr.

"Why not? I want something tangible."

"I got the picture. I didn't need explicit details," said Bikr.

"The truth!" roared Sulayman. "I want the truth, so that I can do what has to be done."

Looking back at Radwana, he commanded, "Tell me everything that happened."

Again she burst into tears and he waved his hand crossly, then turned toward Khidr and asked him in exasperation, "What did you do?"

"Nothing. As God's my witness," he mumbled.

"I want to know everything. A storm like this doesn't blow up for no reason."

Here Saniyya spoke for the first time: "It was just a misunderstanding."

"Shut up," said Sulayman ferociously.

"Satan's causing trouble among us," she sighed despairingly.

"Satan only interferes if you let him," said Sulayman wrathfully.

"We're cursed," wailed Saniyya.

"Let the curse fall on the one who deserves it," declared Sulayman.

Suddenly Khidr stood up and left the room.

"Come back, son," called Sulayman.

But he was gone and Bikr said triumphantly, "Don't you see now, father? He's running away."

"You're confessing to it now, are you?" shouted Sulayman, getting to his feet.

But Khidr did not come back and nobody went after him.

23.

The scandal in the Nagi family was on everybody's lips. The harafish regretted the passing of the old Nagi covenant, and considered what had befallen Sulayman and his sons just punishment for his waywardness and treachery. They repeated that Ashur was a saint whom God saved through a dream and would bless through all eternity. Those who bore a grudge said that Khidr was no more than the most recent product of a dissolute, thieving line.

Sulayman confronted the disaster with a ferocity which transformed him for the second time. He paced the alley, a potbellied giant, waiting to pounce on anyone who slipped up, until even his closest associates were afraid of him. He no longer looked the part of clan chief: he was bloated and indolent, addicted to stimulants and luxury. His stomach swelled out in front, his buttocks drooped behind, and he ate so much he would fall asleep as he sat in his accustomed place in the café.

24.

One morning Sulayman stood talking to Sheikh Said al-Faqi, slowly sinking into the mud that had accumulated at the sides of the alley following heavy rain in the night. "God always tests the faithful," the sheikh was saying.

Sulayman tried to answer, but was suddenly transfixed by the specter of an enemy rushing to attack him. He crashed to the ground, as rigid as a minaret. He tried to get up several times without success. Then he drifted into semiconsciousness. Said and several passersby rushed up to him; he emitted vague sounds but was unable to speak.

They carried him to Saniyya al-Samari's house like a sick child.

25.

Paralyzed down one side, he lay helplessly in bed. Everyone who saw him realized that Sulayman al-Nagi was finished. Fathiyya and his daughters turned their backs on him like strangers. Saniyya nursed him with sad patience and was forever muttering, "We're cursed!"

Several years went by before he could move again. He learned to walk by dragging his paralyzed half along with the help of two sticks. To relieve the monotony of his life he would sit in front of the house or in the café, speaking a couple of words from time to time and looking around with an absent gaze; the sense of things had gone from him.

26.

Atris stood in for Sulayman during his illness. At first he was loyal
to him, visiting him, bringing him his full share of the protection
money and controlling the clan effectively in his name. "You are
our lord and master," he reassured the sick man.

However, his new duties began to keep him away—or so he
said—and he stopped coming to the Samari house except to bring
Sulayman's money. Then he declared himself chief of the clan and
appropriated Sulayman's share; none of his men batted an eyelid,
perhaps even hoping that with him in charge they would be freed
from their few remaining obligations to the harafish.

The clan reverted to what it had been before the days of
Ashur al-Nagi, controlling the area rather than working for it,
content to concentrate its energies on defending itself against attacks by other gangs. Atris was forced to call truces with some of
his enemies and make alliances with others, and he actually paid
protection money to the chief of al-Husayn to avoid a battle he
knew he would lose. The more he was despised outside, the more
arrogant and overbearing he became toward his own people. He
neglected his sister Fathiyya, and married and divorced a succession of wives. He and his men kept the protection money for themselves, imposing restrictions and punishments on the harafish and
reducing the notables, as Sheikh Said said, to the station allotted
them by Almighty God.

27.

Sulayman had not only lost his position as chief but his identity as
well. He was nothing; his motivation had gone and things made no
sense. He clung on to vague hopes of a cure. "Is there really no
potion to help someone in my condition?" he asked Radwan.

"I've tried everything in my power," the herbalist answered,
hiding his contempt. To himself he added, "He wants to regain his
strength and become chief of the clan again. To hell with him and
the whole family."

Sulayman visited all the saints, dead and living, secretly entertaining high hopes. He continued to drag himself around on two sticks or sit motionless on his seat in the café like a big pot of beans simmering on the fire. For the first time in his life he was struck by the truism that man is a bad joke and life a dream. Atris and his men ignored him, and so did the harafish: they felt no pity for him and considered him the chief author of their present ills.

The misery penetrated his own house when Saniyya seemed to tire of being close to him, let a maid take over the job of looking after him, and wore a morose expression, reflecting the gloom of life around her. She never for a moment forgot her fugitive son Khidr, and so naturally her relationship with Radwana suffered. She began to be out of the house a lot, trying to amuse herself with the neighbors. Her absence was extremely painful for Sulayman; he observed that it was as if the sun had vanished behind the clouds, and that a helpless man could obviously expect no favors.

"You're out too much," he reproached her one day.

"There's nothing here for me anymore," she snapped back.

He often thought of divorcing her but was afraid that in Fathiyya's house he wouldn't get the rest he needed, so he swallowed the humiliation with as much patience as he could.

28.

Said al-Faqi sat with him in the café one day, his expression friendly, his heart full of the old hidden resentment. In an affable tone he said, "Master Sulayman, it's not easy for us seeing you in this state."

Sulayman stared at him blankly and the sheikh continued, "But we have a duty to be truthful to you."

What did he want?

"In my opinion you should divorce Saniyya."

His eyelids twitched and the hand holding the coffee cup trembled visibly.

"That's my advice as an old friend," said Said.

"Why?" mumbled Sulayman.

"I'm not saying another word," the sheikh answered.

29.

Sulayman no longer felt capable of strong reactions. His pain had become abstract. Nothing made him laugh or cry. But he would have to divorce her, go right along the road to its dead end.

From the café he went to the apartment he had rented for Fathiyya after his momentous about-face. There, he summoned the legal official and divorced Saniyya.

Bikr was devastated when he heard. "That didn't have to happen," he lamented.

"It's up to you to look after your mother now."

"Damn these lying busybodies!" fulminated Bikr.

They parted on the verge of quarreling. Sulayman began to live off his savings. "God let me die before I do Bikr a mischief," he prayed.

30.

In the midst of all this, Bikr's business affairs prospered. Radwana bore him three children, Radwan, Safiyya, and Samaha. His mother's divorce had shaken him; painful rumors reached his ears until he was forced to talk to her about her behavior and the reactions it provoked. Saniyya was furious and cursed the alley, calling it all the names she could think of and continuing to act with as few inhibitions as ever.

To add to his troubles, Bikr was anxious about his marriage. He had never felt that he possessed Radwana completely although he continued to be infatuated with her. She was not obliging, or communicative or responsive, and there was an anger in her, the causes of which were a mystery to him, but it grew worse as time passed. She had everything she wanted but never seemed grateful or happy, and when she rebuffed him or argued with him the world was unbearable. The thought that she didn't love him as much as she ought to drove him mad. What more did she want? Wasn't he an exemplary husband? He went to great lengths to

avoid provoking her but still she flared up for reasons he could not
have foreseen. The fact that they lived together and had children
together appeared to have no effect. He nursed a festering sore
which made his private life turn sour on him.

31.

"Radwana, you could make this house a nest of happiness."

"Isn't it one already?" she replied vaguely.

"You forget about loving me."

"You only think about your own pleasures. Remember I've
got three children to look after."

He said sadly, "I love you so much. I'm only asking for a bit
of affection in return."

She laughed halfheartedly and murmured, "You're greedy. I
do the best I can."

The breakdown of relations between his mother and wife
compounded his misery. Since Khidr's disappearance Saniyya had
changed and Radwana was quick to respond by changing even
more drastically in her behavior toward her mother-in-law. On one
occasion they were quarreling violently and Saniyya shouted in an
accusing voice, "Something tells me Khidr was innocent all along."

"You'd do better to think about preserving your reputation,"
replied Radwana furiously.

Saniyya lost her head and hurled a little candlestick at her and
missed. When Bikr returned from the shop he found Radwana
blazing with hatred and anger. He reproached his mother for what
she had done when they were alone together, but she answered
coolly, "I advise you to divorce her."

Bikr was amazed and said nothing. Saniyya said scornfully,
"She's the scourge that's done for us all." Her voice began to tremble with anger, as she went on, "The devil himself couldn't have
done as much harm. Even you, descendant of the great Ashur al-
Nagi, pay protection money to a bum who ran errands for your
father."

"We're well and truly cursed," said Bikr to himself.

The wheel of the days kept turning as usual. Old Samari died and his daughter Saniyya inherited a fair sum of money. She let Bikr use part of it to increase his capital and he seemed well on the way to making a vast fortune. To forget his worries he began immersing himself in work, plunging into successful ventures and dangerous speculations, until his lust for money had reached the point of lunacy. He hoarded it as if he were fortifying himself against death, sadness, and his lost paradise. From his entrenchment deep in the mire of sorrow, he threw himself into battle, defying pain and the dread of the unknown. Bikr wasn't entirely generous, nor entirely mean. Outside the house he didn't spend a penny unless it benefited him directly, but at home he spent lavishly, not counting the cost: he showered Radwana with jewels, renewed the furniture and hangings, and collected curios and objets d'art until the place was like a museum.

"If only money could buy happiness," he would say, regret gnawing at his heart.

32.

Radwana's father, Radwan al-Shubakshi, was finally declared bankrupt. The man was extravagant, passionately fond of all kinds of entertainment and long nights of pleasure, and he had lost sight of his businessman's sense of moderation and plunged into ruin. Bikr welcomed the opportunity to prove to his recalcitrant wife how affectionate and generous he was, and when the Shubakshi house was put up for auction he bought it for some monstrous sum to help his father-in-law cover his debts. He employed Ibrahim, Radwana's youngest brother, as his manager and secretary. All the same the shock was too much for old Radwan and he died of heart failure. Bikr arranged a fitting farewell for him with the full three days of mourning ceremonies. After this he expected Radwana to change, or become a little more pleasant, but she was unbending like steel, and sorrow made her more listless and reserved than ever. Finally Bikr admitted to himself that nothing was ever going to make her change.

33.

When his mother disappeared from the house and the alley, total darkness eclipsed his world. In the face of this disaster he was helpless. He soon found out that she had taken all her money and run off with a young water carrier. It nearly broke him. He washed his hands of her and did not even bother to find out where she had gone, taking refuge behind his dossiers and frequent business trips.

Atris sought him out to offer his help. He hated the sight of him, but masked his feelings with a grateful smile. "Thanks for the offer," he said, "but let's leave her to her own devices."

The world appeared gray as ashes, shading into a bloody red. "Why do we love life and cling on to it so eagerly?" he wondered. "Why do we submit to its harsh will? Surely we deserve to have the scum of the earth as our leaders? To hell with Ashur al-Nagi and his false mystique! To hell with the crazy dervishes and their incessant singing!"

Something had gone monstrously wrong but he didn't know what.

34.

One evening Sulayman al-Nagi sent for him. He remembered he hadn't visited him for months and felt embarrassed. Sulayman had been paralyzed for ten years now and had spent the last year in bed, cared for devotedly by Fathiyya. Bikr went in to him, kissed his hand, and sat down by his bed, apologizing for having been too preoccupied to come more often.

"I haven't got much longer, Bikr," said Sulayman.

Bikr protested weakly and his father went on, "I dreamed of your grandfather Shams al-Din three times on three successive nights."

"That doesn't mean anything, father."

"It means everything. He told me that life was worthless if you didn't give your soul to it."

"God have mercy on him."

"What's past is past," he said regretfully, "but I want to ask you which of your sons would be suitable?"

Realizing that he was talking about the clan chief's position, Bikr hid a smile and replied, "They're still young but they'll never be right."

"What about one of your stepsisters' sons?"

"I don't know, father," he said hesitantly.

"Because you don't know a thing about them." He sighed deeply, then said, "I'm leaving this world like a prisoner. I leave you in the care of the Everlasting!"

35.

That same night Sulayman died. Despite his lengthy seclusion, the whole neighborhood turned out for his funeral, even Atris and his men, and he was buried beside Shams al-Din.

Bitter sorrow was reawakened in the hearts of the Nagi family and the harafish and painful memories flooded over them.

36.

A new, unaccustomed burst of activity, emerging suddenly to disrupt the routine flow of events and interchangeable days, like a meteor blazing across a pale sky.

"What's the man doing?" Radwana asked herself, perplexed.

Bikr took her by the hand in an uncharacteristic gesture and led her all around the great house, floor by floor. He was serious and preoccupied, as if he was preparing for a business trip or some important deal.

"What are you doing, for God's sake?"

He didn't answer, or even smile, but led her from room to room, gallery to gallery, great hall to great hall, circling choice pieces of furniture and rare artworks, examining carpets, curtains, rugs, candelabras, lamps, ornaments, looking into the children's bedrooms.

"I'm tired of this," she muttered irritably.

He turned to a mirror framed in solid gold occupying an

entire wall. "There's not another like it in the country," he said. Then he gestured in the direction of a chandelier of vast proportions, encrusted with stars. "One of only three in this entire city." Then to a multicolored glass dome with the light pouring through. "That took a whole year to make and the cost would have supplied an army!" Then with an expansive movement, palms outspread, to a huge carpet covering the floor. "Exported specially for me from Persia!"

He sang the praises of every piece of furniture, made obeisance to every gem and precious stone. At last Radwana ran out of patience, and detaching her hand from his, she asked, "What's this all about?"

He folded his arms on his chest and gave her a strange look, then said, "I'm adored by fate."

"What do you mean?"

"Fate loves me passionately and cares for me day and night."

"You seem to be in a very strange mood."

"Have a good look at me. Study me for as long as you can. I am the world, no more and no less."

"My nerves can't stand any more of this."

He smiled for the first time and said, "What it's all about, my beloved, spoiled Radwana, my dear little rebel, is that Bikr Sulayman Shams al-Din al-Nagi is bankrupt!"

37.

She couldn't take it in; she refused to believe the impossible. She banged her head against the furniture. The world appeared to her in the guise of a woman winking her left eye spitefully. Radwana prepared herself for the flight to never-never land. Bikr's face appeared unnaturally beautiful, impossibly miserable. A sob escaped from her lips and immediately took on the shape of a scorpion.

"It's the truth, Radwana," muttered Bikr.

He watched her turn to stone, the image of stupefaction, and cried in a despairing, angry tone, "I'm not clan chief. I'm not rich. I'm not happy."

Her mouth dry, she asked, "How did it happen?"

"Like a stroke, a scandal, death. Why are you so surprised? It was just a venture that went wrong."

"People were always warning you," she whined.

He answered contemptuously, "People who know nothing about business like to criticize and hand out expert advice mainly because they're envious. To hell with them!"

Silence fell. Terrifying specters danced in the shadows. Impossible dreams crashed against the walls of a somber, unyielding reality.

"What happens now?" she asked.

"The business will go into liquidation. They'll auction off the assets. And after that . . ."

He stopped and she prompted, "After that?"

"After that we'll join the beggars and scroungers!"

"I suppose you're trying to frighten me."

"I'm trying to make you aware of what's going on, that's all."

"It's the price of folly."

"It's just business," he mocked. "Fate's the partner you don't see."

"You took the risks, not fate."

"And you always refused to show interest. But that didn't affect the market."

The tears rained down her cheeks. "Now I know how my father died!" she moaned.

"He was lucky," he said bitterly.

"What will happen to the children?"

"Let's leave them to sleep in peace."

38.

Normal activity came to a halt as people flocked to see the auction of goods belonging to a man who had been the richest of them all before he slid into ruin.

There were clouds racing across the face of the sun. Bikr stood surrounded by former business partners lately become his creditors. Polite smiles were frozen on their lips; their cheeks were pale with anxiety, embarrassment, and anticipation but their clenched jaws betrayed their determination.

Sheikh Said leaned toward Uthman al-Darzi, the bar owner, and remarked scathingly, "I wonder why he didn't have a dream showing him the way to salvation like his famous ancestor!"

"When you eat too much you only have nightmares!" Uthman whispered back.

Just before the auction was due to start there was a loud jingling of bells. All eyes turned to the alley entrance: a carriage was approaching. Could it be a prospective bidder from outside the area? The carriage came to a halt near the crowd and a young man in a black coat and turban stepped down. He was tall and graceful and looked strangely familiar.

Several voices shouted almost simultaneously, "It's Khidr Sulayman al-Nagi!"

39.

A wave of anticipation swept through the gathering. Whispering filled the air like the buzzing of hundreds of flies. Said al-Faqi hid a smile. Bikr turned pale and gave an involuntary shudder. Khidr raised his hand in greeting and was gratified by the response.

"You're just in time!" said Sheikh Said.

"Have you come to bid in the auction?" inquired Uthman.

"No. To save what can be saved," replied Khidr sadly.

Everyone noticed that he was speaking with strength and confidence and had obviously made a success of his exile, and grown wealthy. The creditors' spirits revived and a voice called, "God bless you!"

"Let's postpone the auction and try to come to an agreement," said Khidr.

"No!" shouted Bikr.

All eyes turned to him in surprise. "Time will never erase your crime," he screamed at his brother. "Get the hell out! You're not welcome around here."

He was pelted with a flurry of objections like a squall of rain.

The galloping clouds had caught up with each other and joined to form a canopy of darkness.

"Let me do my duty," begged Khidr.

"I'd rather be ruined than saved by you," raved Bikr.

"One shouldn't squander a gift from on high," intoned Tulba al-Qadi, imam of the mosque.

"He's only come to gloat and have his revenge," protested Bikr.

The creditors surged around Bikr, trying to calm him down and persuade him to listen to his brother, and Sheikh Tulba said, "Let's postpone the auction until we reach a decision we won't later regret."

40.

Bikr finished his account of the events and looked at Radwana. "That's the story," he said.

He waited eagerly for her comments but she was embarrassed and subdued and could find nothing to say. She sat trapped by his fierce, inquisitive gaze.

"What's wrong with you? Why don't you say something?" demanded Bikr.

She retreated deeper into silence, regaining her self-possession. "Tell me what you think," insisted Bikr, the irony in his voice becoming more pronounced.

Escaping his eyes, she stared at a text framed in gold hanging on the wall and said with a desperate energy, "What do you expect me to say when my children look likely to become beggars on the street?"

"Tell me straight what you really think."

Some of her defiance had returned, and she said, "I think he wants to save the Nagis' reputation."

"If he'd been bothered about that, he wouldn't have been after his brother's wife."

"Perhaps he's trying to make up for it," she said awkwardly.

"Since he has no conscience, that's not a possibility."

"Why would he sacrifice his money, then?"

A wave of anger swept over him. "Perhaps it's you he wants to save," he said sullenly.

"Never!" she protested with an angry wave of her hand.

"What do you mean?"

"I believe he's trying to save his family's name."

"You're lying," he shouted in a fury.

"Don't make matters worse," she retorted, exasperated.

"I'm justified in doubting everything, even you!"

"You're not in a state to discuss anything," she cried.

"I'm perfectly lucid," he replied. "Perhaps wealth can make you mad, but the trials of bankruptcy give you back your reason. You're just a slut who's still got her eye on her old lover."

"You've lost your mind," she shouted.

"It's a miracle it's taken this long, living with you. All I ever got from you was dislike, rejection, suppressed infidelity. I gave you everything and got fresh air in return. You were the curse that drove me to folly and ruin. Now it's your turn to pay for what you've done."

She uncurled slowly and menacingly from her seat like a tongue of flame. "Hold your filthy tongue!" she shrieked in his face.

Then he went crazy. He beat her, slapped her, kicked her until she sank unconscious to the floor. Through the anger blazing in his eyes, he stared at her in astonishment. He thought she was dead, or dying. So that was how easy it was to escape from the uncertainty that had plagued him all this time. He leapt the wall of reality and left the room, fired with deadly resolve.

41.

Khidr was having a meeting with the creditors in Sheikh Said's shop when Bikr rushed in. He held a knife in his hand and was drunk with rage.

"I've killed her, and now it's your turn," he yelled.

He lunged at his brother. Thanks to the intervention of some of the onlookers the knife missed its target, and pierced Khidr's turban harmlessly. They pinioned Bikr's arms to his side, wrested the knife from him, and threw him to the floor.

"He's gone mad!"

"He's a murderer, you mean."

Bikr raised his head a little off the floor and shouted, "You're just after money and you don't care where it comes from!"

"Let's hand him over to the police," said Sheikh Said.

"He's killed his wife," exclaimed Khidr brokenly.

"Get him to the police station."

Bikr began shouting again: "Bastards! Sons of bitches!"

42.

The truth soon came out: Radwana wasn't dead as Bikr had thought. They let him go and he fled from the alley.

Khidr settled accounts with the creditors as agreed. The business was put into liquidation but the Samari and Shubakshi houses remained in Radwana's possession.

Fathiyya invited Khidr to stay with her until he had organized his life. He obviously intended to stay in the alley and lost no time in taking steps to buy back the grain merchant's and become active in business again. He also thought about buying the Samari or Shubakshi house, to provide himself with a suitable place to live, and at the same time enable Radwana and her children to live comfortably on what she made from the sale.

"You've always been generous," remarked Fathiyya.

"I never forgot my family. They were in my thoughts all the time I was away," he replied mildly.

The alley too. And he had learned in his exile that the Nagi name meant something in the world outside while the Samari name was of little significance. He discovered that true heroism was like musk: it sweetened people's lives and stimulated them, even if they never had the chance to be heroes themselves. But was this the sole reason he had come back to the alley?

"Why haven't you married?" asked Fathiyya.

"I hated the idea of marrying in exile," he answered hurriedly.

43.

He suddenly felt inspired to go and see Atris. The meeting took place in Atris' luxurious house. The clan chief welcomed him effusively. "We're honored to receive the son of a family of heroes," he said.

Khidr replied modestly, "I'm simply coming to pay my respects to the chief, as I intend to settle in the alley."

"You people are always a force for good," said Atris, relaxing.

This encounter ensured that suspicions were nipped in the bud.

44.

Was he waiting for something particular? He was working as a grain merchant again, and suffering conflicting emotions. Now the hot southerly winds of spring were lashing the alley walls once more, raising clouds of dust, muddying the hot, thick air. Soon the summer would be here with its easy majesty, honest heat, and sticky breath. Was he waiting for something to happen? Radwana had sent someone to thank him; and he had replied pleasantly. Fathiyya reported to Radwana on his behalf that he thought this use of emissaries made them seem like strangers. Finally he sent Fathiyya to arrange a meeting with her. He went at night to avoid prying eyes, so that memories of the past would not become topics of discussion once more. Although his feelings were in turmoil, he was filled with secret determination.

Radwana received him in the salon, modestly dressed, with her head bowed and a black veil as if she were in mourning. They shook hands and their eyes met only for an instant, but in that short space they gave off sparks like two stones rubbing together. Then they sat, silent and uncomfortable, each wishing the meeting was over.

"This is an opportunity for me to thank you in person," said Radwana.

Relaxing a little, Khidr said, "And for me to tell you that I'm here to help you if you need anything."

"What about Bikr?"

"I haven't forgotten my duty to him, but there hasn't been a trace of him so far."

"When do you imagine he'll come back?"

"I know he's very proud. I'm afraid he may stay away a long time. How are the children?"

"As well as can be expected."

Khidr hesitated a little, then said, "I want to buy the Shubak-shi house, if you'll let me."

She frowned slightly. "That's your way of helping a bankrupt woman, I suppose."

"I need somewhere in a hurry," he said uncertainly. Then, resigning himself, "We're all in the same family anyway."

"Thank you for your good intentions," she said, giving him a long look. Then after a moment's silence she asked, "Have you forgotten my past faults?"

"The past'll trip you up if you let it hang around," he answered too promptly.

"But do you really think it's possible to forget?"

"Of course. When it's for the best."

"I don't know . . ."

"If I hadn't thought that I wouldn't have come back. And we wouldn't have met like this."

A wary look came into her beautiful eyes. "Did you really come about buying the house?" she demanded.

A feeling of confusion threatened him for a moment. Suppressing it, he answered, "Of course."

"But you know it still belongs to Bikr!"

He flushed and said, "We can find a way around that."

She shook her head doubtfully.

"Let me help you at least," he pleaded.

"There are enough precious objects in the two houses to guarantee us a very comfortable life," she said haughtily.

"But I'm responsible for you too."

"I don't need any help, thanks," she said with an unfathomable look in her eyes.

He looked down, acquiescing, and made a gesture to imply that it was time the meeting ended.

"Did you have another aim in mind?" she asked anxiously.

He stared at her in astonishment and she said boldly, "I mean did you come to tell me off or punish me?"

"God forbid! Such an idea never entered my head," he protested.

She said nothing and he went on heatedly, "I've been honest with you the whole time."

The tension around her mouth disappeared and she looked peaceful all at once. Changing the subject abruptly she said, "You prospered in exile."

"Yes. I took all my savings with me and put them to good use."

"We're all pleased for you."

He paused, then said, "Success doesn't always make you happy."

"I know that only too well. But what's to stop you being happy?"

There was a heavy silence, then she said in some confusion, "We stopped being happy too."

"There's a curse . . ." he muttered.

"Saniyya was always saying that we were cursed."

She realized from the way he avoided asking about his mother that she knew what had happened to her, and regretted mentioning her. But Khidr said, "Perhaps she was right."

"She thought I was the curse," sighed Radwana.

"We always exaggerate when we're upset," he said in a low voice.

"I admit I was wicked. I really treated you badly."

"What's done is done," he grunted.

"Nobody takes proper account of what their feelings tell them," she asserted defiantly. He could think of nothing to reply, so she went on, "Even if they're sincere."

This was the moment he'd been desperately hoping for. The reason why he'd come. Perhaps the reason why he'd returned to the alley. Why he'd never been happy elsewhere.

He let the feeling of pleasure wash over him. "Sometimes people deny their feelings on purpose," he said.

Her face lit up. Thoughtfulness and eager curiosity shone in her luminous blue eyes. "What do you mean?" she demanded.

He was silent, tormented by guilt.

"What do you mean?" she repeated.

"What did I say?" he asked in confusion.

"That people sometimes deny their own feelings deliberately. Don't try to get out of it now."

He was silent.

Intoxicated with sudden joy, she said, "I didn't deny mine."

Still he said nothing and she continued passionately, "Speak! Why did you come?"

He said brokenly, "I've told you."

"I mean the last thing you said."

"I talked more than I ought to have done," he said, as if making a confession.

"Ought to have done! Ought to have done!" she shouted, out of her mind. "Why did you come? You know very well it was purely to say that."

He was sinking rapidly. "First it was a curse, now it's madness," he said.

Her beauty reasserted itself, sweeping away her distress. "Tell me honestly and plainly."

"You know it all."

"That doesn't matter. I want to hear you saying it."

He looked at her softly, confessing, acknowledging. Her heart sang and her beauty blazed out suddenly, superb in its moment of triumph.

"So it wasn't you who said no?"

"Part of me did."

"What about the other part?"

Very seriously he declared, "I loved you. I still do. But we have to think carefully."

In the dignity of the night silence fell. Both of them wanted it this time. The sound of their hearts beating drummed in their ears.

45.

If permanence were possible, why would the seasons change?

46.

Waiting is an ordeal: it tears the soul apart; time dies, aware of its own dying. The future is based on clear premises but may turn out to be full of contradictions. Let anybody desperately waiting for something to happen wallow in anxiety to his heart's content.

She was married, unmarried, and in love as well. She called upon holy men, consulted lawyers, driven crazy by thinking about what she should do next.

In the grain merchant's he conducted his business efficiently, debated passionately with his feelings, hid his desires, fought violently against temptation, and bombarded heaven with prayers.

People watched, remembered, counted the sidelong glances and the veiled intentions, misinterpreted what they thought they saw, anticipated the confirmation of doubts—all in the guise of piety and innocence.

"Respectability is a mask," Sheikh Said would say. "The dissolute man is more ingenious than the devil himself."

"Why hasn't Khidr married yet?" Uthman al-Darzi would ask his customers in the bar.

47.

The creeping sorrow enfolded Ibrahim, Radwana's brother and Khidr's agent, in its tentacles. Rumors hit him like sparks from a fire. He had lost his status and now he was losing his honor. The days slowly passing contrived to give him a sense of impending disaster.

One day, unable to bear it any longer, he interrogated Khidr.

"Wouldn't you be within your rights if you claimed the Shubakshi and Samari houses in repayment for the debts you soaked up?"

"The thought never crossed my mind," answered Khidr in astonishment.

"It's nice of you to look after Bikr's responsibilities even when he's turned his back on them," Ibrahim remarked slyly.

"His children are my children," said Khidr innocently.

Fine words, but what was behind them?

48.

Ibrahim found himself in a diabolical situation. There were no obstacles ahead; life looked promising and trouble-free, but some anonymous impulse was thrusting him toward difficult terrain. He advanced with his eyes open, his mind as sharp as a knife blade, and he realized he was fast approaching some unnamed terror.

One evening he went to visit his sister Radwana. They had always been loving and protective to one another, but he felt compelled to tell her what was being said about her. She was plainly annoyed. "That's how people are. They won't change."

"It's our duty to put a stop to these rumors," protested Ibrahim.

"I'd like to cut their tongues out," she said savagely.

"It's all we can expect when your husband vanishes like this," said Ibrahim schemingly. "He's a bastard."

"True," she slipped in quickly, while he paused for breath, "and I shouldn't put up with it."

"What do you mean?" asked Ibrahim, his apprehensions re-kindled.

"I'm perfectly entitled to ask for a divorce."

"A divorce!" he cried angrily.

"That's right. Why are you getting so cross?"

"Respectable women don't do things like that."

"*Only* respectable women do things like that!"

"What grounds have you got?"

"He left me without any means of support."

"And will divorcing him give you an income?" he asked slyly.

She realized she had gone too far, and looking a little flustered, she mumbled, "At least I'll be breaking off a relationship that no longer makes sense."

"Put it off for a little while, please," he begged. "It's a complicated procedure that we know nothing about."

"Not at all, according to the lawyer!"

"You've consulted a lawyer already?" he asked in surprise.

There was an awkward silence.

"You should be ashamed!" he shouted. "Behind my back too!"

"I was simply asking for advice. There's no harm in that."

"So people are justified in saying that you're trying to get a divorce so you can marry Khidr!"

"To hell with them!"

"But it's very damaging to our reputation."

"I've done nothing wrong."

He stared savagely into her face. "It'll look to them—not without reason—as if you were his partner in crime."

"They'll always find something to say."

"But it's very damaging. Our reputation will be blown to pieces."

"I'm not a child, Ibrahim," she protested angrily.

"A woman is a child all her life."

Startled by his wrath she said, "Let's postpone this conversation till another time."

"Out of the question," he said obstinately.

"Leave me alone!" she cried irritably.

"Now I'm sure you're in league with him."

"Have you forgotten what happened?"

"And I also know the story of Joseph and Potiphar's wife."

"As far as I'm concerned, I've got nothing to be ashamed of."

He stood up, pale-faced, and asked, "Answer me honestly, do you intend to marry Khidr?"

"I won't be interrogated and accused of things I didn't do."

"It's one catastrophe after another!"

Now it was her turn to stand up and demand, "Isn't marriage a lawful relationship?"

"Sometimes it can be as bad as adultery."

"I haven't heard that before."

Suddenly calm, he said, "So you do intend to marry Khidr?"

She was silent. Her limbs were trembling.

"You're going to marry Khidr. It's true, people have an unerring instinct for such things."

"You needn't have anything more to do with me, Ibrahim. We can go our separate ways."

"We will, Radwana."

He threw himself at her in a frenzy and grabbed her by the throat and squeezed with all his might. Intoxicated by the violence of his feelings, he squeezed harder, bent on destruction. Radwana fought helplessly for her life, lashing out blindly, emitting soundless screams, inaudible cries for help, prayers that went unheeded. Her despair scattered the light into a million particles and strewed objects around the room.

She went limp, submitted, weakened, and grew still as she slid into nothingness.

The Fugitive

The fourth tale in the epic

of the harafish

The sun rose, the sun set, daylight came, darkness fell, the anthems sounded in the dead of the night. Radwana had vanished into the bowels of the earth, Ibrahim into prison, Bikr into the unknown.

Nobody lamented the murdered woman, but there was plenty of sympathy, even respect, for Ibrahim. Khidr nursed his sorrows privately, sharing them with nobody. People exchanged all the old sayings about woman's corrupt nature, quoted proverbs on the treachery of brothers, and agreed sanctimoniously that a curse must have fallen on the Nagi family.

The office of clan chief had passed out of their hands; Atris continued to hold it with pride until he died and was succeeded by al-Fulali, the most powerful of his followers. Ashur, Shams al-Din, and Sulayman became figures of legend.

Their elder statesman, Khidr, sat in the grain merchant's, growing richer day by day, paying taxes to the clan chief when required, cut off from all notions of heroic valor.

He had a new house built, devoted himself to bringing up Radwan, Safiyya, and Samaha, remained single until he was approaching forty, buried Fathiyya, his father's first wife, and attended the funerals of Tulba al-Qadi, the imam of the mosque, Sheikh Said al-Faqi, and Uthman al-Darzi, owner of the bar.

In the end Khidr married Diya al-Shubakshi, Radwana's youngest sister. She bore some resemblance to Radwana, and her beauty was comfortingly familiar. He soon discovered that she was unusually good-hearted, with a simplicity and candor verging on stupidity. She made little contribution to the running of the house and had no children. Elegant clothes and makeup were alien to her and she left her looks to nature. Khidr was satisfied with his lot and never thought of taking a second wife. He began to favor a more pious and devout way of life and often spent his evenings in the square at the monastery gate, like Ashur before him.

Safiyya married Bakri, owner of the timber yard. Radwan worked as his uncle's assistant in the grain merchant's, taking Ibrahim's place. He soon showed that he was steady and reliable, with a flair for business, and his future looked bright.

Samaha, on the other hand, seemed as if he was going to be a problem.

2.

Samaha was of medium height and powerful build, overflowing with life and energy. He had the typical local features of his grandfather Sulayman and the fine head and clear skin of his mother Radwana.

He was educated at the Quran school, and from that virtuous world acquired decency, kindliness, and some basic piety, but he was ablaze with the recklessness of youth, and adulated the world of heroes. He found the work in the grain merchant's uncongenial and appeared to have no talent for it. He made friends with some of al-Fulali's gang and sat up with them in the hashish dens or even wandered through the bar sometimes.

This worried Khidr. He would often say to him, "You need a lot of willpower and concentration."

Samaha would look curiously over to his brother Radwan and say, "I wasn't made for business, uncle."

"What do you think you were made for, Samaha?" his uncle would ask apprehensively.

His eyes would waver uncomfortably and Khidr would say, "Roaming around with the gangs having fun won't get you anywhere."

"What did our ancestors do?" he retorted.

"They were true chiefs, not thugs," said Khidr seriously. "Our only hope is to gain prestige in society through business."

He wanted to give him guidance, point him in the right direction, out of love for Radwana; he had focused his thwarted paternal instincts on her three children. True, she was only a memory, but one that refused to die.

3.

Khidr learned eventually that Samaha had joined al-Fulali's gang. The chief was delighted that a descendant of al-Nagi had declared his allegiance to him, and considered it his greatest triumph in his own alley. The harafish, on the other hand, thought of it as a new phase in the tragedy which was slowly grinding them down. Trying to explain it to themselves, they said that God was sometimes capable of producing worthless scoundrels from the loins of heroes, and that Ashur who had dreamed a dream, escaped miraculously, and returned to rule with perfect justice was an extraordinary phenomenon that would never recur.

Khidr was deeply distressed and suffered from a bitter sense of failure and disgrace.

"You're dragging the memories of Nagi, Samari, and Shubakshi through the dust," he said to his nephew.

"I've got a head full of dreams, uncle," said Samaha.

"What do you mean?"

"One day the Nagis will reign again in all their glory!"

"Are you tempted by the idea of becoming chief?" asked Khidr uneasily.

"Why not?" replied Samaha, full of confidence.

"You don't have the strength for it."

"That's what they thought about Shams al-Din," said Samaha vehemently.

"You're not him."

"Wait till the fight for the succession."

"Watch out for al-Fulali," Khidr interrupted. "He's a cunning devil. Your exploits will disgrace us and finish us off for good if you're not careful."

"Forget about your ambitions," advised his brother Radwan. "Al-Fulali's got eyes everywhere. He's taken you under his wing so that you can't make a move without him knowing about it."

Samaha smiled, and his dreams glowed in his eyes like the rosy red of a sunset sky.

4.

That night Khidr sat in the monastery square. He hid his fears and anxiety in the blessed darkness, contemplated the stars, gazed in reverence at the dim outline of the ancient wall, and prayed to the monastery's imposing door. He looked sadly along the path to the graveyard, then greeted the vague forms of the mulberry trees, remembering with emotion the dead at rest in their graves and those lost in the unknown. Burning passions which had never tasted the nectar of life. Vanished hopes. Dreams released from the valleys of silence like meteors. The throne of love poised above the uncertainties of good and evil.

What did the future hold? Why was Ashur the only one to have visions to guide him?

The melodies rose in the air like the cries of hoopoes.

Ananke khaq ra benazar kimya konand
Aya bovad keh koshahe cheshmi bema konand.

5.

Khidr thought he should find Samaha a suitable girl to marry. He was convinced he was going through a reckless, dangerous period and should be made to listen to reason. If he married into a respectable family he would have to reconsider his way of life. Living in a luxurious house, fathering a handful of fine children, acquiring kinship with people of a superior class would create a new world around him and make him see things differently. He thought he had found what he was looking for in Unsiyya, the daughter of Muhammad al-Basyuni the herbalist. He went to test the water, and found an even friendlier welcome than he had anticipated.

"I've found a nice girl for you to marry," he said to Samaha.

"Shouldn't we start with Radwan? He's older," said Samaha in surprise.

"We'll start with the headstrong one!" retorted his uncle.

"The fact is that I beat you to it," said Samaha in unruffled tones.

"Really?" He bowed his head, seemingly unmoved, but asked in some trepidation, "Who's the lucky girl?"

"Mahalabiyya," answered Samaha with a defiant smile.

Diya burst out laughing, her innocent eyes devoid of either pleasure or sorrow at the news, but Radwan repeated in amazement, "Mahalabiyya!"

"The daughter of Sabah, the exorcist," agreed Samaha calmly.

Khidr frowned and flushed with anger. Diya shook an imaginary tambourine, laughing heartily.

"Why are you tormenting us like this?" demanded Khidr.

"Uncle, I love you, and I love Mahalabiyya too," answered Samaha gently.

6.

He had noticed her for the first time at the Feast of the Dead sitting beside her mother on a donkey cart. Later when he was at Shams al-Din's graveside he saw her jump lightly to the ground. Her skin was dark, almost black. She was slim, with sharp features, well-proportioned limbs, a smiling face, and she exuded life and femininity. He felt a surge of burning desire to be joined with her. Their eyes met in mutual curiosity, responsive like fertile earth. The scorching air, the heavy sighs of grief, the fragrance of cut palm leaves, basil, and sweet pastries for the festival fused with their secret desires. He inclined toward her like a sunflower. The death all around spurred him on.

He was not surprised by what had happened. He had always felt intensely attracted to black women, and his first sexual encounters had taken place in their arms, in the gloom of the archway or in the derelict buildings behind the bar.

7.

He acted alone. He chose the most disreputable man he could think of, Sadiq Abu Taqiya, to ask about Mahalabiyya and her mother.

"I never leave the bar," he said, "but I get unsolicited gossip all the time." He thought a little. "The girl's got quite a few admirers, but I've never heard a bad word said against her."

Samaha felt glad, reckoning that such an obvious scoundrel would probably give the most accurate kind of evidence. However, he was not entirely convinced and went to consult the imam of the local mosque, Sheikh Ismail al-Qalyubi. "Her mother's trade is damned in the eyes of God," he declared.

"I'm asking about the daughter."

"Why choose your wife from a house haunted by demons?" asked the imam testily.

But Muhammad Tawakkul, the local sheikh, was unequivocal. "The girl's reputation is spotless."

She seems more respectable than my grandmother Saniyya, thought Samaha.

8.

Samaha went to visit Sabah in her home overlooking the animal trough. At first she imagined he was a prospective client and her mind went to Diya al-Shubakshi.

"Welcome to the son of our glorious heroes," she said effusively.

He looked at her mildly, lulled by the fumes of Sudanese incense which filled his nostrils. His eyes roamed over the tambourines of various sizes, the whips and swords, and the robes encrusted with colored pearls, all of which were jumbled together on the sofa or piled up on shelves around the room, then returned to rest on her body which bulged in front of him like a sack of coal.

"At your service, my lord," she said.

"It's not what you think," he muttered.

"What can I do for you, then?"

Fixing his eyes on the patterned rug at his feet, he said, "I want to marry your daughter, Mahalabiyya."

She was astonished at first. Her bearing suddenly changed. Her face broke out into a broad smile, revealing even white teeth.

"Fancy that!" she muttered.

He raised his head, smiling, and said, "I hope you'll say yes."

"None of your family's with you," she said significantly.

"I decided to start things off by myself," he said vaguely.

"Really? How I like free men!"

He smiled encouragingly.

"Fine!" she murmured, and they joined hands and recited the prayer to confirm the agreement.

9.

Khidr did not want to let go of Unsiyya, the herbalist's daughter, so he married her to Radwan and ensured his line would be established on a reliable basis.

Samaha asked his uncle, "Will you come to my wedding?"

"You're one of us and the nail clings to the flesh," answered Khidr without hesitation.

Reassured, Samaha asked Radwan the same question. "I'll always be beside you," answered his brother enthusiastically.

But nothing could efface their hidden sorrow.

10.

"Welcome to Nagi, lord of us all!" cried al-Fulali, surrounded by his henchmen in Tirbasa's smoking den. This was how he always greeted him. But Samaha wasn't stupid. He knew instinctively never to drop his guard. He felt there was always someone registering his movements, studying his expressions. He had the impression of being constantly under surveillance. But he played the role to perfection. He hurried up to the chief, brushed his shoulder with his lips deferentially, and took his accustomed place on the mat, among the lowlier members of the clan.

"I came to invite the chief and the brothers to my wedding party," he announced cheerfully.

Al-Fulali guffawed in delight. He turned to Hamouda, his private pimp and right-hand man. "Let's hear it, you son of a gun!"

Hamouda trilled for joy, more exuberantly than any loose woman, and al-Fulali went on, "Congratulations. When's the big day?"

"Next Thursday, God willing."

"And who's the lucky girl?"

"Sabah's daughter."

The men were speechless. They turned to their chief with startled expressions. In the feeble lamplight they looked like grotesque specters. Al-Fulali broke the silence: "Sabah only has one daughter as far as I know!"

"That's the one I mean, master."

All that could be heard was a stomach rumbling quietly from time to time, a stray cough. Vague secrets swirled in the smoky haze.

"By the prophet Husayn, the greatest of all the martyrs!" cried al-Fulali expansively. Then he confronted his men: "The world can play some funny tricks, can't it, lads?"

They moistened their lips nervously, aware of the warning implicit in his words, and uttered lame expressions of surprise.

"It's a funny old world!"

"Amazing!"

Al-Fulali gave Hamouda a friendly slap and said, "You'd better tell our hero the secret!"

Hamouda turned to Samaha. "Can you believe it? No more than an hour ago the chief decided to send you as his emissary to ask Sabah for her daughter's hand."

Samaha was dumbfounded. The ground rocked beneath him. A gaping hole opened at his feet. He was unable to speak.

"Fate," declared al-Fulali. "I only made up my mind yesterday. And I decided to choose you as my messenger an hour ago."

The moment of truth was here. Al-Fulali had accepted him into the clan without any kind of trial, but he had been waiting for the right occasion to test his loyalty. Now it had arrived; it loomed starkly before him. He was at the crossroads of life and death. But whatever choice he made he was finished.

Al-Fulali looked at his men. "What shall we do?" he asked.

Random voices answered him: "Who would challenge the sun's place in the sky?"

"Is the eyebrow beneath the eye?"

"What an honor to be the chief's messenger!"

"When are you going to speak, Samaha?" demanded Hamouda.

He had to say something. The atmosphere crackled with tension. He was expected to sink out of sight. Accept annihilation. Swallow the deadly poison.

"To hear is to obey, chief," he said.

11.

He rejoined his family shortly before midnight.

"Diya was telling us about a dream she had," said his uncle.

Samaha did not listen. Unsiyya, Radwan's wife, continued, "She saw you astride a mule. You were laying into it with a whip, but it refused to budge."

"A woman's dreams generally mean something, you know," teased Radwan.

"He's getting married. Don't antagonize him," soothed Diya.

Samaha sighed audibly. Radwan examined him with concern. "You're a different person, Samaha," he murmured.

"That's what I thought. I was trying not to notice," said Khidr.

Samaha told them the whole story. A heavy weight descended

on his audience. Terror was visible even on Diya's pretty, bland face.

"I always warned you," said Khidr.

"The presence of people like you in a gang is bound to arouse fears," said Radwan. "Even if al-Fulali himself isn't affected, it'll be enough to undermine the pretenders to the throne. It must have been them who kept up the pressure and caused the rift between you and the chief."

Khidr nodded in agreement. "That's why he's pushing you into a corner—so you won't be able to escape without losing either your honor or your life."

"You'll have to be on your guard more than ever now. That man can see into every nook and cranny!" said Radwan.

"The mule refuses to budge," said Diya sadly.

"What have you decided to do?" asked Unsiyya.

But Samaha, looking wretched, remained silent.

"Don't consider any form of resistance," Khidr warned.

12.

Samaha went to visit Sabah early next morning. On his way he felt the eyes burning into him like red-hot coals. Sabah kissed him on the forehead and said, "Only two more days until happy Thursday!"

He smiled weakly. "Things have changed."

She stared hard at him, full of apprehension.

"I'm only al-Fulali's messenger," he said tersely. "He wants to marry your daughter, Mahalabiyya."

The words slid over her mind without leaving any impression. He repeated them and asked her to call Mahalabiyya. He recounted the story to the two of them and they listened despondently. Then silence descended like a lead weight.

Samaha was the first to break it. "I'm the one to suffer most from his decision," he said.

Sabah swore vehemently, convinced of his sincerity.

"We have to work things out," went on Samaha.

"He's terrorizing us!" said Sabah.

"What do you want to do?" Mahalabiyya asked him.

In spite of the discouraging situation he felt excited by her presence. "I want to know how both of you feel," he said.

Sabah answered at once, "No one in their right minds would stand up to al-Fulali, son."

"You think we should give in!"

"It's the only reasonable way to look at things."

He shifted his gaze to Mahalabiyya.

"What do you think?" she asked him.

"I can't give you up," he declared simply.

"It'll be the end of us," cried Sabah in alarm.

"I'm staying with you," said Mahalabiyya, her eyes resting on his face.

His heart pounded and a violent surge of pleasure went through him.

"It's pure madness," said Sabah.

"Let's run away," said Mahalabiyya.

He nodded his head in agreement.

"What about me?" demanded Sabah.

"You'll have nothing to do with it. You'll be quite safe."

"Do you think people who want revenge act according to reason?"

"Come with us!"

"My livelihood's here."

"You can earn your living anywhere."

"We'll take cash with us," said Mahalabiyya.

"You'd be mad to consider it seriously," wailed Sabah.

But Samaha was already working out a more detailed plan of action.

13.

He went straight back to al-Fulali, kissed his shoulder, and said cheerfully, "Congratulations, master."

Al-Fulali stared at him briefly, then grunted, "Well done, lad."

14.

He crouched in the gloom of the pathway between the old city wall
and the monastery boundary. Here, generations before, Ashur had
been found, nameless and shapeless, wrapped in a shawl, oblivious
to the anthems washing over him. A merciful hand had reached
out to pluck him from nothingness. The same anthems scaled the
waves of night now:

> *Darin zamane ratiqi keh khali as khelalast*
> *Sarahiye meye nab o satineye ghazalast.*

Mahalabiyya would come wrapped in shadows. Her heart
would shine through the darkness with the longing for life and
love which kept it beating. They would meet and touch on the
pathway, the pathway of eternity, paved with burning hopes.

He was anxious all the same. Several times he had folded back
his gallabiyya to urinate. He listened intently, dreaming of escaping
to safety, fighting off fears and misgivings. He vowed to sacrifice a
sheep if he succeeded, remembering the example of his uncle Khidr
who had fled in despair and returned as a man of wealth and
status. Perhaps one day he would return to restore the glorious age
of al-Nagi.

Al-Fulali would be fast asleep now, dreaming of his wedding
day, lulled by the joyous trilling, the pledges of loyalty, the smiling
faces. Mahalabiyya would be creeping along close to the wall
toward the archway. Perhaps at this very moment she was crossing
in front of the monastery to the sound of the anthems, driven on by
the heat in her body, guided by her pounding heart. The melodies
would mingle with her heartbeats, protecting her, driving away the
loneliness of the dark night.

15.

A scream broke loose from the kingdom of darkness. A frenzied
sound of terror and despair. It took on the shape of a hunted

creature, robbed of the joy it had scarcely had time to know. It raised protesting eyes to the brilliant stars, hurled itself against the waves of song, and finally submitted to the harsh, mocking grip of silence.

16.

Samaha leapt from his hiding place like a scalded cat. Mahalabiyya. It couldn't be anyone else. He rushed toward the square, throwing caution to the winds. The sound of running feet reached his ears, threatening violence. Somehow the secret had got out. An army of clubs and knives separated him from her. It was pointless to go on. He stood motionless, then retreated as the footsteps came closer. Halfway along the footpath he heard pounding feet from the direction of the graveyard. He was surrounded. Death loomed. The old city wall was impossibly high. The monastery wall had jagged glass embedded in the top of it. With all his strength he jumped and clung to its side, then hauled himself up and lay sprawled over it, his belly, chest, and limbs pierced by its needles of fire. Beyond human endurance.

The two groups met and spoke together in angry sentences.

"Where's the snake got to?"

"Must have slipped out into the square."

"There's no sign of him there."

"No sign of him here either."

The pain tore at his body and spread into his soul. Hope faded and death seemed sweet.

17.

The clouds came down and hung in the air like mist, broken every now and then by the gleam of a star. Souls danced like phantoms. The water carrier distributed water skins full of tears. Ashur al-Nagi searched the empty alley, grieving for the victims. Then he took the plague by the scruff of the neck and danced a victory dance. In the monastery square he met Saint Khidr. "I've come to take you to Paradise," said the saint, and Ashur went off arm in arm with him along a beam of light from a bright star.

Shams al-Din refused to grow old. He left senility begging on his doorstep, hoisted the fountain onto his shoulders, and went off toward the archway. The beggar never moved from his spot. Shams al-Din danced a victory dance. But where was Saint Khidr? The beggar never left his spot. How stubborn he was! He had no pity for Sulayman's paralysis, was unmoved by his tears, and let him suffer a slow, tortuous decline. Where were the miracles and dreams? Blood filled the animals' trough and the cistern of the fountain and congealed in people's veins. But then the beggar spoke for the first time. "Ashur is not dead," he said. "He will return before the crescent moon is in the sky."

18.

The first thing he felt was his eyelids moving, a sense of being alive at least, a flutter of consciousness. The mist in front of his eyes lifted slightly to reveal the frescoes on the ceiling stretching away to infinity. Merciful God! The murmuring voices, the colors were strangely familiar. Had the world survived? This creature before him was a woman: Diya, his uncle's wife, bending over him in her innocent way, murmuring, "He's dreaming so deeply."

Khidr's house. His good uncle's voice repeating over and over, "Thank God."

Now the memories came flooding over him. He had dragged himself back here, pouring blood. The monastery wall, fortified with glass. How cruel the hearts of the golden voices were! Mahalabiyya's scream in the stillness of the night, the scream which had borne away all their hopes and dropped them lifeless behind the old wall. All that was left was his tormented heart. He heaved a deep sigh. His uncle whispered in his ear, "No one knows you're here."

"If the secret gets out none of us is safe," said Radwan.

The truth had emerged, shamefaced. But who had betrayed him?

19.

His health improved daily. The tale came back to him in all its horror. Mahalabiyya had been murdered. Dozens of witnesses testified that he—Samaha—had enticed her to the square and killed her, resentful that she had chosen al-Fulali over him. Her mother was one of them. To save her skin she said what the real killers wanted to hear. So, according to her, Samaha had done the deed and fled.

"So it was poor Sabah who was forced to tell our secret," said Samaha.

What should he do now? He had no choice but to run like his father, Bikr, and his grandmother, Saniyya. To vanish from sight like Ashur.

So as well as seeing his happiness disappear, he would have to say farewell to the monastery, the archway, the mosque, and the fountain, and all the familiar faces.

"How will you be treated?" he asked his uncle.

"Roughly and with contempt," answered Khidr sadly.

Samaha sighed, but Khidr went on with more energy, "This time we have to make sure no one knows you're leaving."

20.

News reached them confirming that he had been sentenced to death in his absence.

"Now you really have to go," said Khidr.

He felt stifled by resentment at the injustice of it.

"You must lie low for fifteen years," Khidr went on.

"The authorities will be after you," said Radwan, "and so will your enemies. Watch out especially for Hamouda, Dagla, Antar, and Farid. They were the first to testify against you."

He groaned. When would he be on his feet again? When would the pain grow less? When would he forget that he had been unable to save Mahalabiyya? When would he have his revenge? How would he escape the hangman's rope?

The Nagis were subjected to hostile treatment. Even the poorest, most insignificant members of the family suffered. Lads threw mud at Khidr. A cart loaded with grain was stolen from outside the shop. They began barricading themselves in their houses at nightfall. But Khidr was not too pessimistic. "They'll come around in the end," he said. "Money'll do the trick."

21.

Once he was completely recovered, his heart beat with new life. He began to think about the future and make plans. There was nothing to look forward to, but he wasn't beaten. A love of life stirred inside him once more. He felt inspired, full of desire, ready to resist and survive.

22.

When he crossed the Nile he believed he had moved to another country. His face was almost hidden behind a flowing beard and a headcloth worn low on his forehead. He changed his name to Badr al-Saidi, said he came from Upper Egypt, and made a living selling dates, fenugreek, and lentils. He lived in a basement room in Bulaq and was known for his pleasant manners.

A vision of the hangman's rope was always before him, a constant reminder to him that his life hung in the balance. He knew death was lurking, demons dogging his footsteps, and he began to keep a record of the passing days in a private journal and to register all his business transactions. His old world vanished. His family, the people of the alley, his desire to be chief, his lost love, his burning hopes, faded into the past. All he had left was exile, work, and piety.

At first he was lonely in Bulaq. Certainly it had many familiar features: a fountain, a trough, a Quran school, a small mosque, a sheikh. But the people knew nothing of the great covenant of the Nagis and his arrival aroused little curiosity. Bulaq was a river port where numerous sailing boats docked each day. It was thronged with strangers, either passing through or coming to settle. For this reason people fleeing from the law would not take refuge there, and strangers did not cause disquiet. Its network of streets and alleyways covered a large area, unlike his own alley, hidden and cut off from the outside world. A sense of exile and loss grew inside him, but at least it was a secure kind of exile. He had unlimited time to examine his life, study his plans, nurture his constant desire for revenge and justice. So the great dreamer sat in his little shop, treating his customers kindly, protected by their trust, content to earn an honest living, and confronting the unknown without fear.

"It's rare to find someone as honest as you," commented the sheikh one day.

"Here perhaps," he answered politely.

"I'm curious to know why you left Upper Egypt."

He answered suavely, but his heart was beating: "You wouldn't ask if you came from there!"

The sheikh laughed and Badr went on, "Anyway, my ancestors were from Bulaq."

"It's good when a man feels drawn to his roots," remarked the sheikh, going off with a package crammed full of his purchases.

23.

There was a girl on the other side of the alleyway. She was always there. Her name was Mahasin and she sold liver from a portable stall which she could carry herself without much trouble. It consisted of a wooden board on a cylindrical stand made of palm stalks woven together with plaited leaves. Calves' liver and lambs' liver were neatly arranged on it, around a pair of scales and a meat cleaver. The girl was tall, with well-rounded limbs and hazel eyes, as attractive as she was hot-tempered and sharp-tongued.

The stranger longed for company to dispel his loneliness and soothe his anxious heart. He began watching her with interest as she worked, fascinated by her energy and ferocity. All the youths were after her, but she defended herself unhesitatingly with her sharp claws and virulent tongue. This was better than submission, but why had nobody asked to marry her?

He developed an appetite for liver, conscious that he was taking a path strewn with invisible obstacles, driven by a force within himself as much as by what was on the other side of the lane. Mahasin weighed him a pound of liver, wrapped it up, and handed it to him, saying simply, "Here you are, Mr. Beard!"

He was pleased by her teasing and took it as a friendly greeting. With her slim figure, well-shaped limbs, and dark coloring she reminded him of his poor lost Mahalabiyya; he remembered the pitiful way he had failed to save her and all the miseries of that sad slice of his past. But he still enjoyed being alive. Perhaps he had long experience of making the best of it. Whenever death cast its shadow over him, he clung more fiercely on to life.

Meanwhile Mahasin came to him for lentils, beans, and fenugreek. Here you are, Mr. Beard. Give me some of that, Mr. Beard. Here you are, Mahasin, you jewel. He never exceeded the bounds of decorum with her. Perhaps she knew how to read his eyes. Perhaps she was drawn to his good manners, which set him apart from other men.

On both sides of the alley, and in an atmosphere that was above suspicion, a profound affection grew.

24.

One evening after the prayer he tried to find out more about her background from the local imam. "Does she live alone, master?"

"No. With her mother who's old and blind now."

"Is that her only relation?"

"Her father was killed in a brawl. She's got a brother in prison."

"I'd say she's in her twenties. Why isn't she married?"

"Her mother had a bad reputation," said the imam apologetically.

"But is the girl . . . ?"

"Irreproachable," interrupted the imam with conviction.

What recommended her to him was the fact that other men had nothing to do with her: a stranger and a fugitive like him would have been ill-equipped to compete with rival suitors. Marriage would give him links with the place and earn him people's confidence. She was better than a girl with a family who would want to know everything about him. Most importantly, why not admit that he desired her with all the wild energy of his youth?

25.

He seized the opportunity of her presence in his shop, encouraged by her cheerful and coquettish mood that day, to ask her, "What would you think, Mahasin, if a man asked you to marry him?"

She looked at him with interest. Interest which she wrapped around in a radiant, mocking glance.

"Does such a madman exist?"

"Yes. A man of flesh and blood who gets by with God's help."

Their eyes met in calm contentment, then in a burst of merriment she demanded, "Does he have a beard like a sheepskin?"

"That's him."

"What shall I do with his beard?"

"It's tame. Completely harmless," he laughed.

Her face betrayed her pleasure, but she went off without uttering another word. He remembered Mahalabiyya and was filled with sadness.

26.

The engagement was announced and the wedding took place a few months later.

Although the couple had no family, neighbors and customers flocked to the celebration. Badr al-Saidi spared no expense and the wedding procession went off around the neighborhood without incident under the protection of the local clan chief.

A flat was made ready for them, containing a bedroom and a

single living room, and Mahasin and her mother made a respectable contribution toward furnishing it.

Samaha was happy with his choice although his pleasure was marred a little by the presence of his mother-in-law, who occupied the main room day and night. She was old and blind, but her withered features still had traces of beauty. She had a vicious tongue and spat out her words like bullets, with no idea of trying to be polite, even during their honeymoon period. However, their love in its first flowering swept aside all obstacles.

27.

Mahasin became a full-time housewife. She loved her husband, and discovered that he was better off than he chose to appear. When he was at home he also looked much more handsome than outdoors.

"If you shaved off your beard, you'd be the best-looking man ever," she declared one day.

"It's the secret of my success," he replied evasively.

"Use it instead of a broom, girl!" interrupted his mother-in-law with a bawdy laugh.

He couldn't find it in him to like her or overlook her past. "I'll agree if we can use it to sweep you out of the house!" he retorted sharply.

She seethed with anger. "You want to keep your eye on him," she shouted. "He's a bad lot."

He looked at her with hatred, silently numbering her among the misfortunes which hounded him.

28.

Even Mahasin did not escape the old woman's poisoned arrows. She had a spiteful nature, always believed the worst, and would frequently accuse her daughter of maltreating her: "You two get all the delicacies. I just get the leftovers."

"You eat exactly the same food as us," said Mahasin.

"Liar! You can't hide the smell from me. You're as crooked as your husband!"

"What's this got to do with me?" asked Samaha angrily.

"You're the source of all the trouble."

"Give me patience! This can't go on much longer!"

"Don't count on it! You'll go before me," shrieked the old woman.

"We'll be in different places anyway."

She cackled noisily. "I bet you murdered your father in Upper Egypt and came here to escape the rope."

He trembled with pent-up dislike and anger, longing to brain her.

29.

All the same, he was genuinely happy with Mahasin and found refuge from his old worries in her arms. She returned his feelings and seemed content with him. Of course he realized from the beginning that she was not going to be a good, obedient wife. She was bold, impetuous, sure of herself, and her humor was sometimes cruel. She took excessive care of herself, spent hours in the bath, perfumed herself with essence of carnation, but dressed in a way that was almost vulgar. He thought this was one of her charms but couldn't bear any stranger to look at her. This was the reason for their first serious quarrel.

"Don't lean out of the window looking like that," he said one day.

"I've worked on the street all my life," she answered irritably.

"And you had no shame."

"And you saw how I didn't let anyone insult me!"

"Didn't I tell you he had an evil mind?" interrupted the old woman.

"Shut up," he snapped.

"God protect you from a father-killer," she wailed.

He turned away from her, shaking with anger, and said to Mahasin, "She's encouraging you to be immoral."

"There's no chance of that," she said, her annoyance growing.

"In this matter, I demand complete obedience from you."

"I'm not a child, or a servant."

He lost his self-restraint. "I'll throw you out of the window," he yelled.

"I'll stuff your head down the toilet."

"Well said!" shouted her mother.

"Don't you dare ignore my orders."

The quarrel stopped there and was forgotten by the next day. That evening she told him she was going to be a mother.

30.

His mother-in-law died a strange death: she fell from the window overlooking the interior courtyard and her skull shattered. Perhaps it was just as well for Badr that he was at work at the time. All the arrangements went without a hitch and the dead woman was committed to the ground. Badr gave her a good funeral out of respect for Mahasin and as befitted his standing in the community. He felt constrained all the same, because of the deep-seated hostility that had existed between him and the dead woman.

Mahasin wept bitterly.

"Don't cry. You're pregnant," he said.

"Don't you care about her?" she asked reproachfully.

He said nothing.

"Don't bother to hide your joy," she stormed.

"I respect the dead," he protested.

Mahasin said it shouldn't be forgotten that her mother had had many virtues. She loved her daughter, despite her nagging which was just superficial, and worshiped her husband. When he died in the prime of his youth, and then when her son was sentenced to life imprisonment, she was completely shattered. She became addicted to opium, her behavior changed, and she was accused of everything under the sun. To add to her troubles, she went blind, then because she had nowhere else to go ended up in the house of a man who made it plain that she wasn't welcome! In her youth she was the most beautiful girl in Bulaq. She could have married a rich butcher but had chosen Mahasin's father instead. There was nothing commonplace about her.

As Samaha listened to this requiem, he thought of his grandmother, Saniyya, running off with a water carrier young enough to be her son, and wondered sadly where she was living, how the years had treated her and his father, Bikr. What shame and sorrow lay buried in the past!

31.

The summer came with its stifling heat. He loved its light, and was not troubled by the burning rays of the sun. He savored the balmy evenings, adored the dinners of mulukhiyya, okra, melon, and watermelon and took pleasure in bathing every morning at sunrise.

Mahasin gave birth to a boy. He was filled with joy and pride. He would have liked to call him Shams al-Din but was afraid the name might endanger his own safety, so agreed to call him Rummana after Mahasin's father. His business thrived, he grew prosperous, the gold bangles multiplied on Mahasin's arms and life looked good. Each day he recorded the slow passage of time in his secret journal; on these occasions he would always remember the hangman's rope and wonder if he was destined to escape it indefinitely; he would think about his family and the people of his alley and wonder how the passing years had treated them, and recall his enemies: al-Fulali, Dagla, Antar, Hamouda the pimp. Would he beat them one day and restore the covenant of the Nagis to his alley? Would he be able to listen to the anthems again?

32.

After Rummana, Mahasin gave birth to two more sons, Qurra and Wahid. Badr had become an important member of the community, respected by all honest men and enjoying special status in the eyes of the poor.

Mahasin never stopped caring for her appearance, and spent hours bathing as usual. Motherhood did not distract her from her femininity or her love of physical pleasure. She developed a passion

for hashish and it became a regular habit. The first time she tried it
for fun with her husband, who smoked every evening, then she
willingly abandoned herself to its soft, greedy caresses.

The days and years went by and Badr began to believe his
future was secure, and his fears evaporated—or almost.

33.

Strange news reached Bulaq: the clan chief had struck up a friendship with a man called al-Fulali. Badr was dumbfounded; suddenly
a yawning pit opened in front of him and his world was shaken to
its foundations. He asked the local sheikh for more details. "It's
good news," the man said. "It means they'll combine their re-
sources."

Badr pretended to be pleased and the sheikh went on,
"There'll be a few celebrations and good nights out."

"Let's hope so."

"Believe me! They'll exchange visits and that means singing,
dancing, and drinking for us!"

"It should be good," murmured Badr, dry-mouthed.

A serpent had slunk into his tranquil home. Such a possibility
had never occurred to him. He had always thought of the Nile as
an impassable barrier. But al-Fulali and his gang would cross it,
make merry in the quarter. He would be invited to the celebrations. He had escaped the rope by little more than seven years.
There was no hiding the reality from searching eyes. He had to
decide what to do.

A few days before this ritual visit he pretended to be ill. Even
Mahasin believed him and stood in for him in the shop.

34.

On the night of al-Fulali's visit, he crouched at the window, peering through a crack in the shutters.

The world had a different look. Everything gave off strange
signals. The festive lamps shone in the dark, mocking him like the

faces of enchanted creatures. The remains of his peace and tranquillity lay heaped up in the garbage cans. The alley heaved with dancing figures. The smell of fish frying filled the air. It was winter. Why hadn't the rain come? Or the thunder and lightning and rough winds? The sound of flutes and drums rose in the air. Men cheered, women trilled in celebration. The allies' cavalcade was approaching, led by prancing horses with silver crescents jingling merrily on their harnesses. Here was the most hateful creature on God's earth. Al-Fulali. Ugly, mean, overbearing. Linking arms with our chief, flashing his gold teeth as he smiled this way and that. After him came Dagla, Antar, Farid. Where was Hamouda? In prison or dead, most likely. All the rascals gathered together here. Why hadn't fate intervened? It was no use being bitter. They were moving away but the racket was spreading. It was a riotous night, debauched, concealing unspecified agonies, threatening every evil imaginable, blessed by the angel of death. The gallows rope encircled it, strangling his dreams. Those most dear to him Mahasin, Rummana, Qurra, Wahid—became phantoms. They threatened to disappear at any moment. Then pitch-darkness would descend. Lethal despair. Total emptiness.

35.

He went back to work and received the well-wishers come to congratulate him on his recovery. Cowering indoors was unwholesome, stirred up fears, made sorrows grow out of all proportion. Activity brought comfort. Dealing with people face-to-face set his blood moving again and prompted feelings of courage. His enemies had disappeared and death no longer hovered. The wine of life was on his tongue. He cast his fate to the winds and his spirit was refreshed. It seemed possible to hope again, and feel inspired. Take heart, Badr, don't be afraid. Hide behind your beard and have faith in the Lord's justice.

He felt more passionately bound to his wife and children, and to food, drink, worship, life itself. He even loved the clouds of winter. He delighted in everything around him, including the

sounds of people swearing at each other. He was only sorry he
could not tell his children stories of Ashur and Shams al-Din, that
they would grow up ignorant of their blessed roots, of the dream,
of Saint Khidr's friendship. Would Rummana ever know that he
was a Nagi? "Make the most of every new day and don't have any
regrets," he told himself.

36.

He was writing an entry in his private diary when something made
him look up. Muhammad Tawakkul, sheikh of his native alley, was
passing inches away from the door of his shop. He gave it a brief
glance as he went by. Samaha's heart jumped with shock, and
terror cut through him like an ax. Had the man seen him? Did he
remember him?

He noticed him from a distance sitting in the local sheikh's
shop. The two men were talking and laughing, Muhammad letting
his eye roam at will over the passersby. This was certain death. The
man would be only too happy to collaborate with the authorities, to
gladden al-Fulali's heart with the news of his arrest. Even if the
sheikh had been blind, Samaha would not have felt safe from that
day on. Bulaq had become legal territory for his enemies.

News went around that Muhammad Tawakkul wanted to
marry the daughter of the scrap metal dealer. He had probably
accompanied al-Fulali the first time and seen her and he fancied
her as a second wife. Now he would be as much at home in Bulaq
as in al-Husayn. Bulaq was no longer a safe hiding place.

37.

Mahasin gave him a searching glance. "What's on your mind?"

The children were all asleep and she was hovering around
him, beautifully dressed and made-up as usual, sensing a problem.

"Several things," he said.

"Business?" she asked apprehensively.

"Business is fine, but I have to go away for a while."

"To Upper Egypt?"
"Maybe."
"But what for?"
Ignoring her question, he said, "I'll be away for a few years."
"A few years! Take us with you."
"I'd love to, but it's impossible."
She frowned suspiciously.
"It's not a business trip. I'm running away," he said.
"Running away?"
"I'll tell you a story of flight and injustice, Mahasin!"

38.

He said goodbye to his wife and children and slipped out of the house shortly before dawn. By early morning Mahasin was standing in the shop and had embarked on a new life. She was depressed and ill at ease with her secret, uncertain whether to believe her husband's tale. He had deceived her for years. Perhaps he had his reasons, but still he had deceived her. So was he finally telling the truth, or just more lies?

The sheikh dropped in and asked after her husband, curious to know what was keeping him at home.

"He's gone to Upper Egypt," she said miserably.

"I spoke to him yesterday and he didn't mention it," said the man in surprise.

"Well, he's gone," she said listlessly.

"He's very ambitious. But you're not yourself, Mahasin."

"I'm fine, sir."

"When's he coming back?"

She maintained a gloomy silence.

"Is it another woman?" he inquired cautiously.

"Certainly not."

"How long is he away for?"

"Several years."

"Good grief!"

"That's the way it goes."

"But you're hiding something."

"Not at all."

"You never know where you are with Upper Egyptians," he said on his way out.

39.

The sheikh told the news to everyone he met, including Muhammad Tawakkul who was staying with him at the time. To his surprise, his guest showed some interest.

"Is he the Upper Egyptian with a beard?" he asked.

"That's the one," answered the Bulaq sheikh.

Muhammad Tawakkul closed his eyes in thought.

40.

An hour later the alley was shaken by a military raid. A detachment of men stormed Badr al-Saidi's house, while a detective named Hilmi Abd al-Basit conducted an inquiry in his shop. People swarmed around like ants.

"Where is Samaha Sulayman al-Nagi?" Hilmi Abd al-Basit asked Mahasin roughly.

"I don't know anyone of that name," she answered confidently.

"Really! What about Badr al-Saidi?"

"I don't know."

"Liar."

"Don't be insulting. What do you want with an honorable man?"

"Honorable! You know very well he's on the run to escape the gallows."

"God forbid! Everyone around here knows him."

"You're coming with me to the police station," he shouted.

"I've got three children. There's nobody to look after them. What do you want with me?" she wailed.

41.

They searched the house and the shop. Mahasin was interrogated thoroughly, then released. The news spread through the alley like wildfire. People were astonished.

"Badr al-Saidi!"

"The one with a beard . . ."

"The one who was always doing good works!"

"He's a killer, fleeing the gallows!"

"Only his mother-in-law found out, even though she was as bad as him!"

42.

Habit gradually stripped the strange events of their novelty. Mahasin put her children into Quran school, and after school she brought them to the shop where she could watch them while they played. She grieved over her husband and her own bad luck, and despite spells of resentment she never forgot that he had left her reasonably well off, even rich, with a thriving business.

Since the day of the raid the detective, Hilmi Abd al-Basit, often hung around the alley or sat in the sheikh's shop. She wondered if he was still watching her. She felt his eyes on her and his behavior made her uneasy but she pretended to ignore him. He was a rough, boorish man, tall, with a big head, small eyes, a coarse nose, and a mustache like a vegetable chopper. It was an appearance that boded ill, and brought back bad memories. He was watching her, she was sure of it, so what was on his mind? He would pass by the shop and give it a strange look that made her wonder, or sit talking to the sheikh and stare mercilessly at her. What did he want? Her reason and her instinct both demanded to know, and she was ready for a fight.

One day he paused in front of her shop. He stepped up to her, breaking in on her thoughts, and asked, smiling, "Do you really believe your husband is innocent?"

"Yes," she answered, without raising her eyes to look at him.

"The killer insisted he was innocent until the rope was around his neck," he intoned as he went on his way.

43.

One morning she saw Muhammad Tawakkul, the sheikh of the al-Husayn quarter, and invited him into her shop. She received him courteously, then confessed, "Perhaps you know what's bothering me?"

"May God come to your aid," he murmured pleasantly.

"But you're the only one who knows the truth."

"The truth?"

"About the accusation."

Tawakkul said smoothly, "All I know is what was revealed by the inquiry."

"But he swore to me that he was innocent."

"It was established in court that he killed the girl and fled."

Mahasin sighed despairingly, then said, "Tell me about my husband's family."

Muhammad Tawakkul smiled. "They're descended from a line of clan chiefs of the old days. People tell tales of the miracles they're supposed to have performed. But I don't trust our people's imagination. They believe good began and ended in an obscure past and they don't distinguish between dreams and reality. They think with their emotions and their judgments are clouded because of the wretched conditions they live in. They think an angel came down from the skies every now and then to protect their ancestors."

"Is al-Fulali one of them?"

"No. Their reign's over. None of them would even think about it. These days most of them are paupers or small tradesmen, but your husband belongs to the only wealthy branch of the family that remains. His uncle Khidr is a big merchant. So is his brother, Radwan. Do you want to hand the children over to them?"

"Certainly not," she interrupted quickly. "I'll never give them up. I don't need anyone's help. I only asked you because I thought I should know."

"They might come to claim them one day."

"I'll do everything in my power to keep them," exclaimed Mahasin passionately.

"May God come to your aid," he said as he rose to leave.

44.

As the days passed, Hilmi Abd al-Basit became a regular customer at the shop. Was it all part of his strategy for observing her? But she had deceived herself for long enough: these hungry looks were not those of a spy, and she had done nothing to merit being kept under observation. He hovered around her with infatuated glances and an ingratiating smile, his embarrassed manner betraying his hidden intentions. She knew what was going on instinctively but pretended not to notice, feeling an aversion but avoiding a decision, and her anxiety about the future increased day by day.

One day he remarked out of the blue, "God forgive him."

She looked at him curiously, although she knew who he meant.

"He left you alone with three children," he said.

She said nothing.

"And even if he escapes, you've still got to wait eight years."

She frowned.

"And he's not going to escape!" he declared with conviction.

"God is on the side of the oppressed," she said sadly.

"I've never heard of a killer escaping the hangman's rope. They always get caught in the end."

45.

The days passed in weary monotony. The unending effort, the worry, the absence of the person who had filled her life tired her out. She had difficulty stocking the shop and the takings fell, although they were still more than adequate. She began to hold Samaha responsible for what had happened to her, especially when the worry and loneliness became too much to bear. Rummana, Qurra, and Wahid often ran wild in the street with no one to take care of them, until the sheikh of the mosque cautioned her. "Your children are exposed to bad influences, Mahasin."

"What can I do?" she said regretfully. "They're not yet of an age to work in the shop."

"Wouldn't it be better if they learned a trade, even just to keep them off the street?"

She glowered. "I won't leave them at the mercy of people I don't trust."

This conversation served only to make her increasingly annoyed and anxious.

46.

Hilmi Abd al-Basit continued to hover about her. Once he said tenderly to her, "I pity you, Mahasin."

"I'm strong and successful," she answered defiantly.

"But you're not free."

"What do you mean?"

"You're still attached to the hangman's rope."

"I'm quite content," she said, frowning.

"But you should free yourself for your own good and the good of the children."

"What are you trying to say?"

"In a situation like yours a woman can ask for a divorce."

She laughed scathingly, but he went on undeterred. "Some decent man would come along and ask you to marry him. You're really a pearl, you know."

He departed, to avoid hearing an unsatisfactory answer.

47.

A few minutes after he had gone she heard a cry that shook her to the core. She rushed out of the shop in a frenzy and saw Wahid rolling in the dust, his face covered in blood. Two boys were running off in fright. She had to let them go and, wailing, took her son in her arms. She examined his face. "The child's lost an eye!" she screamed.

48.

Troubled clouds massed in the sky. Misery rained down. Sorrow descended on the world. Temptation glowed like a rainbow.

49.

A carriage drew up outside the shop. Mahasin rose from her seat, full of curiosity. A middle-aged man descended from it, followed by a younger man, both of them trailing fine camel-hair cloaks. They came toward her and the older one asked, "Mahasin?"

She nodded.

"I'm Khidr Sulayman al-Nagi, your husband Samaha's uncle, and this is his brother Radwan."

Her heart pounded. She offered them a couple of seats, and murmured a greeting.

"We ought to have got to know one another before, but the news only reached us yesterday!" said Khidr.

"I quite understand."

She was going to say that she had heard a lot about them, but thought better of it.

"We're pleased to meet you. Your children are ours too and we'd like to help you in any way we can."

"I'm grateful to you, Master Khidr."

"We trust in God. The oppressed man will triumph over the wrong done to him," said Radwan.

"Samaha's told me everything. But can't you prove his innocence?"

"We'd be risking our lives for a lost cause," said Khidr sorrowfully.

"Where are the children?" asked Radwan.

"At school." Then the color drained from her cheeks. "The youngest one lost his eye in a fight with some other boys."

Khidr and Radwan looked visibly upset.

"You've had a lot to put up with, Mahasin," remarked Khidr.

"I'm quite strong. But it's bad luck," she responded guardedly.

Khidr could read her thoughts, but still he inquired, "How do you see the future?"

"I suppose they'll work in the shop."

Khidr let his eyes stray around him.

"It brings in more than enough for us to live on, thank goodness," she added quickly.

"Perhaps they'd have a better chance if they came to us," he said gently.

"I don't want to give them up."

"We won't force you, but wouldn't it be wrong to deprive them of the opportunity of a better life?"

She began chewing at her fingernails, unaware of what she was doing. "We won't force you to do anything you don't want to do," repeated Khidr.

"Think of this as just a friendly visit to make your acquaintance," said Radwan.

"To let you know you're not alone," said Khidr. "We're your family too. Take your time, and think over my suggestion. Come with them if you'd like to. Visit them whenever you want. Or keep them here with you. It's entirely up to you."

50.

As soon as the carriage bells had faded in the distance, Hilmi Abd al-Basit appeared in the shop. "What did those gentlemen want?" he asked with interest.

These days it was not unusual for her to talk openly to him. She had long since stopped trying to put him off or stand up to him. He was a regular part of her life. Even his ugliness was no longer repellent or disturbing, and so she confided in him without hesitation.

"It sounds like the right thing to do," he declared when she paused for breath.

"Desert my children?"

"No. Send them to take advantage of their good fortune."

"What do you know about a mother's feelings?"

"Real motherhood means making sacrifices!"

"Perhaps what I really ought to do is go there with them," she said slyly.

"God forbid!"

"They're my family too."

"But you'd be a stranger there! You're from Bulaq and they're from al-Husayn. This is where you're respected and have some status." He looked into her face with his small, greedy eyes and murmured, "And this is where there's somebody who loves you more than life itself!"

51.

Nothing is permanent except change. The eternal circle of suffering and joy. When the leaves turn green again, and the flowers bloom and the fruit ripens, the sting of winter's cold is effaced from the memory.

52.

Events follow their course, and convention and religion cannot ignore them. Inflexible resolve yields to compassion, like a coconut releasing its sweet milk. Rummana, Qurra, and Wahid moved from Bulaq to Khidr al-Nagi's house. The boys had no idea what it was all about. They were on the verge of tears as they said goodbye, and Mahasin wept bitterly. To justify her decision, she claimed that the Nagi family had threatened to take her to court. She made excuses to herself for this behavior, but she was genuinely and profoundly sad. Her heart beat with conflicting emotions, like an apricot with its sweet flesh and bitter kernel. Achieving happiness for her sons at the cost of giving them up. Being faithful to Samaha and yet constantly aware that he had deceived her, then left her on her own. Choosing whether to endure frustration or yield to life's exuberant flow; whether to give in to temptation or legalize greedy instincts by getting married again. She convinced herself that she was a weak woman and as such should take steps to avoid improper behavior. The imam of the mosque, the local sheikh, and most of her neighbors backed her up.

"You'll gain nothing from being faithful to a killer."

"Or from being young and beautiful without a husband."

Could she forget how a bad reputation had clung to her mother all her days? Moreover, marriage to a detective would be seen as highly desirable by most people.

So Mahasin handed her sons over to Samaha's family, and got a divorce from Samaha, the fugitive killer.

53.

Her marriage to the detective, Hilmi Abd al-Basit, took place in an atmosphere of warmth and gaiety. She bought new clothes and furniture but stayed in the same flat, and went on working in the shop to preserve her independence and honor, given that she was the man's third wife. She had some trouble adjusting to life with Abd al-Basit after Samaha, but the new generally obscures the old and dilutes past memories, especially if, as in this case, it has its own considerable merits. So she grew fond of him as time passed and bore his children. She paid regular visits to her three sons at Khidr's house and was received with cordial respect by the family, and with great affection by her children. They quickly grew acclimatized to their new environment, and seemed to have changed, but they did not forget their mother, or their old games and companions, or even their father who had been absent for so long. But as time went by and she had more children with Abd al-Basit, the gaps between visits grew longer. In the end they had become so rare that one day her children came to visit her at Bulaq in the carriage, but the cold reception they were given by Abd al-Basit ensured that they never did it again. Relations between mother and sons flagged until they were almost nonexistent. Even the strongest passions are assaulted, either gently or fiercely, by the passage of time.

54.

Abd al-Basit only spent his money during their honeymoon. After that he announced to her bluntly, "You're rich and I'm poor. Married couples are supposed to help one another."

She protested at this attitude, which seemed like a devaluing of her love, but she achieved nothing. Both of them could be violent and stubborn, and she was not about to sacrifice the benefits of her new married life after having suffered so much to obtain them.

Abd al-Basit was unmoved and borrowed from her whenever he needed money. His debts piled up and there was not the faintest hope of him repaying them. Because of this they often quarreled, exchanging words and blows and becoming extremely violent toward one another. But life went on and caresses and sighs of desire succeeded the cursing and beating with monotonous regularity. She gave birth to one child after another until she ended up with six. The one thing unaffected by change was the constant care she gave to preserving her beauty and femininity.

55.

The days passed, life burgeoned, and the fates gathered on the horizon.

56.

Samaha Bikr al-Nagi endured his life listening to the creaking of time's wheel behind him all the time. If waiting for an hour is hard, what must it be like when life consists of nothing else? From the beginning Samaha decided not to stay in one place. He worked as a peddler, moving from village to village, let his beard and mustache grow and wore a patch over his left eye. He continued to record the passing days in his secret diary, and also noted the ages of his three sons. In his spare time he focused all his thoughts on Mahasin and the children, and as he fell asleep after a hard day's work he would console himself with dreams of the day he would be free from the threat of the gallows and return to his family; the day he would go back to his alley brandishing his stick to put the world to rights, resurrecting the famous justice of the Nagi covenant from out of the present iniquities. Sometimes when his heart pounded with longing, he had an irresistible urge to disguise himself as a woman and visit his family, but he suppressed it at the thought of the disastrous consequences which could result and invalidate his years of patient waiting.

He lived alone, or rather in the company of specters that never left him. Specters of injustice, tenderness, deprivation, and of the continual fear of discovery. He grew used to conducting dialogues with himself and with these specters either in silence or loud enough for the trees and the river to hear. Once he went crazy because he thought he saw Mahasin. Another time he dreamed he met Muhammad Tawakkul in the market. His best dreams were those where he saw Saint Khidr, but to his surprise all that stayed with him afterward was a heavy heart, a sadness, and some vague hope. "It's always a good sign when he appears," he told himself. "There's no such thing as meaningless suffering. One day the light will break."

Although he'd lost everything, his strength and courage hadn't weakened. Perhaps his perseverance had made them more pronounced, and they had helped him endure. But what had become of Mahasin and his sons? He would go back one day and find they were grown men working in the shop. They would look at him in surprise at first, but they couldn't have forgotten him altogether.

With each year that passed he heaved a sigh and said, "Now the rope's a little slacker!"

57.

The last year was the worst of all. With every passing day the torment grew. He tried desperately to be patient, praying that he would hold out until the last minute, relentlessly fighting the pain. He occupied his mind with everyday concerns, but all the while he

was taken up with the passage of time and each moment seemed
like an eternity, frozen solid, and motionless.

58.

Only one day remained. The next morning it would all be over.
Work would take his mind off it. But he was incapable of working.
All he could do was follow time like a lover, his will dissolving and
evaporating. Out loud, as if the sound of his voice would give him
the strength to defy existence, he declared, "I'll sleep the night here,
and go home in the morning."

But his nerves rebelled against this scheme of his, and made a
mockery of his defiance, sending their orders to his limbs, which
ceased to work. No food or drink passed his lips. No dreams came
to keep him company. He watched the bruised disk of the sun sink
in the sky. The last drop of patience ran out.

He would spend the night in the bosom of his family. He
launched himself toward his hopes.

59.

Mahasin heard a faint knocking at the door.

The children were asleep on cushions in the living room and
she had done her face and was ready for bed.

Who could be at the door? It was almost midnight. She
opened it just enough to see a figure standing there. "Who is it?"
she cried.

He pushed the door wide open and pounced on her—or so it
seemed to her. Before she could scream he put a hand over her
mouth. They fused into a single being in the light of the lamp
burning in the window. With his hand still clasped over her
mouth, he raised his head and said, "It's Samaha, Mahasin. Samaha's come back."

Then he took his hand away and she stared in amazement at
his hairy face.

"You're safe now. Samaha's come back. The suffering's over!"

She went on staring at him in astonishment.

"It's over. The fifteen years. There are only a few hours left, but I couldn't wait any longer."

At this point, Hilmi appeared in the bedroom doorway, armed with a big metal washbowl. "You've had it. Give yourself up."

The sight of him was like a heavy blow landing on Samaha's skull. "Who's this?" he mumbled. "A man in your room! What does this mean, Mahasin?"

Mahasin took refuge at her husband's side, swallowed, and said, "It's my husband." Then, indicating the children, whom Samaha noticed for the first time, she added, "Their father."

Samaha raised his left arm, then let it sink down on his head in a gesture of confusion. The ground swayed beneath his feet. "Really? Your husband? I hadn't imagined anything like this!"

Hilmi brandished the washbowl, saying, "Give yourself up. I'm a police detective."

"Really?" Samaha was seized with a sudden fit of laughter.

"If you resist I'll smash your head in," roared Hilmi.

"Let him go," whispered Mahasin.

"Go to the window and shout for help," he ordered her.

In a flash, Samaha swooped on one of the children. He hauled him to his feet with one hand and grabbed him around the neck with the other. The child began to scream. "If anybody moves or makes a sound, I'll throttle the child."

"Put my son down, you criminal!" shrieked Mahasin.

"Nobody moves or screams for help. You don't attack a wounded snake."

"Put the boy down."

"He'll be fine as long as nothing happens to me."

"Rummana, Qurra, and Wahid are being looked after by your uncle," ventured Mahasin.

He nodded. "That's good, but don't let anyone think he has a duty to hand me over to the executioner."

"Let him go," Mahasin begged her husband.

"He can go to hell," said Hilmi, the fight gone out of him.

"First throw down the washbowl."

Hilmi threw it down. Mahasin rushed to snatch the child

away from Samaha. Quickly Hilmi picked up the bowl again and threw it at Samaha. His aim was poor and it barely grazed the top of Samaha's head. Samaha seized it and flew at Hilmi and brought it down squarely on the back of his neck. Hilmi sank to the floor, unconscious.

Samaha was out of the door in a single bound, pursued by Mahasin's screams. When he reached the street a few people, still out and about at that hour, were hurrying in the direction of the screams for help. He made with all speed for the road leading down to the Nile. The hunt was on all over again. He leapt into a boat and began rowing away from the shore. When he was halfway across, he heard a familiar voice.

"Give yourself up, Samaha. You've killed the detective," shouted the Bulaq sheikh.

60.

"Samaha. At last!" cried Khidr al-Nagi, gazing at his nephew.

They embraced warmly, then Khidr exclaimed, "I've dreamed of this day for so long. Thank God you're safe. Let me wake Radwan."

But Samaha grasped his hand and murmured, "Where are the children?"

"Wait till the morning. You should shave your beard before you see them."

Again Samaha whispered, "The children. I want to see them."

61.

He approached them, staring at their faces as they roamed in the mysterious valleys of sleep; mouths slack, half-open, masks freed from the grip of time, youthful features betraying adolescent ardor, ripe seeds containing the germs of a future rich in contradictions.

Affection shone from his tear-filled eyes, a rush of longing welled up in him, and his limbs trembled, making him gasp out loud. He pushed his mustache and beard away from his lips.

Khidr whispered in his ear, "You'll scare them."

But Samaha kissed their cheeks lightly and gracefully, watching out for any tiny flickers of movement, then he stood back gently, cautiously, sadly.

62.

"You must get some sleep," Khidr said to him.

"There's no time," he answered, shaking his head.

"But you're very tired, Samaha."

"I've got a lifetime of weariness ahead of me."

Khidr told him al-Fulali had died two years before, and al-Faskhani had taken his place; Dagla and Hamouda were dead too, and Antar and Farid in prison. Samaha listened without interest, then rested his hand on his uncle's shoulder and said, "I'm still on the run."

"Isn't the time up?" asked Khidr, suddenly agitated.

"I was forced to kill some foolish devil an hour ago."

63.

As he went on the run for the second time, Samaha paused in the square in front of the monastery. The perfumed breath of the alley filled his nostrils, but where was the feeling of intoxication? He had so often dreamed of standing here as a prelude to a new beginning: taming the villains and restoring justice. Instead it was the start of a new journey into suffering and exile. If he came back at all it would be as a weak old man.

He went toward the path. The voices were chanting in the darkness:

> *Darde mara nist darman al-ghiyath*
> *Hejre mara nist payan al-ghiyath.*

The Apple of My Eye

The fifth tale in the epic
of the harafish

1.

*T*he emotions of the Nagi family and the harafish were set in turmoil by the unexpected return and sudden disappearance of Samaha. His sons were probably the least affected of anybody because he came and went while they were asleep and anyway, as far as they were concerned, he was no longer much more than a faint memory, like their mother in Bulaq. His story was told far and wide, and became a legend and a cautionary tale.

2.

Rummana, Qurra, and Wahid worked in the grain merchant's with their uncle Radwan and their great-uncle Khidr. A strange piece of news went around the neighborhood: Hilmi was not dead as everybody had supposed. He recovered from the blow and resumed his life as a detective, sponging off Mahasin. The folly of Samaha's flight was exposed and people grieved for him more than ever; Khidr set out to find him. He enlisted the services of the officer in charge of the Gamaliyya police station and tried to negotiate with al-Faskhani, the clan chief, increasing the protection money he paid him and promising a large reward to anyone who found his nephew.

His activities aroused al-Faskhani's suspicions, and when some of his older followers reminded him of Samaha's ambitions he grew increasingly anxious, along with many of the alley's notables.

Early one morning Khidr was found beaten up in the lane outside the kebab seller's where he had sat up late the night before. Nothing could be done for him and he died two days later. Although most people agreed that the killers should be tracked down, inquiries were met with a wall of silence, as usual in such cases, and Khidr vanished from sight like a grain of sand.

3.

The Nagi family was shaken by the killing of its chief and considered such an ignominious end typical of the lamentable state of their fortunes. However, they submitted to their fate, acknowledging their impotence, all except for Wahid—Samaha's youngest son —who flew into a fury which threatened disastrous consequences.

"Our uncle's killer's having a good laugh at this very moment," he exclaimed bitterly, "and his name's al-Faskhani! Did Ashur al-Nagi imagine that his descendants would end up like this?"

Khidr's widow, Diya, was as upset as Wahid, but in her own way. The crime pushed her into the embrace of the unknown. She shunned the world of human beings, learned the languages of the stones and the birds, and took shelter from the knives of suffering in a cave full of spirits. She became a sorceress, interpreted dreams, read tea leaves and coffee grounds, made mysterious prophesies. She liked to wear a white dress and green veil and, swinging a brass censer, would saunter the length of the alley in silence as night fell, with wisps of perfumed smoke rising from her. A servant girl followed a short distance behind, and curious eyes stared.

Some of the clan mocked her. "That's safer than wanting to be clan chief," they sneered.

Her behavior pained the young men of the family in particular, but they could do nothing to control her. Wahid in his anger even said to her, "Stay indoors, and show some respect for your husband's memory."

She looked at him stupidly. "I saw you in a dream, riding a green locust."

Wahid despaired of having a reasonable conversation with her.

"Do you know what that means?" she persisted.

He paid no attention and she answered herself, "That you were made for the open air!"

4.

Such was the strength of his anger that Wahid broke through the barriers of prudence. He was so bored with the grain merchant's, felt so far away from Rummana and Qurra. The old woman said he was made for the open air. Did this mean he was fit to mount a challenge?

He was of medium build, handsome in spite of being blind in one eye, and strong, but next to al-Faskhani he was like a kitten beside a sheep. He was not normally headstrong, but felt disturbed now by a sense of vague uneasiness and disquiet. His uncle Radwan warned him constantly to beware of his fantasies and get on with his work, while his aunt Safiyya said, "Don't make Diya's dreams mean what you want them to mean."

He went against his family and made friends with Muhammad Tawakkul, the local sheikh, in spite of their age difference, spending many a long evening with him in al-Sanadiqi's hashish den. From time to time he took to frequenting the bar, and in the course of his visits he developed a good relationship with the owner, Sadiq Abu Taqiya. He had a young man's predilection for drinking and fighting but never missed the Friday prayer. The sheikh of the mosque, Ismail Qalyubi, asked him one day, "Can God allow the mosque and the tavern to coexist harmoniously in a single heart?"

"Murderers can live happily in their houses, while innocent men suffer in exile," countered Wahid.

5.

After a night of excess he had a long dream: he was in the monastery square, even though he had no particular love of the place. A dervish came to him and said, "The Great Sheikh wants you to know that the world was created yesterday at dawn."

Wahid felt unbelievably happy. He was carried through the alley in a howdah, watched by the crowds who lined either side. He saw his mother, Mahasin from Bulaq, waving a hand in his direction and commanding the howdah to rise.

The howdah lifted him high in the air, and the wind carried him to a stretch of open country enclosed by a red mountain.

"Where is the man?" he found himself asking.

A giant of a man descended from the mountainside and hailed Wahid: "Stand firm in the place of salvation."

"It's you, Ashur," Wahid declared with certainty.

The giant took hold of his arm and rubbed some ointment into it. "This is the magic you need," he pronounced.

6.

When Wahid woke up, he felt inspired. Strength, optimism, and victory were his to command. He had no doubt that he was capable of miracles, that he could jump off the roof and come to no harm. Allowing himself to be swept along by the hurricane, he dressed and went straight to the café where al-Faskhani held court.

"I'm offering you a challenge, you thug," he said, staring him in the eye.

The chief raised his heavy lids, as if he thought Wahid was mad, but he welcomed the chance of a clash with one of the Nagis' young lions. "You're drunk, you son of a whore," he taunted.

Wahid spat in his face. Al-Faskhani leapt to his feet. A crowd was gathering to watch. Wahid did not hesitate: he swooped on the chief and hit him with all his force across the back of the head. Al-Faskhani fell back, gasping for breath. Wahid snatched the chief's club and hit him around the knees, immobilizing him, then grappled with his followers, felling them with amazing strength and speed.

Before the day was over, Wahid was chief of the clan.

7.

The news took the alley by storm. The hearts of the harafish quickened with hope. The notables were beset by uneasy fears. The Nagi family dreamed of the throne of light. Wahid began to tell of his dream, the miracle which had given him his enchanted arm, his supreme confidence in his victory which had made him able to confront death with ease. He quickly became aware of the ardent hopes pinned on him by some, and the chilly dread he inspired in others, but he preferred to go slowly and carefully, and let things proceed in their accustomed way, although he gave generously to the most impoverished inhabitants of the neighborhood.

"When will you realize your exiled father's dream?" his uncle Radwan asked him.

"I'm taking it step by step," he said cautiously, "otherwise I'll lose control of the clan."

"That's the behavior of a politician, not a hero, nephew."

"May God be merciful to a man who knows his limits," he remarked obscurely.

Still Radwan did not lose hope, while Wahid continued to bide his time. As the days passed and he experienced the glory of being chief, the ease and comfort of wealth, the fawning of the notables, he began to abandon himself to the lure of seduction, and his selfish impulses grew stronger as heroic dreams of restoring the Nagis' golden age faded. He was soon building a house of his own, enjoying all the good things of life, becoming increasingly addicted to drink and drugs and so steeped in depravity that his perversions became public knowledge.

"It would have been better if he hadn't been one of us," commented Radwan bitterly to his wife, Unsiyya.

The harafish recalled Sulayman's decline and observed that only the faults were handed down in the Nagi family. Qurra was as distressed by Wahid's behavior as his uncle Radwan, but Rummana said, "At least we've got back some of our standing."

Rummana was like his brother Wahid in his avid desire for pleasure and the scant regard he had for the family's past glory. Wahid gave himself the title of "The Visionary," but he was known privately to the harafish as "The One-Eyed." His perversions were well known: he had never married, and he surrounded himself with young men like the Mamelukes.

This was established as the pattern of Wahid the One-Eyed's reign.

8.

Radwan grew tired at heart. Although he was not yet forty, work began to exhaust him: at the slightest effort he was bathed in a cold sweat and the world would turn black before his eyes. He was weighed down by sorrow, because of the tragedy which had befallen his brother Samaha and his nephew's dismal conduct, and so he withdrew from active life, preferring solitude and meditation. He left the running of the grain merchant's business to Rummana and Qurra.

9.

The brothers occupied the director's office together, two completely different characters sharing the same job. Qurra was handsome; his eyes radiated charm, and he had his mother Mahasin's delicate features and graceful physique which, along with his good manners and integrity, made him seem like Shams al-Din, without his strength. Rummana, on the other hand, was short and stout as a barrel, with dark skin and coarse features and a crude recklessness about him. Qurra was the better manager and businessman, and more straightforward in his dealings with the workers, who liked him for his tolerance and generosity. Rummana used to socialize with his brother Wahid in the hashish den, only too pleased to be involved in his escapades and, when he was drunk, to criticize his brother Qurra with envious sarcasm.

One day he said to Qurra, "You squander your money to buy the men's affections. What's the sense in that?"

"Affection isn't a business deal," said Qurra.

"What is it, then?"

"Try it, Rummana!"

Rummana laughed scathingly. "You're just a manipulator."

Although Qurra was a year younger than Rummana, he felt responsible for him, and even for Wahid. The two brothers were irritated by his perfectionism.

"You're lords of the alley now. Before you were the riffraff. Don't you give me credit for that?" Wahid challenged him one day.

"We only lost our reputation because of you," retorted Qurra angrily.

"Don't believe these fairy tales!" said Wahid with uncontrolled rage.

"Aren't you 'The Visionary'?" asked Qurra sarcastically.

Wahid turned on his heel and strode off in a fury.

Rummana's amorous adventures also pained Qurra. "Why don't you get married?" he implored. "Out of respect for us!"

"You're a year younger than me," said Rummana angrily. "You can't give me orders."

Radwan was upset by the differences he noticed between the brothers and said to Qurra, "It's important to me that you preserve good relations with each other."

"We've got enough trouble as it is," added his aunt Safiyya, "and you're never going to change the world."

Through it all, Diya continued to sway down the alley with her incense burner early each evening, communing with the other world, her eyes full of tears.

10.

Qurra was going home one night when an old woman accosted him in the gloom. "Good evening, Master Qurra."

He returned the greeting in surprise and she said, "There's someone waiting to see you in the monastery square."

"Who?" he asked, his curiosity mounting.

"Aziza, the daughter of Ismail Bannan."

11.

He followed the old woman through the darkness of the archway and out into the dim starlight of the square. It was summer. A pleasant, languid breeze blew and the air was filled with the sweet sound of dervishes chanting. The old woman led him over to a dim figure standing in the shadow of the ancient wall. He could not make out her features and had never heard of her before.

She said nothing and after some time he whispered encouragingly, "Can I help you in some way?"

"Thank you," came her soft, tremulous voice. Then, as if remembering her reasons for being there, she went on in a pleading tone, "Don't think badly of me."

"Of course not."

The barrier of silence descended once more. He sensed her courage had deserted her, and his suspicions took a hold of him. Involuntarily, he urged her to speak. "I'm listening."

"You're known as an honorable man," she said with mounting agitation. "I only want a brief word with you. I pray God I can put this in the right way."

"You have my full attention."

"Your brother, Rummana . . ."

She broke off as if the word choked her, and his heart gave a sickening lurch. His suspicions disappeared and darkness descended in their place.

"My brother Rummana?" he whispered, barely audible.

She seemed unable to continue the conversation and the truth emerged dimly, like an insect crawling toward him through the darkness.

Then the old woman whispered suddenly, "He promised to marry her."

"So that's it!"

"If he doesn't honor his promise immediately, we're finished."

The two shadowy figures moved away and the sound of sti-fled sobbing set like a plaster cast around his eardrums.

12.

He ate his evening meal with his uncle and aunt. Diya stayed in her own quarters, and Rummana was always out at night.

"You're not your usual self," remarked his uncle.

"I'm fine," he murmured.

"Your uncle's right," Unsiyya persisted.

How could he begin to tell them? They should be the first to know, or so he had thought on his way home from the square, but now he found himself drawing back. Something was stopping him, cautioning him against it. The girl had entrusted him with her secret and he felt obliged to keep it safe. He would have to bring the subject up with Rummana first, however unappealing the idea.

13.

The whole household was asleep except Qurra. Rummana returned an hour before dawn, his eyes reddened and heavy with drink. Qurra realized at once that he had a difficult task ahead of him, and wondered how best to set about it when he knew that at first light he had to get up and open the shop, and that the manager's office was no place for such a conversation.

"What woke you?"

Qurra led him into his room. Rummana threw himself down on the divan and went on with a wary attempt at jocularity, "The dawn prayer?"

Ignoring this sarcasm, Qurra said gently, "I've got something important to tell you, Rummana. I want you to give me your full attention."

"Really?"

"Really."

"On condition that it has nothing to do with morals," said Rummana apprehensively.

"Everything has to do with morals."

"Then I refuse to listen," said Rummana obstinately.

"Be patient. It's not what you imagine. It's something that concerns you more than it concerns me, and you can't pretend it doesn't exist."

"You're making me curious."

Resting his hand lightly on his brother's shoulder, Qurra said in a low voice, "It's about Aziza."

Rummana's head went back as if a stone had hit him. "Aziza," he muttered.

"Ismail Bannan's daughter."

"I don't understand. What are you trying to say?"

Calmly and yet firmly Qurra said, "You must marry her. Without delay."

Rummana pushed back his headcloth, freed himself from his brother's hand with an abrupt movement, and exclaimed in anger, "Where's her shame? How did she get in touch with you?"

"That doesn't matter. The main thing is to avoid a disaster."

"The only disaster is in your mind," retorted Rummana scathingly.

"I think it's all too real."

"I won't do it. I've got no desire to marry her," fumed Rummana.

"Why not? You must have liked her once upon a time! And her father's a respected member of the community."

"I don't trust girls who give in like that," said Rummana coldly.

"Never mind what you think, there are times when you have to do the decent thing."

"The decent thing! People who talk like that make me sick!"

"You must avoid disgrace," pleaded Qurra. "When that's taken care of, you can do what you like."

Rummana shook his head, seemingly at a loss, and said, "There's a complication."

"What?"

"Her sister, Raifa. She and I are in love."

"You can't kill off one and marry the other," said Qurra uneasily.

Rummana muttered vaguely and Qurra went on, "And Raifa may get to hear about this one day."

"She already has done."

"And she's prepared to agree to what you want?"

Rummana nodded.

"She must be a bad lot," observed Qurra.

"Not at all. She's like me. She despises women who give in."

"But she's her sister!"

"Real hatred only exists between siblings!"

Qurra recoiled for a moment, then shouted at his brother in fury, "You're to marry her at once!"

"I won't have you ordering me about," shouted back Rummana.

He rose to his feet aggressively. As he turned to go, he added over his shoulder, "If you pity her so much, marry her yourself!"

14.

The rain falls on the earth, and does not disappear in space. Shooting stars gleam brightly for an instant, then plunge to extinction. The trees remain in their places, and never fly through the air. The birds circle around for a time, then return to their nests among the branches. There is a power at work, enticing everything to dance to a single rhythm. Nobody knows what suffering this causes—for example, when the clouds collide and peals of thunder explode in the sky.

Qurra had thought at length about his problem. He had told himself that he would be doing nothing wrong if he went about his business, that he had already done all he could. But he found it impossible to turn his back. Aziza's cry for help rang in his ears whenever he heard the chanting from the monastery, as immovable as the ancient wall. The sound of her sobbing had set hard around his eardrums. He was responsible. So was the whole Nagi family. Even Ashur the miracle worker. He couldn't shrug his shoulders and walk away. The force drawing him to act in a certain way perplexed him: he would never be any freer than the birds, the stars, the rain. It was taking him to the heart of pain and suffering, the torture of conflicting, equally weighted demands.

"If you pity her so much, marry her yourself!"

The bastard was challenging him, putting him to the test, having his revenge. Did he deserve such a marriage? No! A thousand times no! But how could he get out of it? He too despised girls who gave in, but at the same time felt there was something sacred about suffering. Fate seemed to stand obstinately in his way. But hadn't he said to Rummana, "Avoid disgrace at all costs. Apart from that, do as you think best"?

Just so. First save face. Afterward reconsider.

15.

"I've decided to get married!" he announced to his uncle Radwan.

His uncle laughed. "Rummana's beaten you to it. Just an hour ago!"

Qurra's heart beat wildly in the hope that his brother might have had a sudden change of heart. "Who does he want to marry?"

"Raifa, Ismail Bannan's daughter."

Crestfallen, he said nothing.

"What about you?" asked Radwan.

Fixing a smile on his lips, he feigned astonishment and exclaimed, "What an extraordinary coincidence! Can you believe it, uncle, I want her sister, Aziza!"

Radwan laughed loudly. "God bless both of you. I'm delighted. Ismail's a good neighbor and an honest businessman."

16.

Taking this decision did not rid him of his apprehensions. His euphoria was mixed with anxiety and distaste, like limpid rain sinking into the mud. The fact that Rummana and Raifa knew his secret made matters worse. He was also afraid that Aziza would refuse his charitable offer and cause a calamity, but she accepted. The cruel, clean blade pierced him to the marrow. Arrangements were made with a speed which astonished everyone and provoked ribald comments.

17.

The two couples had a joint wedding ceremony and the whole alley celebrated. Qurra saw the two sisters for the first time in his life. Their similarity appalled him: they were like twins, both average build, with rosy cheeks, clear skins, very dark eyes, and unusually regular features. He searched for differences and was rewarded by discovering that Aziza, who was the older, had a dimple in her chin and fuller lips. But the real disparity was in their eyes: Aziza's had a steady, calm, reassuring expression, but Raifa's had a nervous glint in them, as if she was constantly trying to fathom people out, and they shone with malign intelligence. He quickly became convinced of his feelings of dislike for her. She did not try to hide her sense of triumph, although he was possibly the only one who noticed this; Aziza kept her eyes fixed on her white shoes with their satin ribbons and sequins. He told himself that she was unhappy like him, and that this would make it easier for them to separate at some time in the future. He led her to their private quarters, accompanied by the beat of the tambourines and the voice of the female singer hired for the occasion, and wondered all the while what he had done to himself.

18.

When they were alone together he found her consumed by embarrassment; she did not attempt to look at him or make the slightest gesture. Helpless, without honor, she was the victim of his magnanimous act. He felt a powerful rush of tenderness for her, intensified by the seductive effect of her melancholy beauty. But he hadn't forgotten that her heart was closed to him, that she was a complete stranger, and that her wedding dress was no better than prison overalls as far as she was concerned. This was a stage to be gone through, temporary by definition. At this very moment Raifa would be safe in Rummana's arms, full of triumphant desire. What should he say? She came to his rescue murmuring softly, "Thank you."

"I'm sorry about what's happened," he answered, his feelings of tenderness growing.

"I know it must be a burden for you."

"But you're carrying a greater burden," he said playfully.

"That's my fault."

What a conversation for a wedding night! Neither of them made a move. Even the veil had stayed in place. However, her downcast eyes gave him the freedom to examine her face at leisure and he was more impressed by her beauty and charm than ever. He confessed to himself that had it not been for the oddity of the situation, he would have gladly fallen on her. He said gently, "While you're under my roof you won't be forced to do anything you don't want to do."

"I know you're an honorable man," she said warmly, then paused awkwardly, before rushing on, "but I assure you, all that's left of the past is a painful memory."

What did she mean? What could she be thinking of? Didn't she understand the terms? When could he be completely open with her, and be free of the uncomfortable power of her femininity? Changing the subject, he remarked, "Your sister's no better than my brother!"

"They're made for one another," she replied scornfully.

"How do you get on with her?"

"Badly."

"What's the reason?"

"She wants to monopolize everything. Talent. Love. But I beat her to it. She imagined that my parents loved me more than her, so she began to harbor these feelings of spite and resentment toward me. She's terrible."

"So's my brother." Then, remembering, "But you . . ."

He was silent, and she said vehemently, "It's over. I've had my eyes opened."

O Lord! She's obviously living in a dream. And she's sincere, yes, really sincere. Where will it get her? His was a hard mission. He was terrified of the effect of her beauty. The weakness in him threatened to overpower him. For the first time she was raising her eyes to meet his. The candle burned down in the silver candlestick.

"I'd like to know what's going on in your mind," she said resignedly.

The summer's night was so warm! He said nothing.

She went on, "You think I'm not good enough for you."

"You seem sincere and respectable," he protested.

"Thank you for being kind. But that's not enough to base a marriage on."

He considered his options, struggled, resisted temptation. "What do you think about it?" he asked.

Encouraged by the tone of the conversation, she answered, "I'm free, absolutely free, but it all depends on you."

"Don't forget you asked to marry him," he said frankly.

"Fear made me do it. I didn't want to. You must believe me."

"I believe you," he said cautiously.

"But you have every right to act as you see fit," she concluded lamely.

A chasm yawned at his feet. What temptation, what madness wreaking havoc in his heart! He had reservations, but longed to suppress them. In the torment of insomnia, the victim takes the drowsy poppy and his brow relaxes to admit the gentle fingers of sleep.

19.

The burning days of summer passed. Qurra abandoned himself heart and soul to his passion for Aziza, trusting that love would defeat the legacy of the past. Aziza and Raifa played the part of affectionate sisters to perfection, and Unsiyya noticed nothing untoward. In the office of the grain merchant's, Qurra and Rummana continued to work together, confining their conversation to business matters. So love and loathing coexisted.

Aziza was soon found to be pregnant. Both families rejoiced, only Qurra wishing that it could have happened later, wondering exactly when the pregnancy began. An insect bored into the heart of the flower. The shining temple darkened with the breath of evil.

The poisoned needle of doubt. But Aziza did not read his thoughts. She blossomed in innocence and love. He could no longer hold back. He was free, honest, and in love; he was also a believer with great faith in God. He became well acquainted with both joy and sorrow.

20.

Why wasn't Raifa pregnant? The question echoed anxiously around both families. Raifa was worn down by it, and her eyes brimmed with hatred. Pregnancy was only slow to come if there was some defect; nature knew no delays. Suspicion, as usual in such cases, hovered around Raifa. Her mother was agitated and consulted the midwife, who made one suggestion after another. As the days passed, fear and apprehension took root and sorrows gathered like storm clouds.

"What a fuss," sighed Rummana in the bedroom one night, when he was drunk.

"They won't leave it alone. It's hellish," said Raifa angrily.

"You're like two peas in a pod. So what've you got missing?" grumbled Rummana.

Overcome with rage, Raifa demanded, "I suppose you have it on divine authority that it's my fault?"

"There's nothing wrong with me," he answered angrily.

"That's what men always say."

"Shall I try myself out on another woman?" he roared in a drunken fury.

Her head went up and she looked away with a snakelike twist of her neck. "Drunkard," she muttered disdainfully.

"Perhaps there's a baby of mine inside another woman."

"You're mad!"

"Don't call me names!"

"You ought to talk! Filthy son of a bitch!"

He rose to his feet threateningly and she backed away, ready to defend herself. He stayed where he was. "You barren witch," he said venomously.

It was the first quarrel of their marriage and its violence astonished him. But the desire which bound them together could resist any passing storms.

21.

Sheikh Muhammad Tawakkul was sitting with the bar owner, Sadiq Abu Taqiya, when Diya went by with her censer. Sadiq chuckled and whispered, "A Nagi's chief of the clan again. I wonder why that old imbecile keeps on crying!"

22.

In early spring, when the vendors of roast chickpeas and melon seeds were out crying their wares once more, Aziza gave birth to a son whom they named Aziz. When things were calm again and Aziza was lying resting, Qurra bent over the newborn child and examined him with conflicting emotions. Aziza gazed at him, tender, weary, and proud. "He's so like you," she murmured.

Why did she need to confirm that? As far as he could see the baby had no definable appearance, but she was talking innocently. She had completely forgotten the past and was absorbed in the loving present. His two companions, joy and sorrow, were competing for his attention, but he was determined to be happy.

23.

To preserve appearances, Rummana and Raifa paid them the customary visit and gave their nephew a gold-bound Quran. Rummana congratulated his brother and Raifa gazed at the baby for some time, exclaiming over his beauty. Aziza's heart jumped when she saw Raifa's expression as she hung over Aziz. Qurra behaved like any delighted father, all the time praying inwardly that God would show him the right path, enlighten him with the truth, that his love would not be put to the test as a result of misguided fears, that he would come to be as innocent and sincere as Aziza, and not cast himself voluntarily into hell.

24.

One night he took the child well wrapped up to the monastery square. He was greeted by a flood of melody as the anthems started up, and prayed God to graft the little one onto the tree of good men and heroes, to make him a vessel for sacred dreams and not a victim of destructive passions. His thoughts strayed to the narrow passage where Ashur had been left when he was the same age as his son. Like a cloud passing in front of the moon, dark thoughts invaded his mind. He remembered what had been said by his enemies about Ashur and his origins and was suddenly swamped by a sense of dreariness and decay. He took refuge in the anthems, letting them wash him clean of its rancid sweat, muttering to himself, "God give me strength."

The melody wrapped itself around him:

> *Naqdha ra bovad aya keh ayyari girand*
> *Ta hame sume'e daran peye kari girand.*

25.

As he emerged from the archway on his way home he heard a harsh voice asking, "Who's there?"

He recognized the voice of his brother Wahid, the clan chief, and answered, smiling, "Qurra Samaha al-Nagi."

The chief laughed. They stood, two shadows in the darkness. "Were you sitting up in the square like our noble ancestors?" he taunted.

"I was taking the baby to see it."

"Congratulations. I was going to come and see you in the shop tomorrow."

"Why don't you visit me at home?"

"You know I avoid the place."

"It's your home too," said Qurra gently.

In a different tone of voice, Wahid said, "I wanted to talk to you about something else as well."

"Nothing serious, I hope?"

"Our brother, Rummana."

Qurra sighed and said nothing.

"He's spending money foolishly. I don't want to preach, but I know only the clan chief can afford to spend like that!"

"He doesn't take kindly to being told. It just makes him angry."

"It's suicide," said Wahid angrily.

26.

It seemed that whatever bound Rummana and Raifa together was more powerful than good and evil, and made their fights irrelevant. Neither thought of abandoning the other, however fiercely they quarreled. They bickered and made up continuously, mixing violent abuse and sweet talk, nagging and loving sighs, accusations and kisses. She believed he was infertile; he thought it was her. She never looked at another man, and he never dreamed of remarrying.

"It's fate," he would declare when he was drunk.

27.

Radwan died after a short illness. He had kept himself so isolated that people had forgotten all about him and when he died they remembered him again for a few days. His share in the grain business went to Rummana and Qurra, and the rest of his inheritance was divided between his wife Unsiyya and his sister Safiyya.

28.

Rummana was no longer satisfied by drink and drugs and gradually turned to gambling to take the edge off his boredom. One day Qurra's patience ran out and he confronted him in the office. "You're spending money like water."

"It's my money," said Rummana coldly.

"Sometimes you have to borrow from me."

"I always pay you back, don't I?"

"But it's harmful to the business, and we're meant to be part-ners," said Qurra irritably. "What's more, you hardly do any work these days."

"That's because you don't trust me with anything."

Qurra hesitated, then said, "It's better for both of us if we go our separate ways, and set up independent businesses before we go under together."

29.

The family was upset by the news of the breakup, but Wahid visited Qurra and advised him frankly to do what he thought was in his interest. "Your son's growing older by the day," he said, and added scathingly, "Rummana's a pig like our stepfather."

Safiyya had a meeting with Qurra and Rummana to put for-ward her proposal. "Qurra could run the business on his own and Rummana would receive a percentage of the profits to do what he liked with."

"I'm not a child, auntie," protested Rummana.

"The honor of the Nagis is in your hands," she told them, her eyes brimming with tears.

"Honor!" repeated Qurra sorrowfully. "One of us is chief and it means nothing. Our father's disappeared and my brother's either drinking, gambling, or getting stoned."

"You're our only hope, Qurra," she said pleadingly.

"That's why I want to run my business alone."

30.

Raifa was alarmed at the thought of the split and announced her fears to Rummana.

"So you don't trust me either!"

"It would be easier to trust you if you gave up some of your bad habits," she said appeasingly.

"I'll give them up automatically when I have to accept responsibility."

"Do you really know the work?"

He frowned questioningly.

"You need time to train, Rummana. Don't be stubborn and foolhardy. It's always your brother who makes the decisions. He does the deals, goes on the trips—he's everything. And you, sitting hunched at your desk, are nothing!"

He felt a surge of hatred. "What do you suggest we do, since he's already made up his mind?"

"He has to be stopped at any price," she replied, malice dancing in her eyes.

"By force?"

"At any price. Do you know what it means if you go out on your own now? You'll be bankrupt in a matter of days or weeks. One brother a notable, another clan chief, and the third a beggar!"

"So what do you suggest?"

"Make friendly overtures. Change the way you live. Share in the work. Then we'll think again."

He was silent, a sullen expression on his face, and she reiterated, "You'll lose out badly. What will you have left if you split up now? Think about it, and remember too . . ." She paused, then went on, "Remember too that nothing's impossible."

31.

Qurra was preparing to set off on an urgent business trip. Rummana suggested postponing their breakup until his return. He said, with uncharacteristic graciousness, "You might find me a different person when you come back."

32.

That night the matter came up as Qurra and Aziza talked. "He doesn't deserve to be trusted," said Aziza in a matter-of-fact way.

"I know, but there's not time to arrange to dissolve the partnership now."

"Fair enough. But don't delude yourself. He has no affection
for you. He and his wife want to see us finished!"

She watched Aziz as he played with a white cat. Her eyes
softened. She gestured toward Aziz and murmured, "Your family
dreams of him becoming clan chief."

"That's the Nagis for you," he smiled.

"Whereas I think there are many ways to lead a good life."

"What about Ashur?"

"Not him again! Don't tell me you share their dreams."

"I'll raise him the same way Khidr raised me, and then it's up
to him."

"It would be such a relief for you all if you'd only try and
forget you were descendants of Ashur."

"We are, whether we like it or not."

Then his eyes rested on Aziz, and he said, "When will I be
able to have him working with me in the office?"

33.

The driver took his seat in the carriage. Qurra said his goodbyes:
Wahid, Rummana, Sheikh Ismail al-Qalyubi, Muhammad Tawakkul, and others were there to see him off. Muhammad Tawakkul
took Rummana's hand and asked Qurra ponderously, "Who will
be there to take your place at times like this, master, if each of you
opens up separate businesses?"

Qurra ignored the innuendo and continued his conversation
with Sheikh Ismail. Diya went by at that moment swinging her
censer, her eyes full of tears. Her family was no longer enraged at
the sight of her. "Diya's come to bless you," cried Wahid.

They all took turns to shake his hand, then he climbed
aboard. "Safe journey," called Rummana.

The bell tinkled merrily and the carriage moved off toward
the main square.

34.

Such trips normally lasted a week. A week went by and there was no sign of Qurra. As they sat at home in the evening, they voiced their thoughts in turn.

"He must have his reasons," said Rummana.

"You can't calculate the time of a journey to the precise minute," murmured Unsiyya.

"Once he was two days later than he said he'd be," offered Raifa.

Aziza said nothing.

35.

Another day went by. The reassurances were repeated. "There's nothing worse than being worried when you don't know what it is you're worrying about," said Aziza to herself.

36.

The carriage went to the port at Bulaq every morning and returned empty each evening. Aziza stayed awake till dawn.

37.

The alley began asking questions about Qurra's absence. Aziza sent for Wahid. "What do you think, master?" she asked her brother-in-law desperately.

"I've decided to go and look for him myself," declared the chief.

38.

Wahid was away for three whole days. When Aziza saw his face, her heart sank. "It must be bad news," she cried.

"His agents confirmed that he never reached them," said Wahid despondently.

"What can it mean?" demanded Aziza, white-faced.

"Something tells me he's fine," said Unsiyya, with a confidence she did not feel.

"Something tells me the opposite," retorted Aziza.

"Don't succumb to morbid thoughts," said Rummana.

"There are more of your family missing than there are here," shouted Aziza.

"God grant these forebodings come to nothing," said Unsiyya fervently.

"Amen," murmured Raifa.

At this Aziza let out a wail. "What can I do? I'm a woman. I've got no power!"

"I've taken the first step. There are other avenues to explore," said Wahid.

"He doesn't have any enemies," said Unsiyya.

"That's true," agreed Rummana quickly, "but things can happen on the road."

Aziza sighed, and Wahid said, "I'll leave no stone unturned."

39.

One week followed another. The days went carelessly by. People gave their attention to the weather, to work, sleep and food, certain now that Qurra would never return to the alley.

40.

Aziza fought persistently against indifference and oblivion. Qurra's disappearance was a disaster happening anew each morning. She was full of sorrow and anger, refusing to believe that the laws of existence could change in an instant. Worn out by emotion, she fell ill and lay in bed for a week. Again she summoned Wahid and told him, "I'm not going to let this rest, however long it takes."

"You don't know how distressed I am, Aziza," said Wahid.

"It's a matter of shame that this should happen to the chief's brother."

"I won't shut up."

"All my men have been told to give priority to the search, and I've asked the chiefs of friendly neighborhoods for help." He paused, then continued, "I went to my mother in Bulaq. She's blind now but she came with me to the Bulaq chief. The whole world's looking for Qurra."

41.

Her father, Ismail Bannan, went to the local police chief, who promised to help in any way he could. The father tried to console his daughter and encourage her not to give up hope, but she said, "I feel I know the truth in my heart of hearts."

Reading her thoughts, he said apprehensively, "Take care you don't malign innocent people."

"Innocent!"

"You should watch your tongue!"

"Those two are our only enemies."

"A brigand is everyone's enemy!"

"They're our only enemies."

"You have no evidence except your past suspicions."

"I'm not going to let this rest, however long it takes," she persisted.

42.

She rushed into Diya's apartments, something no one normally dared to do, and found her sitting cross-legged on her mattress, absorbed in the patterns on the rug. She threw herself down at her side, but the woman did not look in her direction and seemed not to notice her. "Diya, tell me what you think," she pleaded.

Her voice did not penetrate Diya's enchanted world. "Say something to me, Diya," she whispered eagerly.

But Diya neither heard her nor felt her, and made no response.

Aziza felt she was struggling to reach an inaccessible place, making a ridiculous assault on the unknown.

43.

She lived in her apartments in semi-isolation with Aziz, even eating alone there. Rummana and Raifa came to visit her, their sorrow at Qurra's disappearance conspicuously on show.

"The way you keep yourself apart makes us doubly sad," began Raifa.

"I'm not in a fit state to mix with other people," she declared, avoiding their eyes.

"We're your closest relations," murmured Rummana.

"Sadness is like an infectious disease that needs to be isolated."

"Mixing with people cures it," said Rummana, "and you must remember we haven't stopped looking."

"Yes. We have to find out who the killer is," she said determinedly.

"I don't believe he was murdered," exclaimed Raifa.

Aziza fought back the tears proudly. She was unconvinced by their kind words and the meeting brought her no comfort. She kept in contact with Wahid and her father, and did not allow despair to sap her will. The days passed and Qurra melted into oblivion.

44.

Publicly Qurra was said to have been the victim of a highway robbery, but in the bar and the hashish den most of the suspicions were focused on Rummana. People said he had got rid of his brother before he could divide up the business and make Rummana a bankrupt. Now he was running the grain merchant's, disposing freely of his own money and his nephew's. He had given up riotous living and gambling so that people wouldn't say he was wasting an orphan's money, and was careful not to cross Wahid, the chief of the clan. All the same the business was not the giant success it had been; Rummana put it down to his lack of commercial skill and expertise. "I can't do any better than I am doing," he complained to his brother. "I'd be happy for you to come in with me if you want."

"You know I have no experience in such things," returned Wahid coldly.

45.

Aziza paid little attention to the declining fortunes of the grain shop. She dreamed of the day Aziz would take his father's place, break away from his uncle, and restore the business to its former glory. To this end she devoted herself to his education, sending him to the Quran school at an early age and having him tutored privately in accounting and commerce. She told him tales of his maternal forbears and even, out of loyalty to Qurra, extolled the heroic deeds and legendary glories of Ashur al-Nagi. Consciously and unconsciously she taught him to be wary of his uncle and aunt and avoid their company, and plied him with accounts of the hostility between his father and uncle and the suspicious nature of his father's disappearance.

Qurra was forgotten, living only in Aziza's heart, and to a lesser extent in Aziz's imagination. Aziza had a daydream which she loved to replay in her mind; she would roam the world in search of him, and either find him, or establish beyond doubt who had killed him; then she would take revenge to restore justice to the world and peace in his heart, and recover her own peace of mind.

46.

When Aziz turned ten Aziza asked if he could become an apprentice in his father's business. Rummana agreed at once. "Welcome to the dear son of my dear brother," he enthused.

Shortly after that Aziza's father died and she inherited a considerable sum of money. She decided to keep it for Aziz to invest in his business when he was free of his uncle.

Eighteen months later Unsiyya died and the house was empty

of loved ones. Only Rummana and Raifa were left, and Diya if she could be counted. She was no longer capable of her daily promenade through the alley and lived in total isolation in her apartments. Every day shortly before sunset she would hang the censer out through the wooden latticework at her window, dry-eyed; even the tears no longer came to her aid.

47.

In his free time Rummana watched attentively. Aziz now sat in his father's place in the manager's office. He walked with firm steps, showing remarkable composure for one just approaching adolescence. He was a handsome boy, full of life, tall and slender with pleasant features and eyes which were thoughtful, sometimes anxious. Uncle and nephew were outwardly courteous to one another, without showing any real affection. Behind the polite words and sweet smiles lurked antipathy. The deceptive sweetness of a bitter April. He was full of his mother's poisoned breaths, and could be a dangerous enemy one day! He kept telling himself that the boy could be his son, even though he looked like an exact mixture of Aziza and Qurra. But what did it matter? His spirit was the decisive factor, not his blood. He was his brother's son, and his enemy. He couldn't love him, even if he did think he might be his—which he probably wasn't anyway. If the boy had known what was in his mind, he would most likely have hated him more.

"You're turned in on yourself, Aziz. Why?" he asked him one day.

The boy stared blankly at him as if he hadn't understood.

"Where are your friends?" persisted Rummana. "Why don't I see you around with them?"

"I invite them to the house sometimes," he replied uncertainly.

"That's not enough." Rummana laughed. "I never hear you calling me uncle."

Aziz looked embarrassed.

"I'm your uncle, and your friend."

Aziz smiled obligingly. "Of course."

Rummana assuaged his fears with a neat plan: he decided to begin taking his nephew along to male gatherings, in order to draw him out of his defensive shell and prise him from his mother's grip.

He returned to his accounts but was quickly distracted by overwhelmingly powerful images: he saw Aziz at death's door after an accident or illness.

48.

He revealed his misgivings to Raifa. "I've always warned you that snake was planning something," she said.

"I don't need you to warn me," he said irritably.

"And you don't need someone to tell you what you ought to do," she returned.

They had quarreled about the same thing so often. There was the devil looking through her beautiful eyes again.

"We might not always be so lucky," he grumbled.

She laughed scornfully. "All right. Let's just wait and see what happens!"

"He's begun to discuss business with me, so there's hope!"

"Do you imagine you'll be able to snatch him from his mother's arms, when she's so fired up with hate?"

"He still doesn't know the pleasures that exist in the world!"

"The snake has burrowed deep inside him."

He exhaled bad-temperedly. The silence crackled with murderous thoughts. From the alley came the sound of boys shouting, followed by a pattering on the wooden lattice.

"It's raining again," muttered Raifa.

Idly, he prodded at the coals in the stove with an iron poker. "How cold it is!" he shivered.

Breaking in on his thoughts, she said suddenly, "There's a remote chance . . ."

"What?"

"It's not impossible that a boy like him would be tempted by the thought of restoring the past glories of the Nagis."

"Aziz?"

"Yes. He's a dreamer like your father."

He gazed at her, bewildered. He feared her as much as he admired her. But he said listlessly, "He doesn't trust me."

"You can prime him without him knowing you're doing it." She sighed pleasurably. "Then Wahid can be warned of his intentions at the appropriate time!"

What was the point of it all? He sometimes felt a deep dissatisfaction. But he enjoyed passing the time with his bloodthirsty daydreams.

49.

Rummana took his nephew to male gatherings on the pretext of introducing him to the employees, and Aziza could not object.

The water pipe was passed around but he never invited the boy to partake. "It's obligatory for men on these occasions," he told him, "but you should keep away from it. It's not suitable for you."

Aziz got to know a great number of people. It pleased him that they still remembered his father with genuine affection.

"He was the most gentle and reliable of men."

"He always put morals first and business second."

"He had the same attitude to business as his ancestors had to being clan chief!"

"Too bad the glorious age of the Nagis has gone!"

"One day someone will put them back where they belong."

Such sentiments were repeated at every gathering. On the way home Rummana would say to him, "These people never stop dreaming." Or, "If it weren't for your uncle Wahid, we'd count for nothing around here."

Once Aziz replied, "But Wahid isn't like Ashur."

"Nobody's like Ashur. The age of miracles is past. We should be proud that a Nagi is chief again."

He wanted to look into his heart. When they were sitting with the men he would steal a glance at him and feel a sort of delight at the enthusiasm shining in his eyes.

50.

One evening Aziza said to Aziz, "The time has come."

He realized what she meant, but he waited, and she went on. "You can stand on your own two feet now. You're not a child any longer. Go into business on your own. I've got enough money to guarantee you'll be as successful as your father."

He nodded, but not with the enthusiasm she had anticipated.

"Get away from your father's enemy," she urged. "He's had enough of your money."

"I've said I'll do it."

"You don't seem too keen."

"I am. I've waited for this day for a long time."

"You'll do it at once?"

"Of course."

"You seem preoccupied. I've noticed it a lot recently, and put it down to problems at work."

"That's it."

"Come on, Aziz," she said skeptically. "I can tell from your eyes that there's something else."

"Don't make a mountain out of a molehill," he laughed.

It was as important to keep his secret from her as from his uncle Wahid. He knew exactly what her attitude would be.

"Don't hide anything from me, Aziz," she said anxiously. "We're surrounded by enemies. You must tell me everything."

"I'll do what we've agreed," he said with forced cheerfulness. "The rest is just a dream."

"What do you mean? I've had enough of these fatal dreams."

He shuddered at her perception, born of a mother's instincts and love and fear together.

"It's nothing," he mumbled evasively.

"Don't drive me crazy!" she cried passionately. "I'm perpetually sad. I've had to put up with more than a faithful wife should. You're my only hope. The one who's going to console me for my years of waiting. Wake me up from the long nightmare. We've been forced to live in this vile, underhand atmosphere. Our poison will always be fed to us in sweetmeats. You've no need to fear overt hostility. But what you must be on your guard against are the sweet smiles, the pleasant talk, the false remedies, the interminable masks of sincerity."

"I'm not stupid, mother," he said, squirming under the impact of this onslaught.

"But you're innocent and innocent people are the natural prey of rogues."

"He's got nothing to do with it." The words slipped out, before he realized what he was saying.

"Rummana?"

"Yes."

"Tell me what it is. Have I become so cut off from my heart and soul that all I know about the most vital matter is random snippets of information that come my way?"

"I don't want to keep anything from you, but I know you have misgivings."

"Be honest with me. This is killing me!"

He sighed and began pacing up and down the room, then came to a halt in front of her.

"Don't I have the right to think about glory?" he demanded.

Fearful thoughts assailed her. "Think of the consequences. That's what counts. Your grandfather Samaha dreamed of glory and now he's wandering the country like a tramp and nobody knows what's become of him. Tell me what your ideas of glory are, Aziz."

In confessional tones he told her about his encounters with the employees. She listened to him, her face pale at first, yellow as death by the time he had finished.

"Your uncle Wahid will see it as deliberate provocation," she observed in a faltering voice.

"I'm not stupid."

"I can tell Rummana's in this somewhere."

"He hasn't said a thing," interrupted Aziz. "He's on Wahid's side. He's always cautioning me."

"Don't trust him. The men are just repeating stuff that he's fed them. Have you talked to them about your plans?"

"Of course not, I told you before, I'm not stupid. I told them I wouldn't betray my uncle Wahid."

"That's good. Did you say anything different to Rummana?"

"No. I pretended to agree with him."

She gave a deep sigh and her eyes filled with tears. "Thank God." Then fiercely, "They've given me some rope to play with. Now what you have to do is concentrate on your work. Get free of your father's enemy—his murderer!—and devote yourself to your work. They've given me some rope . . ."

51.

There was a lull presaging a storm. The expression in Aziz's eyes boded ill. Since his nephew had left childhood behind, Rummana had been waiting for the blow to fall. He had not succeeded in winning his confidence. Aziz had been friendly only as a polite response to his attempts at communication. Despite all his efforts to soften him up, he had progressed without faltering, and now he was ready to take his revenge.

"Uncle!" he addressed him one day.

This was the first time he had used the title and Rummana was convinced it was a bad sign.

"What, nephew?"

With an offensive calm which reminded him of his brother in some of his moods, Aziz said, "I think it would be a good idea if we split the business."

Although he had expected this, expected it for a long time, his heart sank. "Really?" he stammered. "Of course you're free to do so. But why? Why fritter away our strength?"

"My mother wants to go into partnership with me."

"She can. And we can still preserve the existing arrangement."

"My father wanted it, as you know."

"So he said one day, out of the blue, but he wasn't set on it, otherwise nothing would have stopped him."

"What stopped him was his mysterious disappearance," remarked Aziz coldly.

Rummana's heart missed a beat but he pretended not to notice the barb and said, "He could have delayed his trip." Then, patently irritated, "Don't believe everything you hear."

With more boldness than he had shown previously, Aziz retorted, "I believe whatever's worth believing."

"I repeat you're free to go," said Rummana despondently, "but it's bad for both of us."

"Not for me."

This was another painful twist of the knife; he burned with resentment and thought to himself that if Aziz had really been his son, he would never have reached the point of being so scathing and hurtful to him. What could he do to restrain the devil in his heart that was bent on revenge? "The way you're talking doesn't become you," he said aloud. "Won't you think about it for a bit?"

"It's all decided," Aziz answered, as gently as he could.

"Even if I were to beg you to change your mind?" said Rummana despairingly.

"I'm sorry. I can't."

"Is it because of your mother?"

"She wants to go into partnership with me, as I've said."

"All this suspicion breeds a dislike which is based entirely on illusions."

Aziz hesitated a little. "They're not illusions. The accounts are hardly convincing, and the partnership arrangements aren't favorable to me."

"From now on you'll have as much power as you want!"

"You're wasting your time," murmured Aziz in annoyance.

"This is hatred!" cried Rummana in a fury. "Vicious spite! The curse which has hounded the Nagi family!"

52.

Rummana went back home shattered to Raifa, and told her everything. "The seed of hatred has brought forth its poisoned fruit," he concluded.

"Wahid's our only hope," said Raifa, her face gripped by venom.

"But the cunning little devil hasn't fallen into the trap yet."

"Don't wait for him to fall."

"It's not as easy as you seem to think." Then, coolly, "Your legacy is the only thing that can save us."

"My legacy!"

"Aziza's going to give hers to her son."

"That's because she's been priming him for revenge."

"With what you inherited I can make a new start."

"What about your money?" she demanded in surprise.

"There's not enough left to set up a respectable business," he answered hopelessly.

"So it's all gone on gambling!" she exclaimed.

"This isn't the time for recriminations."

"I didn't hoard my legacy like that snake, and you want me to squander what's left of it just so that I can end up on the streets with you?"

"I'll turn over a new leaf," he said defiantly.

She laughed scornfully and his anger flared. "So I've no choice but to tell him he's my son."

"Talk sense!" she shouted, enraged herself now. "Haven't you accepted that you're sterile yet?"

"You're the one who's sterile."

"The midwife found nothing wrong with me."

He went to strike her but she was ready to defend herself, like an angry lioness. Not convinced that he had backed down, she continued her invective. "Our enemies must be gloating. Perhaps it was your stupid fantasies about being a father that stopped you getting rid of him all these years!"

Shaking his head in amazement, he answered, "You think murder is some kind of pastime!"

At this point the maidservant entered to announce Sheikh Muhammad Tawakkul.

53.

Rummana waited for him in the reception room on the first floor. The man entered in an anxious flurry and Rummana's heart jumped uneasily.

He sat down and asked without preamble, "Have you made Wahid angry?"

"We're on excellent terms," answered Rummana, shocked.

"I saw him just now in the bar, raging drunk, cursing and swearing and accusing you of setting Aziz against him."

"That's a complete fabrication!" shouted Rummana in sudden panic.

"You'd better go and convince him of it as fast as you can."

"How do you mean?" queried Rummana aggressively.

"If you don't hurry, there's no telling what might happen to you!"

"But he's my brother!"

"It's not unusual for brother to kill brother in this alley," replied Tawakkul innocently.

Rummana swallowed agitatedly. "True," he muttered.

"Sorry to alarm you, but you'd better get moving."

54.

Rummana didn't dare confront Wahid when he was drunk, so he decided to wait till next morning. However, Ismail Qalyubi, imam of the little mosque, burst into the house at midnight with a warning from Wahid that if he set foot outdoors he'd be exposing himself to certain death.

Rummana realized that Aziz was the one who'd driven a wedge between himself and Wahid and rushed into his apartments, hurling abuse. The two were about to become embroiled in a violent punch-up. In desperation, Aziza confessed that she'd suspected Rummana of plotting against her son, and had expressed her fears to Wahid. Rummana turned his anger on her, and she screamed in his face, "Get out of my sight! You killed Qurra!"

The house erupted in a blaze of hatred and anger in full view of the servants.

Aziza and Aziz moved out immediately to the Bannan's house, leaving Rummana, Raifa, and Diya alone in the Nagi house.

Aziz took over the grain shop, restored it, and made business bloom again as it had in Qurra's day. Wahid lost all his misgivings about Aziz, reassured by what Aziza had told him, visited him to wish him well, and publicly offered him his approval and protection. Aziz abandoned his dreams, sadly, half despising himself for it, and compensated by being good to his employees, agents, and customers, and any of the harafish who threw themselves on his mercy.

55.

Rummana cowered in the house, condemning himself to voluntary imprisonment, beleaguered by fear, his heart heavy with shame. He had gone through his and Raifa's money. Boredom was killing him. He escaped from it into drugs and drink, and took his anger out on the servants, the walls, the furniture, the mysteries of the unknown.

Relations between Raifa and him became more strained, and worsened from day to day. She despised his cowardice, his inactivity, his stupors brought on by drink and drugs, his noisy outbursts. As their quarreling grew more frequent, a mutual antipathy replaced the domestic harmony. Every time an argument flared up she asked him for a divorce, until one day he lost his head and gave her one. It was a foolhardy decision, since neither of them could do without the other's love; but rage makes people mad, pride makes them outrageous, and obstinacy can become a chronic sickness. As if each wanted to establish that the other was sterile, Raifa married a relative almost immediately after the divorce, whereupon Rummana married one of the servant girls. But they soon found out almost for sure that they were both sterile. Rummana married a second, third, and fourth wife until he had drunk the cup of despair to the last drop.

He and Raifa each lived in hell, in a world of tedium.

56.

One morning a stranger arrived in the alley. His head was swathed in a black turban, his body in a purple cloak, and he was clearly blind, tapping his way along with the help of a stick. He had a

white beard and an impressive brow. People regarded him indifferently and left him to his own devices, some wondering what had
brought him there.

When he had progressed a little way along the alley he called
out, "Hello there!"

Sadiq Abu Taqiya, owner of the bar, answered him. "What do
you want?"

"Lead me to Khidr Sulayman al-Nagi's house," he said in a
melancholy voice.

Sadiq looked hard at his face. It was like a vision. The past
rushed in on him. "Merciful God!" he shouted in amazement.
"Master Samaha!"

"God bless you," said the blind man gratefully.

People rushed forward, with Wahid, Aziz, Muhammad
Tawakkul, and Ismail Qalyubi leading the way. They embraced
the newcomer feverishly, uttering expressions of welcome.

"This is a happy day, father."

"A day of justice, grandfather."

"A day of light, master."

"God bless you. God bless you all," repeated Samaha, his face
lighting up with joy.

Everyone wanted to invite him home, but he said obstinately,
"Khidr's house is my house."

The news spread. The merchants called out from their shops
and the harafish congregated around their shacks and derelict
buildings. The street rang with cheers, then a chorus of joyful
trilling broke out from the women at the windows and wooden
lattices.

"Glory be to God!" cried Sadiq Abu Taqiya. "No absence is
eternal, no injustice everlasting."

57.

Samaha sat cross-legged on a divan. Wahid, Rummana, and Aziz
sat facing him on cushions. Thus, they were united in specious
calm, side by side like balm and poison in an herbalist's workshop,

the rivalries temporarily blotted out in the presence of the suffering father, martyr of purity.

"We've prepared a bath and food for you," said Wahid.

"Not straightaway," murmured Samaha gently. "Let me set my mind at rest first."

He moved his head in an uneasy gesture. "Where's Khidr?"

"Only God is everlasting," sighed Wahid.

His face clouded for a moment, then he asked, "And his wife, Diya?"

"In her apartments. She's off in her own world."

Samaha hesitated sympathetically, then inquired, "And Qurra?"

There was a silence. Samaha sighed bitterly.

"That's too young. I always used to dream a tooth was being pulled."

He extended his palm. "Your hand, Aziz."

He took the proffered hand affectionately and asked Aziz, "You remember him, of course?"

"The Almighty took him when I was just a child."

"God rest him! And who's your mother, my son?"

"Ismail Bannan's daughter."

"A good family. Where is she now?"

"She and my aunt Safiyya are on their way."

"How about you, Rummana?" he asked.

Rummana and Wahid exchanged rapid glances and Rummana said, "I've got four wives who are waiting to look after you."

"How many children?"

"None so far."

Samaha took a deep breath. "It's God's will. And you, Wahid?"

Silence returned until Samaha moved his head agitatedly and asked again, "And you, Wahid?"

Wahid scowled. "I'm not married yet."

"What I'm hearing is very strange. So there was a reason for all my nightmares! What's become of Radwan?"

"God rest his soul."

"Really? Only the names remain."

He was silent for a while, digesting the news, unaware of the tension gripping the assembled company.

"Who's chief of the clan these days?" he asked finally.

"Your son, Wahid," declared the latter, taking heart for the first time.

"Really?" exclaimed Samaha with a shudder of excitement.

"Really, Father."

He told the tale of his dream and the way he had seized power, and Samaha's face brightened. "The first piece of good news!" he cried.

He crossed his arms on his chest in a gesture of gratitude. "So the age of Ashur has returned!"

They were plunged into confusion, but Wahid echoed boldly, "The age of Ashur has returned!"

"A blessing from the skies!" shouted the blind man excitedly, his pleasure showing on his face and in his delighted gestures. "May Ashur rejoice with the angels, and Shams al-Din in the gardens of Paradise."

Nobody thought for a moment of wakening him from his dream or pouring scorn on his happiness. He seemed to have forgotten his exile and banishment and be exulting in this happy ending. "Now for a bath and food," he said peacefully, "and may God's blessings fill the earth."

58.

Samaha slept for the rest of the day and sat up at night in the monastery square, finding his way to it by sound, smell, and touch. He summoned up the images of the monastery building, the mulberry trees, and the old wall, using the power of his imagination. As the melodies filled his heart, a blessed happiness washed over him. He spread his palms, and prayed, "Thanks be to God who has allowed me to be buried beside Shams al-Din. Thanks be to God who in his mercy has allowed justice to prevail in our alley. Thanks be to God who has let my son inherit the supreme qualities of strength and goodness."

His song of thanks was overshadowed by the poetry of the chant:

Har ankeh janibe khoda negahdorad
Khodash dar hame hal azbala negahdorad.

Royal Jelly

The sixth tale in the epic
of the harafish

1.

Samaha's health deteriorated rapidly and he gave up the ghost one morning as he was drifting back to sleep after the dawn prayer, as if he had only returned from exile to be buried next to Shams al-Din. He died happy, under the illusion that he was merely exchanging one paradise for another.

"We hid the reality from him," commented Aziz. "So all of us, including Wahid, have acknowledged that our life is something ugly, to be kept from decent people."

2.

The cereal business was hugely successful and Aziz grew wealthy. He contented himself with being heroic in a limited sphere, having faith in people, and doing good when the opportunity arose. He abandoned his dreams of glory, preferring security and appeasing his conscience by telling himself that he was not cut out to be a hero.

Aziza arranged a marriage between him and Ulfat al-Dahshuri, daughter of Amir al-Dahshuri, the iron merchant. He was content with his mother's choice: she was his muse and the guardian of his stability and success. The wedding was celebrated a year after his grandfather's death. He set up house with his bride in the Bannan's old house which he had purchased for himself and completely refurbished. She was a big, tall, good-looking girl, well versed in the household arts. She was all that he could desire, and a strong bond of affection grew between them. They embarked on a life of happiness and produced a string of children.

3.

Rummana remained incarcerated in his house even when there was no longer any need for it. It had only taken Samaha's return to make Wahid drop his threats, but Rummana hated the outside world and his absence went unremarked and unlamented. He lived more or less cut off from his four wives, could never rid himself of Raifa's memory, and gave himself up increasingly to drink and drugs.

One evening, more drunk than usual, he staggered into Diya's apartments. He weaved around her, spluttering with laughter. "You're the reason for this foolishness and misery," he told her scathingly.

The old woman remained in a world of her own, so he continued, "I need your money. Where do you keep it, you old cripple?"

He grabbed hold of her hand and pulled her up. Startled, she struck him in the face with the incense burner. He gripped her around the neck in a demented rage and squeezed violently until there was no life left in her.

4.

The house trembled with fear. The news took the alley by storm and the new sheikh, Gibril al-Fas, reported the crime to the police. Rummana was arrested, tried, and sentenced to life imprisonment. Before he was transported to the penitentiary he sent for

Aziz. "I admit that I was behind your father's murder," he told
him.

"I know," replied Aziz sorrowfully.

"He's buried in the clothes he was wearing next to Sheikh
Yunis' tomb."

5.

Aziz exhumed Qurra's body in the presence of the sheikh and a
detective; Wahid and Aziza were there too. When his skeletal
frame appeared, the old sorrows were renewed. He was wrapped
in a shroud, and given a proper funeral and reburied in Shams al-
Din's tomb.

"Now my heart can be at ease," said Aziza. "It was always my
dream to be beside him when my time comes."

6.

Aziz's conscience began to trouble him again. As Wahid's reputation worsened, Aziz felt the burden weigh heavier on his own
shoulders. The clan chief's depravity and greed had become pro-
verbial in the whole area, not just his own alley. A few years after
his father's death he died of a heart attack as a result of an over-
dose.

All this time Aziz was actively looking for a suitable candidate for clan chief from among the many descendants of al-Nagi, in
the hope that such a man could make that dead age live again, but
he found the Nagi family had been absorbed into the ranks of the
harafish, ground down by poverty and misery, and robbed of what
was best in them. So when Wahid died, there was no one ready to
take over from him. At once Aziz was confronted by an extremely
delicate question: should he be buried next to Shams al-Din? His
heart told him no.

"He was your uncle, after all," remonstrated his wife,
Ulfat.

But he was adamant and had him buried in a pauper's grave

in the Nagis' plot. Oddly enough, this behavior did not go down well in the alley.

"He was careful to be pleasant to him while he was alive. He waited till he was dead to take his revenge," remarked Sanqar al-Shammam, the new owner of the bar.

7.

Nuh al-Ghurab filled the vacancy with alacrity. He was coarse and insolent and grasping. He called a truce with neighboring clan chiefs and dominated the alley through brute force so effectively that he became one of the richest men around in the space of a year. The people bore his oppression with indifference. No one grieved for the Nagis' reign, now that their sweet dreams had come to nothing at the hands of Wahid. The notables were delighted. The harafish entered a new phase of enforced idleness and wretchedness.

8.

The sun followed its course, sometimes shining out of a clear sky, sometimes hidden behind the clouds. Aziz renovated the small neighborhood mosque and chose a new sheikh, Khalil al-Dahshan, following the death of Ismail al-Qalyubi. He also restored the fountain, the animals' drinking trough, and the old Quran school.

Raifa became a widow and lived alone in her house with the servants. She inherited a small fortune from her second husband but she and her sister Aziza never saw each other and were like strangers, even enemies. She saw Aziza as the reason for all the ills that had befallen her, and claimed she had breathed an unlucky spirit into her when they were together in the cradle. The conventions of the alley were seriously breached when she started visiting Rummana in prison, thereby openly declaring that she still loved him, despite all that had happened.

So the years passed, with not much that was good and incalculable evil.

9.

One day Aziz learned that an employee had met his end while transporting a load of cereal. His name was Ashur and he had considered himself to be a Nagi as he was related to Fathiyya, Sulayman's first wife. Aziz' kind heart was filled with sorrow and he gave the man a decent burial and arranged for his wife to be paid a monthly allowance. When he made inquiries he learned that the man had several married daughters and a little girl of six called Zahira who still needed to be cared for. Aziz suggested that she could be taken into his household to work as a maid for Madame Aziza, and the girl's mother accepted the offer gladly. Zahira moved into Aziza's apartments and it was as if she had been transported to Paradise. For the first time her natural color appeared, as she benefited from good food and proper clothes, and learned household tasks. She won Aziza's sympathy and the mistress treated her more kindly than the other servants and even sent her to the Quran school for a while. Aziz was not interested in seeing the girl. He entrusted her to his mother. "Don't forget she's a Nagi," he teased.

10.

Zahira's mother visited Aziz in the director's office. He had forgotten all about her. She reminded him who she was, and of his worker, Ashur, who had died ten years before, and thanked him effusively. "May you always live in plenty," she concluded. "Abd Rabbihi wants to marry Zahira."

Aziz recollected the girl, whom he had also forgotten. "Do you think he's suitable for her?"

"He's perfect," she answered proudly. "And he earns enough to support her."

"God be with you, then," he agreed indifferently.

11.

At the supper table he told Madame Aziza and Madame Ulfat of the episode. Ulfat burst out laughing. "Abduh the baker! He's an idiot."

"She's an excellent girl," protested Aziza. "She deserves better than that."

"Are you expecting a rich merchant to try for her?" joked Aziz.

"Her looks qualify her."

"This lad's good enough for her," said Aziz carelessly. "It wouldn't be right for us to let a definite offer go for the sake of some fantasy that may never be realized." Then, conclusively, "I assured her mother I had no objection. It's up to her to decide."

12.

Madame Aziza fitted her out with furniture, clothes, and a set of copper pans. "Such a shame," she lamented repeatedly.

Aziz was sipping his morning coffee before he went off to the shop when Aziza brought Zahira to say goodbye.

"Come along, Zahira," she was calling as she came in, "come and kiss your master's hand."

"There's no need for that, mother," protested Aziz in a whisper.

The girl came in, covered in embarrassment and confusion, and stopped at the door. He looked up to give her an encouraging glance, and found that for a few moments he could not take his eyes off her. Quickly he recovered himself and looked away, conscious of the need to preserve his dignity in front of his mother and his wife, struggling to master his violent astonishment. How had this treasure remained buried in his mother's apartments for so long? Her posture was more graceful than any dancer's, her skin miraculously clear, the enchantment in her eyes intoxicating. She was the embodiment of lethal beauty. He noticed Ulfat engrossed in the child at her breast, controlled himself, and said, clinging to this image of security, "Congratulations, Zahira."

"Kiss your master's hand," insisted Aziza.

He proffered his hand. She was so close that a fleeting scent of carnations from her abundant black hair took his senses by storm. He felt the imprint of her lips on the back of his hand. As she retreated he had a powerful intuition that one day a miracle would happen.

13.

It was his habit to go each morning in the carriage and pray at the mosque of al-Husayn, then take a turn along New Street and through the goldsmiths' and coppersmiths' quarters before returning to his business. He dreamed all the way. His soul floated in heaven, leaving his body empty in the carriage. Had he found out at last why the sun rose? Why the stars shone at night? What the songs from the monastery were talking about? Why madmen are happy? Why people are sad about death? This beauty had lived under his roof for ten years! How had his wife and mother escaped her charm? Did the girl have any idea what riches she possessed, or was she like the wind, unaware of the havoc she wrought? Was her mother mad that she could accept Abduh the baker's offer so blindly? Could he stop the rain falling? He pitied all the ignorant hearts!

On the eve of the wedding her mother came to thank him. He studied her face curiously and saw an old woman with traces of past beauty lingering still on her features. He stared at her in suppressed anger. "Is everything all right?" he asked.

"Thanks to God and yourself."

"Why are you in such a rush?"

"She's been engaged to him since she was born," she said resignedly.

As she went he cursed her silently, and wondered sadly what stops people doing what they want to do.

14.

Zahira married Abd Rabbihi the baker in a modest ceremony. He
had not seen her since she was six but had grown used to thinking
of her as a wife. When he saw her on their wedding night he was
shocked by her beauty, but he was charged with traditional knowledge and advice which obliged him to assume a firm and lordly air.
He was twenty-one years old, tall and muscular, a typical local man
with his prominent cheekbones, flattened nose, and thick mustache.
His head was shaved smooth and shiny as a pebble except for a
luxuriant lock of hair at the front. He recited a few prayers, then
assumed a brusque, somewhat rough manner to appear intimidating and hide the sweetness inside.

She marveled at his virility, succumbed to the heat of his
passion, and yielded to him as if to fate.

She found herself living in a basement flat, consisting of one
room and an entrance hall which served as both kitchen and bathroom. She thought about the paradise she had lost but her instinct
told her that she had been a visitor passing through, not a permanent resident there. This basement was her home and her destiny.
Here she possessed a man, and would realize her dreams and find
peace of mind.

15.

Love had taken over Abduh's heart and almost destroyed his cover,
but he went to great lengths to demonstrate his masculinity. Before
the first month was out, he asked her, "Are you going to sit at
home all day like a lady of leisure?"

"What would you like me to do?"

"Satan finds work for idle hands!"

16.

That was how Zahira became an itinerant seller of sweetmeats. Enveloped in a blue work gallabiyya, she paraded the streets crying, "Turkish delight! Come on, boys and girls!"

By being free to wander the streets, Zahira discovered who she was. She became aware of her power and charm. Eyes devoured her, tongues sang her praises, her appearance enchanted and provoked. She was strong, spoiled by nature, and pampered and flattered by the people she met. She rebuffed amorous advances with disdain, and her self-confidence grew.

17.

The bond between her and Abd Rabbihi grew stronger. He was her man and she was his goddess. He treated her with conventional male superiority but found her as tough as she was affectionate, as quick to anger as she was loyal and faithful. She bore him a son, Galal, and the sweet wine of motherhood flowed through her veins, bringing her new happiness.

18.

Abd Rabbihi used to deliver bread to Madame Raifa.

"Why do you let your wife roam the streets?" she asked him one day.

"We have to make a living, madame," he said humbly.

"There are many ways to earn a living. I'm on my own and I could do with a maid. Working for me would pay better and keep her away from the wickedness of the streets."

Abd Rabbihi was taken aback and asked in some confusion, "What about the child?"

"I'd never separate a mother and child," she said coaxingly.

His ambition got the better of him and he said quickly, "Mother, father, and child are at your service."

19.

"Madame Raifa!" murmured Zahira apprehensively.

"She's very rich and she's all alone," said Abd Rabbihi.

"But she's Aziza's mortal enemy!"

"That's nothing to do with us, and working for her is easier and more lucrative than begging in the alley with a basket on one arm and a child on the other."

"I'd prefer to work for Aziza."

"But she hasn't asked you, which means she doesn't want you," said Abd Rabbihi irritably.

Zahira said nothing but her dream of paradise was reawakened.

20.

Aziza erupted in fury when she heard the news. "That girl's always in a rush!" she exclaimed.

"She didn't mean to annoy you. She's just trying to earn a living," said Ulfat.

"We should have priority!"

"She has a child who's not old enough to be left," protested Ulfat, "and if he came with her he might bring germs."

Aziz followed the conversation with interest. He sensed that his wife would not be happy if Zahira came back and felt a pang of unease, as if an accusing finger was pointing at him.

"Ulfat's hit the nail on the head," he declared resolutely.

21.

Zahira was combing Raifa's hair in the sitting room when a servant came in to announce the arrival of Muhammad Anwar. From comments of Raifa's, Zahira knew that the visitor was her stepson and that he remained loyal to her even after her visits to Rummana in prison had become common knowledge. The man entered shortly afterward, greeted them, and handed her a neat package, saying, "Caviar for madame!"

Raifa beamed with delight. Muhammad was a young man of average height with pleasant features, wearing a beautiful cloak and caftan.

"You're good to me, Muhammad," she said.

"I wanted you to taste it before any of my customers," he declared gaily.

"When are you going to let me pay for it like the rest of the caviar lovers?" she teased.

"When the sun rises in the west," he said.

He drank from a glass of cinnamon tea full of nuts. Raifa burst out laughing. "You're a good man, Muhammad," she repeated.

As he sipped the tea, his eyes fell on Zahira, still busily arranging her mistress' hair. He could hardly believe what he saw, and fastened his eyes on his glass as if to escape the vision. "God protect me from His creation," he breathed.

"How's business?" asked Raifa.

He extricated himself from his reverie. "Excellent, thanks."

Zahira noticed him looking at her with shining eyes, imploring, and smiled inwardly.

22.

Muhammad Anwar frequented Raifa's house at every possible opportunity. His visits became a matter of routine for Zahira, like his passionate glances. He was careful to avoid rousing the slightest suspicion in Raifa's mind, according her household the loyalty and respect it deserved. Every man who saw Zahira went crazy over her. She became convinced that she was the best-looking woman in the alley. And she was a Nagi like the great merchant Aziz! It was strange how people's lives turned out. One woman ended up in a big house, another in a basement. One got a rich businessman, another a baker. She herself had decided her fate when she was blind. Even her instinctive attachment to her husband did not satisfy her. Life wasn't a cycle of desire and motherhood. It wasn't poverty and hard work and pretending to enjoy serving a rich old lady. It wasn't possessing an amazing strength, then squandering it doing servile work. Inside she was changing, slowly but persistently. A movement each day, a jump each week, and a great bound each month. She was discovering herself layer by layer. From within her sprang all sorts of creatures, resolute and ready for action. In her imagination she interrogated her mother and her husband, questioned her home, her lot in life. She resented everything that demanded her to be content: the handed-down wisdom, the old lady's kindness, her husband's male prowess. She had drunk a burning draft of elixir which had inflamed her imagination, intoxicated her, and made a new dawn blaze into life.

"Have you heard the news?" said Muhammad Anwar to Raifa one day. "A woman's the new clan chief in Birgawan!"

"I'd like to see a woman toppling the men," laughed Raifa.

Zahira gave an admiring smile and inside her a secret fire stirred. Muhammad Anwar flung her a desperate, entreating look and she suddenly wondered if it would take a man like him to realize her dream. Her heart gave her no indication of the answer. She appraised him dispassionately and was struck forcibly by the idea that a woman's weakness is her emotions; and that her relationships with men should be rational and calculated. Life is precious, with vast possibilities, limitless horizons. Love is nothing more than a blind beggar, creeping around the alleyways. She sighed and said to herself, "The only thing worse than having bad luck is putting up with it."

23.

Zahira was feeding Galal when Muhammad Anwar suddenly rushed into the room. She thrust her breasts inside her dress, and pulled the veil more tightly around her head and face, full of embarrassment. He looked agitatedly at her, then asked, "Where's Madame Raifa?"

She was sure he was being devious—he must have seen Raifa

passing his shop in the carriage, but she answered politely, "She's gone out."

He hesitated, then said, "Perhaps I'll wait for her. No, I should come back later, shouldn't I?"

"Goodbye, then," she answered firmly, not bothering to go through the motions of courtesy.

But he had no intention of going. He was transfixed by an overwhelming force. He moved closer, his eyes wild, full of frantic desire. She stepped back, frowning. He moved closer again.

"No," she said sharply.

"Zahira!" he muttered derangedly.

"If you don't go, I will!" she exclaimed.

"Have pity on me. I . . . I love you."

"I'm not a whore."

"God forbid! I love you." He retreated, scared by the specter of Raifa, and as he turned to go, he sighed, "How can I marry a woman who's already married?"

24.

She lived in a whirl of revolt and anticipation. Life had to change. She possessed the strength to alter the boundaries of her existence. Every minute without change was a victory for submission and hopelessness. But how could she start to fight? She seized her chance when Raifa was suffering a bad headache. "I could stay the night," she volunteered.

"What would your husband say?"

"He won't die of fright if he spends the night alone!"

Two hours after the time she normally returned from work, Abd Rabbihi came to find out what had happened.

"Madame's ill," she explained.

He was silent, unsure what to say. "Don't you think you should have let me know?" he said at last with some bitterness.

"Madame's ill! Can't you understand?" she snapped back angrily.

25.

When she returned to the basement the following evening, Abd Rabbihi realized that Raifa had only been slightly unwell and there had been no need for Zahira to spend the night with her. A wave of anger engulfed him. "She didn't really need you. She's got a house full of servants," he said.

She reacted furiously, looking for any excuse to be angry with him. "Is that my reward for doing someone a kindness?" she retorted.

"Your behavior gets worse every day. You're not to go back to that house," he said resolutely.

"Aren't you ashamed of yourself?"

"To hell with the house and its mistress!" he shouted.

"I'm not ungrateful like you," she screamed back.

He struck her across the face and stormed out.

Zahira was beside herself with rage. Her suppressed resentment burst to the surface. She threw a final dismissive glance around the room. The blow preoccupied her entirely and grew in her mind until it took over her emotions and deadened her senses. Indifferent to Galal's screams, she drummed her fists on the bed.

She walked away from the basement with the child, consigning the past to oblivion.

26.

Madame Raifa was surprised at her returning so quickly, only an hour after she had left.

"Have you got room for me, madame?" asked the girl.

"Why, for goodness' sake?"

"I can't live with that man any longer," she said miserably.

Raifa shook her head wonderingly, and Zahira went on, "He was going to stop me working for you."

"How ungrateful of him!" burst out Raifa angrily.

"And he hit me."

"He's a beast. He doesn't know what a treasure he has." She

thought for a little, then said, "But I don't like to break up families."

"I know what I'm doing," insisted Zahira.

Raifa smiled. "Make yourself at home then, Zahira."

27.

Abd Rabbihi the baker fidgeted with embarrassment under Madame Raifa's gaze. He mumbled apologetically but remained fixed on his goal, stubborn, full of male pride.

"So what if I hit her?" he said. "She's not permanently damaged."

"You're at fault, and you're stupid too," she said virulently.

"She must come back with me now," he insisted, still polite.

"When you've learned her worth and not before," said Raifa sharply.

He forced himself to leave. He had begun to see his surroundings through a red haze of anger.

28.

Abd Rabbihi sat in the bar taking deep swigs from the calabash and wiping his mustache on the sleeve of his blue gallabiyya. All he could talk about was Zahira. "She's run off and taken the boy with her."

"You've got no guts," said a drunk.

"Madame Raifa encouraged her," he objected angrily.

"Act like a man," advised Sanqar al-Shammam.

"What do you mean?"

"Divorce her!"

His face twitched with anger. "I could kill a woman with no trouble at all."

Nuh al-Ghurab, the clan chief, guffawed loudly and slapped him good-naturedly on the back. "What a hero!"

His anger subsided and he said meekly, "I'll take advice from my master."

"Trample her underfoot until she's like a wornout rug," said Nuh, his eyes red from drink and drugs.

"Divorce will bring you peace of mind," said Gibril al-Fas.

"Divorce is useless in a case like this," said Nuh.

"Who said that marriage is half of religion?" demanded Abd Rabbihi. "It seems more likely to make you commit sins!"

29.

Abd Rabbihi went reeling through the darkness and came to a halt under Madame Raifa's windows. He was inflamed with drink and anger. The conventions of masculinity and the overwhelming urgings of his love struggled against one another in his overloaded heart. "Come down here, Zahira," he shouted hoarsely.

He was having difficulty keeping on his feet and the strength began to flow out of him. He called again: "I've got the fire of the baker's oven and the demons from the archway on my side."

A window opened and Khalil al-Dahshan, the imam of the mosque, looked out.

"Who's that madman out there?" he demanded angrily.

"It's me—Abd Rabbihi, the baker."

"Get out of here, you drunkard."

"I want my wife. The law's on my side."

"Stop making such a racket around the houses of respectable people."

"Will I only get justice from the devil then?"

"Go to hell."

Abd Rabbihi flung himself at Raifa's door, beating on it with his fists, until Sheikh Gibril came down from his house and hauled him away, protesting, "Stop it! You're crazy! Come with me. I'll try and put in a good word for you with madame."

30.

Gibril found Raifa in a wild fury. Now Zahira was not the only one to have a quarrel with Abduh.

"That miserable baker," she fumed.

"He's only too ready to serve you," said the sheikh.

"Didn't you see his effrontery? Am I going to hand her back to him and let him have his revenge?"

"I really think he loves her."

"Animals don't know what love is!"

"What if he tries to use the law to make her go back?"

"Let him do his worst!"

31.

Nuh summoned Abd Rabbihi to the café where he held court. He looked hard at him, then said imperiously, "Divorce the woman!"

Abd Rabbihi was astounded. Despair engulfed him. He realized that Raifa knew how to get her own back. The chief found his silence oppressive and roared, "Have you lost your tongue?"

"Didn't you say, sir," he began modestly, "that divorce was useless in a case like mine?"

"You're useless," mocked the chief.

"The law's on my side, sir."

"Divorce her, Abd Rabbihi," said the chief in a dismissive tone.

32.

The divorce took place. Abd Rabbihi was dragged toward it like a condemned man to the gallows. The dream was over, the precious jewel lost. Zahira was drunk with victory and the joy of freedom. At the same time she felt a twinge of regret inside her for the passion that was lost to her forever. She held Galal tightly to her breast, fruit of a love she knew had been precious. Her ambition quickly reasserted itself and her personality was clearly revealed: hard, steeped in pride and suffering.

"I get what I want when I make up my mind," boasted Raifa happily.

True. She was a strong, influential woman. But she would not have had her way without recourse to the clan chief. The power of the clan chief: eternal subject of fantasy, fatal source of unhappiness for the Nagi family, summit crowned with shining stars!

33.

She smiled encouragingly.

"Congratulations on regaining your freedom and honor," said Muhammad Anwar, the man with the caviar.

Taking his chance when Raifa went to attend to some business he whispered, "I'm waiting." His eyes gleamed with desire and he persevered with his plea: "I want to do it legally."

How did he view her? As a merchant views his servant? She didn't really like him. She'd always seen him as weak and servile. But he had the power to give her some kind of status and class. Could she hope for anything better than him?

She smiled at him encouragingly.

34.

Abd Rabbihi got so thoroughly drunk that the floor of the bar moved beneath his feet. "Is it shameful for a man to cry?" he asked Sanqar al-Shammam.

The bar owner snorted with laughter. "If he's the size of a mule, like you!"

Abd Rabbihi cradled the calabash in his hands and began rocking it from side to side as if he was dancing. "Take yourself away, Abd Rabbihi," he said out loud. "Go and hide yourself in the darkness. Even the dust in the alley has more strength than you. The only time you test your strength is pushing dough into the oven. God have mercy on you!"

"What's got into your head?"

"Divorce. I divorced her. With a single word, I ruined everything. Even a louse puts up a fight. How your enemies must be gloating, Abd Rabbihi!"

"It's an honor to obey the clan chief," cautioned Sanqar.

"Then I thank God," he muttered hurriedly, taking fright

even though he was drunk. "But there's something else weighing
on my mind," he added with a sigh.

"What's that?"

"I still love the damned woman."

"That's what really disgraces a man," laughed Sanqar.

"Strange, by God, it's strange," sang Abd Rabbihi in a voice
like a donkey braying.

"Keep singing! Singers have always been crossed in love, from
what I can make out!"

35.

Abd Rabbihi went back to delivering bread to Madame Raifa's
house after several well-disposed people had put in a good word for
him.

"I hope you're not angry with me anymore?" he ventured
timidly one day.

"I'm ready to let bygones be bygones," she said coldly.

He hesitated, then implored, "Leave me alone with her for a
minute."

She looked warily at him. "No."

"I'll talk to her in front of you then."

She pondered briefly, then called Zahira who appeared in a
navy dress, looking as fresh as a flower. They gazed at each other
and she did not blink or lower her eyes. She seemed like a stranger,
distant and cool. A picture quite at variance with the struggle
raging in the depths of her soul.

"I never meant any harm. Let's forget what happened."

She said nothing.

"I'm sorry for what I did."

"Say something, Zahira," prompted Raifa.

"I want you back. Our life together must mean something,"
said Abd Rabbihi.

"No," mumbled Zahira.

"We can't forget we were man and wife, or say it doesn't
matter anymore. We had some good times."

She lowered her gaze for the first time and said resolutely, "We no longer have any hold over each other."

36.

Muhammad Anwar slipped into the house when Raifa was out. He confronted Zahira impatiently. "I know I shouldn't be here, but I'd risk anything for you. Come with me now and we'll get married."

"What makes you so sure I want to marry you?" she demanded haughtily.

"I love you, Zahira," he declared humbly.

"So why are you asking me to run away like a thief?"

"There's no other way. Madame Raifa would never agree."

"Have you discussed it with her?" she asked in astonishment.

He hung his head sorrowfully. "She's stubborn and arrogant." Cut to the quick, she said proudly, "I'm a Nagi!"

"She's stubborn and arrogant. She ordered me to stop visiting her—I was born in this house!"

A wave of anger rushed over her. "I'll come with you straightaway," she said.

37.

Zahira married Muhammad Anwar, the caviar merchant. Raifa was furious and accused her of malice and treachery. The news took the alley by surprise. People talked of nothing else; words like good luck, destiny, the marvels of love, were bandied about. Zahira took Galal with her and Muhammad welcomed him, thinking himself the happiest of God's creatures.

For the first time Zahira was mistress in her own home, a richly furnished flat with many rooms, and a bathroom and a kitchen and a storage tank, which was replenished daily by the water carrier. She had dresses, rich wraps, gold-embroidered veils, necklaces, earrings, gold bangles, and silver anklets.

Her table was laden with delicious food, almost as good as the food served by Aziza and Raifa. She ran the household and was its cook at the same time.

Scarcely a month had gone by before she decided to break free and come out of seclusion, going to visit her mother or a neighbor or al-Husayn mosque. People saw her in her finery and muttered admiringly to themselves.

38.

Married to Zahira, Muhammad Anwar was happy beyond his wildest dreams. He made no secret of his love and passionate devotion, and indulged her without restraint. From the beginning he was uneasy at her going out and exposing her dazzling beauty to all and sundry. Very tactfully he let her know how he felt, but she was visibly irritated and he quickly backed down and went to even greater lengths to please her. He discovered he could put up with anything but seeing her angry or miserable. He knew he was weak where she was concerned, that he was flying in the face of traditional advice, but he submitted readily, not allowing himself even to contemplate resistance, and yet fully aware that he was at the mercy of love's whims and caprices.

A terrifying feeling haunted him, like a monster from a fairy tale, that he did not yet fully possess his darling and perhaps never would, that she would always elude his grasp. It was the sickly feeling of defeat. He invented excuses, sought comfort in his illusions, and smothered his bitterness with gifts and sweet words. He was love's slave, valued for what was in his hand rather than for his heart or his body. The red of sunset and the red of dawn were all the same to him, so he lost nothing by acting gentle and sweet to win a smile from the parted rosy lips, a glance from the dark eyes, a satisfied toss of the graceful head.

39.

One day Zahira visited her benefactress Aziza. "I was forced by circumstance to live in someone else's house, but my heart is loyal," she assured her, kissing her hand.

Aziza was gladdened by her words. She brushed her cheek with her lips, made her sit down beside her, and treated her as an

equal. A warm gust of happiness and pride filled her. They drank
cinnamon tea and ate almonds and slices of watermelon. Aziza
asked how she was, inquired about her husband and Galal. Then
Ulfat came to greet her.

"Your beauty has found its reward, and beauty is the key to
many different worlds," Aziza told her.

"No. It's your prayers and kindness, madame," answered
Zahira.

40.

"Won't you visit Raifa too?" was Muhammad Anwar's comment
when Zahira returned.

"That arrogant woman! To hell with her!" retorted Zahira,
almost choking with annoyance.

"She'll go crazy!"

"Let her."

"There's no telling what she'll do," he muttered anxiously.

"What kind of a man are you?" she teased with a mocking
glance from under lowered lids.

His heart sank and he was silent.

41.

That afternoon the alley witnessed an unforgettable scene.

Zahira was promenading along in her fine clothes when
Raifa's carriage stopped beside her. Raifa's head poked out and her
voice could be heard, reproachful, but with a touch of affection in
it: "Zahira!"

Zahira turned in confusion.

"Traitor!" said Raifa.

Zahira had no choice but to approach her, holding out her
hand, in full view of the numerous bystanders, including Gibril al-
Fas, Khalil al-Dahshan, and Abd Rabbihi the baker.

"When are you coming to visit me?" demanded Raifa.

"As soon as I can," answered Zahira, her confusion mounting.

"The only thing stopping me was . . ." She tailed off in embarrassment.

Suddenly hostile and aggressive, Raifa said, "I'd be happy to welcome my faithful servant."

At once Zahira's anger blazed. "I'm the same as you now!" she shouted.

She rushed off, blinded by emotion.

42.

Abd Rabbihi was getting drunk in the bar while the March winds raged outside.

"Yesterday I had a strange dream," he said.

Nobody asked him what he had dreamed, but he went on anyway. "I dreamed the khamsin winds blew at the wrong time of the year."

"A diabolical dream!" laughed Sanqar al-Shammam.

"Doors came off their hinges, dust fell like rain, hand barrows flew through the air, turbans and headcloths blew away."

"What happened to you?"

"I felt as if I was dancing on the back of a Thoroughbred stallion!"

"Tuck the cover tightly around your arse before you go to sleep!" advised Sanqar.

43.

Muhammad Anwar felt fear creeping over him. Dangerous ghosts danced in the corners of his constricted world. Was he going to suffer the same fate as the baker Abd Rabbihi? He began stealing glances at Zahira's face, gathering his resolve. At last he managed to speak. "You're four months pregnant, Zahira. It's better for you to stay indoors."

"I'm not helpless yet," she answered scornfully.

He turned to Galal and started playing with him to soften the impact of his words. "You've challenged a power that isn't to be trifled with. It would be prudent for us to lie low."

"It's as if you're scared," she said frostily.

"Not at all. I just want to safeguard our happiness," he said, trying to hide his irritation.

"I've got every right to go out."

"The truth is, I'm not happy about it."

"The truth is, I can't bear what you're trying to make me do."

"But I'm your husband."

"Does that mean you can trample me underfoot?"

"God forbid! But I have undeniable rights."

A scowl appeared on her face, clouding her beauty. "No," she said fiercely.

He hesitated, uncertain whether to persist or say nothing, but he felt her scorn and was provoked to repeat angrily, "I have my rights."

"Your rights are giving me a headache."

"You owe me obedience," he burst out with unaccustomed heat.

She stared at him in astonishment.

His fury mounted. "Complete obedience," he repeated.

Zahira's features set hard in an expression of refusal and the atmosphere was thoroughly spoiled.

44.

Muhammad Anwar drew courage from his despair. In his heart he was afraid of losing her, and so when he saw her emerging into the street from his shop, he abandoned his composure and rushed to block her path.

"Go back home," he said firmly.

"Don't cause a scandal," she whispered in astonishment.

"Go home," he repeated stubbornly.

She felt the eyes slithering toward her, snakelike, and was forced to go in, seething with rage.

45.

In the evening when he went home Muhammad Anwar was met
by a tempest. He had fully expected it. The last thing he wanted
was to continue being angry, to create a bad atmosphere, to see the
beauty he adored destroyed through hostility and resentment. He
showed a willingness to accept any compromises, provided Zahira
gave in to his single legitimate demand.

"Don't imagine that I enjoy humiliating you," he said to her.
"All I want is for us to be happy."

But she came at him like a dust storm, her face sickly yellow,
her expression transformed, and sparks flying from her eyes. Her
anger had materialized into black loathing, pride darted out at him
like a viper. "God protect me from the evil in your heart," he said
to himself. "Think what I've made of you! Doesn't that work in
my favor?"

46.

Zahira found herself in a hellish situation. She refused to accept
defeat. She would not forget the painful confrontation in the alley.
She didn't love him, had never loved him. But what could she do,
and where would she go? In a situation like hers the wife returned
to her family, but she had no family. She had a choice between
submitting and preserving her status or walking the streets. There
would be no shortage of people waiting to gloat, including Abd
Rabbihi in his basement.

She remembered her first benefactor, Master Aziz, a leading
notable and her husband's friend. At least her husband would
know that she was not entirely without family support.

She slipped out to the cereal merchant's. A fine rain fell on her
black wrap and her cheeks, prominent above the veil. She burst
into his office and found him alone. He had an attractive dignity
about him, as always. His mustache was prematurely gray. He
knew her at once, in spite of her veil. He had no need to remember

those fascinating eyes, looking at him from either side of the gold nosepiece of her veil. He felt that this was fate storming his defenses. He heard the sweet voice. "You're the only person I can turn to in my trouble."

"It's nothing serious, I hope?" he inquired, struggling to control his conflicting emotions.

"My husband."

"He's a good man, as far as I know."

"But he's started treating me much worse recently."

"For no reason?"

"He wants to control me." She told him the story of the incident in the alley. He looked thoughtful for a moment, then said, "He behaved rather foolishly, but there's no denying he's within his rights."

"There's not a woman in our alley who has to stay imprisoned in the house!" she declared fervently.

Master Aziz smiled. "I'll talk to him about you since you're a Nagi, but you'll have to agree to be sensible."

47.

Aziz' intervention achieved very little. She had no choice but to submit, even if it was only for a while, and grudgingly. However, the meeting with Aziz had revealed possibilities which had never crossed her mind before. Exciting, crazy, wonderful possibilities that plunged her into a world bursting with dreams. She said to herself that Aziz liked her. No, it was more than that. His eyes had acknowledged his fascination. When had this begun? Every man that saw her was fascinated by her, but Aziz was not like the rest! Furthermore, he was married and so was she, and he was also middle-aged and renowned for his high-mindedness and untarnished reputation. A man like him wouldn't look at a married woman, the wife of a friend. And she had no interest in an illicit relationship. What would be the point? She was bent on getting her due and in the process had suppressed her emotions mercilessly, although she had tasted a rush of sublime frenzy sometimes in a glass of blessed wine. Aziz Nagi had appeared to her in a rosy dreamlike glow: she had no idea how this could materialize in the real world. Could she, some magical day, become Ulfat's co-wife, and almost a daughter to Madame Aziza, preside over a magnificent house and have her own carriage with a tinkling bell?

Muhammad Anwar dwindled, until he turned into a smut blowing away down a road that stretched endlessly into the distance.

48.

When the peasant women arrived in town celebrating the flooding of the Nile and selling their dates, Zahira was giving birth to her second son, Radi, in considerable pain.

Muhammad Anwar's happiness distracted him from his other worries and he hoped the baby's birth would be the beginning of a new era of prudent, successful matrimony.

Umm Hishim, the midwife, tended Zahira each day until she had fully recovered. On her last visit she dropped her voice to a whisper and said, "I've got a message for you."

Zahira looked inquiringly at her.

"A letter from heaven!" announced the old woman.

The notion that it was from Aziz flashed through her mind. "Who's it from really, Umm Hashim?" she urged.

Umm Hashim's features wore the pale mask of sin. "Nuh al-Ghurab, our local chief," she said.

Zahira's heartbeat quickened in surprise. She had expected a comet from the east and one had come from the west instead. "Can't you see that I'm a wife and a mother?" she said crossly, regaining her composure.

"The sun rises and sets every day," declared the old woman. "Don't shoot the messenger."

49.

Muhammad Anwar soon relented. He forsook the hard character he had temporarily assumed and retreated into his natural state of weakness. He was finally convinced that Zahira was a jewel with-

out a heart who would slip through his fingers like the wind. Yet
he could not imagine life without her. She was its breath, its guid-
ing habit. She was also very dangerous, and there was not one part
of her that he trusted. How could he forget what had happened to
Abd Rabbihi the baker? The more his confidence was shaken, the
more he longed to cling to her and keep hold of her at any price. If
he failed in that it meant his whole life was a failure. In this world
and the next. The quarrel between her and Raifa would remain a
source of annoyance to him for all time. He was aware that he was
the most wretched of men and should be ready to make any sacrifice required of him.

They were sitting together in the evening as usual, Zahira
feeding Radi on the divan, Muhammad smoking a water pipe, and
Galal playing with the cat. He could no longer stand Galal. He had
always liked him and been kind to him in the past, but as soon as
Radi came along he began to hate him and wished he would cease
to exist. But he treated him the same as he always had done. He
was cheerful and fatherly, but it was false now, an added worry in
his catalogue of griefs.

He had decided to do the impossible to win her over. "I've got
a surprise for you," he announced.

She looked at him without interest.

"A peace offering."

She smiled, and he went on, "A formal contract making you
the owner of the house!"

She flushed. "What a generous man you are!" she exclaimed
in delight.

It was a three-storied house with a shop selling ful beans on
the ground floor.

Muhammad was glad at her obvious pleasure and felt somewhat reassured. She was genuinely grateful to him for making her
into a property owner, grateful too that he had implicitly acknowledged her strength and regretted provoking her. But she still despised him and thought constantly about Aziz and Nuh al-Ghurab.
Aziz was rich, Nuh powerful. Aziz had power too, while Nuh's
wealth was increasing all the time. Aziz had one wife and Nuh had
four, and a troop of children. You couldn't do without power or

money. One created the other. How would things turn out? She believed she had hardly started yet. Her mind wandered, envisaging the various scenarios as she lay next to Muhammad, listening to his regular breathing.

50.

Muhammad Anwar decided to safeguard his happiness through Nuh al-Ghurab. He paid him a formal visit at his house and sat before him in the guest hall like a boy in front of his schoolteacher. Without a word he handed him a promising bundle of notes. The chief took it and began counting it. "You've already paid your dues," he said, "so why this enormous sum?"

"I need your protection," said Muhammad.

"Do you have enemies?"

"It's just a preventive measure!"

Casually Nuh returned the money. He smiled. Muhammad's heart began to beat violently and his eyes widened in fear.

"Fate has beaten you to it," murmured Nuh.

He groaned inwardly. Raifa had played her cards well, or so he imagined, since it did not occur to him that Nuh was acting on his own account.

"I was about to send for you . . ." began Nuh.

"What's going on?" interrupted Muhammad, his mouth dry.

". . . to advise you to divorce your wife," finished Nuh, odiously calm.

His heart plunged in his chest and he felt the touch of death. "Divorce her?" he demanded in amazement. "There's no reason why I should."

"Divorce your wife," pronounced Nuh conclusively.

51.

Muhammad left Nuh's house robbed of his five senses. Was it his turn to be treated like Abd Rabbihi? Had a respectable merchant ever endured such treatment before? Were his life, his happiness, his honor, to be disregarded as if they were worth nothing?

A desperate anger seized him, blowing away his indecision, concentrating his thoughts. "I'll do what nobody around here's ever done before," he vowed, beside himself with rage.

52.

Gibril al-Fas, the alley's sheikh, approached Nuh at one of his regular sessions in the café. He greeted him. "The inspector wants to see you at the police station."

Nuh looked startled. "Why?" he demanded, frowning.

"I don't know. I'm just delivering the message."

"What if I refuse?" asked Nuh aggressively.

"Perhaps he wants to enlist your services in some matter of security," said the sheikh amicably. "You shouldn't be unnecessarily hostile."

The clan chief shrugged his shoulders scornfully and said nothing.

53.

The police inspector, Fuad Abd al-Tawwab, gave the clan chief a cordial reception. Nuh sat facing him across his desk, smiling as pleasantly as he could. The smell of leather filled his nostrils.

"I'm delighted to meet you, inspector," he said.

The inspector smiled. He was stout, of average height with a bushy mustache and handsome features.

"Delighted to meet you too. The clan chief is really one of us!"

"Thank you, inspector."

"The clan chief is the brave knight and protector of the alley, the embodiment of chivalry and honor, the hands and eyes of the police in his domain . . . that's how the Ministry of the Interior regards you."

"Thank you, inspector," repeated Nuh, his anxiety mounting.

With a firmness which belied his flattering comments, the police inspector went on, "Therefore, I expect Muhammad Anwar to be safe with you."

"Has he complained to you about me?" asked Nuh, flushing with anger.

"I have my ways of finding out what's going on. And suppose he did come to me for help? He's entitled to. And it's my duty to guarantee his safety, but I'm quite happy to let you do that for me!"

A silence descended between them. He recognized the threat in the inspector's friendly manner.

"What do you say?" asked the inspector after a long pause.

"We're the first to respect the law," answered Nuh, suspiciously calm.

"I consider you responsible for him."

54.

Nothing like this had ever happened in the alley. The police only came near it in extreme emergencies. The clan chief's numerous crimes were usually unattributed, thanks to the testimony of false witnesses. Was Inspector Fuad Abd al-Tawwab going to do what nobody had done before him if Muhammad Anwar's body was discovered on the path or under the archway? How had Muhammad had the insolence to go to the police for help, and why had the inspector been ready to challenge Nuh in this underhand way? It seemed that for the first time a police inspector was measuring himself up against a clan chief, and challenging his elaborately contrived prestige.

But there was an aspect which people were unaware of, and that was the personality of Fuad Abd al-Tawwab. He was a fearless, stubborn man. In the countryside of Upper Egypt, before his transfer to Cairo, he had been known as The Killer. Had he not been hindered by the interior ministry and its long established policy toward clan chiefs, he would have embarked on a bold initiative to wipe them out altogether.

So as soon as he heard that Muhammad felt threatened, he decided on a show of strength which shut people's mouths and made their hearts tremble violently. One morning the alley woke up to find itself invaded by a detachment of armed men with the

inspector at its head. Military orders rang out and people rushed to
look. Gibril al-Fas appeared, surrounded by police officers, then
came the officer in charge of the local station, the inspector in his
official uniform, and, bringing up the rear, a huge column of
soldiers bristling with arms. The procession moved forward slowly
and determinedly through the archway and into the monastery
square. There they performed some noisy maneuvers before returning slowly the way they had come. The street was lined with
people as if it was the day the pilgrims left for Mecca. The inspector showed no interest in them, but every now and then his eyes
strayed to the windows crowded with women's faces. A little way
from the fountain Sheikh Gibril went up to him and drew his
attention to Zahira, the focus of the quarrel, standing in her window.

Nuh al-Ghurab did not move from his customary seat in the
café, while Muhammad Anwar crouched petrified in his shop, fearing the worst. Abd Rabbihi followed the procession in astonishment, remarking to those around him, "The Day of Judgment's on
its way!"

55.

Zahira often noticed the inspector contriving to meet her apparently by chance on New Street, as she came back from al-Husayn
mosque. His eyes bored into her, fierce, defiant, hungry.

"Even the inspector," she murmured to herself.

The big square at the end of the alley mocked her, full of
temptations, like a magician's bag, writhing with cats and mice and
snakes. Her body swayed to the music of pride. It seemed to her
that she was astride an eagle that was beating its wings powerfully,
inspired by the spirit of creation. Aziz . . . Nuh al-Ghurab . . .
Fuad Abd al-Tawwab. Enchantment, love, the glorious summit
crowned with stars. Her heart pounded, strong and regular, and
with every beat a shining image formed, transcending anything she
had ever seen before.

56.

The inspector summoned Muhammad to a meeting in absolute secrecy. He sat him down and said, "I gave them a demonstration of the strong arm of the law like they've never seen before. Do you feel safer now?"

Muhammad shook his head uncertainly. "I don't know."

"You're right," said Fuad Abd al-Tawwab. "I feel the same. The truth is, I'm frightened for you."

"Life isn't worth a penny around here," said Muhammad apprehensively.

"You're right. Any miserable thug could come along and kill you. What good would it do you then if we crushed the chiefs and wiped out the whole clan system?"

"What good indeed!"

"Can I give you some advice, even if it sounds odd?" asked the inspector.

"What is it?"

"Divorce your wife."

"Is that really what you advise?" muttered Muhammad in amazement.

"I find it as distasteful as you do. But I fear for your life."

"I think I'm going crazy, inspector."

"It'd just be a temporary measure, to give me time to deal with the tyrant," said the inspector slyly.

"A temporary measure?"

"Then everything would return to normal."

"I'll give it serious thought," said Muhammad, after a long pause.

57.

He returned home confused and despairing. But from the depths of his despair inspiration came to him.

"Gather up anything valuable that's light enough to carry," he

said to Zahira. "We're going to run away tonight when everybody's
asleep."

"Run away!"

"Even the inspector advised me to divorce you."

"The inspector!"

"He admitted he was powerless to protect me. Our only hope
is to run away."

She guessed what was behind the police inspector's advice, but
could not think how to act toward her husband. "Where would we
go?" she asked in alarm.

"The world's a big place and I've got plenty of money. We'll
start a new business."

She swore to herself. He was about to scatter all her dreams in
one go. To make her a fugitive and bind her to him forever, compel
her to bury her newborn power, her new existence. Melt into the
darkness of hardship and misery like Samaha. Who could tell?
Maybe she would be forced to do manual work again like a beggar.
Let the coward run by himself, get out of her life forever!

"There's no time to lose."

"Why don't you think about it a bit more?"

"I've thought about it a hundred times, and there's nothing
else we can do."

"No!"

"What do you mean, no?"

"It's impossible."

"It's quite possible. As you'll find out before the sun rises."

"No!" she repeated obstinately.

He looked at her in astonishment.

"We'd be tramps. It would be the end of us," she said.

"I've got enough for us to live on," he said suspiciously.

"No."

"Don't you understand my life's in danger?"

"You did wrong and you know it."

"There was nothing else I could have done."

"Why should I suffer for it?"

"A wife has to go where her husband goes," he said, a frenzied note coming into his voice.

She appeared hard, antagonistic, ready to dodge out of his reach, full of hatred simmering just below the surface.

"You don't have the strength to protect me," she said.

"You snake!" he shouted, beating his chest with his fist.

She stepped back to the window instinctively.

"You want to play the same game you played with the baker!"

She read death in his pale, desperate face, his clenched fists, his taut muscles, and screamed through the window at the top of her voice as he sprang toward her like a tiger.

58.

The door was broken open. Nuh, Aziz, and Gibril rushed in. Muhammad retreated Zahira fell unconscious to the floor. The children's cries rose in the air.

The men busied themselves with reviving Zahira. Muhammad had vanished without trace. Nuh looked pointedly at Gibril.

"Attempted murder and evading arrest!" pronounced the sheikh in official tones.

"Let him go," muttered Aziz.

"What about the crime he's committed?" asked Nuh.

"It was as clear as day, and we're witnesses," said Gibril.

"You must spend the night with my mother," said Aziz, turning to Zahira.

59.

Muhammad Anwar had disappeared without divorcing her. She went back to her own flat the next day. At first she was drunk with the sense of freedom, but she quickly realized that she was still bound to her husband by the ties of marriage. She longed to break away. The breath of golden dreams swept over her. She was determined not to lose a moment of her life. She visited Aziz al-Nagi.

"He's taking his revenge on me by keeping me imprisoned from a distance," she complained.

Aziz realized what she meant and it was like sweet magic stirring in him. His head spun with delight and hope.

"How will you manage?" he asked.

"The income from the house will give me just enough to live on."

"You're not alone. I assure you of that."

She inclined her head gratefully. "Thank you. But I want to protect the children's future."

"What do you have in mind?" he asked, his heart pounding.

"I want to ask for a divorce on the grounds of attempted murder and desertion," she declared boldly.

So it was that the door of the unknown opened to him and his life was thrown into turmoil.

"We'll have to think about that," he said.

60.

Aziz made it his business to follow Muhammad Anwar's trial in absentia and engage a divorce lawyer for Zahira. He was still anxious, torn between his desire and his reputation, his emotions and his respect for Ulfat and his friend Muhammad. Meanwhile the events which heralded the unleashing of wild, heated passions were unfolding behind the scene.

61.

The first night visitor arrived. She opened the peephole in the door, saw a shape, and smelled a smell which aroused both yearning and disgust. "Who's that at this time of night?" she inquired suspiciously.

"Abd Rabbihi the baker," came the familiar voice.

Her insides moved with desire and anger at the same time. "What do you want?" she asked sharply, to hide her weakness.

"For us to try again," he begged drunkenly.

"You're drunk, and you're out of your mind."

"I'm your only real husband."

"Go away, or I'll shout for help."

She shut the little window, her chest heaving with anger and determination.

62.

That same night Gibril al-Fas slunk up to her door. He entered, cloaked in apprehension and fear. As soon as he sat down, he announced, "God protect me from the devil. I'm obliged to give you a message."

"What is it?" she asked, guessing the reply, and guessing also why he was so afraid.

"The inspector wants to marry you."

She was right. And he was frightened that Nuh al-Ghurab would suspect him of being the go-between. But what was the inspector? What would he give her except a new name and a new look, both meaningless? Aziz was probably the best of the three but Nuh was a force to be reckoned with. He had the real power and unlimited authority.

"What's your answer, Zahira?"

"Won't Nuh al-Ghurab have something to say?"

"The inspector'll take care of him!"

"I've got two children," she ventured slyly, "and a miserable income, and the inspector's married with children of his own."

"He knows what he can handle."

"And I know what I want," she declared after a moment's hesitation.

"So you'd rather be al-Ghurab's lover than the inspector's wife?"

"I'm the most respectable woman in the alley," she returned ferociously.

63.

Before Gibril was out of the way, Umm Hashim the midwife arrived. Zahira ushered her hurriedly into another room.

"There's nothing to stop us now!" exclaimed the old woman when they were alone.

"It has to be Nuh al-Ghurab. But he's got four wives already."

"You can replace one of them."

"Zahira doesn't share her husband with other women," she said with angry pride.

"You mean he should divorce all four?" asked Umm Hashim in astonishment.

"That's for him to decide," answered Zahira stubbornly.

64.

Nuh al-Ghurab divorced his four wives.

The neighborhood was convulsed by the news, the families of the four women were shattered, and Zahira's name was on everybody's lips, a byword for tyranny and heartlessness. The inspector bit his lip in rage. Aziz was amazed but kept his grief to himself.

By chance, news of Rummana's death in prison arrived on the day of the wedding, and Raifa was so distressed that she committed suicide hours afterward by setting herself alight.

Nuh al-Ghurab had a huge wedding procession which progressed through the surrounding quarters of the city, protected, so it was thought, by his alliances with neighboring chiefs. However, in Darasa the chief of the Atuf clan and his men attacked the cortege out of the blue, violating all pacts and treaties.

How this happened and why, nobody knew, but a bloody fight flared up, and the police quickly intervened, as if they had been waiting for just such an opportunity.

They broke up the disturbance without pity.

A bullet hit the bridegroom and he was killed instantly.

65.

The alley was set ablaze with news of the event and they gave their chief a grand funeral. Zahira was more frightened than sad, worried that this horrific event should be linked to her wedding, and sorry that she had only enjoyed her new position for a few hours. The envious—and there were many of them—pointed out that her marriage had coincided with the twin disasters of Rummana's death and Raifa's suicide, and decided she had the evil eye. Muhammad Anwar's disappearance, Nuh al-Ghurab's quadruple divorce, and his death were all connected directly with her. What other bad luck would this beautiful woman bring with her insatiable desires? This speculation depressed her, but she banished it from her mind with her iron will, and under her shell of mourning joyfully calculated the riches which would come to her. Her sense of shock quickly passed and she felt pleased with life again. She could enjoy the prestige associated with the clan without paying the price for it to a man for whom she felt no affection. She acknowledged gratefully to herself that he had been killed at the right moment, before he had violated the sanctity of her beautiful body. He had received the punishment a filthy despot like him deserved. Imagine the disgrace for the great al-Nagi if his beautiful descendant had submitted to a corrupt criminal in chief's garments. You could not blame a proud wind for uprooting a dead, worm-eaten tree.

66.

Word went around that Inspector Fuad Abd al-Tawwab was behind the carefully planned operation that ended in al-Ghurab's death, and that he had removed him, not in the interests of security but to get his hands on the chief's enchanting new wife, Zahira.

People's opinion of him worsened when he intervened in an unprecedented way to prevent a new clan chief being chosen. For the first time in its long history, the alley had no chief to control its day-to-day life, and the people felt more humiliated than they had ever done before.

The curious among them wondered when the inspector would come out from behind his mask and propose to Zahira.

67.

Sheikh Gibril asked to see her. She guessed why at once. She appeared lukewarm in the face of the inspector's approaches, for she was richer now than him and his whole police station. Aziz Samaha al-Nagi was a precious pearl, worthy to crown her dreams. His only fault was that he had inherited his ancestor's sense of

honor without his strength and daring. Ashur al-Nagi had married
the woman his sons were fighting over, but Aziz kept his love a
secret, withdrew into himself, avoided doing wrong, and grew
steadily older. Perhaps she could entice him and possess him, but
what would be the use when there was a stubborn, wicked man in
the offing who would have no scruples about dealing with Aziz
just as he had dealt with Nuh?

O radiant hope, mad breeze beyond the clouds!

68.

"Remember, I won't be a co-wife," she repeated to Gibril al-Fas.

"As everyone knows, the inspector's wife is old enough to be
his mother, but she's rich. Will you fill the gap?"

"Why do I have to?"

"It's one of the calamities of the age," said the sheikh apologetically.

She concealed her anger. Her imagination worked frenetically
and her resolve hardened.

"Let him wait till the mourning period is over, then I'll marry
him," she said, pretending to give in.

The sheikh beamed. "Thank God," he murmured.

69.

She set to work immediately, bursting into Aziz's office like a
breeze, drunk on dew and perfume. Her appearance was elegant,
yet sad, and she looked at him beseechingly, captivatingly. She
noticed his flushed cheeks, his unsteady eyes, his agitation, and said
softly, pleadingly, "What choice did I have? I've no one but you to
turn to when I'm in trouble."

Everything but his tongue was confessing his love.

"Welcome, Zahira."

Delighted by his good manners, she asked, "What shall I do?
Hand myself over to The Killer?"

"Has he asked for your hand?" asked Aziz in horror.

"With no inhibitions."

He frowned.

"What a way to end up for a poor woman who's never ever had the freedom to choose her partner in life," she said.

"Don't agree to something you'd hate," he said with obvious emotion.

"To tell you the truth, I'm frightened of him."

"You mustn't be," he said fiercely.

"Everyone knows he's bad. He was the one who killed Nuh al-Ghurab."

"One criminal killing another!"

"Yes," she agreed placidly. "If the Interior Ministry questioned the Atuf clan, they'd get at the truth."

She paused and looked into his face, then went on, "It needs somebody who commands respect, who'll be listened to by the Interior Ministry."

The summer clouds passed to reveal the sun's face.

70.

Inspector Fuad Abd al-Tawwab was ordered abruptly back to Upper Egypt. The sky cleared, storms no longer threatened, and summer came to stay, bedecked with melons and grapes. Samaka al-Allaj became clan chief. Zahira, drunk with pride, was convinced she was the real chief, the instigator of events.

"I am intelligence, will, beauty, achievement," she told herself.

Then, looking fondly at Galal and Radi, she whispered, "May you be more glorious than them all!"

71.

She visited Aziz without delay to thank him for what he had done.

"If only there were more men like you," she declared, clearly relieved.

The man smiled, enraptured. "I'm glad to see you happy," he murmured.

"I've been saved from the plague, like our ancestor," she remarked playfully. Then she added sadly, "I don't know about happy . . ."

He looked at her curiously, and she went on, "What is this happiness we think we deserve?"

"Perhaps we know it instinctively."

"How could a woman in my position ever be described as happy?"

"You have everything you want," he said, hiding his confusion.

She rose to her feet gracefully, and looked steadily at him until his resolve almost collapsed. "I'm lacking the most important thing in human life," she said as she went away.

72.

Aziz submitted to his fate, acknowledging his weakness with extraordinary strength, like the old wall or the monastery gate, or like his ancestor one evening in the bar. What curious madness can strike a man in middle age! He stole a glance at his mother, Aziza.

"Mother," he murmured finally.

She sensed an alien quality in the atmosphere. "Say what's on your mind."

"It's God's will that I should marry again," he said, trying to sound calm.

Aziza was amazed. She stared at him. "Really?"

"Yes."

"Who is it?"

"Zahira," he replied after a moment's hesitation.

"No!" protested Aziza.

"It's the truth."

"The snake!"

"Mother, don't judge her too hastily," he implored.

"The snake!"

"You always loved her, mother."

"So did Ulfat. But she turned out to be poisonous."

"She's had a hard time."

"Another Raifa," murmured Aziza with a sad smile.

"Don't go by appearances."

"You're so sensible. How did she manage to charm you?"

"I know exactly what I'm doing."

His mother sighed. "And what about Ulfat, your proper wife?" she asked.

"She'll continue to be the lady of the house and the children's mother," he said firmly.

"Tell me, do you still respect your mother?"

"Absolutely, mother."

"Then give up this idea."

"I can't."

"She's bewitched you, son."

"You should be happy because I'm happy."

"Have you forgotten what happened to Abd Rabbihi or Muhammad Anwar or Nuh al Ghurab?"

"They all oppressed her," he said irritably.

"She's the oppressor. You're storing up trouble for yourself."

"It's good intentions that count," he murmured in a conciliatory tone.

"That low-class creature," sniffed Aziza spitefully.

"We're from the same line, mother," protested Aziz.

"You can be proud of what's good in your line, but not the violence. What about Rummana who killed your father? Or Wahid?"

"What must be . . . ," he said tranquilly.

73.

Zahira married Aziz al-Nagi. Madame Aziza boycotted the celebrations, did not acknowledge the marriage, and lived in her apartments with Ulfat and the children, in a permanent sulk. Aziz bought Nuh al-Ghurab's house for Zahira, changed the furniture, carpets, and ornaments, and turned it into a glorious love nest. He respected all Ulfat's rights, heaping care and affection on her and the children. But only now, in late middle age, had he found true love.

74.

Zahira enjoyed an exquisite, unreal feeling like a glow of inspiration: it was the majesty of achievement, the splendor of a dream fulfilled. A big house, wealth, prestige, a leading notable for a husband. She did not mind about Aziza's anger or Ulfat's sadness, and if there were people who looked down on her, she could be more arrogant than anyone and with more justification, thanks to her God-given beauty and intelligence. She believed she was the clan chief in a woman's skin and that the blessed life was only for the strong. For the first time she found herself with a husband she respected, admired, and did not want to leave. She still suppressed all feelings of love in the interests of something greater and more glorious. "I'm not weak like other women," she would remind herself frequently.

She took full advantage of her status: a little before sunset she would sit Galal and Radi in front of her in the carriage, and drive down the street at a leisurely pace, the silver bells ringing gaily, proud as a queen, her eyes flashing behind her light silk veil. People would stare at her in a mixture of admiration, envy, and astonishment. She savored the beauty of each moment with all her being, inspired by a heavenly draft which swept her along on wings of delight, transforming the world into a diamond whose many facets reflected back at her an image of her irresistible beauty.

She would drive to al-Husayn, rejoice as the beggars crowded around her, and grandly distribute alms and gifts.

75.

She gave Aziz a son, Shams al-Din, and the world looked even more beautiful. As she blossomed and her beauty shone brighter than ever, Aziz declined into a premature old age. To her own family she was generous beyond all expectations, and her mother and sisters lived a life of ease. One question troubled her constantly: what did she have to do to make her story unique, different from that of any woman before her?

76.

One day she left the mosque as usual in a crowd of beggars and madmen. She sat Galal and Radi on their seats and was about to climb aboard when a voice at her elbow whispered, "Zahira."

She turned and saw Muhammad Anwar looking at her with a face of death. In a panic, she tried to haul herself into the carriage, but the man raised his heavy stick and brought it down with all his force on her noble, beautiful head. She collapsed on the ground, crying out in pain. He hit her savagely, indifferent to the children's screams, until her head was smashed to a pulp.

All that remained of that magnificent, brilliant face was a web of shattered bones submerged in a pool of blood.

King Galal

The seventh tale in the epic
of the harafish

1.

Zahira's death dealt Aziz a cruel blow, for which there was no
cure. At her funeral he appeared bereft of all hope, a ghost banished from the body of life. His pain was only equaled by his public
self-control. The world was a vicious, cunning old woman with
endless cruel tricks up her sleeve, and he began to mistrust and
loathe all her beguiling promises.

His mother came to visit him. He received her unenthusiastically, hiding his resentment. She wept and clasped him to her
breast.

"We mustn't quarrel. We should face the blows of fate together," she whispered in his ear. Then she kissed his forehead and
continued with a sigh, "It's as if I was only created for sorrow and
grief."

Her words of comfort glided over his heart, leaving no trace.

2.

A few months after Zahira's death Aziz became ill and was left
half-paralyzed. He died a few weeks later. Aziza was devastated. It

had never occurred to her that she would bury her illustrious son
and live on after him. Her sadness returned, even worse than it had
been when she lost Qurra. It was as if she was some awesome
creature whose true glory was revealed only in the vast expanses of
a great sorrow. The beautiful, respected Aziza who had stubbornly
insisted on carving out her own path in life had, it seemed, sowed
patience only to harvest pain.

In accordance with Aziz' wishes, she took Radi and Shams al-
Din into her house. Although she looked after Shams al-Din as
well as she could, he died when he was eight months old, and then
Abd Rabbihi took Galal.

3.

The alley was shaken by Zahira's death, by the struggle of luck
against fate. They went over the events tirelessly, trying to learn
from them. Why do people laugh, dance in triumph, feel recklessly
secure in positions of power? Why do they not remember their true
place in the scheme of things, and their inevitable end? The inhabitants of the alley felt some sorrow, but this was quickly submerged
in a flood of anger and resentment. They cursed volubly and declared that the oppressors had got their just deserts. No one respected the noble Aziz' grief: he was accused of snatching Zahira
away from Abd Rabbihi. At his death he was not lamented as he
deserved to be. The harafish said that the Nagi family had become
like actors in a tragedy—a warning and deterrent to others—as a
punishment for their betrayal of their mighty ancestor, the blessed
miracle worker.

All at once the late spring weather changed. The sky clouded
over and a strange rain fell, followed by a wave of bitter cold.
People were disconcerted. Their hearts stirred fearfully. "May this
be a good omen, Lord!" they murmured uncertainly.

4.

No child seemed marked out for trials and sufferings like Galal,
the son of Zahira and Abd Rabbihi. The sight of his beautiful

mother's shattered head was imprinted deep in his soul, a permanent nightmare, tormenting his waking hours and troubling his dreams. How could such cruelty exist, such magnificent beauty meet such a horrific end? Why was his mother silent, gone forever? What had he done to be robbed of her beauty and affection, the splendor of the life which sprang from her? Why couldn't time go backward? Why did people lose what they loved and have to endure things they hated? Why were events governed by such harsh laws? Why had he been moved from luxury to Abd Rabbihi's squalid dwelling? Who was Abd Rabbihi anyway? Why was he supposed to call him father? His mother was his only parent: she'd given birth to him and raised him, and he didn't love anyone else. She was his soul and his lifeblood. Her image was stamped on his face, her voice sang in his ears, and the hope of getting her back one day lived in his heart.

The shattered bones drowning in a pool of blood would never be forgotten.

5.

Abd Rabbihi's world had also changed. Thanks to Galal's inherited wealth, he was able to move from the basement room to a respectable flat. He bought the baker's oven from its owner in his son's name and began running the business himself, incompetently, due to his addiction to alcohol. He took to wearing a white gallabiyya and a brightly colored cloak, with a brocade headcloth, and for the first time in his life his rough feet were hidden from view in red slippers with turned-up toes.

"You might as well benefit from Zahira's status now," he told himself with a shudder, half morbid, half defiant.

Nobody was prepared to speak out and accuse him of wasting Galal's money and despite the wine and the grief he was attached to the little boy. He gazed dumbfounded at Zahira's beauty emblazoned on his features, reminding him simultaneously of his happiest and most wretched times. He spared no effort to be friendly to him, reassure him, and win his affection. Such a handsome, prickly little boy!

6.

Galal woke up crying one morning a little before dawn and the sound roused his drunken father. Anxiously he stroked the boy's smooth black hair. "Did you have a bad dream?" he asked.

"When's my mother coming back?" sobbed the boy.

He felt a sharp burst of annoyance despite his befuddled state. "After a long, long time you'll go and join her," he answered curtly, "but I shouldn't be in too much of a hurry."

7.

Zahira's story came up one evening in the bar.

"That's the first time a woman's been the cause of a clan chief's death," observed Samaka al-Allaj, the new chief.

"She paid for it," said Abd Rabbihi, trying to sound manly.

"Don't pretend you're cured of your love," said Gibril al-Fas.

"I'm just afraid her murder will atone for the evil she did, and she'll go to heaven," retorted Abd Rabbihi aggressively.

"You want her to go to hell, so you can be sure of meeting her again," teased the bar owner, Sanqar al-Shammam.

Abd Rabbihi groaned, abandoning his front. "It's such a pity! Is all that beauty really feeding the worms?"

He paused, then said gruffly, "She practically worshiped me. But she was off her head!"

He began to sing in a voice like a donkey braying.

> *Hey you with the fancy cap*
> *Tell me who made it*
> *My heart's ensnared*
> *May yours be too.*

8.

Galal went to the Quran school, a pleasant, intelligent boy, extremely lively and strongly built. One day he was taught the verse, "Every soul will taste death."

"Why do people die?" he asked.

"It's the will of God, Creator of all things," answered the sheikh.

"But why?" persisted Galal.

The sheikh grew angry. He tied him down by his feet and flogged him. The boy shouted and cried. His rage stayed with him all day long. None of this would have happened if his mother had still been alive and the world aglow with her presence.

9.

In school and out in the alley Galal was the victim of vicious attacks. The boys insulted him. "Zahira's son!" they would jeer. Always that name. Is it a swear word, you bastards? They pelted him with fragments of her life history which he had never heard: cheat, two-timer, husband collector, tyrant, servant, social climber.

He rushed off to his father. "Why do they insult my mother?" he demanded.

"She was an angel," he said, gently consoling. "If you don't react, they'll soon stop."

A vengeful frown transformed his handsome face. "Don't react?" he protested.

His father gave him an uneasy look.

10.

His mother's story filtered through to him, a word here and a word there. He refused to believe what he heard. On the occasions when he was forced to believe, he refused to see anything shameful in his mother's actions. She would always be an angel, whatever she did.

What was wrong with someone reaching for the skies? But such logic had no effect on the hooligans in the alley.

As a result, Galal was forced into one fight after another. He would have preferred things to be different. He had an affectionate nature and tried to be on good terms with everybody. The other boys despised this outlook and picked quarrels, so he grew hard in the face of their provocation, stood up to impossible challenges, and cultivated harsh defenses which were alien to his nature. He responded to a word with a blow, became involved in more and more punch-ups, and was always certain to win. He was transformed and became known as a devil. Power raised him up and silenced his adversaries, so he grew drunk on it and worshiped it.

11.

At Quran school he met up again with his brother Radi. He was the murderer's son, but also his victim, a gentle, polite, weak child. The other boys taunted him and called him "Zahira's son" too, and he burst into tears. Galal sprang to his defense and dealt with his tormentors. The boy grew fond of him.

"You're my brother and I'm proud of you," he announced. Radi did not have Galal's strength and beauty, but he had good manners.

"I want you to come to lunch with me," he said one day.

12.

That was how Galal found himself visiting the house of the late lamented Aziz. Madame Aziza, old and patrician, was there, and Ulfat. He kissed their hands, and they greeted him cordially, marveling at his health and good looks. Aziz' youngest daughter, Qamr, was there too. She was beautiful and vivacious and he watched her enraptured throughout the meal and afterward. When he was alone with Radi he asked, "Don't you think Qamr is as beautiful as our mother?"

Radi shook his head uninterestedly and Galal said, "You're lucky to live in the same house as her."

"The only thing I like about her is her voice," replied Radi.

13.

Galal approached puberty. He had discovered all aspects of his background, good and bad. He persisted in believing that his mother was the greatest woman the alley had known, and that he was a descendant of the famous al-Nagi whose disappearance remained a mystery to that day. He had not been a clan chief like Samaka al-Allaj, but a saint, a friend of the great Saint al-Khidr. In his dreams, Galal battered heads full of evil obsessions, befriended angels with golden wings, knocked at the monastery gate and was welcomed inside; anxiety stalked him wrapped in the shadows of night, and Qamr beckoned to him from behind the carved wooden lattice.

"What did my mother do wrong?" he asked himself confidently. "She was looking for a man like me, but she had no luck in her short, miserable life."

14.

Abd Rabbihi made him a partner in the bakery and he proved his worth, with his intelligence and enthusiasm. His father was so pleased with him that he gradually handed over all responsibility to him, abandoning himself to the calabash in Sanqar's bar. He went downhill rapidly, the huge sums of money he spent accelerating his decline. He observed his son with pride and admiration, as he dominated the bakery workers through the strength of his personality, earning their respect in spite of his mother's bad reputation. He watched his muscles hardening, his limbs growing strong, his frame filling out, until his whole body exuded vitality and his face glowed with extraordinary beauty.

The bakery was all that Galal had left, and painful memories of the past. He was not deceived by ingratiating smiles, knowing

for sure that there were malicious whispers about his beautiful
mother jostling angrily behind them. But the future augured well
for someone so handsome and strong, and Qamr's image inspired
the sweetest hopes.

15.

After work he would sit in front of the bakery watching the cockfighting, betting on his own bird. This was his favorite pastime.
Occasionally he cast passionate glances at Qamr as she went by in
the carriage with Ulfat, and remembered his childhood and going
to play at Madame Aziza's with Radi and Qamr. Happy times that
ended abruptly when he sensed that Aziza and Ulfat would rather
he stayed away. Why did they make this distinction between him
and Radi, both of them Zahira's sons? No doubt out of respect for
Aziz' last wishes, but also because he developed such a marked
resemblance to his mother and reminded the two women of someone they loathed and would prefer to forget.

From then on a huge gulf stood between the baker with a bad
reputation and Aziz' radiant, well-bred daughter. But he still loved
her with a love that dominated his reason and his senses, and found
a response in her glowing eyes. Was he going to be afraid, like
cowards were, when good luck came his way?

16.

He soon realized that his father had squandered his inheritance,
and he was bitterly angry. He forbade him to have anything to do
with the business.

"I'll make sure you have enough to live decently," he assured
him.

But his father was an endless source of annoyance. His addiction to alcohol was ruining his health and dignity. He spent every
evening in the bar, amusing himself by broadcasting complaints
about his son.

"He treats me as if I was the son and he was the father," he said. "He blames me for everything."

Or, chuckling, he would ask, "Have you ever heard of a son telling his father off for having a few too many?"

He talked affectionately, without malice.

"Has he forgotten our Lord's commandment about honoring your parents?"

Galal failed to make a respectable man out of his father, something he had wanted to do out of love for him, but also to remove one of the obstacles standing in the way of his love for Qamr. Abd Rabbihi was sorry he had unintentionally caused offense to his handsome son.

"It's your mother's fault," he said apologetically one day. "Look what became of the other men who loved her."

Galal frowned protestingly but Abd Rabbihi went on, "Muhammad Anwar was hung, Nuh al-Ghurab murdered, the inspector banished. Aziz died of grief. I'm the luckiest of the lot."

"Don't speak badly of my mother," implored Galal.

"Don't get upset," murmured Abd Rabbihi. "But think about it. You want to marry Qamr. I'm not the problem, son. It's your mother. How do you think Ulfat could give her daughter to Zahira's son?"

"Don't rub salt into the wound!" cried Galal.

"I advise you not to marry a woman you love," said his father sympathetically. "And not to love the one you marry. Be content with companionship and affection, and steer clear of love. It's a trap."

17.

One night Galal learned that his father was causing a commotion in the monastery square. He rushed there at once and found him imitating the anthems in an atrocious voice. He took his arm and led him home.

"That's the one thing the alley won't put up with," he said.

When his father was asleep, Galal felt a fierce desire to return

to the square. He had never been alone at the monastery gate
before. The night was pitch-black. The stars were hidden by thick
wintry clouds and it was bitingly cold. He drew his cloak tightly
around him and pulled his headcloth over his face. The anthems
washed over him in warm, slow waves. He thought about the
Nagis who had frequented the place, since the first one who had
vanished mysteriously into thin air. A voice whispered to him that
men only gain distinction by challenging difficulties and he felt his
limbs bursting with inspiration at the thought of human beings and
their achievements. He made a pact of friendship with the darkness, the chanting voices, the cold, the whole world, resolving to
soar above the obstacles like a mythical bird.

18.

Radi bought the cereal business with the money he had inherited
from his mother and married Naima, Nuh al-Ghurab's granddaughter. Encouraged, Galal approached Madame Aziza.

"Noble lady, I want to marry your granddaughter," he said
determinedly.

Her tired eyes regarded him at length, then she said with the
frankness of old people, "I once suggested that Radi should marry
her, but Ulfat refused."

"It's Galal asking to marry her this time," he said with confidence.

"Don't you know why she refused?"

He was silent, scowling, and she went on with the same bla-
tant frankness, "Even though Radi's a better bet!"

"I'm not a pauper," he said angrily, "and what's more, I'm a
Nagi."

"I've told you what I know," she said irritably.

"Tell her mother that I asked," he persisted stubbornly.

"That's for you to do."

He left, his disappointment choking him like a mouthful of
earth.

19.

But there was a surprise awaiting the late Aziz' household: Ulfat refused Galal's request, whereupon Qamr hid herself away as if she was ill.

"Do you want to marry him?" asked Madame Aziza.

"Yes."

"He's Zahira's son!" shouted Ulfat, flying into a rage.

Qamr shrugged her shoulders indifferently. However, her mother ignored her wishes with cruel obstinacy and accepted a suitor for Qamr from her own family, the Dahshuris. Qamr refused him without a moment's hesitation.

Ulfat heaped blame and recriminations upon her daughter but she replied obstinately, "I won't get married at all."

"You've got the spirit of that devil Zahira in you!" shouted Ulfat.

Qamr wept, but Ulfat showed no signs of softening and said, "Don't get married then. That's the best solution as far as I'm concerned!"

20.

Madame Aziza's health declined suddenly due to sadness and old age. She withered away, her color faded, and she was soon paralyzed and confined to bed. Ulfat did not leave her side. She was alarmed at the loneliness threatening her in the big house.

"Don't be afraid," Aziza said. "God will grant me a cure."

She believed her as she always had done, but then her mother-in-law muttered as if she was a completely different person, "This is the end, Ulfat."

Her sight grew weaker until she could no longer see. All the same she stared into the void and called out for Qurra and Aziz. Ulfat shuddered and felt that death had stormed into the bedchamber and was waiting ready in a corner, the most powerful presence there.

"God have mercy on us," she muttered tearfully.

"How I've suffered," moaned Aziza. "The Almighty is my last hope."

"O God! Spare her too much suffering!"

"I have two requests," began Aziza.

Ulfat stared attentively at her and the old woman went on, "Don't be cruel to Qurra's granddaughter."

She paused and sighed deeply, then finished, "Or to Aziz' daughter."

Then death came and her soul departed, crowned with love and nobility.

21.

Six months of the year of mourning went by. Ulfat wished the year would never end, but she respected Aziza's dying wish. She allowed herself to entertain the vague hope that Qamr would change of her own accord, but this hope came to nothing.

Radi summoned his brother Galal. "Congratulations. You've been accepted," he said.

A tide of heavenly joy swept through him, leaving him speechless.

Radi suggested that the engagement should be announced immediately but the wedding delayed till after the mourning period.

This moment would remain embedded in Galal's memory forever.

22.

Scarcely two months later, Galal begged that the marriage should be allowed to take place, and the contract signed, promising that he and Qamr would delay the celebration and not live together as man and wife until the year's mourning was up. It was as if he wanted to have control of his peace of mind, stamp out his forebodings, and forestall any untoward twists of fate. He became the very picture of happiness and his praiseworthy characteristics developed to the full. He no longer called his drunkard of a father to account. He spoiled his employees and their families and hummed to himself while he was working or watching the cockfighting. He blossomed and grew immensely strong, and stayed up at night in the monastery square, listening to the singing and praying his own prayers.

Nearly every day he visited his bride and took her presents. From her he received a rosary of cornelians set on a gold chain, sweetly scented. She became his life, his hope, his happiness, his golden dream. To him she was the most beautiful creature on God's earth, although many thought him more striking. But in her there was an incomparable sweetness.

Madame Ulfat stopped being so unenthusiastic and expressed some satisfaction and friendliness. She called him her good son and began drawing a new picture of the future, suggesting that he used Qamr's money to go into partnership with Radi in the cereal business.

"The Nagi family's greatness has come out in many ways. This time it's love," said Galal to Qamr one day.

She smiled coquettishly. "Love makes miracles happen."

"Don't forget my part in making this miracle happen!"

He held her close, beside himself with passion.

23.

He brought his father to visit Madame Ulfat and Qamr. He was sober, but he seemed drunk, his eyes heavy and unfocused, his voice unsteady, his head shaking. He realized he had to act the part of a respectable citizen, a role which was quite alien to him. He looked at Madame Ulfat in awe and felt as if he was undergoing a metamorphosis, amazed that once upon a time he had possessed beauty that made all this look paltry.

"You know what I am, madame," he began, "but my son's a jewel."

"You're a good man," she murmured graciously.

Such respect had never come his way before, and it shook him.

"He deserves to be happy," he said, indicating Galal, "as a reward for all his kindness to his father."

He laughed loudly, for no reason, then regained his composure, embarrassed.

"Why didn't you give the bride her present?" Galal asked his father as they left the house.

He thought of the present Galal had given him to give the bride, and said nothing.

"Did you forget?" persisted Galal, annoyed.

"I needed that jewelry much more than your bride," he said gently.

"Have I ever failed to give you what you needed?" demanded Galal reprovingly.

His father patted him on the back. "Never. But life makes a lot of demands on us."

24.

The year of mourning ended in a fair autumn of surpassing sweetness. The gauzy clouds were puffed up with dreams. Qamr caught a cold but carried on with her energetic preparations for the wedding. The cold took an unexpected turn. Her temperature rose, she had difficulty breathing, she was in greater pain. The blooming rose withered as if a vicious pest had mounted a cunning, treacherous attack. She had no strength to get out of bed. The light died in her eyes, her face grew waxen, and her voice weak. She lay there moaning, hidden by piles of covers, fed on lemon and caraway tisanes, vinegar compresses on her forehead. Ulfat lay awake at night, her head twitching with uneasy thoughts. Galal was anxious, tired of waiting for the illness to pass.

A strange feeling hung over the house, of something waiting, never quite ready to reveal itself. Memories of the last moments of Aziz and Aziza floated in Ulfat's mind. Almost frantic, she felt that an unknown creature had taken up residence in a hidden corner of the house with no intention of leaving.

One night Galal dreamed that his father was singing in his mocking, uneducated fashion in the monastery square. He woke up with a heavy heart, then noticed a noise in the street. A singular

kind of noise, unconnected to the chanting in the monastery. A
clamor in the depths of the night, announcing the ascent of a soul
to its final resting place.

25.

Galal felt that some monster had taken over his body. He possessed
other senses and saw an unfamiliar world. His mind worked according to new laws. The blinding reality revealed itself to him. He
gazed at her body prepared for burial. He pulled back the cover
from her face. It was like a memory, not reality. It existed and did
not exist. Still and remote, separated from him by an unbridgeable
gap. Quite unfamiliar, coldly denying all knowledge of him. It was
on a loftier plane, inaccessible to human understanding, submerged
in the unknown. Unfathomable, mysterious, already moving away
on a journey of its own. Treacherous, mocking, cruel, suffering,
disconcerting, intimidating, infinite, alone.

"No," he murmured, shocked, resisting.

A hand replaced the cover and closed the door of eternity.
The world collapsed around him. A voice was mocking him. An
enemy moving in to fight him. He would not cry out. He did not
shed a tear, say a word. His tongue moved again. "No."

He saw his mother's shattered head, a vision that came and
went, then remained imprinted on the fringes of his consciousness.
He saw the cock gouging out its adversary's eyes with its pink
beak; the skies alight with the fires of damnation; the blessing of
red blood. The unknown promised him he would understand everything if he pulled the cover back once more. He stretched out
his hand, but a hand grasped it and a voice intoned, "There is no
god but God."

Lord, was there someone with him? Were there other people
in the world? Then who said the world was empty? Empty of
movement and color and sound. Empty of reality. Of grief, sorrow,
and regret. In fact, he was liberated. No love, no sadness. He could
never suffer again. Peace had come. His insolent powers had had a
cruel friendship imposed upon them. A salutary gift for one who

wanted the stars as friends, the clouds as soul mates, the wind as drinking companion, the night as comrade.

"No," he murmured for the third time.

26.

Galal left the work to his manager. He found peace in walking. He strolled through the alley, the quarter, around the gates in the city walls and the citadels, or sat alone in the café, smoking a water pipe.

At night he stood looking at the monastery. The melodies floated past him. He knocked contemptuously at the door, not expecting a reply. He knew they never replied. They were death everlasting, which never stooped to reply.

"Don't they know about being good neighbors?" he wondered.

He listened to the chanting. The sound streamed sweetly through the air:

> *Sobh dam murghe chaman ba gole no khaste goft*
> *Naz kam kon kah dar in baghbi chun tu shekoft.*

27.

One day Khalil al-Dahshan, imam of the alley's small mosque, hailed him with a benign smile. "There's no harm in exchanging a few words."

Galal looked at him coldly.

"God only tests his faithful servants," the sheikh went on consolingly.

"Tell me something I don't know," retorted Galal disdainfully. "That's what the cock shouts every morning."

"We all have to die like our fathers before us," the man said.

"No one dies," declared Galal with conviction.

28.

He was walking past the bar late one night when he saw a figure staggering out. He recognized his father, and took him by the arm.

"Who's that?" demanded Abd Rabbihi.

"It's Galal, father."

"Son—I'm ashamed," said the drunk man after a brief silence.

"What of?"

"I deserve to go more than she did."

"Why?"

"Justice would have been done."

"There's only one thing that's real, father," said Galal scornfully, "and that's death."

"I know I shouldn't be drinking at this time," said Abd Rabbihi apologetically, "but I can't help it."

"Enjoy your life, father," said Galal, holding him up.

29.

Autumn passed and winter arrived, triumphant and cruel. Cold winds buffeted the walls and stung people to the bone. Galal watched the dark clouds and longed for the impossible. Once he caught sight of Madame Ulfat emerging from the graveyard. He felt a profound hatred for her, and in his imagination he spat on her swollen form. She had accepted him grudgingly, got rid of him thanks to death. For her death was a cluster of rites, and special pastries for the wake. All of them sanctified death, worshiped it, encouraged it until it became an eternal truth. She had certainly been enraged when Qamr had left him money. That was why he had taken it all, then distributed it secretly to the poor. He told himself it would be a nice token of his recovery if he were to smash the arrogant old woman's skull.

30.

"You're always coming and going, Galal," called Sheikh Gibril al-Fas to him as he passed him in the street. "What are you looking for?"

"Something I can't find, and I find what I'm not looking for," replied Galal disparagingly.

31.

One night he sat up alone in the monastery square, not seeking benediction, but defying the dark and cold. Here was where Ashur had found solitude. Here was a void. He told himself he was no longer in love. No grieving over a lost love. I don't love. I hate. Hate, and only hate. I hate Qamr. That's the truth.

She's pain, madness, disillusion. If she'd lived she would have become just like her mother, ruled by empty values, laughing with inane companions, imitating princes. Now she's just a handful of dust. What does she look like in her grave? An empty bag of skin exhaling foul gases, floating in poisonous liquids where the worms dance. Don't grieve over a creature so quickly destroyed. She broke her promise. Didn't respect love. Or hang on to life. She welcomed death with open arms. We live and die by our strength of will. There's nothing more revolting than a victim. People who invite defeat. Cry out that death is the end of life. The ultimate truth. This outlook is the product of their weakness and their illusions. We are immortal. We only die as a result of betrayal or weakness. Ashur is alive. He worried about people confronting his immortality, so he disappeared. I am immortal. I've found what I was looking for. The dervishes only keep their doors closed because they're immortal. Has anyone seen them holding a funeral? They're immortal. They sing about eternity, but nobody understands them.

He was drunk on the frosty night air.

He went off toward the archway. "Oh, Qamr," he murmured.

32.

His frenzied thoughts took on the form of a hovering eagle, with a harsh cry that flattened buildings.

"When are you going to pay protection money to Samaka al-Allaj?" his father asked him one morning, yawning noisily.

"That's for weaklings and cowards," he answered brazenly.

His father stared at him in horror. "You'd defy the clan chief?" he demanded.

"I am the clan chief, father," said Galal coldly.

33.

He walked deliberately past the café when the chief was holding court as usual. The reaction was not slow in coming. The waiter hurried up to him. "The chief asks after your health."

Loudly and clearly, Galal answered, "Tell him it's fine and can stand up to imbeciles."

The answer burned the chief like a tongue of flame. Immediately Khartusha—the only one of his men who happened to be there with him—rushed toward Galal. Quick as lightning, Galal seized a chair and brought it squarely down on his head. He crashed over onto his back, unconscious. Then Galal brandished his club, and stood waiting for Samaka, who was descending on him like a wild beast. Spectators streamed in from all around and the chief's men gathered behind their chief. The two men began to exchange blows, but it was all over in seconds. Galal's strength was phenomenal. Samaka sunk to the ground like a slaughtered bull.

34.

Galal stood, his giant form bathed in a glow of defiance and anger. Fear invaded the hearts of Samaka's men, for the only one fit to take over from Samaka was Khartusha, who lay prone beside him. Some of the men, who secretly hated the hard core of the gang, began hurling bricks at them, showing their support for Galal. Victory went to the one who deserved it.

Galal Abd Rabbihi, son of Zahira, took the title and it reverted to the Nagi family.

35.

"I never dreamed you'd become clan chief, in spite of your great strength," said his father, beaming with joy.

"Nor did I," smiled Galal.

"I was strong like you, but to be chief you need the stomach and the ambition," said Abd Rabbihi proudly.

"You're right, father. I was planning to be a respected member of the community, then I had a sudden notion . . ."

"You could be Ashur himself, you're so strong," laughed his father. "So be happy, and make the people of your alley happy."

"Let's not talk about happiness yet," he said in measured tones.

36.

He began to act, inspired by his strength and visions of immortality. He planned out a route for himself. He challenged the chiefs of neighboring alleys to put his excess strength to use, and won Atuf, Darasa, Kafr al-Zaghari, Husayniyya, and Bulaq. Every day a piper paraded down the alley, announcing a new victory. He became chief of chiefs, all-powerful, like Ashur and Shams al-Din.

The harafish rejoiced, pinning their hopes on his reputed generosity and benevolence. The notables were uneasy, anticipating lives poisoned by restrictions and hardship.

37.

Abd Rabbihi swaggered about, proud and dignified. In the bar he announced that a new era had begun. These days he was received with admiration and respect. The drunks hung around him, sniffing out news.

"Ashur al-Nagi has returned," he announced. He emptied the calabash down his throat. "Let the harafish rejoice. Let all who love justice rejoice. The poor will have plenty to eat. The notables will learn that God is truth!"

"Did Galal promise that?" asked Sanqar.

"It was his sole aim in wanting to become chief," declared Abd Rabbihi confidently.

38.

Friends and enemies alike owed Galal allegiance. No power challenged him, nothing worried him. He had supremacy, status, and wealth. Feelings of boredom and inertia crept up on him. He thought seriously about himself. His life appeared to him in sharp relief, the features and colors clearly visible, right down to its ludicrous, definitive ending. His mother's shattered head, his childhood trials and humiliations, Qamr's ironic death, his unlimited power and dominance, and Shams al-Din's tomb awaiting one funeral procession after another. What was the point of being sad or happy? What did strength mean, or death? Why did the impossible exist?

39.

"People are wondering when justice will be done," said his father one morning.

Galal smiled with some irritation. "What does it matter?"

"It's everything, son," cried his father in astonishment.

"They're dying like flies all the time, and they don't complain," he said scathingly.

"Death has rights over us, but you have it in your power to eradicate poverty and indignity."

"Damn these stupid ideas!" shouted Galal.

"Don't you want to follow al-Nagi's example?" asked Abd Rabbihi sorrowfully.

"Where is he now?"

"In Paradise, my son."

"That's meaningless."

"God preserve us from losing our faith!"

"God preserve us from nothing at all," he said savagely.

"I never imagined my son would go the same way as Samaka al-Allaj."

"Samaka al-Allaj is finished, the same as Ashur."

"Not at all. They took power and lost it in completely different ways."

Galal sighed angrily. "Don't make things worse for me, father. Don't make demands on me. Don't be deceived by my achievements. Just understand that I'm not happy."

40.

Abd Rabbihi despaired and stopped talking about the promised utopia.

"God's will is supreme," he declared, completely drunk, "and we just have to accept it."

"If we'd been more cagey about him in the past, we'd be content now," lamented the harafish.

The notables were reassured by the relative tranquillity, paid the protection money, and showered him with gifts.

Galal went about with the winds of despondency and anguish blowing through his empty heart, although he continued to exude power, strength, and voracious ambition from his dazzling exterior. He gave the overwhelming impression of someone dominated, almost against his will, by a passion to make more money and acquire more possessions. Not only was he in partnership with his brother Radi in the cereal business, but also with the timber merchant, the coffee merchant, the spice merchant, and others. He could never have too many ventures on the go, and the other merchants were only too happy to make him one of them, to bind him firmly to their world of respectability and power. He became the most powerful clan chief, the most successful merchant, the wealthiest of the wealthy, and still did not think it was beneath him to collect protection money and accept presents. Apart from his gang members, the only people to prosper were those who were uncon-

ditionally and abjectly loyal to him. He had many tenement buildings constructed, and a dream house to the right of the fountain,
aptly known as The Citadel, because it was so large and imposing.
He filled it with magnificent furniture, adorned it with curios and
objets d'art like a fantasy of the immortals, sailed around in rich
silks, and always traveled in a carriage. Gold flashed from his teeth
and gleamed on every finger.

He was uninterested in the state of the harafish or the Nagi
covenant, not from egotism or weakness in the face of life's temptations, but because he despised their concerns and found their problems trivial. The strange thing was that he was naturally inclined to
asceticism, and scorned the demands of the flesh. Some blind, face-
less power was behind his desire for status, money, and possessions,
at the heart of which was anxiety and fear. It was as if he was
fortifying himself against death, or strengthening his ties with the
world, fearful it would betray him. Although he was submerged in
the vast ocean of material existence, he never overlooked its capac-
ity for treachery, was not lulled into oblivion by its smiles, nor
captivated by its sweet talking. He was acutely aware of its pre-
planned game, the end it had in store for him. He did not drink,
take drugs, have love affairs, or become addicted to the chanting
from the monastery. When he was alone sometimes, he would sigh
and say, "My heart, how you suffer!"

41.

"Why don't you get married?" asked his brother Radi, who was
perhaps the only friend he had.

Galal laughed and did not reply, so Radi went on, "A bachelor's always the subject of speculation."

"What's the point of marriage, Radi?" he asked scathingly.

"Pleasure, fatherhood, perpetuating your name."

Galal laughed noisily. "What a lot of lies people talk, brother."

"Who are you gathering all this wealth for?" demanded Radi.

A good question. Would a man like him not be better off as a
dervish? Death chased him all the time. Zahira's crushed head and
Qamr's waxy face loomed before his eyes again. Neither The Cita-

del nor an army of clubs would be any use. The splendor would
fade. The edifice of strength and pride would crumble. Other people would inherit the wealth, and make sarcastic remarks about
him. The magnificent victories would be followed by everlasting
defeat.

42.

He sat cross-legged on the chief's traditional wooden sofa in the
café. An image of beauty and power, dazzling eyes, inspiring
hearts. No one was aware of the deepening shadows inside his
skull. A ray of light penetrated this darkness in the shape of a
brilliant, seductive smile of greeting, and left its glowing traces.
Who was the woman? A prostitute living in a small flat above the
moneylender's, with many eminent customers. She always greeted
him deferentially as she passed, and he neither turned away nor
responded. He did not deny her soothing effect she had on him in
his tormented state. Medium build, luscious body, attractive face.
Zaynat. And because she dyed her hair gold, they called her Zaynat
the Blonde. He did not deny her soothing effect but was reluctant
to respond to her advances. His desires were constantly held in
check by his preoccupation with fighting, putting up buildings,
amassing wealth, and embracing boredom.

43.

One evening, Zaynat the Blonde asked to see him. He received her
in the guest hall and let her marvel at the furniture, the objets d'art,
the ornamented lamps. She removed her wrap and veil and sat on
the divan, armed with all her weapons of seduction.

"How should I justify my presence here?" she asked adroitly.
"Shall I say that I was trying to rent a flat in one of your new
buildings?"

He found himself being pleasant, trying to put her at her ease.
"No one's going to ask you to justify yourself."

She laughed contentedly. "I said to myself, I'll go and visit him, since he can't decide to come and see me!"

He sensed he had taken a step down into the abyss of temptation, but did not let it concern him. "That's as good a reason as any. Welcome!"

"I was encouraged by the nice way you received me each afternoon."

He smiled. Behind the smile he was wondering as he so often did what Qamr looked like now.

"Don't you like me?" she asked with unusual boldness.

"You're exquisite," he replied truthfully.

"And is a man like you content to have this feeling and not act on it?"

"You're forgetting certain things," he said in embarrassment.

"You're the most powerful man around. How can you sleep like the poor people?"

"The poor sleep deeply," he said sarcastically.

"What about you?"

"Maybe I don't sleep at all!"

She laughed sweetly. "I've heard from people who know that you've never drunk or smoked in your life, and never touched a woman. Is it true?"

He was at a loss to know how to reply, but had the feeling she would find out what she wanted.

"Love and pleasure—they're what life's about," she continued, undaunted.

"Really?" he replied, feigning surprise.

"The rest we leave to others when we go!"

"We leave love and pleasure too," he said angrily.

"No! They're absorbed by the body and soul, so no one else can have them!"

"What a farce!"

"I haven't lived a single day without some loving or enjoyment," she said passionately.

"You're an astonishing woman!"

"I'm a woman, that's all."

"Aren't you worried about death?"

"We all have to die, but I don't like how it happens."

Have to? Have to? "Do you know anything about the life of Shams al-Din?" he asked her abruptly.

"Of course," she answered proudly. "He's the one who fought old age."

"He resisted it for all he was worth."

"The lucky ones are really the people who enjoy a quiet old age," she said softly.

"The lucky ones are those who never grow old."

She was taken aback at the change in him. "This moment's all you've got for sure," she said provocatively.

He laughed. "That sounds like an appropriate homily when night's approaching."

She closed her eyes, listening to the wind whistling and the rain beating on the shuttered windows.

44.

Zaynat the Blonde became Galal's lover. People were shocked but said in any case it was better than what happened to Wahid. Her former lovers stayed away from her, and he had her to himself. She taught him everything, and added a gilded calabash and ornately embellished water pipe to the other luxurious objects in the house. He had no regrets, and thought this way of life had a certain appeal. Zaynat loved him with a love that possessed her heart and soul, and was tantalized by a strange dream that one day she would be his lawful wife. To his surprise his old love for Qamr was reborn too, like an unchanging memory filled with sweetness. He realized he would never escape it. Nothing would cease to exist. Not even his love for his mother. He would remain indebted to Zahira's shattered head and Qamr's face for his knowledge of the tragedy of existence, the faint, recurrent melody of sorrow beneath the facade of bright lights and brilliant victories. He had no idea of Zaynat's age. She could have been the same age as him, or older. It would remain a secret. He grew attached to her. Was he in love again? He grew attached to the calabash and the water pipe. To them he owed this inner ecstasy which gave rise to both joy and anguish, and he had no qualms about abandoning himself to the current.

45.

His father cornered him alone, looking concerned.

"Why don't you marry her? Surely it's better to make it legal?"

He didn't answer.

"If you married Zaynat," went on his father, "you'd be following Ashur's example."

He shook his head.

"In any case, I've definitely decided to marry again."

"You!" exclaimed Galal in amazement, "but you're in your sixties, father!"

"So what?" laughed Abd Rabbihi. "I'm in excellent health, in spite of everything, and I've got high hopes—God willing—of the herbalist's potions."

"Who's the lucky girl?"

"Zuwayla al-Faskhani's daughter," he boasted. "A nice, respectable girl in her twenties."

"Wouldn't it be better to choose a lady nearer your own age?" smiled Galal.

"No. I need someone young to make me feel young again."

"I hope you'll be happy," murmured Galal.

Abd Rabbihi began singing the praises of the herbalist and his magic powers, and how he could restore a man's youth.

46.

Farida al-Faskhani married Abd Rabbihi, and the couple set up house in a wing of The Citadel. Galal thought constantly about the magic powers of the herbalist, Abd al-Khaliq. One night he invited him and they got stoned together and ate fruit and sweetmeats.

"What passes between us here must be kept secret," said Galal earnestly.

Abd al-Khaliq promised that it would, pleased with the new status bestowed on him by the chief.

"I've heard you give mature men back their youth," began Galal tentatively.

The herbalist smiled confidently. "With the help of the Almighty."

"Perhaps it's easier for you to stop people aging?"

"That goes without saying."

Galal's face brightened. He looked visibly relieved. "You see why I sent for you?" he murmured.

The man thought for a moment, awed by the burden of trust. "The herbalist's potions aren't everything," he said finally. "They must be used in conjunction with the will to act sensibly."

"What do you mean?"

"You must be honest," said Abd al-Khaliq cautiously. "Have you experienced any kind of weakness?"

"I'm in perfect health."

"Splendid. Then you must stick devotedly to a regime."

"Don't talk in riddles."

"You have to eat, but excessive eating is harmful."

"Anyone in my position should be able to understand that," said Galal, relieved.

"A little alcohol is a pleasant stimulus but too much is bad for you."

"Obviously."

"You shouldn't try to exceed your capabilities when it comes to sex."

"Not a problem."

"A sound faith is highly beneficial."

"Fine."

"When all that's taken care of, the herbalist's prescription can work wonders."

"Has it been tried before?"

"By many of the notables. Some of them have preserved their youth so well that people who know them have started to get scared and wonder what's going on!"

Galal's eyes gleamed delightedly.

"If someone follows my advice, God willing, he should be able
to live to a hundred," continued Abd al-Khaliq. "And there's nothing to stop him going on beyond that, until he actually wants his
time to be up!"

Galal gave a gloomy smile. "Then what?"

"Death comes to us all," shrugged the herbalist.

Galal cursed to himself at this general conspiracy to venerate
death.

47.

One evening as he and Zaynat were sitting together, relaxed and at
ease with one another, she asked suddenly, "Why don't you do
something to fulfill the expectations of the harafish?"

He looked at her, startled. "What does it matter to you?"

She kissed him and said frankly, "To stop people being jealous. That's fatal."

He shrugged his shoulders indifferently. "To tell you the
truth, I despise them."

"But they're poor and miserable."

"That's why I despise them!"

A spasm of disgust distorted her pretty face.

"All they think about is getting enough to eat."

"Your ideas frighten me," she said pityingly.

"Why don't they resign themselves to hunger, like they do to
death?"

Memories of her youth swept over her like a choking dust
storm.

"Hunger's more terrible than death."

He smiled, half closing his eyes to hide the cold scorn in them.

48.

The days went by and Galal grew more powerful, more beautiful,
more glorious. Time slid over him leaving no trace, like a trickle of
water on a polished mirror. Zaynat herself changed, like everything
else, despite the great care she took of her beauty. Galal realized

that he had begun his sacred struggle of resistance against the passage of time. How sad that it was bound to end! He might delay it for a while, but there was no escaping destiny.

49.

The ties of friendship grew firmer between him and Abd al-Khaliq. The herbalist claimed that if his potions did not cost so much, the alley would be full of centenarians. Galal thought often of sharing the magic potion with Zaynat, but always abandoned the idea. Perhaps he had begun to fear her power over him and her charm, and was loath to immunize her against the tyranny of age. He loved her most of the time, but every now and then he felt like getting his own back and ejecting her on to the nearest rubbish heap. His relationship with her was not simple or clear-cut. It spread and merged into a complex web of relationships, indivisible from his memories of his mother and Qamr, his hostility toward death, his self-respect, his dependence on her which held him captive. What annoyed him most of all about her was her deep-seated assurance, her seemingly boundless confidence. And yet she was worn out by drink and sleepless nights, her cheeks aflame with makeup. Could he detect sly glances of envy in his direction?

50.

"I suppose you've heard the tale of Ashur al-Nagi?" he asked Abd al-Khaliq one day.

"Everyone knows it by heart."

"I believe he's still alive," said Galal after a pause.

Abd al-Khaliq was shocked and didn't know how to reply. He knew that Ashur was a saint for some, a crook for others, but they all accepted that he was dead.

"That he didn't die," persisted Galal.

"Ashur was a good man. Death doesn't spare good men."

"Does a person have to be evil to live forever?" protested Galal.

"We all have to die. A believer shouldn't try and live forever."

"Are you certain of that?"

"So they say. God knows," said Abd al-Khaliq, taking fright. "Why?"

"I think people can only live forever if they associate with jinns."

"Tell me what you mean," demanded Galal, ablaze with a sudden fierce interest.

"Associating with jinns means you become immortal, and damned forever. You sign an everlasting pact with the devil."

"Do you think that's drivel, or is there some truth in it?" asked Galal, his interest mounting.

Abd al-Khaliq hesitated. "It may be true," he said eventually.

"Let's hear more details."

"Why? Are you really thinking of taking such a risk?"

Galal laughed edgily. "I just like to know everything."

"It's said that . . . Shawar . . ." began Abd al-Khaliq slowly.

"The mysterious sheikh who claims to read the future?" asked Galal.

"That's what he does on the face of it. But he knows some terrible secrets."

"It's the first I've heard of it."

"He's scared of believers."

"Do you think there's anything in it?"

"I don't know, but the whole business is cursed."

"Immortality?"

"Mixing with jinns!"

"You're scared of immortality!"

"That's not surprising. Imagine if I survived long enough to witness the world I know ceasing to exist, all my friends and family gone, leaving me surrounded by strangers, permanently on the move, rejected. I'd go mad and long to be dead."

"You'd preserve your youth forever!"

"You'd have children you had to avoid. With each generation you'd have to start all over again, lose a wife and children all over again. You'd be classified as a permanent alien, have no true links of any kind."

"That's enough!" cried Galal.

They laughed uproariously.

"But what a dream," murmured Galal.

51.

Shawar lived in a large basement directly opposite the animals' drinking trough. It had several rooms, including one reserved for women and another for men. He himself was a mysterious character whom no one had ever seen. He received his clients in a dark room at night. They heard his voice, but saw no sign of him. Most of them were women, but a few may have been men driven to consult him on the advice of knowledgeable women. After the consultation the client was expected to leave an offering with an Ethiopian maid called Hawa.

Galal sent for the sheikh, but was told he lost his magic powers if he left his room, so he had to make his way there under cover of darkness, late enough to ensure that he was the only customer.

Hawa showed him into the room, sat him down on a soft cushion, and vanished. He was in pitch-darkness. He peered around him but could see nothing. It was as if he had lost all sense of time and space. He had been warned to keep quiet, not to initiate conversation and answer all questions briefly and to the point. The time dragged by oppressively. They seemed to have forgotten all about him. It was ridiculous. He had not been slighted in this way since he had become chief. What had happened to Galal the giant? Could he really be this resigned creature, patiently waiting? It would be the worse for mankind and the spirit world if this escapade came to nothing.

52.

"What's your name?" asked a calm, sonorous voice from the darkness.

Galal gave a sigh of relief. "Galal, the clan chief," he answered.

"Answer the question," repeated the voice.

He stuck his chest out. "Galal Abd Rabbihi al-Nagi."

"Answer the question."

"Galal," he said dryly.

"And your mother's name?"

His anger flared dangerously. Lurid demons danced in the darkness.

"Your mother's name?" asked the voice, mechanical yet threatening.

He swallowed, suppressing his rage. "Zahira."

"What do you want?"

He hesitated, but the voice did not allow him this respite. "What do you want?"

"To know about associating with jinns."

"What do you want?"

"I've just told you."

"What do you want?"

Anger seized him. "Don't you know who I am?" he said menacingly.

"Galal, son of Zahira."

"I could flatten you with a single blow."

"I think not." This was said with absolute confidence.

"Shall we try?" shouted Galal.

"What do you want?" asked the voice, cold and indifferent.

"Immortality," answered Galal, surrendering on all fronts.

"Why?"

"That's my business."

"The believer does not challenge God's will."

"I'm a believer, and I want to be immortal."

"It's risky."

"Too bad."

"You'll long to die and be unable to."

"Too bad," he said again, his heart pounding.

The voice fell silent. Had he gone away? Once again Galal lost all his bearings, and waited impatiently, his nerves on edge. He peered desperately around him, but could see nothing.

53.

After a period of agony, the voice returned. "Are you ready to do whatever is required of you?"

"Of course," he replied with alacrity.

"Give my maid Hawa the largest building you own so that I can atone for my sin by providing her with a good source of income."

"I agree," he said after a brief pause.

"Build a minaret ten stories high."

"On to the present mosque?"

"No."

"A new mosque?"

"No. A freestanding minaret."

"But . . ."

"No arguments."

"I agree."

"Spend a whole year in your private apartments seeing no one and being seen by no one except your manservant. Avoid all distractions."

"I agree," he said, feeling his heart contract.

"On the last day of your seclusion your pact with the Evil One will be sealed and you will never know death."

54.

Galal made his largest building over to the Ethiopian maid, Hawa. He hired a contractor to erect a giant minaret on a piece of waste ground. The man agreed to this strange commission out of a mixture of greed and fear. Galal put Mu'nis al-Al in charge of his men, leaving him numerous instructions, and announced that he was withdrawing from public life for a year to fulfill a holy vow. He entrenched himself in his rooms, recording each passing day as Samaha had done in exile, and stayed away from the calabash, the narghile, and Zaynat the Blonde in the firm hope that he would triumph in the greatest struggle known to man.

55.

His decision hit Zaynat the Blonde like a death blow. A painful severance, with no preliminaries, no satisfactory reason given for it. It evoked bitterness, fear, desperation. Hadn't they been like butter and honey, blending sweetly? She had been sure he was hers forever, and now he was shutting the door in her face like the dervishes in the monastery, leaving those who loved him hurt and confused. She wept inconsolably when the servants prevented her entering his room. She went to visit Radi, but found him equally perplexed. She sat with Abd Rabbihi in his room. The old man had changed. These days he seldom visited the bar and had become proper and modest. He too was troubled about his son.

"I'm not allowed to see him, even though we're living under the same roof," he said.

Zaynat lived a tormented existence. She was not short of money but had lost her lord and master. Her self-confidence was shaken, and the future loomed threatening and mysterious.

56.

The clan was thrown into disarray. No one was content with Mu'nis al-Al, but they were obliged to obey him. They wondered what vow Galal had made, why he had handed over the leadership of the clan, and entrusted his business and property to his brother.

The dangerous news leaked out to rival chiefs. As time passed, they announced the resumption of hostilities. Mu'nis al-Al suffered his first defeat at the hands of the men of the Atuf clan, followed closely by the gangs from Kafr al-Zaghari, Husayniyya, and other neighborhoods. Eventually he was forced to pay out protection money to safeguard the alley's peace and security. The men wanted to tell Galal of the disastrous turn of events, but they were prevented as surely as if death had snatched him from them and buried him in a sealed tomb.

57.

The people watched the strange minaret going up in astonishment. It rose higher and higher toward infinity, straight from its firm foundations in the ground. There was no mosque beneath it. No one knew its function or purpose. Even the man responsible for building it knew nothing about it.

"Has he gone mad?" people asked one another.

The harafish said a curse had fallen on him for betraying his great ancestor's covenant and ignoring his true people in pursuit of his insatiable greed.

58.

As time went by, he sank deeper into isolation. Gradually he pulled up the roots attaching him to the outside world—his power in the clan, money, his beautiful lover—and abandoned himself to silence, to patience, to his conscience. He was worn out by the hope of being the first human being to achieve the impossible dream. Every day he stared time in the face, alone with no diversions, no drugs or alcohol. He confronted its inertia, its torpor, its solid weight. An obstinate, unyielding, impenetrable mass, where he floundered like someone in a nightmare. A thick wall, oppressive and gloomy. Time was unendurable without the aid of work or companionship. As if we only work, make friends, fall in love, seek amusement to escape from it. Seeing time pass too quickly is less painful than seeing it grind to a halt. When he achieved immortality, he would try everything, unhindered by fear or laziness. He would rush into battle without stopping to think. Scorn reason as much as folly. One day he would be at the forefront of the human race. Now he crawled over the seconds and begged for mercy, palms out-stretched. He wondered when the devil would come, how he would form a bond with him. Would he see him in the flesh, hear his voice, or be joined with him like the air he breathed? He was exhausted, bored. But he would not succumb to weakness. He was not going to fail. It didn't matter if he suffered, or gave in to tears. He believed in what he was doing. He could not turn back. Eternity did not scare him. He would never know death. The rest of the world would be subject to the changing seasons, but for him it would be eternal spring. He would be the vanguard of a new form of existence, the one to discover life without death, the first to reject eternal repose. A secret power made manifest. Only the weak are afraid to live. However, living face-to-face with time is an unimaginable torment.

59.

On the last day of the appointed year, Galal stood naked in front of an open window. The sun's rays, cleansed in the moist air of winter, struck him full in the face, and the cool wind played gently over his body. The time had come for him to reap the fruits of his patience. The weary, lonely night was over. Galal Abd Rabbihi was no longer an ephemeral creature. A new spirit breathed in him, intoxicating him, inspiring him with strength and confidence. He would talk to himself and to others too, and listen to the voice of his conscience with no misgivings. He had triumphed over time by holding out against it, unaided. He was no longer afraid of it. It could threaten others with its ominous passing. He would never be afflicted with wrinkles, gray hair, or impotence. His soul would not betray him. No coffin would ever carry him, no tomb shelter him. This firm body would never disintegrate and become dust. He would never know the grief of parting.

He strolled naked around the room, repeating serenely, "This life is blessed indeed."

60.

The door opened agitatedly and Zaynat the Blonde rushed into the room. She flew at him in a frenzy of longing and they melted in a long, passionate embrace. She began to sob convulsively. "What did you do?" she asked him reproachfully.

He kissed her on the cheeks and lips.

"How did you pass the time?"

He was overcome by a rush of yearning for her. A precious, transient feeling. He saw her young and beautiful, old and ugly in turn. A sweet deception. As if fidelity had become impossible.

"Let's forget what's happened," he said.

"But I want to know."

"Think of it as an illness that's over now."

"You're so deceitful."

"You're so nice."

"Do you know what happened while you were away?"

"Let's talk about that later."

She took a step back. "How beautiful you look," she said admiringly.

He felt a pang of guilt and looked at her regretfully. "I'm sorry for making you suffer."

"I'll be fine again in a few hours. But I want to know your secret," she said stubbornly.

He hesitated, then said firmly, "I was ill and now I'm cured."

"I should have stayed with you."

"Isolation was the cure!"

She held him close and whispered amorously, "Show me if love's still the same. I'll tell you my troubles later."

61.

He received Abd Rabbihi and Radi in the salon and embraced them warmly. They were followed by Mu'nis al-Al and men from the gang. They kissed him respectfully.

"It's all gone. We were powerless to stop it," said Mu'nis pitifully.

Escorted by his men, Galal emerged into the alley and made for the café. The whole alley turned out to greet him, friends, enemies, admirers, detractors. He leaned toward Mu'nis. "Do some people think I'm crazy?" he asked.

"God forbid, chief," murmured Mu'nis.

"Let them get back to work. Tell them we're grateful," said

Galal, gazing at the crowd contemptuously. Then he muttered, "How much hatred there is. How little affection!"

62.

He visited the minaret, accompanied by Abd Rabbihi and Radi. It was firmly planted in the waste ground, with the rubble and litter cleared from around about it. It had a square base the size of a large room with an arched door of polished wood. Its sturdy bulk rose endlessly toward an invisible summit, towering above the surrounding buildings. Its sharp sides evoked power, its red color strangeness and terror.

"If we accept that this is a minaret," asked Abd Rabbihi, "then where's the mosque?"

Galal did not answer.

"It cost us an inordinate sum of money," said Radi.

"What's it for, son?" persisted Abd Rabbihi.

"God knows," laughed Galal.

"Since it was finished, people talk of nothing else."

"Don't pay them any attention," said Galal disdainfully. "It's part of my vow. A man may do a lot of stupid things in the course of becoming unusually wise."

His father was about to repeat his question, but he interrupted him in a decisive tone. "Look, you see this minaret? It will still be here when everything else in the alley is in ruins. Interrogate it. It'll answer your questions if it pleases."

63.

Taking the herbalist aside, he asked him with terrifying solemnity, "What did you think of my year's retreat?"

"I took what you told me at face value," said the man sincerely, his heart beating with fright.

"What about the minaret?"

"I suppose it's part of your vow," he said hesitantly.

"I thought you were a man of sound judgment, Abd al-Khaliq," scowled Galal.

"I'm damned if I've breathed a word of our secret," he said hurriedly.

64.

At dead of night he crept along to the minaret and climbed the stairs, floor by floor, until he reached the balcony at the very top. He braved the winter cold, armored in his absolute power over existence. He craned up at the festival of bright stars spread like a canopy above his head. Thousands of eyes sparkling down at him, while beneath him everything was immersed in gloom. Perhaps he had not climbed up to the top of the minaret, but simply grown to the height he ought to be. He had to grow higher, ever higher, for there was no other way to achieve purity. At the top the language of the stars was audible, the whisperings of space, the prayers for power and immortality, far from the exaggerated complaints, the lassitude, the stink of decay. Now the poems from the monastery sung of eternity. The truth revealed many of its hidden faces. Destinies were laid bare. From this balcony he could follow successive generations, play a role in each, join the family of the celestial bodies for all eternity.

65.

He led his men out to teach his enemies a lesson and restore the alley to its former status. In a short space of time he had won brilliant victories over Atuf, Husayniyya, Bulaq, Kafr al-Zaghari, and Darasa. He hurled himself at his adversaries and they scattered before him, crushed by the humiliation of defeat. He was known to be invincible. No amount of strength or courage could work against him.

66.

He changed his style of life. He began to eat, drink, and smoke to excess. Whenever a whore flirted with him, he responded discreetly. Zaynat soon lost her hold over him and became no more than a pretty rose in a garden full of roses. Reports of his escapades reached her ears and she was consumed by a frenzy of jealousy and loss. In the mirror of the future she saw her face fading away in the murky gloom of oblivion. She had always seen him as an innocent child with some unorthodox beliefs. His innocence had opened the doors for her to a faraway hope: she was sure of love and hoped for marriage. Perhaps it would be easier to give up life itself than to lose him, the embodiment to her of strength, beauty, youth, and boundless glory. But his year's isolation had made a different person of him: a creature smitten with power and beauty, and terrified of change, of madness, of being treated with contempt, of having to acquire wisdom the hard way. She felt herself growing small, thin, feeble, almost ceasing to exist in the face of his dreadful, mysterious domination. She could only confront him with weakness, pleading, and a sense of failure. But he met her with haughty gentleness, exulting in his arrogance, clothed in cold tenderness, fortified by a bottomless sense of superiority.

"Be content with your lot," he told her. "Many would envy you."

She saw him blossoming as she withered, and realized they were going opposite ways. Her heart swelled with love and despair.

67.

Abd Rabbihi had a son, Khalid, and tore himself away from the bar once and for all. He found happiness in prayer and meditation, and Sheikh Khalil al-Dahshan became his friend and confidant.

He was desperately anxious about Galal, and even more so about the terrible minaret. It seemed to him that his relationship with his son was destroyed, that he had become a stranger unconnected to him. He was an alien presence among the people of the alley, like the minaret among its buildings: strong, beautiful, sterile, and incomprehensible.

"I shan't rest easy until you marry and have a family," he told him.

"There's plenty of time, father."

"And until you revive the glorious covenant of the Nagis," he entreated.

Galal smiled without answering.

"And repent and follow God."

Remembering his father's distant and not so distant past, Galal let out a guffaw like a drum roll.

68.

The passing days and changing seasons held no fears for him. His inflexible will dominated the aggressive forces of nature. The unknown no longer scared him.

In the pit of despair and sorrow, Zaynat the Blonde received a summons to love. She had been waiting for it, yearning for it all along, preparing for it in her battered heart.

Now he was granting her one of his precious nights. She made her way to his house, outwardly pleased at the way she was being treated. She removed the drapes, flung open all the windows in her old rooms to allow the May breezes to circulate, and met him cheerfully, hiding her sorrows. She had learned to treat him with caution, apprehensive of his reactions. She prepared a tray with drinks and glasses.

"Drink up, my love," she whispered in his ear.

"How kind you are!" he said, gulping down the wine.

She observed to herself that he had lost his heart along with his innocence and that, like winter, he gloried in his power, oblivious to his cruelty. She also acknowledged that she was willfully destroying herself.

He stared at her, already fairly drunk. "You're not your usual self," he murmured.

"It's the solemnity of love," she said gently.

He laughed. "Nothing is solemn." Playing idly with a lock of her golden hair, he went on, "You're still in a very powerful position. But you're such an ambitious woman!"

"I'm just a sad woman," she cried impetuously.

"Remember what you said about seizing life's pleasures while you can . . ."

"That was in the days when you loved me."

"I'm following your advice, and I'm grateful for it."

He did not know what he was saying, she thought. She was much better acquainted with the mystery of life than him and knew that evil raised a man against his will to the ranks of the angels. She gazed at him passionately, restraining a desire to cry. Lulled by the breeze, she thought what a treacherous month this was. Soon the khamsin winds would blow, transforming it into a demon which would wreck the spring. He took her in his arms and she clasped him to her with frantic strength.

69.

He freed himself from her arms and began stripping off his clothes until he stood naked, like a statue of light. He walked around the bedroom, laughing at his unsteady progress.

"You've drunk a whole sea," she said.

"I'm still thirsty."

"Our love's over," she murmured, as if to herself.

He staggered a few more steps, before collapsing onto a divan, shaking with laughter.

"You're drunk."

He frowned. "No. It's more than that. It's as if I'm sleepy." He tried to rise to his feet, without success. "I'm falling asleep just when I don't want to," he muttered.

She bit her lip. The world would end like this one day. The most pitiful people were those who sang victory songs in their hour of defeat.

"Try to stand up," she said hoarsely.

"There's no need," he answered, languorous yet dignified.

"Are you sure you can't, my love?"

"Quite sure. There's a burning like the fires of hell, and I'm sleepy."

She leapt to her feet and stepped back into the center of the room, staring wildly at him, all the softness gone. She was a mass of taut muscle, ready to spring, but there was an air of bitterness and sorrow about her. He looked at her dully, then his eyes swam out of focus.

"Why am I falling asleep?" he said thickly.

She spoke in the tones of someone making a sacred confession. "It's not sleep, my love."

"So it must be the bull that carries the world on its horns."

"It's not the bull either, my love."

"You're acting the fool, Zaynat. Why?"

"I've never been more serious. I'm killing myself."

"Huh?"

"It's death, my love."

"Death?"

"You've swallowed enough poison to kill an elephant."

"You mean, you have?"

"No, you, my love."

He burst out laughing, but quickly fell silent, too weak to continue.

"I killed you to put an end to my torment," she said, starting to cry.

He attempted another laugh. "Galal is immortal," he muttered.

"I can see death in your beautiful eyes."

"Death has died, stupid woman."

Gathering all his strength, he rose to his feet, dominating the room. She drew back, terrified, and rushed out of the room like someone possessed.

70.

It was as if he was carrying the dreadful minaret on his shoulders. Death charged at him like a bull, blind with fury, charging solid rock.

"What terrible pain!" he cried, still without fear.

He staggered outside, stark naked.

"Galal can feel pain, but he cannot die," he muttered as he emerged into the dark alley.

He inched forward in the pitch-darkness, mumbling inaudibly, "I'm on fire. I want some water."

He began to move slowly in the gloom, groaning faintly, believing he was filling the alley with his cries. Where was everybody? Where were his men? Why didn't they bring him water? Where was Zaynat, the criminal? This must be a terrible nightmare, weighing down on him with all its odious force, but it wasn't death. The mysterious powers would be working at full strength now to restore him to his mocking, immortal self. But what terrible pain! What unbearable thirst!

As he stumbled along, he bumped against a cold, unmoving mass. The animals' drinking trough! A wave of joy and relief swept over him. He bent over the edge of the trough, overbalanced, stretched out his arms. The water closed over them. His lips touched water full of animal fodder. He drank greedily, dementedly, then let out a cry which rang out around the alley, a sound distorted by the savage pain. The top half of his body vanished in the murky water. His knees sagged and his lower half sank down into the mud and droppings. The dark shadows of that terrible, eventful spring night closed around him.

The Specters

The eighth tale in the epic

of the harafish

1.

It took a long time for the alley to forget the spectacle of Galal's body draped over the side of the drinking trough, a giant white cadaver among the straw and excrement. The huge frame suggested immortality; its emptiness in its wrecked state confirmed death. Above it in the light of the torches the air was charged with terrible derision.

The proud strength had ended in its prime. Gone its protective shadow with a hundred eyes and a thousand fists. His father Abd Rabbihi and his brother Radi carried him into The Citadel. An immense cortege accompanied his body to the tomb of Shams al-Din. He was remembered as one of the great clan leaders, despite his demonic characteristics.

He took his good and bad deeds with him to the grave but the legends lived on.

2.

Mu'nis al-Al took over the clan. Although Galal's death evoked a general feeling of relief, the alley lost its sense of equilibrium and was beset by new fears. It relinquished its elevated status in the neighborhood and became just another alley, and its chief no longer reigned supreme. Mu'nis al-Al made alliances, fought battles and lost, and was again obliged to buy peace with protection money and bribes. No one in the alley expected him to honor the covenant which Galal, descendant of the Nagis and miracle of triumphant power, had himself betrayed.

3.

Abd Rabbihi and Radi were the sole inheritors of Galal's vast fortune. Galal's death was attributed to drugs and alcohol. The fact that he had ended up lying naked in straw and dung was considered a divine retribution for his arrogance and his high-handed treatment of his fellow human beings. No one inherited the minaret, and with its exaggerated structure and sterility of purpose it continued as a symbol of insolence and folly.

4.

After some time had elapsed, the herbalist Abd al-Khaliq opened his mouth. In whispers he told of Galal's strange enterprise, his association with demons, the role played by the mysterious Shawar. The secret was out, and Zaynat the Blonde confirmed people's suspicions by telling the tale of Galal's belief in his own immortality. Shawar and his maid vanished, escaping the general anger. Many proposed demolishing the minaret, but most people were scared that it was haunted by the devil and that its demolition would lay the alley open to undreamed of evil. So it was left standing. People gave it a wide berth, cursed it as they passed, and abandoned it to snakes, bats, and demons.

5.

The harafish declared that what had happened to Galal was a fair punishment for someone who had betrayed the great al-Nagi's covenant, and forgotten his immortal prayer that God would grant him strength to use in the service of others. Every time descendants of al-Nagi betrayed his name, they were cursed and destroyed by insanity. Even Abd Rabbihi and Radi earned the scorn of the harafish, and their ample wealth was of no use to them.

6.

Zaynat the Blonde lived for a while in terrified anticipation, but nobody thought of accusing her. Even those who had their doubts about her part in Galal's death brushed them aside, grateful to her for her anonymous deed. Zaynat did not enjoy her revenge. She lived abstemiously by herself, with no zest, no sense of repose. Sometime after Galal's death she discovered that their love had borne fruit, and guarded this germ of life with all the strength of her undying love. She was filled with a sense of pride despite the fact that the child would be illegitimate. She gave birth to a boy and, defying the traditions, boldly named him Galal.

7.

She gave him love twice over: as her son and as her dead lover's child. She brought him up in humble surroundings with no desire to return to the life of a rich woman. She never forgot that he was the true heir to Galal's fabulous wealth and pestered Abd Rabbihi and Radi to give up part of their inheritance in favor of her little boy. But they rebuffed her angrily, insinuating that they suspected her of playing a decisive part in Galal's death.

"How can a woman like her know who's the father of her child?" scoffed Radi.

8.

Galal grew up as just another alley child whose father's identity was unknown. He was taunted and called a bastard, as his father years before had been taunted and called "Zahira's son." But as he grew older, it became obvious to anyone with eyes to see that he was Galal's son and nobody else's. He did not possess his strength and grace, but there was no mistaking his origins.

9.

Galal attended the Quran school for two years, then went to work for al-Gada, the carter. Zaynat had used up her savings and could not afford anything better for him. She was proud of her son and pleased with herself for holding out and living an honest life. Although she was well past forty she was still beautiful enough for al-Gada to have ideas about adding her to his harem. She did not welcome his interest, but at the same time was afraid he would take it out on her son if she rejected him. However, the man abandoned his pursuit of her when Mugahid Ibrahim, who had succeeded Gibril al-Fas as sheikh, exclaimed to him one day, "How can you trust a woman who killed her lover!"

Galal found out as time went by that he was the son of the man who had built the minaret, and grandson of the famous Zahira; that Abd Rabbihi was his grandfather and Radi, the notable, his uncle. He learned the sad story of his origins and the glorious history of al-Nagi. But he was doomed to be known as a bastard forever.

"Watch you don't start using violence," al-Gada cautioned him one day. "Just put up with the insults. Otherwise you can look for another job."

"Mu'nis al-Al is watching you with interest because you're a Nagi. Don't be tempted to use your strength, or you've had it," warned Sayyid Osman, the new imam.

So Galal controlled himself and kept out of trouble, and his diligence and reliability earned him the respect of his boss.

10.

The days passed and hopes were rekindled. Encouraged by al-Gada's obvious liking for Galal, Zaynat went to ask him for his daughter's hand for her son.

The man was blunt. "He's a good lad, but I'm not marrying my daughter to a bastard."

Zaynat wept bitterly, but Galal bore the blow with stoicism.

11.

Al-Gada died after eating a baking dish of beans with onions and tomatoes and a tray of vermicelli pastries and sweet cream. He was over seventy. Zaynat waited until the year's mourning was up, then asked his widow for her daughter's hand for Galal. She accepted because she had noticed her daughter was fond of the young man.

So it was that Afifa al-Gada married Galal Abdullah.

12.

Through marriage Galal rose from being a driver to running the carter's business, even though Afifa was not, properly speaking, the proprietor. He was a success, his living conditions improved, and his joy was complete when he became a father. In the happy time that followed, Afifa gave birth to several daughters and then a son, whom he promptly named Shams al-Din Galal al-Nagi, thereby disclosing the fierce pride that was hidden in him like fire in flint. Everyone accepted the name, although the important members of the Nagi family—such as Radi—were annoyed by it. However, nobody had forgotten that Galal was the illegitimate son of the madman who had built the satanic minaret.

"What a lot of Ashurs and Shams al-Dins there are in our alley!" exclaimed Anba al-Fawwal, the bar owner, who had taken over when Sanqar al-Shammam died.

It was true that all that was left of the immortal Nagi heritage were the names. The deeds and promises lived on in the imagination along with the legends of miracles overlaid with grief and pain.

13.

The days went by pleasantly and mundanely in the lives of Galal
Abdullah and his family. He was known for his goodness, honesty,
even temper, and piety. He made a good living, adored his devotions, and became a close associate of Sheikh Sayyid Osman, the
imam of the alley's small mosque. He was faithful to Afifa and
satisfied with her company, raised Shams al-Din well, and remained a loyal son to Zaynat despite the bad reputation and the
troubles she had bequeathed to him. All the signs were that this
family would lead a tranquil and uneventful life.

14.

When Galal was fifty his life was changed by a series of unexpected
events descending on him from out of the blue. First his mother
died. She died suddenly, aged eighty. What was strange was that
although Galal was a middle-aged man and his mother an old
woman, her death came as a violent shock which threw him completely off balance. He sobbed like a child at her funeral and was
sunk in such deep depression for the next three months that people
thought he was going into a decline. Many found his grief incomprehensible and made fun of him. He even said himself that although he had loved her a great deal he could not have imagined
her death would have such an effect on him. More remarkable than
that was what happened to him after the depression had lifted. A
new person was there in his place, like an apparition discharged
from a haunted archway. The love he had felt for his mother
seemed to him an odd, misguided sentiment, as if he had been the
victim of black magic. It had evaporated into the air, leaving a cold
hard stone behind it. Not a trace of sorrow or loyalty was left in his
heart. A voice whispered to him that she was the source of all the
hostility and dislike he had encountered in his life; and that he was
her eternal victim.

"Was I really sad when she died?" he wondered to himself.
"It must have been some crazy, illogical reaction to death."

He was sitting with Sheikh Mugahid Ibrahim one day. "My mother had some loathsome characteristics," he announced suddenly, "and a bad reputation, and evil intentions."

"I can hardly believe what I'm hearing," said the sheikh in astonishment.

"Now I think she really did kill my father. She was a debauched, loudmouthed drug addict. I'm revolted by her memory."

"Don't speak ill of the dead."

"There's nothing good to be said," he cried with uncharacteristic ill feeling. Then, his fury mounting, he added, "She had a long, happy life, which she didn't deserve."

15.

His behavior went downhill to the point of complete collapse.

He stopped praying, abandoned the mosque, was prone to violent outbursts. One night he stormed into the bar for the first time in his life. Mu'nis al-Al and some of his men were sitting there. "At last the donkey's found its stall!" jeered the chief.

The bar erupted into laughter. Galal merely smiled, somewhat embarrassed, and raised the calabash to his thirsty lips.

"What prompted you to behave like a man?" inquired Mu'nis.

"It's the right way to be," answered Galal cheerfully.

When the chief left, Galal began to sing:

> *At the gate of our alley*
> *Sits Hasan the coffee man.*

He was thoroughly drunk. "Last night I dreamed I slipped out to my father's minaret," he declared convivially. "A handsome creature carried me to the top and invited me to play hopscotch with him. I lost my balance and fell down the stairwell. But I wasn't the least bit hurt."

"You should try it when you're awake," remarked Anba al-Fawwal, the bar owner.

Galal began to sing again:

At night I hear songs
Of passionate virgins
My strength is destroyed.

16.

He found Afifa waiting up for him. He had never stayed out like
this before. The bar smells hit her in the face. She beat her chest
with the flat of her hand.

"You're drunk!" she cried.

He executed a few dance steps. "I'm a man, my beauty!"

17.

The news spread. People said, "He's crazy, just like his father."

Sheikh Sayyid Osman went up to him in the street one day.
"What's taken you away from us?" he asked.

Galal said nothing.

"Is it true what they say about you?" persisted the sheikh
sorrowfully.

Galal walked off up the street leaving him standing.

18.

When he was drunk and didn't know what he was doing, he was
the prey of new temptations, as if he had developed the instincts of
a stranger. He was violently attracted to adolescent and even
prepubescent girls. He pestered them, flirted with them, and if he
found himself alone with one of them felt as if a ravenous beast was
struggling to escape from his skin. He avoided getting drunk in the
daytime, fearing the consequences, and at night he slunk around
waste ground and derelict buildings like a hungry wolf.

One night he ended up with a prostitute called Dalal and gave
his passions their head.

19.

He became thoroughly dissolute and devoted great energy to pouring scorn on everything around him. What bound him to Dalal was probably the fact that she was young, with a face that still bore the imprint of childhood, and tolerated his strange whims, indulging them without criticism.

"I love people who are crazy and don't give a damn what people say about them," she declared one day.

"At last I've found a woman as great as my grandmother Zahira!" exclaimed Galal.

He lay sprawled on his back, relaxed and contented. "One morning I woke up drunk, even though I'd had nothing to drink," he confessed to her. "There was a new heart beating in my chest. I hated my present and my past, even the thought of working at my trade and making money. My married daughters' problems depressed me. So did my son's lack of spirit. He's quite happy to work as a driver for me. One donkey driving another! I was fed up with his mother, who protects him every step of the way, and bleeds me just like my mother used to, only using different tactics. My heart, my head, my guts, my prick, and my balls rose up in protest and I yelled out my good news to the devils."

"You're the sweetest man in the world," laughed Dalal.

"I've heard that men are reborn at fifty," he said confidently.

"And sixty. And seventy," she agreed.

He sighed. "If it hadn't been for a spiteful woman's jealousy, my father would have lived forever."

"If you hadn't been a miracle, I wouldn't have loved you at all."

20.

The blows continued to land on Afifa's head. Her world crumbled around her, her dreams evaporated, her happiness vanished. She was convinced her husband was under a spell, and made the rounds of saints' tombs and fortune-tellers. She followed all the

advice she was given, but Galal persisted in his erring ways and
showed no signs of repenting. He neglected his work, was always
rowdy and drunk, clung to Dalal, and damaged his reputation
running after girls.

Had she not been scared of the consequences she would have
complained about him to Mu'nis al-Al. But in her isolation she only
had her son, and she turned to him to tell him of her distress. "Talk
to him, Shams al-Din," she said. "Perhaps he'll be more ready to
listen to you."

Shams al-Din and his mother had a surprisingly close relationship. He was sad for her reputation and her honor, and summoned the courage to tell his father openly. His father grabbed him
by the shoulders and shook him violently. "Are you trying to tell
me what to do, son?" he demanded in a fury.

After that the boy kept his worries to himself. In his physical
strength, pleasant manner, and good character he resembled his
father before his abrupt transformation. He was at a loss. His feelings were in a state of turmoil: his respect for his father and his
mild nature were both under threat. His mother complained constantly, and he was the one who had to take her blasts of venom
and bitterness.

"He'll squander it all," she would say ominously. "You'll be
out on the streets."

To him, his family seemed permanently cursed. They all
ended up mad, debauched, or dead. His heart shriveled, as the love
and loyalty began to ebb away, and he adopted a more combative
attitude toward the future. "Why did my mother marry a man like
that?" he wondered in astonishment.

21.

Things went from bad to worse, like a summer's morning advanc-
ing to the blazing heat of high noon. Shams al-Din's heart hardened, as his feelings of antipathy and rage mounted. Sitting in the
café one night, he was told that his father was dancing half-naked
in the bar. He rushed there in a frenzy, sick at heart, but determined to take action. He saw his father gyrating drunkenly, clad

only in his underpants. His inebriated audience clapped along with him. "Float on the water," they sang at the tops of their voices.

Galal did not notice his son's arrival and remained completely absorbed in his dancing. Some of the drinkers saw Shams al-Din, stopped clapping and singing, and tried to warn the others.

"Let's watch this. It should be good," urged one of them with malicious pleasure.

As the clapping and singing died down, Galal stopped dancing with an aggrieved air. Then he noticed his son. He saw he was angry and ready to make a stand, and this infuriated him. "What brings you here, lad?" he shouted.

"Please put your clothes on, father," said Shams al-Din politely.

"I said what brings you here, you cheeky son of a bitch?"

"Please get dressed," persisted the boy.

His father lunged unsteadily at him and gave him a slap that ripped through the silence of the bar.

A chorus of voices egged him on approvingly.

The man fell on his son again, but he was so drunk that his strength soon gave out and he collapsed on the floor, unconscious.

There was a short burst of laughter, then silence returned to the bar.

"You've killed your father, Shams al-Din," a voice called.

"He didn't even have time to say his prayers!"

Shams al-Din bent over his father to put his clothes back on, then slung him over his shoulder and carried him out in a hail of coarse, mocking laughter.

22.

Galal came to shortly afterward lying on his bed in his marital home. His red eyes roamed around him and fell upon Afifa, Shams al-Din, and the familiar features of the room he hated. It was nighttime and he should have been in bed with Dalal. This boy had made him the laughingstock of the drunks in the bar and not shown him the respect owing to a father. He sat up in bed, fuming with rage. Then he leapt to the ground. He lunged at Shams al-

Din, and began pounding him with his fists. Afifa threw herself between them, sobbing loudly. Galal turned on her in blind fury. He grabbed her around the throat and squeezed hard. Vainly the woman tried to struggle free, giving every sign that she was being choked to death.

"Leave her alone. You're killing her," shouted Shams al-Din.

Intoxicated by the savagery of the crime, Galal paid no attention. In desperation Shams al-Din seized a wooden seat and brought it down on Galal's head with demented energy.

23.

A heavy calm took the place of the shouting and hysteria. Galal lay supine on the bed, soaked in his own blood. The neighbors came rushing to see, closely followed by Sheikh Mugahid Ibrahim. The barber gave first aid and stopped the bleeding, while Shams al-Din cowered in a corner, abandoning himself to his fate.

Time was absent altogether. One mocking instant had spread out far and wide, bursting with possibilities. A single haphazard moment, more influential than all the thought and planning in the world. Afifa and Shams al-Din each realized that the present was thrusting away the past, destroying it, burying it.

"What cruel fate would play games with a father and his only son?" muttered Mugahid Ibrahim.

"It's the devil," wailed Afifa.

Silence hung over Galal like a mountain. His chest continued to rise and fall.

"Galal!" called Mugahid Ibrahim.

"God have mercy on us!" cried Afifa.

"What can you find?" the sheikh asked the barber.

"It's in God's hands," answered the barber, still intent on his work.

"But you have your expertise as well."

The barber approached the sheikh. "No one could survive such a beating," he said under his breath.

24.

Galal opened his dim eyes. He could scarcely recognize anybody. Still he said nothing, until the nerves of those around him were at breaking point, but gradually he began to recover consciousness.

"I'm dying," he murmured.

"Don't say such things," gasped Afifa.

"The shadows don't frighten me."

"You're fine."

"God's will be done."

Mugahid Ibrahim approached the bed. "Galal," he said. "It's Mugahid Ibrahim. Speak before these witnesses."

"Where's Shams al-Din?" asked Galal in a weak voice.

Mugahid Ibrahim summoned him to the bedside.

"He's here beside you."

"I'm dying."

"What happened?" asked the sheikh.

"It was an act of God."

"Who hit you?"

Galal said nothing.

"Tell us," insisted the sheikh.

"I'm dying."

"Who hit you?"

"My father," sighed Galal.

"Dead people don't hit you. You have to tell us."

He sighed again. "I don't know."

"How's that?"

"The alley was dark."

"Did someone attack you in the alley?"

"On my own doorstep."

"You must know who it was."

"I don't. The darkness hid him. He didn't want to be seen."

"Do you have any enemies?"

"I don't know."

"Do you suspect anyone?"

"No."

"You don't know who did it and you don't suspect anyone?"

"I called to my son to help me and then I lost consciousness."

Mugahid Ibrahim was silent. All eyes were on Galal as he lay dying.

25.

Shams al-Din listened in astonishment to his father's last words. His courage failed him and he said nothing. He received the dying man's affection with humility, cowardice, and regret. He avoided meeting Mugahid Ibrahim's eyes, then buried his face in his hands and wept. Throughout the funeral and the days immediately following it, when people flocked to offer their condolences, he never closed his eyes in sleep and moved among them like a ghost pursued by the shades of hell. His grandfather and great-grandmother had gone mad; one of the line had been a foul pervert; but he was the first of the cursed Nagi family to kill his father.

When he was finally alone with his mother she said encouragingly, "You didn't murder your father. You were forced to defend me." Then she added, "Don't forget. God knows the whole truth." Then, impassionedly, "The way he protected you is enough to atone for all his sins. He'll meet his Lord as pure and innocent as a newborn baby!"

Shams al-Din dissolved in tears, murmuring, "I've killed my father."

26.

Abd Rabbihi invited Shams al-Din to The Citadel, former home of Galal, the builder of the minaret. Shams al-Din knew he was his great-grandfather and that he was about a hundred. He found an old man who no longer left his house, or even his room, but who, for his age, was astonishingly healthy, lively, and dignified, and saw, heard, and understood what went on. Shams al-Din marveled at the way he had remained in such good shape and outlived both his son and grandson, but felt not one jot of love or respect for him and did not forget how he had treated his father.

Abd Rabbihi scrutinized him for some time, his face a few inches away from Shams al-Din's. "My condolences," he said at last.

Shams al-Din responded coldly.

"You resemble your grandfather," said Abd Rabbihi.

"You severed all connections with my father," said Shams al-Din icily.

"Things were complicated," replied Abd Rabbihi.

"You mean you wanted the legacy to yourself," he said fiercely.

"Apart from Ashur's legacy, inherited wealth is a curse."

"But you're enjoying it right up till the end."

"I invited you here to express my sympathy," said the old man, troubled. "Take your share if you want it."

"I refuse to accept any kindness from you," said Shams al-Din, as if expiating his sin.

"You're stubborn, my child."

"I don't want anything to do with a man who disowned my father."

The old man closed his eyes. Shams al-Din left the house.

27.

Shams al-Din had to confront life. His features were stamped with a gravity which aged him by fifty years. He tried to behave devoutly and honorably. He took his father's place at the head of the carting business and immersed himself in work as a means of escape. He was known in the alley as a father-killer, a curse on two legs, corresponding to that stationary anathema, the minaret. What would you expect of a young man who was the son of a bastard and the grandson of the man responsible for building the minaret? Shams al-Din resolved to brave his ill luck with a stern face and an inflexible will, nourished by the regret which filled his heart. He followed his religion faithfully, gave alms to the poor, behaved amicably to his customers, but led an outcast's existence. His eyes wore a look of permanent melancholy. He hated all forms of merriment, singing, music, the bar, the hashish den. Since people caused him anguish, he hated them too, but he clung on to life.

28.

Marriage was the best remedy Afifa could come up with. Sadiqa the bean seller's daughter pleased her and she went to propose the engagement, commending her son's reliable occupation and illustrious forbears, but the family declined to marry their daughter to a father killer. Shams al-Din was not much interested in marriage, but this refusal rubbed salt into his wounds and he determined to marry at any price.

There was a dancer called Nur al-Sabah al-Agami, a girl of easy virtue whose background nobody knew. He liked the look of her and visited her after dark one night, not to sleep with her as she had expected but to propose to her! The girl was amazed and assumed he must be planning to make her work for him.

"No, I want you to be the lady of the house in every sense," he told her sincerely.

Her face lit up with pleasure. "You're a fine young man, and it's no more than I deserve."

29.

Afifa was upset. "She's a whore," she protested.

"Like my grandmother Zaynat," said Shams al-Din sullenly. Then he added sarcastically, "Our distinguished family seems to be full of them!"

"Don't give up so easily, son."

"She's the only one who'll have me without bad feeling."

30.

Nur al-Sabah married Shams al-Din Galal al-Nagi. Emerging from his seclusion he gave a party for his employees and his mother's family, ignoring those who ignored him. The alley sneered at the marriage. The names of Zaynat and Zahira were frequently on people's lips as they recounted snippets about the family that had descended from the heavens and was finally rolling in the mire.

The bar owner Anba al-Fawwal declared boldly, "Ashur himself was an abandoned baby, wasn't he? And the mother of his children worked in this very bar."

31.

The marriage was destined to succeed. Nur al-Sabah metamorphosed into a housewife. Shams al-Din was happy with her and part of him was more at ease. All that clouded the serene atmosphere were the sporadic quarrels between Afifa and Nur. Afifa was stern and intolerant, Nur sharp-tongued and fiery. But these did not shatter the conjugal harmony and Nur gave birth to three girls and was finally blessed with a boy, Samaha.

32.

With the passage of time Shams al-Din became less aware of his worries, and the painful memories of his crime faded to the back of his mind, although melancholy had become part of his nature. Samaha did not have the good looks of his father and grandfather, but rejoiced in a more powerful physique. His mother and grandmother doted on him, guarding him like a precious treasure. He did badly at Quran school. One day he was fighting with a schoolmate and hit him in the face with a slate, almost blinding him. This landed his father in a lot of difficulty and he could only extricate himself by paying a considerable sum in compensation. Back home he thrashed the boy savagely, much to the sorrow of his mother and grandmother, then dragged him to work in the stable prematurely, saying, "Let's hope you learn some manners from the donkeys."

Samaha grew up under his father's gloomy eye and rapidly reached adolescence.

33.

Although the boy was never out of his sight from the moment he awoke until bedtime, he was uneasy about him, sensing a willfulness there and anticipating trouble.

Then one day Sheikh Mugahid Ibrahim remarked spitefully to him, "Give them an inch and they take a mile!"

He had the feeling he meant Samaha but found it hard to believe since he kept such a firm hold over him. He pressed the sheikh to be more explicit.

"Did you know your son was Karima al-Anabi's lover?"

Shams al-Din was shocked. When did the boy get the chance? "He's never out of my sight till bedtime."

"Then while you're asleep he slips out of the house," laughed the sheikh.

Still Shams al-Din could not take it in. Karima al-Anabi was a widow approaching sixty and his son was a teenager.

"Take care he doesn't get used to all that sophistication and maturity!" teased Mugahid Ibrahim.

34.

Shams al-Din lay in wait in the darkness outside Karima's door. He had ascertained that the boy's bed was empty. An hour before dawn the door opened and a shadowy figure slipped out. He walked straight into his father's arms. He was afraid at first and got ready to strike out at his assailant, but then he recognized the voice and capitulated.

"Filthy pig!" Shams al-Din dragged him furiously after him and caught a whiff of his breath. "You're drunk too."

He struck him a blow that drove the cheap brandy right out of his head. Once he had got him home he started to beat him so savagely that Nur and Afifa woke up, and learned the story through the words and blows.

"Stop, father! My face!" shouted Samaha.

"I should kill you! You went behind my back!"

"I swear I won't do it again! Please stop!"

"She's older than I am. Sinful creature!" snorted Afifa.

Shams al-Din gestured toward Samaha. "He's the guilty one. Nobody else."

35.

Shams al-Din thought to himself that such beginnings threatened much worse to come. If you began by making love to a woman old enough to be your grandmother, where did you go from there? He had seen Madame Karima on her outings around the alley, and been appalled by her youthful dress and garish makeup, coupled with her exuberantly overweight body. He was convinced, in any case, that it was a complete disaster for an adolescent youth to get used to being kept by a woman.

At this time Mu'nis al-Al died and Suma al-Kalabshi succeeded him as clan chief. Conditions in the alley were more degrading and unjust than ever. The harafish accepted these misfortunes as the inescapable blows of fate. The whole clan system—regardless of who the chief was—had become one long-standing calamity.

36.

Grandfather Abd Rabbihi died and was given a big funeral which neither Shams al-Din nor Samaha attended. Afterward they learned that he had left Samaha five hundred pounds, but when the boy asked for it, his father told him to wait until he was officially an adult. He watched the boy more closely than ever and made his life miserable. One day when they were working together in the stable he happened to look over at him and caught an empty, blank expression in his eyes that made him feel dispirited. "The boy doesn't love me," he said to himself. He sighed. "He's stupid. Doesn't he realize I'm doing it for his own good?"

37.

Events rushed by like the dusty foam on the river. One morning as Shams al-Din sipped his coffee he detected a dreadful anxiety enveloping Nur and Afifa. His heart pounded. "Where's Samaha?"

He was met with an uneasy silence and his fears grew.

"What's he done now?" he asked sharply.

Nur started crying and Afifa said in a tremulous voice, "He's not in the house."

"So he's started creeping around in the night again?"

"No. He's left us."

"Run away?" Heavy with apprehension, he went over to the strongbox and found the legacy gone. "He's a thief as well," he bellowed.

"Don't be hard on him, son. It's his money," said Afifa.

"A thief and a runaway," declared Shams al-Din emphatically. He shifted his eyes suspiciously between the two women. "What's going on behind my back?" he demanded.

38.

He presumed he would take refuge with Karima al-Anabi. Mugahid Ibrahim made inquiries.

"Not a trace of him anywhere in the alley," he reported several hours later.

Shams al-Din was convinced that God was punishing him for his crime. He'd have to pay, just as he'd already paid for the sins of others. His son would probably kill him one day. Why not? The boy was completely cynical about the world. Shams al-Din threw a ferocious glance at the minaret. "Why don't they demolish that obscenity?"

39.

Not a trace was found of Samaha even though Shams al-Din charged his drivers to be on the lookout and make inquiries wher-

ever they went. The boy was following in the footsteps of all the
other men and women in the family who had disappeared leaving
no clues behind them.

The years went by. Afifa died after a long illness. Nur's life
had turned sour. Shams al-Din learned to bear his burdens, muttering, "What will be, will be," whenever things went wrong.

40.

However, unlike Ashur and Qurra, Samaha did not stay away for
good. He returned to the alley one day, a grown man. A grown
man, who had lost many precious things forever. His body was full
of brutal power. His beauty was hidden by a mask of severity and
an uneven tissue of scars and bruises. Had he been hiding out with
bandits? Even his own father failed to recognize him at first glance.
When he realized the truth and was hit by a great wave of mingled
joy and sorrow, he was uncertain whether to be relieved or resentful. He was torn between love and rage. In the stables among the
bustle of drivers and donkeys they exchanged a long look.

"What have you been doing all this time?" he asked pityingly,
taking him aside.

He repeated the question, while Samaha remained silent, his
appearance speaking for him.

"Did you spend the money?"

Samaha bowed his head. Ah! Some make their money work
for them, others fritter it away. He heaved a deep sigh and muttered, "Perhaps this has taught you a lesson." Then, irritated by his
silence, "Go and see your mother."

41.

The feeble flicker of hope in Shams al-Din's heart quickly died. He
recovered from the fierce wave of paternal feeling which had swept
over him. He saw in his son obstinacy, deviousness, and stupidity,
united in a sort of inflexible, cruel strength he had never encountered before. Still he did not despair altogether. "Back to work,

son," he said gently. "You have to prepare to take over this business one day."

Nur encouraged him with her affection, her entreaties. Samaha refused to work as a driver, so his father kept him at his side letting him help in the essential running of the business. But he was restless and kept asking for more money. His father could no longer treat him like a child and he spent his evenings in the bar, the hashish den, with prostitutes, but he never went near his first mistress.

"You ought to think about getting married," Shams al-Din said to him in his mother's presence.

"There isn't really a girl worthy of a descendant of the great al-Nagi!" he teased.

"Do you realize what this name implies?"

"People who perform extraordinary miracles like building a haunted minaret!" he said brazenly.

"You're crazy!" cried Shams al-Din in a fury. Then he gave up and walked off, muttering, "He hates me, that's for sure."

He shook off his forebodings for a while but could not help thinking gloomily, from time to time, "He'll kill me one day."

42.

Shams al-Din discovered that a considerable sum of money had gone missing. He knew at once what this meant and realized he would end up going bankrupt. He went straight off to the bar. Samaha was sitting with Suma al-Kalabshi and his men as if he was one of them. He gestured to his son to accompany him but he did not move. Lost in a fog of alcohol, he stared at his father aggressively.

Shams al-Din swallowed his anger. "You know why I'm here," he said.

"It's my money just as much as yours. And I'll spend it as I think fit," retorted Samaha coldly.

"Well said," put in Suma al-Kalabshi.

"You'll ruin me," said Shams al-Din, ignoring the clan chief's remark.

"You have to spend money to make money," answered Samaha with heavy sarcasm.

"This boy talks sense!" said Suma.

Anba al-Fawwal moved close to Shams al-Din. "Count to ten," he warned in a low voice.

But Shams al-Din succumbed to his anger. "You are all my witnesses," he shouted. "I'm throwing this ungrateful son of mine out of my house, and I disclaim all responsibility for him from this moment on."

43.

For Nur al-Sabah this was a dreadful calamity.

"I'll never give up my son," she cried.

Shams al-Din hated her at that moment with the full force of his anger and resentment. "He won't enter this house again as long as I live."

"My son! I won't let him go!"

"It's your sordid background coming to the surface," he said, beside himself with rage.

"There are no whores or madmen in my family!"

He struck her, knocking her to the floor. Crazed with anger, she spat in his face.

"Get out of here! I'm divorcing you," he roared.

44.

Nur and Samaha went to live in a separate flat together. Samaha joined Suma al-Kalabshi's gang, but because he was so extravagant he was never content. He made no attempt to hide his hatred for his father and denounced the Nagi family vigorously, as if he was their worst enemy.

Shams al-Din lived alone. He no longer felt secure and expected to end up like his father or worse. He went to enormous lengths to protect himself, heaping generosity on his employees to win their hearts, keeping his doors and windows firmly locked, making donations to Suma and being as friendly as possible to him.

45.

One day Mugahid Ibrahim visited him. "I'm here to give you a piece of advice," he announced.

"What do you mean?" asked Shams al-Din with foreboding.

"Stop being so hostile. Give him some money."

Shams al-Din could think of nothing appropriate to say so the sheikh continued, "Yesterday in the bar I heard him promising his companions a few good evenings, once . . ."

He hesitated and Shams al-Din finished gloomily for him, "Once I die or someone kills me off."

"Murder wasn't mentioned. But there's nothing sadder than seeing a son wishing his father dead . . . or vice versa."

"But I don't wish him dead."

"We're only human," said the sheikh, making his meaning plain.

46.

Shams al-Din felt fear like a bird of ill omen hovering over him. He set off to see the clan chief, resolved on a singular course of action. He saluted him respectfully, then said without further pre-amble, "Do me the honor of granting me your daughter's hand."

The chief stared hard at him, then said, "There's no law against a girl of sixteen marrying a man in his forties."

Shams al-Din bowed his head humbly and Suma continued, "You're from good stock and you've got plenty of money!"

Shams al-Din continued to look deferential, satisfied with his reception so far.

"What would you pay for her?"

"Whatever you ask," answered Shams al-Din with secret trep-idation.

"Five hundred pounds."

"It's a vast sum, but she's worth more than money," he said sagely.

The chief held out his hand. "Let's make that official."

47.

Sanbala Suma al-Kalabshi married Shams al-Din Galal al-Nagi.

The whole alley came to the wedding. Shams al-Din found himself in an eminently desirable and secure position. Sanbala was not beautiful but she was young and strong. She was also the chief's daughter.

48.

Nur and Samaha were in a state of panic.

"I might as well say goodbye to my inheritance," said Samaha.

"But your rights won't be affected," said his mother, as if she didn't have much faith in what she was saying.

"Do you imagine Kalabshi will bother with the law?"

"Life's more precious than money," Nur admonished.

"The man has me watched day and night," exploded Samaha. "I'm the successor to the terrible Nagis. And this new alliance will make him more wary than ever."

Nur sighed. "Watch out for yourself, son. To hell with your father! And God preserve you."

49.

Samaha was convinced his life was still in danger, because his death would make Sanbala sole inheritor after Shams al-Din and enable the chief to consolidate his position once and for all.

It was strange, but Shams al-Din himself did not enjoy the lethargy of his newfound security for long. What was there to stop Samaha taking revenge on him? He knew his son's wild, rash nature better than anyone. And Suma al-Kalabshi had all the cards in his hand now. His fear of dying had thrust him right into the lion's jaws. The chief would not rest until he had taken his last penny off him. He felt no real affection for Sanbala, and his yearning for Nur returned with a vengeance. But he had to endure this union along with the other irritations in his life. A simple truth was embedding its claws in his flesh: the past would never return.

50.

Suma al-Kalabshi visited him one night. He signaled to his daughter to leave the room and Shams al-Din feared the worst. What did it mean, this nighttime visit? Suma's face, round as a ball, covered in scars, repelled him. He hated his easy manner, as if he was in his own home. The chief began to talk about amazing coincidences, odd twists of fate, the obscure forces controlling men's destinies. Shams al-Din was at a loss, until finally the chief said, "For example, look how a particular person's existence is equally inconvenient for both of us!"

Instantly Shams al-Din realized where the man's speculations had been heading. An image of his son rose up before his eyes. He was more alarmed by this complicity with his secret desires than he was afraid for Samaha. He decided to act the innocent. "Who do you mean?"

"Come on!" said Kalabshi scathingly. "What kind of fool do you take me for?"

"Do you mean Samaha?"

"So do you!"

"He's my son."

"You were your father's son!"

He winced. "You're powerful enough. You shouldn't be afraid of anyone."

"Cut it out. Are you really that stupid?"

"Perhaps you should make yourself clearer."

"Put everything in your wife's name, then Samaha will give up and go away."

His heart sank. "Or finally decide to have his revenge on me," he said desperately.

"As long as I'm alive, no harm will come to you."

He saw the trap open wide, the hunter baring his teeth. Poverty or death or both at the same time. Impossible to accept, impossible to refuse.

"Give me time to think," he implored.

The chief glowered. "I've never heard anything like it."

"A little time," he begged.

"Tomorrow morning. That gives you all night," said the man, getting to his feet.

51.

Shams al-Din couldn't sleep. Sanbala, all beautifully dressed and made up, tired of waiting for him and fell asleep. He put out the light and sat huddled in his cloak against the cold. He saw the specters in the dark. All the specters from the past. Why this sudden disintegration after he had persevered so long? Hadn't he borne his burdens serenely? Paid for his sins without complaining? Always been serious, reliable, patient? So why this to take away all he'd struggled for? It was because he had plunged into an abyss of fear. Fear was at the root of the misfortune. He had been frightened of his son and driven him out, then divorced his wife, then gone running into the devil's lair. Without stopping to think rationally. Because he had panicked. When he had fought fear and beaten it, he had faced life with his head held high. His family's bad reputation, his own foul crime, the alley's scorn, had not defeated him. He had faced life boldly, put despair to work for him. On immoral foundations he had built a respectable home. He had prospered in his business, gained power and wealth. Now he was being asked to give up his riches. Next Samaha would kill him and be arrested for his crime, then Kalabshi would have wealth and security. A specter in the darkness said, "Don't kill your son. Don't make your son kill you. Don't submit to a tyrant. Don't let fear get the better of you. Put despair to work for you. If life becomes impossible, seek consolation honorably in death."

The winter wind wailed mournfully. Intoxicated by his reveries, he pictured Ashur listening to the same wind one night long ago in his immortal basement room.

52.

In the morning a light rain had begun to fall, breathing the pure, capricious, rebellious spirit of the late winter season, and the cold chilled people to the marrow of their bones. Shams al-Din made his way over the slippery ground with the aid of his stout stick. Suma welcomed him, sitting cross-legged on his sofa in the café. "Good to see you, Shams al-Din!" He motioned him to sit beside him, and murmured, "Shall we start proceedings for the sale?"

"No," replied Shams al-Din with frightening calm.

"No?!"

"There's no deal."

The chief's face grew livid with anger. "This is an insane decision."

"It's the voice of reason."

A grim mask of evil etched itself on Suma's features. "Don't you depend on your alliance with me?"

"Apart from God, I depend only on myself," said Shams al-Din with the same resolute calm.

"Are you challenging me?"

"I'm explaining my position, that's all."

Anger seized Suma and he slapped him hard. Enraged, Shams al-Din returned the blow with even greater ferocity. The two men jumped to their feet in a single moment, brandishing their clubs, and began to fight savagely. Shams al-Din was strong and ten years younger than Suma, but he didn't have the habit of fighting. Suma's men appeared on all sides with amazing promptness. Samaha was among them. In deference to the traditions, they surrounded the combatants but did not intervene. Suma al-Kalabshi had the upper hand and summoned his strength to deliver the decisive blow. At that moment Samaha suddenly leapt forward and brought his club down on the chief's head. Suma's legs gave way beneath him and he crashed over on his back. This all happened at lightning speed. The men shouted and fell on Shams al-Din and Samaha. But there was another surprise in store. A group of

Suma's men crossed over to join forces with Shams al-Din and Samaha.

"It's a mutiny!" cried several voices.

The two groups fought one another with savage enthusiasm. Clubs clashed, bodies made violent contact, loud cracks exploded in the air, curses flew about under the damp rain, blood flowed, hatreds were unleashed. Shutters were closed on shopfronts, carts hurtled along, people gathered at either end of the alley, windows and wooden lattices were crowded with faces. Shouting and wailing rose to the sky.

53.

Shams al-Din's broken body was carried to his house. Samaha managed to drag himself home to bed, where he lay more dead than alive. Suma was finished, his legend destroyed, his men routed.

54.

The same day, the truth was uncovered. Samaha wanted to be chief and had secretly won a group of Suma's men over to his side. He planned to eliminate the chief and gain control over his father. The surprise battle between the two men had given him the opportunity he needed. When he attacked to protect his father he signaled the start of his insurrection. His plan had succeeded, but for the moment he hovered between life and death.

55.

The rain continued to fall throughout the day. The air was dark reddish-brown, steeped in drowsiness. The sticky ground was patterned with animals' hooves. Shams al-Din lay dying, cared for by a neighbor, since Sanbala had fled. He didn't open his eyes or speak a word, only stirred vaguely every now and then. He appeared detached from everything around him, and in the middle of the night he died.

The Thief Who Stole the Melody

The ninth tale in the epic

of the harafish

1.

𝓕ate decreed that Samaha should live. Gradually he recovered his health and strength. The last battle had scarred and disfigured him, and he looked ugly and intimidating. He took over as chief of the clan without a struggle and enjoyed unlimited power. Nur rejoiced at her good fortune and her decisive victory over Sanbala, who was obliged to return to her aged father's house to give birth to a son. She named him Fath al-Bab, after her maternal grandfather. Shams al-Din's legacy was divided between his two sons, Samaha and Fath al-Bab, and his widow Sanbala. Samaha appointed himself his stepbrother's guardian. Since no one dared oppose him, most of his father's wealth fell into his steely grasp.

"You abandoned my father," he said to Sanbala, "you left him alone when he was dying. It would be unfair for you to inherit any of his money. Don't expect a penny of Fath al-Bab's share to come your way either. Think of some of it as protection money and the rest as punishment for your sins!"

2.

Samaha created a legend around himself. He declared that he had only entered the battle against al-Kalabshi to defend his father, in spite of the animosity between them, and that the men who had gone over to his side had done so spontaneously, driven by a noble impulse. Nobody believed a word of this. It was widely known that he had been plotting against the chief, had incited some of his men to rebel, and had merely profited from the occasion to seize power. His detractors accused him of not defending his father as he ought to have done, and of being glad when he died. But he knew nothing of this and continued to bathe in his manufactured glory.

His reign hung over the alley like the shadow of a huge mountain, but to his credit he brought the neighboring chiefs to heel, and restored the alley to its former position of power. He built a sumptuous house where he installed his mother, and divided his own time between the bar, the smoking den, and the neighborhood brothels.

3.

Suma al-Kalabshi died and his daughter Sanbala inherited a small fortune which she shared with her ten sisters. Soon afterward she married a moneylender's clerk, who was reluctant to welcome his wife's son by her first marriage. Things grew worse when he and Sanbala had children of their own, and Fath al-Bab grew up in a miserable atmosphere, clinging to his mother and avoiding the master of the house. He felt a growing sense of pain and isolation which was not eased by his excellent performance at Quran school or his gentle nature and good behavior. When he was nine years old his mother took him to the chief.

"Here's your brother," she said. "It's time you took him under your wing."

Samaha examined him. He looked handsome, frail, sad, but his heart didn't warm to him. "What's wrong with him? He looks half-starved!"

"He's not. But he's a delicate boy."

"To see him, you wouldn't think he was descended from clan chiefs on both sides! It's more appropriate for you to take care of him," he said, trying to shrug off the unwanted burden.

Her eyes filled with tears. "He's not happy with me, there's nothing more I can do."

Samaha, feeling obliged to take him, presented the child to his mother. She protested vigorously. "I don't have the energy to look after children anymore."

The truth was that she was horrified at the idea of raising her co-wife's son. Samaha was at a loss, and the boy had to bear his humiliation and distress without a murmur. Seeing his plight, an old woman, a friend of Nur's, volunteered to look after him. Sahar the midwife was a widow without children of her own, and a descendant of the Nagis. She lived in a two-room basement in a building which had belonged to Galal, the minaret man. She was good-hearted, proud of her lineage, and with her for the first time Fath al-Bab had a cozy, untroubled life, which helped him bear the separation from his mother.

4.

One day a pretty young girl caught Samaha's eye. She wasn't his for the taking like his other women. He saw her passing in a carriage and found out where she lived. In her beautiful face he detected a familiarity which made him think some hidden affinity existed between them. He soon discovered why. It turned out that she was Firdus, Radi's granddaughter. His attraction was based on lust for her and a desire to possess her, but it was so powerful that it made him think seriously about marriage for the first time in his dissolute life. Added to that, he was tempted by the fact that she owned the cereal business and was a Nagi like him. His mother was amazed when he asked her to arrange the engagement, but overjoyed at the same time.

"What makes us a good match," chuckled Samaha, "is that we're both descended from beautiful, crazy Zahira, the mankiller!"

He was so ugly, so bad that he deserved to be turned down, but who would refuse the clan chief?

5.

Firdus married Samaha. Beauty united with the Beast. He had been beautiful once until the clubs rearranged his face. But he was endlessly proud of his origins and his unrivaled strength. Contrary to expectations, the marriage succeeded and they were happy. Samaha became manager of the cereal business and its virtual owner. From his office he unleashed his iron will, and ran the business and directed the gang's military operations with equal zeal. Marriage brought pleasant days and youth and beauty into his life, palatial ease, the habits of refined living against a background of fine artifacts and furnishings, and all the splendors and diversions of wealth and luxury. He did not give up his riotous excesses, but confined them to his marriage nest, installing gilded water pipes and calabashes to enhance his pleasure. Managing the cereal business taught him a love of money, and as he began to amass a fortune he decided to follow in the footsteps of the eccentric Galal and impose his authority not only on people but on objects of value.

6.

Firdus demonstrated that she was intelligent as well as lucky. She loved her husband, gave him children with warmth and tenderness, was tireless in her efforts to make him more cultured and genteel and to possess him completely, but she did this gently, stealthily, without a hint of aggression or arrogance. She did not set great store by the office of clan chief, but was happy to enjoy all its privileges. As a Nagi herself, she extolled the virtues of the legendary chiefs of old with their justice and integrity; at the same time, as a member of the bourgeoisie, she had an aversion to such purity which favored heroic poverty and muzzled the powerful and rich. She was happy for the memory to be a blessing and a source of pride, as long as the clan system of the present was there to achieve power and wealth. There was no harm in Samaha doing what he wanted provided that it was in her house, protected by a gilded veil of wealth and respectability.

The days passed; she was happy. The rich grew richer and the poor grew poorer.

7.

Fath al-Bab continued his education in the Quran school, and learned the Holy Book by heart. He was happy in the affectionate atmosphere of his new home. The shadow of fear had lifted from his soul, revealing a wealth of feelings and a prodigious imagination. He was a boy with a clear, light brown skin, jet-black eyes, a dimple in his chin, a graceful physique, and a pleasant, intelligent air. He forgot his mother, just as she forgot him, and centered all his affection on the midwife Sahar. He loved and revered her, and she explained things to him that he'd never thought about before.

As they sat together in the evenings she would say to him, "We're both descended from the blessed Ashur al-Nagi."

Then she would go on to talk with conviction of the distant past as if to her it was a living, breathing reality. "He came from very noble origins, but his father wanted to protect him from the wrath of a tyrannical clan chief. In a dream he was ordered to leave the boy on the path in the sacred shadow of the monastery."

Fath al-Bab cursed those who called his ancestor a foundling.

Sahar recited, "He came from very noble origins. He was raised by a good man and grew up to be a strong and powerful youth. One night an angel came to him and told him to leave the alley to escape from the plague. He called on the people in the alley to flee with him but they laughed at him, and he departed sadly with his wife and child. When he returned, he saved the alley from suffering and shame, just as God had saved him from death."

She would go on to tell the tale of Ashur's life—his return, his sojourn in the Bannan house, his reign as chief, his covenant—until the boy's eyes were filled with tears.

"Then one day he disappeared. He never came back, so people thought he was dead, but the truth is that he never died."

"Is he still alive today?" asked Fath al-Bab expectantly.

"He'll be alive forever!"

"Why doesn't he come back here?"

"Only God knows the answer to that."

"Might he turn up unexpectedly?"

"Quite possibly."

"Does he know what my brother did?"

"Of course, son."

"Why did he keep quiet about it?"

"Who knows?"

"Doesn't he care about injustice?"

"Of course he does."

"So why doesn't he do anything about it?"

"Who knows? Perhaps because he's angry that people seem indifferent to the tyrant that rules them."

Fath al-Bab was silent. "Is all that really true?" he demanded finally.

"Have I ever lied to you?"

8.

As Fath al-Bab went back and forth to school, he saw Ashur everywhere. He made his heart pound, quickened his imagination, set his hopes and passions alight. He saw him in the mosque, the fountain, the animals' trough. He saw him on the path by the old wall that enclosed the monastery garden and in the little square in front of the monastery. Hour after hour Ashur had contemplated those walls, that closed door, the tall mulberry trees, just as he was doing now. The air was still moist with his breath, with the murmurings of his voice. With his desires and dreams. The secret of his whereabouts was hidden in the folds of the unknown, out of reach of the sun's streaming rays. One day he would definitely return. That's what Sahar had said, and she always told the truth. He would wave his rough stick and Samaha with his ugly face would vanish. That would be the end of his black reign of tyranny, his bloody avarice, his hoarded wealth. The harafish would rejoice at the day of salvation and swim in a sea of light. The madman's minaret would come tumbling down and treachery and foolishness would be buried under its rubble for all time.

Or is it really true that he's ignoring us because we let the tyrant get away with it?

He loved his ancestor. He wanted to please him. But where would he get the strength from, when he had been built skinny as a shadow?

9.

When Fath al-Bab reached adolescence Sahar began thinking about his future. She consulted Sheikh Mugahid Ibrahim.

"Find him an apprenticeship," he advised.

"He's one of the best pupils at Quran school," she declared proudly.

"Aren't you Madame Firdus' midwife?"

"Yes."

"Talk to her about him. And I'll prepare the ground with Samaha."

10.

"Fath al-Bab is a remarkable boy," said Sahar to Firdus. "He's your flesh and blood, and the obvious candidate for a job in his brother's business."

Firdus was quite agreeable and promised to talk to her husband.

11.

Samaha examined his stepbrother carefully. "He's made like a girl," he muttered with scorn.

"That's just the way he is. He has a lot of skills."

"Such as?"

"He knows the Quran by heart. He can write and do sums."

He turned to the boy and asked sarcastically, "Are you trustworthy or light-fingered like the rest of our famous family?"

"I fear God and respect my ancestor," declared Fath al-Bab vehemently.

"The one who built the minaret?"

"Ashur al-Nagi!"

Samaha glowered. His face changed.

"He's an innocent child," Sahar said quickly.

"It's your ancestor Ashur who taught us to steal," said Samaha viciously.

Fath al-Bab was surprised and hurt. Scared he would say something detrimental to his chances, Sahar said, "I can guarantee that he's reliable and serious, as God's my witness."

So Fath al-Bab joined the business as assistant storekeeper.

12.

Fath al-Bab threw himself into his work. The warehouse occupied a vast basement with as much floor space as the shop itself. Sacks of cereal were piled up on shelves and on the ground, but they were constantly being shifted, the scales were never idle, and he was kept busy registering the movement of goods all day long. He met with his brother at least once every morning to report to him on the purchases and sales. The chief was pleased with his energy and keenness, and saw that he had engaged someone who would unconsciously keep an eye on the storekeeper.

"I encourage hard workers and stamp on idleness," he said in his normal fashion.

13.

Following Sahar's advice Fath al-Bab called on Nur, mother of his boss, to pay his respects. Nothing remained of her former beauty, and she gave him a chilly reception, making it plain that she could not forget an affront.

"How's your mother?" she asked him.

"I stopped living with her because her new husband didn't like me, and I haven't seen her since."

"Heartless. That's her only excuse."

He left, privately vowing not to see her again if he could avoid it.

14.

Again on Sahar's insistence he visited Firdus. She welcomed him affectionately and he was entranced by her beauty and elegance.

"I've heard nice things about how hard you work," she told him.

But he noticed that she didn't call her children. Perhaps she was reluctant to introduce a simple worker like him as their uncle. This hurt him, but he decided to do his best to forget it. He left, his senses charmed by her. He vowed not to visit her again either.

15.

Through hard work he gained confidence and pride. He began to imitate grown men, grew a mustache, and wore a fine headcloth around his skullcap. He became an habitúe of the mosque and developed a close bond with Sheikh Sayyid Osman. He spent an hour in the café each evening, drinking cinnamon tea and smoking a water pipe, and never went home without taking a stroll around the monastery square, for he had developed a passion for the dervishes' anthems.

16.

A mysterious pain consumed his entrails. His breast overflowed with longing, and burned with a secret fire. The sight of women entranced him, the sound of their voices made his heart tremble. His companions tried to tempt him to become acquainted with the bar, the hashish den, the whorehouses, but the past screamed a warning in his ears. The past burdened with memories of the minaret and the lusts and perversions which had destroyed his family's prestige. As if Sahar could read his thoughts, she said to him one day, "It's time you were married."

He was delighted at the idea; it seemed like the way out he had been searching for.

But before long the horizon grew dark, threatening storms that nobody could have foretold.

17.

Strange rumors came from outside the alley. The Nile was not going to flood that year. People wondered what to make of this. Some said one catastrophe would follow another until nothing was left. Was it true? Food would become scarce. Perhaps there would be a famine. It would be prudent to lay in provisions for the future. Those with money followed this advice. The harafish looked on and laughed, refusing to believe that they would be deprived of the morsel of bread which they snatched by the sweat of their brows, or were given in alms.

The air filled with a humming sound and was tinged a repulsive yellow. Specters of anxiety were on the march day and night.

18.

The wheel of misfortune raced ahead at full speed. Prices rose by the hour. Black clouds darkened the sky. Food shops only stayed open half the day for lack of supplies. Complaints and lamentations jostled together in the air. There were demonstrations in front of the flour and bean shops. People could no longer talk of anything but food. It was the sole topic of conversation in the bar, the hashish den, the café. Sparks flew and a fire was kindled. Even the notables complained openly but no one believed them, and their plump, pink faces let them down.

"It's an epidemic!" said Anba the bar owner.

Prices went on rising, especially the prices of cereals.

"There's not enough left to feed the birds!" cried Samaha.

However one night Fath al-Bab said to Sahar, "What a liar he is! The warehouse is full. The prices he's asking are just protection money in another form."

"Hold your tongue, son," she implored anxiously.

"He's barbaric. He doesn't know what compassion means."

19.

The atmosphere became gloomier, uglier. Prices went crazy. Beans, lentils, tea, and coffee were scarce. Rice and sugar vanished altogether. Bread was hard to find. As nerves grew more frayed, there were signs that people began to stop caring. Thefts mounted. Chickens and rabbits disappeared. At night people were held up and robbed on their doorsteps. The clan went about issuing warnings and threats, calling for good behavior and solidarity, their voices loud and their stomachs full.

Life bared its cruel fangs as the days passed. The specter of starvation loomed large, like the madman's minaret. It was said that people were eating horses, donkeys, dogs and cats, and would soon be eating one another.

20.

In that cold, sickly time a strange day blazed briefly like a glimpse of another world. Ihsan, Samaha's daughter, married the timber merchant's son. It was an extravagant and flamboyant celebration such as the alley had never witnessed before, flying in the face of the hard times and the famine. Firdus announced that she would feed the harafish. The hungry flocked to the wedding, and as soon as the trays appeared, balanced on the servants' heads, they attacked like wild beasts. Massed together like so many grains of dust on a windy day, they grabbed at the food, pulling, pushing, snatching from one another, then arguing and fighting until blood flowed mingling with the meat broth. The people were drunk on the chaos and commotion; a wave of them surged to the door of the bar and rolled through it, devouring all the food in their path, drinking greedily straight from the barrels. Then they rushed back into the alley whooping with delight and threw bricks at the ghosts that inhabited their slums and squats.

The whole alley gave itself over to frantic carousing till daybreak.

21.

The following day the alley was subjected to a revenge attack. Samaha's men were deployed at strategic points, and the chief walked the length of the alley from the archway to the main square. Not one of the harafish escaped without being beaten up and humiliated. Panic spread, people ran for cover, the shops closed, the café, the smoking dens were deserted. That day nobody even went to the mosque to pray.

22.

Fath al-Bab sat with Sahar, dejected and sad. "Ashur will never return," he began.

The old woman gave him a sorrowful glance.

"He's still angry with us," he went on.

"This is worse than the plague in Ashur's time," muttered Sahar.

"And they're still singing hymns to joy in the monastery!"

"Perhaps they're prayers, my son."

"Wouldn't it be proper for them to give some of what they've got to ordinary people?"

"You shouldn't criticize them," she said with feeling.

"They've got the mulberries and the kitchen garden stuffed with vegetables."

She held her hand up in a gesture of warning.

He sighed. "It's Samaha who's the devil incarnate," he finished lamely.

23.

A pinprick of light pierced the darkness. A murmur of compassion broke the silence. The secret did not go beyond the slums and derelict buildings where the harafish lived. They were intent on preserving it, sensing that their life depended on it. Someone had received a sack of food. "From Ashur al-Nagi," a voice had whispered, then a dim shape had melted away in the darkness. The first time it had been under the archway, then on the path by the monastery wall, then several times in the slums themselves. The harafish talked about it in low voices. They knew instinctively that they were being sought out by a secret benefactor, that the food was intended for them. Bread from heaven. A miracle taking place in the darkness of night. A window opening onto mercy. Ashur al-Nagi or his spirit moving among them. The blank, solid walls of existence bursting apart to reveal the unknown.

The blood coursed through their veins and their hearts beat with new life.

A sack of mercy, accompanied by Ashur al-Nagi's whisper.

24.

The joy of newfound happiness loosed their tongues, which danced to the melodies of their wishes and prayers. They repeated Ashur's name until he seemed to acquire a physical presence. They said nothing of the sacks of food, but it was widely rumored that Ashur returned to life under cover of night. Samaha's men ridiculed this fairy story: they were on guard at night and hadn't seen anybody. Samaha summoned Sayyid Osman, the imam of the mosque. "The people have gone mad with hunger," he began.

The sheikh inclined his head.

"Have you heard what they're saying about Ashur's return?" continued Samaha.

The sheikh gave another nod of his head.

"What do you think about it?" demanded Samaha.

"It's not true."

"It's also blasphemy."

"It is indeed," said the sheikh sorrowfully.

"Do your duty then."

So the sheikh addressed the people, warning them against superstition and blasphemy. "If Ashur had really risen from the dead, he would have brought you food," he declared confidently.

25.

The darkness was transformed into a magic arena crisscrossed by a
network of channels linking souls to one another. The air was
drunk with enchanted whisperings. Unknown to the watchmen
secret conversations burst into life, intense and passionate.

"Are you Ashur al-Nagi?"

But the whisperings melted back into the night like a lost soul.
These whisperings roused the sleeper, confirmed that the warehouses were full, cursed greed—greed, not drought, was mankind's
enemy. These whisperings suggested that it was better to take a
risk than die of hunger. Pointed out that there was a time when the
clan slept and were vulnerable. Asked what could stand in their
way, if they all broke out together. Challenged them, demanded
how they could hesitate when Ashur al-Nagi was on their side.

The darkness was transformed into a magic arena. The air
was drunk with enchanted whisperings. The invisible was full of
mysterious powers.

26.

There was another force working relentlessly to uncover the secret
of the manna from heaven. Samaha came upon a scandal at the
heart of his business. Damir al-Husni, the chief's warehouse super-
visor, cried out in fear. "I'm innocent, as God's my witness."

"Half the stuff's gone from the warehouse," said Samaha savagely.

"I'm innocent, chief."

"You're guilty until proved innocent."

"Don't destroy a man who's given his life to serve you."

"You're the one who has the keys."

"I hand them into you every evening."

"And I find them in their place every morning and give them
back to you!"

"Perhaps someone takes them and puts them back in the
meantime."

"Without me knowing?"

"It could be someone who's free to come and go," said Damir desperately.

A cruel light blazed in Samaha's eyes, enough to call the demons from their lairs. His face ugly with malice, he declared, "If you're lying, you're dead. Whoever it is, he'd better start saying his prayers."

27.

Fath al-Bab sneaked out from behind the fountain in the pitch-dark and made for the door of the warehouse. Cautiously he turned the key and pushed the door gently open. He closed it behind him and advanced a few paces, guided by the light of memory.

Suddenly the place was flooded with light. Fath al-Bab stopped dead in his tracks. Terrifying, cruel faces emerged in the lamp's glow. Samaha, Damir al-Husni, some of the fiercest of Samaha's men. His eyes collided violently with theirs. The silence impaled them all, whistled in their ears like the hissing of snakes. The air crackled with the heat released as their wild, primitive instincts asserted themselves. His brother's look engulfed him, transfixed him, dismembered him. He felt the poison coursing through his veins, and a sense of absolute defeat and loss. His hopes vanished and he plunged into despair, waiting for his sentence to be pronounced as if it related to someone else.

The words came cold, scornful, bitter. "What brings you here at this time of night?"

There was nothing for it but to confess, be brave, hope for the best. He spoke with unexpected calm. "You already know."

"What are you doing here at this time of night?" repeated Samaha as if he hadn't heard.

"I've come to save people from death," he declared boldly.

"Is this how you repay my kindness?"

"I had to do this."

"So you're Ashur al-Nagi?"

He said nothing.

"You will be hung by your feet from the ceiling, Ashur," declared Samaha spitefully, "and left to die slowly."

28.

The whispered words took root in the minds of the harafish and were changed into a destructive force. A flood swept through the alley, such as had never been seen before. The harafish divided into groups and broke into the houses of Samaha's men. It was a little before dawn, the time when everyone was sound asleep. Taken by surprise in their beds, they were overwhelmed and defeated by the sheer numbers of their assailants. Their houses were looted. Their aura of magic was stripped away, leaving behind permanent scars and infirmities. The dawn call to prayers was inaudible through their screaming. The harafish streamed out into the alley, stormed the warehouses, sacking and destroying. Samaha's was their prime target. They left nothing standing, and plundered the contents down to the last grain of cereal. They saw Fath al-Bab hanging from a beam, arms dangling, unconscious or dead. They cut him down and laid him on the ground barely alive. When day broke they had control of the alley. People crowded in the windows and behind the wooden lattices and shouted in fear. At the sound of the commotion the chief's door opened and he appeared in the doorway like a wild bear, gripping his club.

29.

All eyes turned toward him. The harafish stood stock-still, resolute, and full of hate, yet keeping silent and waiting expectantly. Here was the terrible beast! But they were drunk with victory and unafraid. However, they hesitated. Perhaps he was waiting for his men to join him, not yet aware of what had happened to them. He'd soon guess, if he hadn't already. He was facing the harafish alone, with only his strength, his club, and his fabled powers to protect him.

"What's the meaning of this?" he shouted, unabashed.

No one answered him. Cries for help floated down from the windows, and tales of looting and pillage.

"What have you done, you sons of whores?" he roared again.

Nobody said a word. They were neither discouraged nor emboldened.

"What've you done, you sons of whores?" he repeated savagely.

Like a stone being thrown into the midst of the silence, a voice cried, "Your grandfather was a whore's son."

There was a roar of laughter and Samaha leapt forward, brandishing his stick.

"Let's see if there's a man among you sniveling lot," he shouted.

Silence descended on them like a lead weight, but nobody retreated. Samaha prepared to attack. At that moment Fath al-Bab appeared, pale and unsteady on his feet. "Throw stones at him," he ordered, leaning on the wall for support.

At once the harafish exploded into life, pelting Samaha with bricks and rubble. The attack halted when the rain began to fall. Blood poured from his wounds, staining his face and clothes. He reeled back, moaning. The stick fell from his hand and he collapsed on his doorstep.

They swooped on his house. Its inhabitants fled over the roofs, while the harafish looted and wrecked until only a heap of ruins remained.

30.

Fath al-Bab's role in the battle quickly became well known. A legend was born and he was invited to be clan chief. The young man was ill at ease. He was not deluded by the victory into having a false view of himself. He had never held a club in his life, and his fragile body could not withstand a beating from bare fists. "We'll choose a clan chief," he said to his supporters, "and oblige him to rule like Ashur."

But they were prisoners of their emotions and roared, "You are our chief. Nobody else will do!"

Fath al-Bab found himself chief of the clan without a struggle.

31.

Thanks to two men in the clan—Danqal and Hamida—the clan preserved its standing in the alley and in the surrounding neighborhood. Danqal and Hamida, like most of the other members of the clan, were survivors of the previous regime, but Fath al-Bab maintained absolute authority through his personal charm and the power of the harafish who came out in force to support him, intoxicated by the triumph of their rebellion.

During this time Nur died and Firdus and her children took refuge with her family—Radi's branch—having lost most of their riches and gone down the social scale.

32.

The people were eager for justice. The harafish were filled with hope and the notables with misgivings. Fath al-Bab was convinced that justice should not have to wait a single day. "We must revive Ashur al-Nagi's ideals," he said to his two aides.

Danqal and Hamida distributed charity, promises, hopes, and the wounds began to heal. Fath al-Bab noticed that they collected protection money and redistributed it in his name, and that the men of the clan still enjoyed their privileges, kept a good part of the money, and lived as heroes and thugs. He was plagued with apprehension. Fearing a gradual return to the old ways, he summoned his men. "What are you doing about justice? What's happened to Ashur al-Nagi's covenant?"

"The situation's changed," said Danqal. "We have to proceed one step at a time."

"Justice can't be postponed," said Fath al-Bab angrily.

"Your men won't be satisfied with living like ordinary people," replied Danqal with a new boldness.

"If we don't begin with ourselves we won't achieve anything," cried Fath al-Bab passionately.

"If we do, the whole clan system will be shaken to its foundations."

"Didn't Ashur live by the sweat of his brow?"

"It's impossible to bring back those days," said Hamida.

"Impossible?"

"One step at a time," said Danqal unenthusiastically.

If he had been a proper clan chief, one word from him would have settled the matter. "What's the point?" he asked himself sadly. "Seeing that I'll never have Ashur's strength."

Had the harafish already forgotten their destructive power?

33.

In a moment of angry despair, Fath al-Bab announced to Danqal and Hamida that he was resigning as clan chief. The two men were anxious and asked him to give them some time, promising to fulfill his demands. They went to their friend, Sheikh Mugahid Ibrahim. "Our chief's angry. We don't share the same ideas. What do you think?"

"He wants to revive Ashur al-Nagi's covenant, doesn't he?" said the old man wrathfully.

"That's right."

"Give power to the harafish, oppress the notables, make us the laughingstock of the neighborhood!"

"But he's threatened to give up being chief," said Danqal gloomily.

"Not now!" exclaimed Mugahid Ibrahim. "Let the image of their hopes remain in place until we can be quite sure that they have reverted to their normal state, and completely forgotten their crazy outburst. Give him half of what he's asking for."

"He wants all or nothing," said Hamida crossly.

Mugahid Ibrahim pondered for a moment with a scowl on his face, then declared firmly, "He must remain chief for a while. Use force if necessary."

34.

Danqal and Hamida went to find Fath al-Bab in his modest dwelling.

"We've done all we can but we've come up against insurmountable obstacles. The men don't like it. They're threatening to get nasty," Danqal told him.

"But you two are the most powerful members of the clan," muttered Fath al-Bab in amazement.

"There are a lot of them and they're the ones who are against you."

"I'll give up being chief," he said decisively.

"If you do that we can't be answerable for your safety," said Hamida.

"Don't leave the house from now on," continued Danqal. "One step outside will cost you your life."

35.

Fath al-Bab realized all too plainly the predicament he was in.

"I'm a prisoner. They've got me surrounded," he complained to Sahar.

"There's nothing you can do. Just keep hoping," sighed the old woman.

"I can't stop fighting for Ashur's beliefs. I'd despise myself forever," he cried in anguish.

"What can you do against their power?"

He paused for a moment, his thoughts confused. "The harafish," he muttered finally.

"They'll kill you if you try and make contact with them."

36.

Fath al-Bab remained under house arrest. Nobody knew the reason outside the clan, and people surmised that he must be ill or have decided to withdraw from the world. He was under surveillance day and night. Even Sahar was not allowed out. He knew for certain that his life depended on the enthusiasm of the harafish, and that he would be of no consequence the day their legend died and they lapsed back into ignominy. The clan grew more vigilant: they kept the harafish under constant watch and committed acts of terror and violence.

One day Hamida jumped on Danqal, thrashed him, and reigned supreme as the most powerful member of the clan. When he felt sure that the harafish were docile he proclaimed himself chief.

Fath al-Bab thought his detention would end, since there was no longer any justification for it.

"What's past is past," he said to the new chief. "Let me lead a normal life and earn my living like the rest of the human race."

But Hamida refused. "I don't trust you. Stay where you are, and you can live without having to work for it!"

37.

So ended the story of Fath al-Bab and his crusade. A brief burst of sunshine in a long, cloudy day. One morning his shattered body was found at the foot of the minaret. Many wept for him, some rejoiced. People said he was demented with sorrow at having the leadership snatched away from him, and had climbed to the top of his mad ancestor's minaret in the night and, in an act of profanity, thrown himself into the void.

So ended the story of Fath al-Bab and his holy war.

The Club and the Mulberry

The tenth tale in the epic

of the harafish

I.

With Fath al-Bab's death the alley awoke from its rosy dreams and came up against the hard rocks of reality. The people nursed their sorrows, while the shadow cast by the butcher Hamida grew darker until it blotted out the sun.

The elite of the Nagi line was reduced to Firdus' three daughters and her son, Rabi. The daughters married and were absorbed into the general population and the son lived in poverty, his mother having no money to speak of. He worked for the coffee merchant and led an extremely simple life, but nevertheless used to recount the glories of the Nagi family. This gained him nobody's sympathy. The harafish were increasingly attached to the legendary exploits of Ashur, Shams al-Din, and Fath al-Bab, but harbored resentment toward the rest of the line for betraying their great ancestors' ideals and joining the ranks of the thugs and criminals.

Rabi wanted to marry into a respectable family but his requests were turned down and he quickly realized that his origins did not compensate for his poverty and insignificant metier. Poverty exposed faults which wealth generally concealed, such as the fact that he was descended from Samaha with the ugly face, Galal

the madman, Zahira the murderess, Zaynat the blond whore, and
Nur the call girl. A lineage eroded by debauchery, crime, and
madness. This realization plunged him into a profound gloom, and
he resolved to spend his life in proud isolation. Firdus died in her
sixties, and he had to go and live alone in a cramped two-room flat.
He found the complete solitude unbearable, and the squalid neglect
which soon prevailed in his bachelor home got him down. So he
looked around for someone to do his chores and kind neighbors
found him a widow in her thirties, a descendant of the Nagi family,
called Halima al-Baraka. She was serious, reliable, passable to look
at, and had a strong personality despite her poverty. She cleaned his
house, prepared his food, and went to her own home to sleep, but
as time went by he developed a liking for her and wanted to make
her his lover. She refused point-blank. "I'm leaving this minute, sir,
and I won't be back," she told him.

He was all alone again, more miserable than ever, unable to
stand the complete absence of emotional attachments, fearing illness and death, and yearning for children. In desperation he proposed marriage to Halima and she accepted with alacrity, all smiles
now.

Rabi Samaha al-Nagi married Halima al-Baraka when he was
fifty-three years old. He was happy in his married life. His partner
was an energetic housewife, God-fearing and pious, proud to be a
Nagi, entranced by the tales of the family's past glories. She bore
him three sons, Fayiz, Diya, and Ashur. Rabi died when Fayiz was
ten, Diya eight, and Ashur six, leaving his family penniless.

                                    2.

Halima was left to face life alone. Her family being from the
poorest of the poor, she resolved to be self-reliant, and use determination rather than tears to get what she wanted. She moved into a
basement, made up of one room and an entry, sold a heap of her
furniture, and employed her talents as a vendor of pickles and
spiced molasses sweetmeats, a beautician, and a door-to-door saleswoman of goods such as women's hankies and underwear. She had
no strong desire to complain and regret the past, and faced her

customers with a beaming smile, almost as if she was happy. Sometimes, she allowed herself to dream sweet dreams of an unknown future.

She sent her sons to Quran school, and when they were old enough Fayiz became a carter and Diya a porter at a coppersmith's. Life became a little easier, although at past fifty Halima was still chasing work.

Fayiz was the first of her sons to confront the world. He found it a hostile, unsympathetic place where he was blamed for the crimes of ancestors he had never known. He was tall and skinny with a prominent nose, small eyes, and a strong jawline. He swallowed the insults, kept his feelings to himself, and went about his business. From his mother he learned the glowing side of the family history but outside in the alley he heard about its darker aspects. At home he learned the significance of the mosque building, the fountain, the Quran school, the animals' drinking trough. In the street he was rudely confronted with tales of the outlandish minaret, and of those splendid houses where his ancestors had lived, which now belonged to unknown merchants and notables. He would stare at them, full of curiosity, and dream, and as he drove his donkey around the old quarter his mind would be full of images of the past.

So this was the world, but how was he supposed to deal with it?

3.

He expressed his irritation to his mother and brothers.

"Ashur was a saint!" said Halima.

"The age of miracles is past," snapped Fayiz, "I'm talking about the property being in other people's hands."

"They were acquired illegally and lost illegally," declared his mother with passion.

"Illegally!" he protested.

"Be content with your lot. What is it you want?"

"I'm just a donkey boy and you're a servant to a bunch of scoundrels."

"We earn our living in an honorable fashion," she said haughtily.

He burst out laughing. He had gone via the bar on his way home and drunk a couple of calabashes of cheap liquor.

4.

The youngest boy, Ashur, worked as an apprentice goatherd for Amin al-Ra'i. He collected the goats from their owners and led them out to pasture in the open country, to graze and play in the wind and sun. Halima's mind was at rest now that her three sons were breadwinners; life smiled at her serenely. The days went by with their little pleasures and familiar sorrows until Fayiz was twenty years old.

"When are you going to get married, son?" asked his mother in a quiet moment.

"There's plenty of time," he replied with a mysterious smile.

5.

One evening Fayiz did not return at the usual time. Near dawn there was still no sign of him. Ashur went looking for him in the bar and Diya in the hashish dens, but they both came back empty-handed. In the morning Halima went to his boss, One-Eyed Musa, looking for news. She found him annoyed and upset. "I've heard nothing from him."

"Have you been to the police station?"

"They've heard nothing either. We'll just have to wait and see."

One day followed another; they waited with uneasy hearts and Fayiz did not return.

"He's stolen the cart and run off," shouted One-Eyed Musa. "Wait till I get my hands on him!"

"Don't you trust him after all these years?" cried Halima in anguish.

"He's a snake in the grass," he retorted angrily.

6.

Halima and her two remaining sons wept bitterly. Days, weeks, months, passed. Everyone was convinced by now that he'd committed the crime and fled.

"Once upon a time they stole big houses. These days it's donkey carts," scoffed Hassuna al-Saba, the new clan chief.

One-Eyed Musa sought legal advice from Galil al-Alim, sheikh of the mosque, and Yunis al-Sayis, sheikh of the alley, and they decreed that Halima and her sons should reimburse him for the donkey and cart. Sad and unprotesting, the family paid a fair price.

7.

Something happened which was not considered unusual by the alley's standards, but it shook the family. Halima did the chores in the clan chief's household for no payment, not even a word of thanks. Nothing strange about that: Hassuna was one of the worst chiefs ever to hold sway in the alley. He exploited even its most poverty-stricken inhabitants, argued with his hands and feet rather than his tongue, and spread terror through the air. For all his strength and villainy, he was as sly as a fox. It was he who forced his followers to take over a little cul-de-sac off the main alley and stop anyone else living there, to prevent an uprising like the one in Fath al-Bab's time. He built a house for himself at the far end of the cul-de-sac.

It happened that Halima was late making a tray of sweets because she was unwell, and when she delivered it he swore violently at her and slapped her across the face. She went home with tears in her eyes, but said nothing to Diya and Ashur. However, Diya was in the bar that evening and the owner, Zayn al-Alabaya, said to him, "Don't you know what happened to your mother?"

Having received this blow to his pride, Diya tossed it raw to his brother, but confined his anger within the walls of the basement room. Ashur was in the depths of despair. He was a powerful young man, his polite, gentle manner belying his strength. He had a noble head, strong features, dark coloring, prominent cheekbones, and a toughness about his jaw. He found it unbearable cooped up in the basement with his grief, and went out into the darkness, drawn by an invisible hand toward the monastery square and the immortal presence of his namesake Ashur. He squatted there, his head between his knees. The air was deathly still except for the murmuring of the anthems. He listened for a long time, then said softly, "I'm suffering so much, Ashur."

The anthems whispered to him in their mysterious language:

Bi mehre rokhat ruze mara nur namandast
Vaz omre mara joz shabe dijur namandast.

8.

The insult settled deep inside the two boys, and they neither absorbed it nor shook it off. Ashur grew at an amazing rate, like a mulberry tree. His giant frame and his heavy, attractive features were reminiscent of the first Ashur. The goatherd began to turn heads. Halima worried that his strength would arouse Hassuna's fears.

"Forget how strong you are," she cautioned him. "Pretend to be a coward. It's easier. If only I hadn't called you Ashur!"

But the boy was intelligent and this made excessive caution unnecessary. He spent all day in the open with the goats and his master, Amin al-Ra'i. He never showed his face in the bar, the hashish den, or the café. He only used his strength to endure and be patient. There was no question that the insult had cut him deeply. He was so angry that he pictured the alley crashing about his ears, the dead rising from their graves. But he kept his head, controlled himself, and never forgot the wary, brutish, cruel force with clubs always at the ready. Every time he felt cast down he went to the monastery square and listened intently to the dervishes chanting. "I wonder if they're praying for us or cursing us," he mused. "Who can solve these riddles?" He heaved a deep sigh.

"They keep the doors shut because we're not fit to cross the threshold!"

He found Diya shouting with fury in the basement room. "If we weren't harafish our mother would never have been insulted like that!"

"It doesn't matter who you are," retorted Ashur. "People will always insult you if you let them."

"What should we do then?"

Ashur was silent. "I don't know," he admitted finally.

9.

Halima feared the consequences of their angry thoughts.

"What happened to me isn't considered an insult in our alley," she declared simply.

She was determined to see them past this ordeal and thought seriously about getting them married. She had lost Fayiz. Time was rushing by, without hope. The boys marrying would inject a burst of energy into their stagnant life. It would make men of them, more sensible, less tempted by rash schemes.

"What do you think about finding nice girls for both of you?"

They were poor, inhibited. So they accepted gladly.

"We'll move to a bigger flat with room for us all," said Halima briskly. "That'll make life easier."

She chose Fathiyya and Shukriyya, daughters of One-Eyed Musa's stableman, Muhammad al-Agal. Neither of the boys had set eyes on his girl before, but they were burning with youthful passion and in their unruly imaginations eager to embrace any female.

So the engagements were formalized.

10.

A stranger came to the alley. His face glowed with health and well-being. He was dressed in a flowing dark brown cloak, red slippers with turned-up toes, and a slip of striped silk wrapped around his head and garnet prayer beads between his fingers. The first to see him was Zayn al-Alabaya, the bar owner. He didn't recognize the young man until he smiled. "Fayiz!" he exclaimed.

All eyes turned to look, but he kept going to the café, where he made straight for Hassuna al-Saba. He bowed low to kiss his hand, then straightened up and waited submissively.

"Well, well. The fugitive's returned," said Hassuna, looking him up and down.

"People always come back to their roots!"

"It looks as if you've done well for yourself."

"That's the Lord's doing," Fayiz said modestly.

One-Eyed Musa entered the café, followed by Sheikh Yunis al-Sayis.

"It's up to you to see justice is done, chief," cried Musa.

"Don't bray like an ass," scolded the chief.

"He sold the donkey and cart, then used my capital."

The chief turned to Fayiz. "What did you do with his money?"

"I swear the cart was stolen while I was asleep. That's why I ran away."

"Liar!" shouted Musa. "How did you get to be so grand?"

"A bit of luck, hard work, God's help."

"Odd business," muttered Sheikh Yunis.

"It's my money. If I'd stolen it, would I have come back? I only came because I was eager to pay what I did owe."

He handed the chief a small bag. "Two years of money due to you."

The chief took it, and smiled for the first time.

"I came first of all to see you," Fayiz told him, "and then to visit my family."

"Are you a thief?" said Hassuna al-Saba. "Never mind. You're a smart operator, anyway. I believe you!"

"What about me?" demanded Musa.

"Halima gave you the price of the donkey and cart," said Sheikh Yunis.

"His money is really mine," persisted Musa.

"Musa deserves the same amount as me," decreed the chief.

Without hesitating, Fayiz handed another bag over to him. The men, delighted by this just ruling, cried in chorus, "God bless him! God bless him!"

But Hassuna kept a firm hold on the second money bag and a despairing look appeared on Musa's face.

"Go and see your family now," said the chief to Fayiz.

11.

He found Halima waiting for him at the door of the basement room. She had been there since she first heard the news. It was like a dream, a fairy tale, a miracle. An impossible happiness, in any case. She held him tight, sobbing and repeating, "Thank you, Lord. Thank you."

Once Diya and Ashur came home the family was reunited. Astonishment mingled with joy again. Fayiz sat in the little room like a diamond in a heap of straw. He gave off light, a light of hope which made the future look more bewitching than in their wildest dreams. The family's perceptions changed. They were reborn.

Fayiz began to speak. "People always envy someone who's made good. They'll invent stories about me. But I'm innocent, as God's my witness."

"I believe you," declared Halima emotionally.

"Why did I go? Very briefly, the cart was stolen while I was asleep. I panicked and decided to make a run for it. Perhaps it was the wrong decision, but that's what happened."

They gazed at him, delighted, credulous.

"I wandered around for some time without a job, until a foreigner rescued me. It's a long story, but I worked for him as a domestic servant and driver, protected him from some louts, and learned how to do business. Then I had a piece of luck. You need luck. I won a lottery and decided to work for myself. I was more successful than I ever guessed I would be."

"What is it you do exactly?" asked Ashur.

"It's not easy to explain. Have you ever heard of brokerage, speculation? Right. No shop or office. We make our transactions in the street, in cafés. It's complicated. I'll come back to it in more detail. But I won't ask you to be my partners! I've got various specific projects planned for the future, whose success is guaranteed."

Their faces flushed with delight and hope and they waited in silent expectation.

"It's God's will that the Nagi family should be restored to its proper place in society," continued Fayiz.

"Are you talking about the leadership of the clan?" breathed Ashur.

"No, no," laughed Fayiz. "Wealth and luxury!"

"That would be splendid," said Diya, his face radiant.

"We have to change this paltry way of life. From today we're no longer harafish. No more shepherds or porters in the family! This is God's will."

"You're the fruit of my love and my prayers!" cried Halima.

"We must think fast," said Fayiz with great seriousness. "My activities require me to make frequent trips away."

12.

Changes took place as definite as the four seasons. In the space of a day Halima gave up being a maid and became a lady of leisure. Diya and Ashur handed in their notice to the coppersmith and the shepherd and the family moved temporarily to a four-room flat while a house was built for them on a plot of waste ground opposite the moneylender's. Fayiz bought a coal yard for his two brothers to run. They sat in the manager's office in ample robes, giving off aromas of musk and amber.

The reality was indistinguishable from the dream. People stared, their eyes transfixed by the dazzling sight. Exchanging their old rags for such sumptuous attire, the brothers felt dazed, afraid, then enraptured. They went into the street as if they were going into battle. The harafish surrounded them. They were greeted by a deluge of conflicting remarks: insults, blessings, wisecracks, solemn advice, taunts, congratulations. By late morning rank had been awarded its privileges and settled in its rightful station, and everyone had submitted to the decrees of fate. But so many hearts were burning with envy, overwhelmed and disoriented, drunk on ill-defined hopes.

Galil al-Alim, imam of the mosque, and Sheikh Yunis al-Sayis were standing exchanging confidences. Ashur went by and Yunis commented, "They say that boy looks like the first Ashur."

"Don't confuse pure gold and gold plate," joked Galil.

13.

A grim obstacle loomed in sight, blocking the smooth path ahead: their engagements to Fathiyya and Shukriyya. They had weighed heavily on them from the beginning.

"Why were you in such a hurry?" Diya asked his mother reprovingly.

Halima didn't know what to say. She was no longer enthusiastic about the arrangement, but she didn't want to do anything she would be ashamed of, and she was a pious woman.

"It's fate," she announced.

"What?"

"The proverb says, 'If you marry a poor woman, God will make you rich,' " she said lamely.

"But God made us rich before we married them!"

"You thought they were all right at the time."

"It's a joke!" muttered Diya angrily.

Ashur remained silent and morose. He was no longer happy at the engagement either but—like his mother—he was God-fearing and hated to dishonor a contract.

"What about you, Ashur?" asked his mother.

"We've promised on the Quran," he muttered helplessly.

"I refuse to go through with it," shouted Diya. "I'm sorry, but there it is!"

"Do what you want," said Halima. "But don't expect me to back you up."

14.

Diya had a meeting with Sheikh Yunis and asked him to convey his excuses to Muhammad al-Agal. The sheikh stared at his small face with its delicate features and inexplicably pale good looks and said to himself that here was a real bad egg, but out loud he commented sycophantically, "What you're doing is perfectly fair. Only someone with a grudge against you would criticize you for it."

"I've no choice," said Diya, concealing his embarrassment.

"What about Ashur?"

"He's good and stupid!"

Yunis al-Sayis laughed. "People will praise him and then ridicule him for being so naive."

15.

Diya breaking off his engagement provoked a storm of anger and sarcasm, to which both the good contributed with their outraged sense of justice, and the spiteful with their jealous envy. Diya's despicable conduct outweighed Ashur's decency, which was quickly overlooked as curses rained down on the family of traitors whose cruelty and egotism had been made manifest; their aura of sanctity melted away in a rush of wildly speculative tales about their past history.

Ashur was on his way to the coal yard when he heard a harsh, commanding voice call his name. He saw Hassuna al-Saba sitting cross-legged on his usual sofa in the café, surrounded by a group of his henchmen. He went up to him at once and greeted him politely. Without inviting him to sit, the chief started haranguing him. "You Nagis are a bunch of rogues and frauds."

Ashur wondered why he did not direct his insults at Diya, and realized that he was testing out the giant of the family. He had not forgotten his mother's advice and with instinctive shrewdness he replied courteously, "May God forgive us our sins!"

"You seem to forget your background very quickly. The madness. The immorality. Isn't Muhammad al-Agal a more honorable man than any of you?"

Suppressing his rage, Ashur replied, "He's an honorable man, and I'll soon become part of his family."

"Oh, no, you won't."

"That's the truth."

"He won't allow one of his daughters to be happy at the other's expense."

"But I haven't broken off my engagement."

"No. He's done it himself. And I'm informing you of his decision."

Ashur was silent, grim-faced.

"You'll have to compensate him for the trouble you've caused him," went on Hassuna.

"We'll do whatever our chief thinks is right."

16.

The heavy fog of resentment, bitterness, and regret lifted. The days went by bathed in happiness and good fortune. The elevated status of Diya and Ashur became a normal part of life. The luxurious household was established opposite the moneylender's. Halima al-Baraka went about in a carriage. But Fayiz, instigator of all the changes, only visited his family and inspected his property every once in a while.

17.

They quickly grew to enjoy their status and accept it without questioning. Ashur was secretly delighted that his engagement had been broken off, especially since he hadn't had to do anything wrong. He savored his comfortable existence and thought of Fayiz as one of the family's miracles, and a genius. He used to admire beautiful girls going by in their family carriages, for he loved beauty, just as he loved the monastery and the true glory of his family whose pure fragrance rose up from the recesses of the past. He gave freely to the clan chief and the sheikh, renewed the mosque, the fountain, the drinking trough, and the Quran school, and gave alms to the harafish.

His mother cautioned him about the harafish. "Don't provoke Hassuna al-Saba. Leave them to me. I can distribute alms to them in secret."

Ashur agreed, knowing that the rebellion of the harafish was still fresh in the clan chiefs' minds.

Diya was perhaps the happiest of the three. He loved the fame and status with all his heart, enjoyed his superior position at work, the luxury at home, and driving about in a carriage. He was wild about elegant clothes and exotic food, and chose the finest wines, hashish, and opium. He secretly worshiped his brother Fayiz, and all the Nagi men, heroes and renegades alike. He used to say proudly, "The important thing is to be out of the ordinary!"

Halima was probably the most frugal of them, but she too reveled in their good fortune. At saints' days and festivals she would smuggle alms to the harafish. She was especially generous to the mother of Fathiyya and Shukriyya, who soon forgot the bad blood between them and became one of her closest friends.

18.

A secret voice kept calling Ashur back to the monastery square to hear the songs, and sometimes out into the open countryside where he used to guard the sheep and goats. His happiness was like a sky with a few clouds that usually stayed out around the edges but sometimes scurried across the face of the sun. In his sweetest moments he was sometimes assailed by vague fears, sapping his zest for life, and he wondered why.

His mother noticed his fluctuating moods. "A man without a wife he can rely on is a poor creature," she declared one day.

"That's true. But it's not everything."

"What more do you want?" asked Diya.

Ashur kissed his brother's hand in a gesture of gratitude. But the chief's insulting behavior was lodged inside him like a dagger. He dared not contemplate his ancestor Ashur. His happiness was lacking some essential component. "How can a man be anxious when God has given him everything?" he demanded.

"It's the devil, son," said his mother automatically.

It was the devil all right. But which devil?

19.

Two girls from old-established families took the Nagi brothers' fancy. Diya got engaged to Salma al-Khashshab, daughter of the owner of the timber yard, and Ashur to Aziza al-Attar, daughter of the biggest spice merchant in the alley. Fayiz appeared at the engagement party dressed like a king.

The days went by, happy and serene.

20.

One night Fayiz arrived unexpectedly.

The family was gathered around the glowing coals of a big copper stove. Halima was telling her rosary, Ashur smoking a water pipe, Diya getting stoned. Outside a cold wind blew, threatening rain.

Fayiz usually came—when he did come—at midmorning, showing off his splendid clothes and fine carriage. They all rose to greet him and noticed immediately that the miracle of the family looked tired and cross. He sat on a divan, pushing his cloak back off his shoulders, despite the cold.

"What's wrong?" asked his mother anxiously.

"Nothing," he said listlessly.

"I know there is, son!"

"I'm not well."

His words tailed off. They all looked at him and saw a hardness in his expression that used to be there in the old days, before he made good.

Halima got to her feet. "I'll make you a caraway tisane."

"Then you can sleep," murmured Diya.

Fayiz let his eyelids droop for a moment, then said, "There are times a man can't help longing for home."

"The winter's been bad this year," said Ashur.

"Worse than you can imagine!"

"And you work harder than most men could bear to."

"Than most men could bear to," he repeated vaguely.

"A man has a right to rest," said Diya.

"I've decided to have a long rest."

Silence fell. He stood up abruptly. "I'm off to bed."

Halima took him his tisane. The candelabra lit up the room. Fayiz lay on the bed fully clothed.

"Why don't you get undressed?" she asked.

Then suddenly the glass slipped from her hand and she let out a piercing scream.

21.

They stood staring with crazed expressions.

His eyes were wide open, his face frozen, as if he had been dead for a thousand years. His left hand hung down over the edge of the luxuriant bedcovers and below it a little pool of blood was forming on the Shiraz carpet. A gold-handled dagger lay on his beige caftan. Diya began to search feverishly behind the divan, under the bed, in the cupboard, combing the room whose windows were closed and shuttered. "It's absurd! What can it mean?" he shouted.

"The Prophet save us!" cried Halima hoarsely.

"The barber!" shouted Ashur, and flew out of the room.

Halima began to wail.

Diya screamed at her. "He's still alive."

"It's over," she sobbed. "My son! Why did you do this to yourself?"

The barber surgeon arrived, followed by Yunis al-Sayis, Galil al-Alim, and members of the Khashshab and Attar families.

He took one look at Fayiz and retreated, muttering, "Only God is immortal."

A demented wind swept through the elegant house.

22.

The police arrived shortly before midnight, interrogated the family and the servants, and examined all the possibilities with scrupulous care.

"Why do you think he did it?" the officer in charge asked the assembled family.

"Until yesterday he was the happiest man alive," said Halima.

"Do you know if he had any enemies?"

"None at all."

"What was his occupation?"

"He was a businessman, a speculator."

"Where did he work?"

"Nowhere in particular. He had a house in Darasa, in the foothills."

"What do you know of his employees and his partners?"

"Absolutely nothing."

"How's that possible?"

"It's the truth."

23.

It was announced that Fayiz had committed suicide for reasons which the inquiry had so far failed to identify. Despite the manner of his death, he was given a splendid funeral and buried beside Shams al-Din.

The three days of the mourning ceremonies passed with the family in a state of shock, unable to find an explanation for this terrible disaster.

24.

Why had Fayiz al-Nagi killed himself? The question weighed on them, plagued their confused, sorrowing minds. The authorities— so Yunis al-Sayis claimed—were taking the inquiry very seriously.

But how had they themselves not known what was happening until the last moment? How had they been so completely blind? He had been absent for long periods, kept most of the details of his work a secret, but his infrequent visits home had filled the house with joy and delight and hope for the future. Until his last visit, when he'd been a different person. What had changed him? How had death become his only way out?

"We're cursed," wailed Halima.

"Why did he do it? I'm going mad," groaned Diya.

"If we do find out why, it won't be pleasant," said Ashur. "People don't kill themselves for no reason."

25.

The two brothers decided to search the deceased's house to try to find the key to his secrets, his business dealings, his sources of finance. The authorities agreed to escort them there. It was an enormous house with extensive land abutting the hills. They were struck by the large number of luxurious apartments, the stocks of drink and drugs, the profusion of furniture and ornaments, but when they forced open the safes and strongboxes they found them completely empty. No documents, letters, ledgers, or cash. The two brothers exchanged bewildered glances.

"What does it mean?" asked Ashur.

"Where's all his wealth?" asked Diya.

Ashur turned to one of the detectives. "Do you know something we don't?" he asked him.

"We'll leave no stone unturned," said the man.

26.

Diya and Ashur returned from their failed journey of discovery utterly confused. The riddle was more obscure and murkier than ever and they were beset by apprehensions. Fayiz had left them secure before he died: they and their mother had inherited the coal yard and two wonderful houses. But what about his own wealth and his mysterious life?

"Perhaps he went bankrupt," said Diya thoughtfully.

"Why kill himself, when he still had the coal business and two mansions?" objected Ashur.

Diya shook his head uncomprehendingly. "Why do people kill themselves at all?"

27.

Fayiz' suicide dominated the interest of the drinkers in the bar.

"Why would a man like that kill himself?" said Zayn al-Alabaya.

"It wasn't because he went bust," said Sheikh Yunis. "What he left would have made him one of the richest men in the alley."

"You must have some more information, being a lawman yourself," goaded Zayn.

Not wanting to announce his lack of information, Yunis said guardedly, "They're following up all his contacts."

"There's a much more telling reason than insolvency," said Hassuna al-Saba sarcastically.

All heads turned respectfully toward him.

"Madness!" he guffawed. "It's in their blood. Even their revered ancestor was a foundling and a thief."

28.

The Nagi family's life dragged by miserably. Naturally, the weddings were postponed. Diya and Ashur carried on with their daily routine, but the spark of joy and creativity had been extinguished in their souls. Halima was practically a recluse and stayed in her apartments, mulling over her sorrows and taking comfort in prayer.

29.

One evening, when winter winds were lashing the alley, Sheikh Yunis arrived at the house with the police inspector and a pack of detectives.

"Who owns the coal business and the two houses?" asked the inspector.

"They belonged to our dead brother. We inherited them."

"Show me the title deeds."

Diya went away and came back with a medium-sized silver box, and the inspector began examining the documents. He looked from Halima to her two sons. "It all belongs to somebody else," he announced.

Nobody took in what he said. Not a trace of emotion crossed their faces.

"All the trade and real estate in your hands belongs to someone else. It never belonged to Fayiz. Therefore you have no rights to it."

"What are you talking about?" shouted Diya.

"You must give up this house and the coal yard immediately."

"There must be some mistake."

"Fayiz had sold everything. The new owner's come forward with the contract and it's all in order."

"Are you telling us the truth?" asked Ashur in disbelief.

The inspector was gentle but firm. "We wouldn't come here at this time of night for fun."

"It's impossible to take in."

"You'd better start trying!"

"So where's the money from the sale?" demanded Diya.

"Only God and the dead man know that." He was silent for a few moments, then went on, "Perhaps it was a fictitious sale. Maybe it was lost in some crazy wager. The investigation will no doubt uncover more dirt!"

"It's impossible to take in," repeated Diya.

"It's quite simple. He was robbed," said Ashur.

"Then why did he kill himself instead of reporting it?"

"There must be some crime involved, inspector."

"A whole string of crimes! The inquiry's still in its early stages!"

30.

The family waited helplessly, the death sentence hanging over them. The inspector repeated, "A whole string of crimes. Bad crimes," then added, "You'll have to come with us."

"Where to?" asked Halima in a quaking voice.

"The station."

"They need you to help with the inquiry," put in Sheikh Yunis kindly.

"Are you charging us?" Ashur asked the inspector.

"Let's wait and see," he replied firmly.

31.

The inquiry was long and exhausting. They were held in the police station for a week while it was going on but eventually it was established that they had no links with the mysterious work Fayiz did when he was away from them and they were released. They returned to the alley, disgraced, homeless.

32.

The facts had preceded them like a rotten smell. Everyone, young and old, friend and foe, knew that Fayiz had begun his escapade by selling the stolen cart, then invested his money in whores, gambling, drugs, and the trappings of debauched luxury. He gambled with money he didn't have and when he lost he would entice his creditor to his house in the foothills with promises of women and drugs, kill him, take his money, and bury him in the grounds. On the last occasion he lost all his liquid assets and was forced to gamble with his real estate in the form of a fictitious bill of sale, and lost that too. This time he had failed to kill his creditor and the man had escaped with his money still on him. Ruined, and threatened with exposure, Fayiz had killed himself. The police had received an anonymous letter—perhaps from a one-time associate—

which had led them eventually to his victims' graves. So the appall-
ing secret of his success and final downfall was uncovered.

33.

They returned to the alley, disgraced, homeless.

Their story was a gem for the spiteful, a nightmare for the
morbidly fanciful and neurotic. Al-Saba, al-Alabaya, and al-Agal
added fuel to the flames. Such was the strength of the hatred directed at them that they were spat upon and punched in the street.
They fled down the archway and along the path by the old city
wall, and ended up in the cemetery.

Sheikh Galil, imam of the mosque, tried to intercede for
them. "Don't punish them for something they didn't do."

"Shut up," roared Hassuna al-Saba, "or I'll strangle you with
your own turban!"

The Khashshabs and the Attars were among the first to wash
their hands of them.

34.

The fugitives took up residence in the mourners' chamber of
Shams al-Din's tomb. They only had a few piastres to their name,
and their immediate troubles made the sorrows of death and bankruptcy recede into the background. Dry-eyed, even Halima, they
huddled close to one another, taking comfort from the closeness of
their bodies, warmed by their collective heartbeat, as the winter
wind growled around the tombstones.

"Bastards!" raged Diya.

"We must think what to do," urged Halima.

"Our only choice is to become gravediggers," scoffed Diya
bitterly.

"The dead are nicer to live with," said his mother.

"Have we really been forced out of the alley?" demanded
Ashur in disbelief.

"Why not go back and wash your face in their spit again!"
said his brother.

"We'll survive anyhow," said Ashur defiantly.

"We could try begging again!"

Outside the winter wind growled around the tombstones.

35.

The next day their misery entered a new stage, distinguished mainly by inertia.

"We've no time to lose," said Halima.

Diya remarked that they had no time, no money, no friends, no nothing.

Ignoring him, she went on, "Where ought we to go?"

"The world's our oyster!" answered Diya.

"Let's stay here, close to the alley, until we can go back," said Ashur.

"Go back?" repeated Diya scathingly.

"Why not? One day we're sure to. And there's nothing for us anywhere else."

"Let's stay here for a little while at least," said Halima peaceably.

"I didn't sleep a wink last night," said Diya. "I thought so much, the dead must have heard my brain humming. I've made up my mind."

"To do what?"

"Not to stay here."

His mother ignored him, and said, "I'll go back to work, and make sure I keep well away from the alley."

"I'll sell fruit in the street," said Ashur.

Annoyed at the way they took no notice of him, Diya repeated loudly, "I'm going, even if it means leaving you here."

"Going where? And what will you do?" asked his mother.

"I don't know," he said, still angry. "I'll take my chance."

"Like Fayiz did," she said sadly.

"Certainly not! There are other ways."

"For example?"

"I'm not a prophet!"

"Stay with us," said Ashur gently. "We need each other more than ever now."

"No. It's too late."

<h2 style="text-align:center">36.</h2>

Diya said goodbye to his mother and brother and left. Halima's eyes were filled with tears but there was no room for sorrow. She and Ashur led a cruel, harsh life. She peddled her sweets and pickles like a beggar woman, and Ashur sold fruit and vegetables from a little basket on his giant shoulders. It was as if they had some unspoken agreement to endure the present and avoid complaining or digging up the past. But for all that the past remained deeply rooted within the two of them: memories of their beautiful house, the opulence, the splendid carriage, the manager's office, generously cut coats, garnet prayer beads, the scents of musk and amber, good conversation. Aziza al-Attar with her yashmak and happy smile. The flattery of Yunis al-Sayis and his customary morning greeting: "God give you a happy day, you whose face shines with light!" Ah, Fayiz! What did you do to yourself, and to us? Even Galal the madman didn't murder people and hide the corpses. What's this curse that hounds the descendants of the saintly miracle worker?

Ashur never tired of spending his rest time in the open air where he used to graze the goats. Where blessed Ashur, giver of the covenant, had sought refuge. The ancestor he loved, whose word he trusted, whose good deeds and strength he venerated. Wasn't he supposed to resemble him? But where had it got him? His ancestor had performed miracles, while he sold cucumbers and dates on the street!

At night he still went to the monastery square, wrapped in darkness, guided by the stars. His gaze wandered over the dim shapes of the mulberry trees and the dark mass of the ancient wall. He sat down in al-Nagi's old spot and listened to the dancing rhythms. Didn't these men of God care about what happened to God's creatures? When would they open the gate or knock down the walls? He wanted to ask them why Fayiz had committed his crimes. How much longer the alley would be poor and oppressed. Why egotists and criminals prospered, while the good and loving came to nothing. Why the harafish were in a deep sleep.

Meanwhile the air was filled with their chanting.

> *Did keh bar joz jur o setam nadasht*
> *Beshkast ahd o zoghame ma hich gham nadasht.*

37.

Halima said to herself that he always seemed distracted, absent-minded. She wondered what he was thinking about. Was it possible to have a life of hard toil with no pleasant breeze to soothe it? "What's bothering you, Ashur?" she asked him tenderly.

He didn't answer.

"Wouldn't it be a good idea if we found you a wife to stop you being lonely?"

"We can barely feed ourselves," he smiled.

"But is there something wrong?"

"Nothing," he answered sincerely.

She had to believe him, but she wasn't convinced. There was a whole secret life inside him, and it made her jealous and afraid.

38.

One night his secrets were weighing him down. It was spring and he had taken to sitting in the open courtyard of the tomb. The sky arched above, brilliant with a myriad of stars. He and Halima were eating a supper of curd cheese and cucumbers.

"I sometimes wonder what Diya's doing," said Ashur.

"He'll have forgotten about us," sighed Halima.

Ashur lapsed into silence and the only sounds were the smacking of his lips as he ate and the barking of dogs around the cemetery.

"I'm afraid he'll do what Fayiz did," he went on.

"But he gave us an example we're not likely to forget."

"People always do forget."

"Is that what's troubling you?"

He bowed his head in the pale light of the crescent moon.

"Why did Fayiz turn to a life of crime?" he demanded. "Why did Galal go mad? Why does the clan chief hunt us down?"

"Don't we have enough to worry about?"

"It's a never-ending chain of worries!"

"It's the devil, God protect us."

"Of course. But why doesn't he have any trouble tempting us?"

"He has no success with believers."

He fell silent again. He had finished eating and began to smoke a pipe of tobacco steeped in molasses. The dogs barked more insistently, some of them almost howling.

"Do you want to know what I think, mother?" he said suddenly. "The devil conquers us by knowing our weak spots."

"God protect us."

"Our love of money and power are our two greatest weaknesses."

"Perhaps they're the same thing," murmured Halima.

"Perhaps. The power of money."

"Even your ancestor succumbed to it."

"My ancestor!"

She stared at him.

"What was wrong with him?" he asked.

"Wrong with him?"

"I mean why did he succumb?"

"It wasn't his fault."

"Of course not," he murmured hastily.

But privately he continued to wonder what Ashur had lacked, and what had thwarted the development of his ideals after his death, or after Shams al-Din's death. If wrong existed, right must exist too. It must be constantly renewable, and if it was possible to suffer lapses, it must also be possible to ensure that they didn't recur.

"Don't you have more than enough to worry about?" asked Halima again.

39.

No. He didn't. He was dissatisfied, as might be expected of somebody who was addicted to spending an hour in the open country every day and an hour or more in the monastery square! In whose heart a torch blazed constantly. Somebody who was kept awake by kaleidoscopic dreams, who continued to think that Ashur al-Nagi was his only ancestor. In the sandy ground of the country he outlined a way. By the light of the stars in the monastery square he imagined it. In his wanderings and in his sleep, he secretly confided in it. Until it existed for him, as strong, solid, and impressive as the ancient wall.

40.

He hung around for hours in the Darasa market. It was here that many of the harafish from the alley loitered, which was why he had previously avoided it and now frequented it. He passed in front of their little groups, singing his wares. Some of them recognized him at once.

"It's Ashur!"

"The killer's brother selling cucumbers!" a voice mocked.

Ashur went toward them with a cheerful expression on his generous features. He held out his hand, saying, "Are you going to refuse to shake it like the others?"

They crowded around to shake it warmly.

"To hell with them," said one.

"You've always been good to us," said another.

"How's your mother? She's a fine woman."

"Seeing you, my wandering spirit has come back home," murmured Ashur.

He spent an hour in their company, a happy hour of affectionate, joyous conversation. From that time on he went regularly to the Darasa market.

41.

Meeting the harafish had set his whole being on fire. His vital energies raced together and his heart pounded as if it would burst its walls. He couldn't sleep, he was so agitated by this upsurge of power inside him. He defied the unknown like Fayiz and Diya; but he took a different path, his sights set on more distant horizons. He stared it in the face, grasped it by the hand, rushed toward it unreservedly. As if he was bound by destiny to gamble and take risks, to pursue the impossible. He was harboring an amazing secret. In his sleep he had seen someone he believed was Ashur al-Nagi. Although the figure was smiling, it had asked him in a tone of obvious reproach, "Is it going to be me or you?"

It repeated the question twice.

"Me!" answered Ashur, as if he had suddenly realized what the words meant.

Still smiling, al-Nagi vanished.

When he woke up, Ashur wondered what al-Nagi had meant by this question, and what he had meant by his answer. He could find no clear explanation, but he was filled with inspiration and fearless optimism.

42.

One day he questioned the harafish in the market. "What could restore our alley's fortunes?"

"The return of Ashur al-Nagi," answered several voices.

"Can the dead come back to life?" he murmured, smiling.

"Of course," someone replied with a laugh.

"When you're alive you're alive, and when you're dead you're dead," he said firmly.

"We're alive but not living."

"What haven't you got?"

"Bread."

"Power, you mean," said Ashur.

"Bread's easier to come by."

"Not at all!"

"You're strong and powerfully built," said a voice. "Do you want to become clan chief?"

"And be transformed like Wahid, Galal, and Samaha!" said another.

"Or be assassinated like Fatḥ al-Bab!" said a third.

"Even if I became an honest, upright chief, what good would it do?"

"We'd live happily under your protection!" said one.

"You wouldn't be honest for long!" said another.

"Even if you were happy when I was there what about after I'd gone?" asked Ashur.

"It would be back to the bad old days."

"We don't trust anyone. Not even you!"

"Wise words," smiled Ashur.

They burst out laughing.

"But you have faith in yourselves!" went on Ashur.

"A lot of good that does us!"

"Can you keep a secret?" asked Ashur seriously.

"Just for you!"

"I had a strange dream. I saw you armed with clubs."

They broke into gales of unrestrained laughter.

"He's definitely crazy," said one of them, indicating Ashur. "That's why I like him."

43.

Somebody knocked on the door of the tomb room. Ashur and his mother were sitting together after supper, wrapped up in blankets to protect them from the biting winter cold. Ashur opened the door and saw a face he knew in the lamplight. "Diya! My brother!" he cried.

Halima jumped up and clasped him to her breast. A few

moments were lost in warm embraces and greetings, then they
came to themselves and sat down on cushions, looking at one another. Diya was in a dark cloak, green leather slippers with turned-
up toes, and a striped silk headcloth, looking the picture of health
and happiness. Ashur's heart twitched apprehensively, and Halima
shut out her suspicions with a smile and let her affections submerge
them. Diya broke the brief silence. "What a long time it's been!"
He laughed. "And yet not long!"

"You forgot all about us, Diya," murmured Halima, her eyes
brimming with tears.

"Life was harder than I could ever have imagined," complained Diya in a tone which managed to convey his inner triumph.

It was time to talk of the present but Halima and Ashur
recoiled from broaching the subject. Diya's appearance reminded
them of someone else whose image they could not erase from their
minds, and they were gripped by a secret anguish. Diya knew just
what they were thinking. "At last the Almighty has taken us by the
hand!" he said.

"Thank God," muttered Halima, for the sake of saying something.

She looked at him inquiringly.

"I'm manager of the biggest hotel in Bulaq." He turned to
Ashur. "What do you think of that?" he inquired cheerfully.

"Wonderful," said Ashur in a lifeless tone.

"I know what's going on in your head."

"Can't you see why I'm worried?"

"But it happened in a very ordinary way. Completely different
from our brother's fiasco."

"I hope so."

"I worked in the hotel as a servant, then I became a clerk
because I knew how to read and write, then I got friendly with the
owner's daughter." He paused to give his words a chance to sink
in, then continued. "I was afraid to ask her father for her hand, in
case I lost everything. But he died. We married and I became
manager of the hotel, and its virtual owner."

"God grant you make a success of it," murmured his mother.

He looked at Ashur. "Are you afraid I'm not telling the truth?"

"Oh, no," said Ashur quickly.

"You can't get the disaster of Fayiz out of your mind."

"I'll never be able to."

"But I've taken a different course."

"Thank God."

"Do you believe me?"

"Yes."

"As soon as I'd made my way in the world, I remembered my mother and brother," said Diya proudly.

"God bless you," said Halima.

"Because I never abandoned an old dream of mine."

"An old dream?" queried Ashur.

"That we should go back to our alley, recover our old status, and be greeted respectfully by those who once spat in our faces."

"Forget it," said Ashur tersely.

"Really? What are you scared of? Money works miracles."

"People stopped having real respect for us while we were still wealthy."

"What do you mean—real respect?"

Should he divulge his own dream? But he couldn't trust him. He might be able to communicate with the harafish, but not with this frivolous snob. "The respect we lost a long time ago."

Diya shrugged dismissively. "In any case, it's time you two gave up living with the dead!"

"No," said Ashur resolutely.

"No! Are you refusing my offer of help?"

"Yes."

"That's nothing short of crazy."

"It's your wife's money. Nothing to do with us."

"You're hurting me."

"I'm sorry, Diya. Leave us be."

"You're still suspicious of me."

"No. I think I've made that clear."

"I'm not letting my mother stay here," he said, his irritation plain to see.

"You're a good boy, but I won't abandon your brother," said Halima quickly.

"You're suspicious of me too!"

"God forbid! But I'm not leaving him. Let things take their course."

"How long do you plan to stay here with the dead?"

"We're not exactly as poor as we were. Things get better each day."

"I can reinstate you in the alley as respected citizens," he said vehemently.

"Let things take their course," implored Halima.

Diya hung his head. "What a disappointment," he muttered.

44.

After Diya had gone, Halima said, "We were hard on him, Ashur."

"There was no other way," insisted Ashur.

"Don't you trust him?"

"No."

"I do."

"I'm certain he must have bent the rules a bit to get where he is."

"Who could fail to learn a lesson after what happened to Fayiz?"

"We could. Our family history's nothing more than a succession of deviations, disasters, lessons not learned."

"But I believe him."

"As you wish."

"And you wouldn't even tell him your secret?"

"No," said Ashur sadly. "We believe in different things."

"He might have joined your group."

"We believe in different things," repeated Ashur patiently.

Diya had certainly come at an inopportune moment, for Ashur was poised—after much hard work—to take the decisive step.

45.

One wondrous day as the alley suffered its normal miserable life and winter prepared to depart, a man stepped out from under the archway. A giant in a blue gallabiyya and brown skullcap, carrying a long stick. He moved calmly and confidently as if he was returning from an hour's trip rather than several years' absence. The first person he met was Muhammad al-Agal. He stared at him in amazement.

"Ashur!"

"God's peace upon you, Muhammad."

At once astonished eyes were fixed on him. From shops, house windows, from all around the alley. He took no notice of anyone and made straight for the café. Hassuna al-Saba was cross-legged on his couch, attended by Yunis al-Sayis and Galil al-Alim. Ashur entered under the shocked gaze of the clientele. He made for a corner table, uttering a general greeting.

No one answered. It was clear the chief expected a formal salutation accompanied by some conciliatory remarks but Ashur sat down without a glance in his direction. The customers waited to see what would happen next.

"What brings you back here, boy?" demanded al-Saba, losing patience.

"I was bound to come here one day," he answered calmly.

"But you were chased out, rejected, cursed," he shouted.

"That was an injustice," he retorted, "and justice must triumph in the end."

Sheikh Galil interrupted at this point.

"Approach and ask our chief's pardon," he said.

"I didn't come here to seek pardon," answered Ashur coldly.

"We didn't know you were rude and conceited," shouted Yunis.

"You said it," mocked Ashur.

Hassuna al-Saba unfolded his legs from under him and sat forward, feet planted firmly on the floor.

"How were you thinking of coming back to live here, if it wasn't with my indulgence?" he asked menacingly.

"By the grace of the Almighty," proclaimed Ashur unruffled.

"Get out of here, or you'll be leaving on a stretcher," roared al-Saba.

Ashur stood up, and his fingers tightened around his club. The waiter rushed outside to summon the clan. The customers rushed after him in fright. Hassuna and Ashur lashed at one another with their long sticks. The shock of contact was like a wall coming down. A cruel, merciless battle broke out.

The men of the clan appeared from different directions, the alley emptied of people, shops closed, and the windows and wooden lattices filled with curious heads.

And then there was a surprise which hit the alley like an earthquake. Nobody was prepared for it. The harafish poured out of the lanes and derelict buildings, shouting, brandishing whatever weapons they had been able to lay hands on: bricks, bits of wood, chairs, sticks. They surged forward like a flood against Hassuna's men who, taken by surprise, were rapidly forced on to the defensive. Ashur struck Hassuna's arm and the club dropped from his fingers. He grappled with him, got him in a clinch, and squeezed him until his bones cracked. Then he lifted him high over his head and hurled him into the alley where he lay senseless and robbed of his honor.

The harafish surrounded the men of the clan and beat them with sticks and bricks. The lucky ones were those who escaped. In less than an hour the only people left in the alley were Ashur and a group of harafish.

46.

The number of combatants made this battle without precedent in the alley. The harafish, the overwhelming majority of the populace, had suddenly joined forces and prevailed over the clubs and long sticks. This sent a violent tremor through the private homes and businesses. The thread holding things in place had been broken. Anything was possible. However, the leadership of the clan had returned to the Nagi family, to a grave giant, whose clan was drawn for the first time from the people who made up the majority. Contrary to expectation, chaos did not follow. They closed ranks around their chief, with dedication and obedience. He towered above them like a lofty building, the look in his eyes inspiring them to create rather than wreck and destroy.

47.

At night Yunis al-Sayis and Galil al-Alim came to see Ashur. They were plainly uneasy. "I hope it won't be necessary for the police to intervene," began Sheikh Yunis.

"How many crimes have been committed under your nose and you never thought of calling the police?" said Ashur angrily.

"Sorry," said the man excitedly. "You understand our position better than anyone. And can I remind you that although you owe thanks to them you'll soon be at their mercy!"

"No one will be at anyone's mercy."

"All that kept them in check in the past was their weakness and lack of unity," Sheikh Galil said apprehensively.

"I know them better than you," said Ashur confidently. "I've lived alongside them in the open for a long time. And justice is the best cure for their ills."

"What will become of the rich and the notables?" asked Yunis, after some hesitation.

"I love justice more than I love the harafish and more than I hate the notables," declared Ashur unequivocally.

48.

Ashur did not flag for a moment in his efforts to realize the dream which had brought the harafish over to his side. He had taught them his interpretation of it in the open air and transformed them from layabouts, pickpockets, and beggars into the greatest clan the alley had known.

He quickly put the notables and the harafish on an equal footing and imposed heavy taxes on the rich. Many of them found

life so unpleasant that they fled to distant parts of the city where
the clans were unknown. Ashur imposed two duties on the
harafish. The first was to train their sons in the virtues of the clan
to maintain their power and prevent it ever falling into the hands
of hooligans or soldiers of fortune. The second was to earn their
living by a trade or a job which he could procure for them with
money from the taxes. He himself continued to hawk fruit and
vegetables and set up house with his mother in a small flat. So
began an epoch in the history of the clan which was distinguished
by its strength and integrity. Sheikh Galil was obliged to praise it
publicly for its justice, and Sheikh Yunis did the same. But Ashur
was suspicious of their inner thoughts, and had no doubt they
grieved for the handouts that had come their way from the notables, or when the protection money was distributed under the old
regime.

Sheikh Galil soon left the alley and Sheikh Ahmad Barakat
was appointed in his place. Since Sheikh Yunis was appointed by
the authorities, it was hard for him to move. Alone in his shop he
would grumble, "There's only rubbish left in this alley."

He confided in Zayn al-Alabaya in the bar.

"How long is this going to last?" the bar owner asked anxiously.

"There's no hope of a change while that barbarian's alive." He
sighed, then went on, "I'm sure people like us had the same conversation in his ancestor's time. We just have to be patient."

49.

Ashur renewed the mosque, the fountain, the trough, and the
Quran school, and founded a new school to accommodate the increase in numbers brought about by the arrival of the children of
the harafish. Then he did what no one before him had dared to do:
he arranged with a contractor to have the minaret demolished. His
predecessors had been afraid of the wrath of the evil spirits which
haunted it but the new chief wasn't afraid of evil spirits. He towered over the alley like a minaret himself, but he was committed to
justice, integrity, peace. He never provoked neighboring chiefs but

brought them sharply into line if they initiated hostilities against him, as a warning to the others. In this way he established his supremacy without having to fight for it.

50.

Diya returned to the alley delightedly with the intention of re-claiming the coal yard and becoming a leading notable under his brother's protection, but he didn't meet with any encouragement and was obliged to stay put in his hotel in Bulaq.

Halima believed that the time had come for Ashur to think of his own happiness, and proposed that he should find a wife. "There are still some respectable families left in the alley who haven't abused their wealth," she said.

Bitterly Ashur remembered the attitude adopted by the Khashshabs and the Attars.

"I get the feeling you hanker for a better life," he said to his mother.

"I don't think there's any justice in being unfair to yourself," she said truthfully.

"No!" he said adamantly.

It was not the strength of a genuine refusal, but a strength assumed to hide the weakness he felt boiling in his entrails. How he longed sometimes for luxury and beauty! How he dreamed of life in a mansion with a soft-skinned woman! That was why he said no with such force. "I'm not going to be the one to destroy the most magnificent structure in the alley!"

He was determined that this refusal should come from within him, and not be the result of pressure from the harafish. He wanted to be better than his ancestor. The first Ashur had relied on his own strength, while he had made the harafish into an invincible force. His ancestor had been carried away by his passion; he would stand firm like the ancient wall. "No," he repeated firmly. That was his sweetest victory: his victory over himself. He married Bahiyya, daughter of Adalat, the hairdresser, after seeing her and making inquiries on his own behalf. When Galal's minaret was torn out of the ground, the alley celebrated with a night of dancing and music. After midnight Ashur went to the monastery square to gather his thoughts alone under the stars in the ocean of songs. He squatted on the ground, lulled by his feeling of contentment and the pleasant air. One of those rare moments of existence when a pure light glows. When body, mind, time, and place are all in harmony. It was as if the mysterious anthems were speaking in a thousand tongues. As if he understood why the dervishes always sang in a foreign language and kept their door closed.

A creaking sound spread through the darkness. He looked at the great door in astonishment. Gently, steadily, it was opening. The shadowy figure of a dervish appeared, a breath of night embodied.

"Get the flutes and drums ready," the figure whispered, leaning toward him. "Tomorrow the Great Sheikh will come out of his seclusion. He will walk down the alley bestowing his light and give each young man a bamboo club and a mulberry fruit. Get the flutes and drums ready."

He returned to the world of the stars and the songs and the night and the ancient wall, grasping at the tail ends of the vision; his fingers sunk into the waves of majestic darkness. He jumped to his feet, drunk on inspiration and power. Don't be sad, his heart told him. One day the door may open to greet those who seize life boldly with the innocence of children and the ambition of angels.

And the voices sang:

> *Last night they relieved me of all my sorrows*
> *In the darkness they gave me the water of life.*

ABOUT THE AUTHOR

Naguib Mahfouz is the most prominent author of Arabic fiction published in English today. He was born in Cairo in 1911 and began writing when he was seventeen. A student of philosophy and an avid reader, he has been influenced by many Western writers, including Flaubert, Balzac, Zola, Camus, Tolstoy, Dostoevsky, and, above all, Proust. He has more than thirty novels to his credit, ranging from his earliest historical romances to his most recent experimental novels. In 1988, Mr. Mahfouz was awarded the Nobel Prize for Literature. He lives in the Cairo suburb of Agouza with his wife and two daughters.